SONS OF
SITA

Ganesa, lead well this army of words

ASHOK K. BANKER

SONS OF SITA

wisdom
tree

for
yashka
ayush yoda
bithika

my beginning
my middle
my end

not necessarily in that order

love, forever
and nothing but love, forever

© Ashok K. Banker, 2012

First published 2012

ISBN 978-81-8328-294-9

Published by
Wisdom Tree
4779/23, Ansari Road
Darya Ganj, New Delhi-110 002
Ph.: 23247966/67/68
wisdomtreebooks@gmail.com

Printed in India

Contents

|arvaci subhaghe bhava site vandamahe tva|
| |yatha nah subhaghasasi yatha nah suphalasasi| |

|Auspicious Sita, we venerate and worship thee|
| |Bless us, endow us with prosperity and bring us fruits abundantly| |

Rig-Veda, Mandala 4, Sukta 57, rca 6

RETELLING THE RAMAYANA

Adi-kavya: The First Retelling

Some three thousand years ago, a sage named Valmiki lived in a remote forest ashram, practising austerities with his disciples. One day, the wandering sage Narada visited the ashram and was asked by Valmiki if he knew of a perfect man. Narada said, indeed, he did know of such a person, and then told Valmiki and his disciples a story of an ideal man.

Some days later, Valmiki happened to witness a hunter killing a kraunchya bird. The crane's partner was left desolate, and cried inconsolably. Valmiki was overwhelmed by anger at the hunter's action, and sorrow at the bird's loss. He felt driven to do something rash, but controlled himself with difficulty.

After his anger and sorrow subsided, he questioned his outburst. After so many years of practising meditation and austerities, he had still not been able to master his own emotions. Was it even possible to do so? Could any person truly become a master of his passions? For a while he despaired, but then he recalled the story Narada had told him. He thought about the implications of the story, about the choices made by the protagonist and how he had indeed shown great mastery of his own thoughts, words, deeds and feelings. Valmiki felt inspired by the recollection and was filled with a calm serenity such as he had never felt before.

As he recollected the tale of that perfect man of whom Narada had spoken, he found himself reciting it in a particular cadence and rhythm. He realised that this rhythm or metre corresponded to the warbling cries of the kraunchya bird, as if in tribute to the loss that had inspired his recollection. At once, he resolved to compose his own version of the story, using the new form of metre, that others might hear it and be as inspired as he was.

But Narada's story was only a bare narration of the events, a mere plot outline as we would call it today. In order to make the story attractive and memorable to ordinary listeners, Valmiki would have to add and embellish considerably, filling in details and inventing incidents from his own imagination. He would have to dramatise the whole story in order to bring out the powerful dilemmas faced by the protagonist.

But what right did he have to do so? After all, this was not his story. It was a tale told to him. A tale of a real man and real events. How could he make up his own version of the story?

At this point, Valmiki was visited by Lord Brahma Himself.

The Creator told him to set his worries aside and begin composing the work he had in mind. Here is how Valmiki quoted Brahma's exhortation to him, in an introductory passage not unlike this one that you are reading right now:

> Recite the tale of Rama…as you heard it told by Narada. Recite the
> deeds of Rama that are already known as well as those that are not, his
> adventures…his battles…the acts of Sita, known and unknown. Whatever
> you do not know will become known to you. Never will your words be
> inappropriate. Tell Rama's story…that it may prevail on earth for as long
> as the mountains and the rivers exist.

Valmiki needed no further urging. He began composing his poem.

He titled it Ramayana, meaning literally, The Movements (or Travels) of Rama.

Foretelling the Future

The first thing Valmiki realised on completing his composition was that it was incomplete. What good was a story without anyone to tell it to? In the tradition of his age, a bard would normally recite his compositions himself, perhaps earning some favour or payment in coin or kind, more often rewarded only with the appreciation of his listeners. But Valmiki knew that while the form of the story was his creation, the story itself belonged to all his countrymen. He recalled Brahma's exhortation that Rama's story must prevail on earth for as long as the mountains and the rivers exist.

So he taught it to his disciples, among whose number were two young boys whose mother had sought sanctuary with him years ago. Those two boys, Luv and Kush, then travelled from place to place, reciting the Ramayana as composed by their guru.

In time, fate brought them before the very Rama described in the poem. Rama knew at once that the poem referred to him and understood that these boys could be none other than his sons by the banished Sita. Called upon by the curious king, Valmiki himself then appeared before Rama and entreated him to take back Sita.

Later, Rama asked Valmiki to compose an additional part to the poem, so that he himself, Rama Chandra, might know what would happen to him in future. Valmiki obeyed this extraordinary command, and this supplementary section became the Uttara Kaand of his poem.

Valmiki's Sanskrit rendition of the tale was a brilliant work by any standards, ancient or modern. Its charm, beauty and originality can never be matched. It is a true masterpiece of world literature, the 'adi-kavya' which stands as the fountainhead of our great cultural record. Even today, thousands of years after its composition, it remains unsurpassed.

And yet, when we narrate the story of the Ramayana today, it is not Valmiki's Sanskrit shlokas that we recite. Few of us today have even read Valmiki's immortal composition in its original. Most have not even read an abridgement. Indeed, an unabridged Ramayana itself, reproducing Valmiki's verse without alteration or revisions, is almost impossible to find. Even the most learned of scholars, steeped in a lifetime of study of ancient Sanskrit literature, maintain that the versions of Valmiki's poem that exist today have been revised and added to by later hands. Some believe that the first and seventh kaands, as well as a number of passages within the other kaands, were all inserted by later writers who preferred to remain anonymous.

Perhaps the earliest retelling of Valmiki's poem is to be found in the pages of that vast ocean of stories we call the Mahabharata. When Krishna–Dwaipayana Vyasa, more popularly known today as Ved Vyasa, composed his equally legendary epic, he retold the story of the Ramayana in one passage. His retelling differs in small but significant ways.

Sometime later, the burgeoning Buddhist literature, usually composed in the Pali dialect, also included stories from the Ramayana, recast in a somewhat different light. Indeed, Buddhist literature redefined the term dharma itself, restating it as *dhamma* and changing the definition of this and several other core concepts.

In the eleventh century, a Tamil poet named Kamban undertook his own retelling of the Ramayana legend. Starting out with what seems to have been an attempt to translate Valmiki's Ramayana, Kamban nevertheless deviated dramatically from his source material. In Kamban's Ramayana, entire episodes are deleted, new ones appear, people and places are renamed or changed altogether, and even the order of some major events is revised. Most of all, Kamban's Ramayana relocates the entire story in a milieu that is recognisably eleventh-century Tamil Nadu in its geography, history, clothes, customs, etc., rather than the north Indian milieu of Valmiki's Sanskrit original. It is essentially a whole new Ramayana, retold in a far more passionate, rich and colourful idiom.

A few centuries later, Sant Tulsidas undertook his interpretation of the epic. Tulsidas went so far as to title his work *Ramcharitmanas*, rather than calling it the Ramayana.

By doing so, he signalled that he was not undertaking a faithful translation, but a wholly new variation of his own creation. The differences are substantial.

In art, sculpture, musical renditions, even in dance, mime and street theatrical performances, the story of Valmiki's great poem has been retold over and over, in countless different variations, some with minor alterations, others with major deviations. The tradition of retellings continues even in modern times, through television serials, films, puppet theatre, children's versions, cartoons, poetry, pop music and, of course, in the tradition of Ramlila enactments across the country every year.

Yet how many of these are faithful to Valmiki? How many, if any at all, actually refer to the original Sanskrit text, or even attempt to seek out that text?

Should they even do so?

So Many Ramayanas

Does a grandmother consult Valmiki's Ramayana before she retells the tale to her grandchildren at night? When she imitates a rakshasa's roar or Ravana's laugh, or Sita's tears, or Rama's stoic manner, whom does she base her performance on? When an actor portrays Rama in a television serial, or a Ramlila performer enacts a scene, or a sculptor chisels a likeness, a painter a sketch, whom do they all refer to? There were no illustrations in Valmiki's Ramayana. No existing portraits of Rama survive from that age, no recordings of his voice or video records of his deeds.

Indeed, many of the episodes or 'moments' we believe are from Valmiki's Ramayana are not even present in the original Sanskrit work. They are the result of later retellers, often derived from their own imagination. One instance is the 'seema rekha' believed to have been drawn by Lakshman before leaving Sita in the hut. No mention of this incident exists in Valmiki's Ramayana.

Then there is the constant process of revision that has altered even those scenes that remain constant through various retellings.

For example, take the scene where Sita entreats Rama to allow her to accompany him into exile. In Valmiki's Ramayana, when Rama tells Sita he has to go into exile, and she asks him to allow her to go with him, he refuses outright. At first, Sita pleads with him and cries earnest tears, but when Rama remains adamant, she grows angry and rebukes him in shockingly harsh terms. She refers to him as a 'woman disguised as a man', says that 'the world is wrong when they say that there is no one greater than Rama', calls him 'depressed and frightened', 'an actor playing a role', and other choice epithets. It is one of the longer scenes in Valmiki's Ramayana, almost equalling in length the entire narration of Rama's early childhood years!

Tamil poet Kamban retells this incident in his more compressed, volatile, rich style, reducing Sita's objections to a couple of brief rebukes: 'Could it be that the real reason [for Rama not taking her into exile] is that with me left behind, you'll be free to enjoy yourself in the forest?'

By the time we reach Sant Tulsidas's recension, Sita's rebukes are reduced to a few tearful admonitions and appeals. Were these changes the result of the change in the socially accepted standards of behaviour between men and women in our country? Quite possibly. Tulsidas's *Ramcharitmanas* depicts a world quite different from that which Valmiki or even Kamban depicts. In fact, each of these three versions differs so drastically in terms of the language used, the clothes worn, the various social and cultural references, that they seem almost independent of one another.

Perhaps the most popularly known version in more recent times is a simplified English translation of a series of Tamil retellings of selected episodes of the Kamban version, serialised in a children's magazine about fifty years ago. This version by C Rajagopalachari, aka Rajaji, was my favourite version as a child too. It was only much later that I found, through my own extensive research that my beloved Rajaji version left out whole chunks of the original story and simplified other parts considerably. Still later, I was sorely disappointed by yet another version by an otherwise great writer, RK Narayan. In his severely abridged retelling, the story is dealt with in a manner so rushed and abbreviated; it is reduced to a moral fable rather than the rich, powerful, mythic epic that Valmiki created.

English scholar William S Buck's nineteenth-century version, dubiously regarded as a classic by English scholars, reads like it might have been composed under the influence of certain intoxicants: in one significant departure from Indian versions, Guha, the tribal chief of the Nisada fisherfolk, without discernible reason, spews a diatribe against Brahmins, and ends by kicking a statue of Lord Shiva. To add further confusion, in the illustration accompanying this chapter, Guha is shown kicking what appears to be a statue of Buddha!

If you travel outside India, farther east, you will find more versions of the Ramayana that are so far removed from Valmiki, that some are barely recognisable as the same story. In one recent study of these various versions of the epic across the different cultures of Asia, an ageing Muslim woman in Indonesia was surprised to learn from the author that we have our own Ramayana in India also! The kings of Thailand are always named Rama along with other dynastic titles, and consider themselves to be direct descendants of Rama Chandra. The largest Rama temple, an inspiring ruin even today, is situated not in India, or even in Nepal, the only nation that takes Hinduism as its official religion, but in Cambodia. It is called Angkor Vat.

In fact, it is now possible to say that there are as many Ramayanas as there are people who know the tale, or claim to know it. And no two versions are exactly alike.

My Ramayana: A Personal Odyssey

And yet, would we rather have this democratic melange of versions and variations, or would we rather have a half-remembered, extinct tale recollected only dimly, like a mostly forgotten myth that we can recall only fragments of?

Valmiki's 'original' Ramayana was written in Sanskrit, the language of his time, and in an idiom that was highly modern for its age.

In fact, it was so avant-garde in its style—the kraunchya-inspired shloka metre—that it was considered 'adi' or the first of its kind. Today, few people except dedicated scholars can understand or read it in its original form—and even the scholars often disagree vehemently about their interpretations of the dense archaic Sanskrit text!

Kamban's overblown rhetoric and colourful descriptions, while magnificently inspired and appropriate for their age, are equally anachronistic in today's times.

Tulsidas's interpretation, while rightfully regarded as a sacred text, can seem somewhat heavy-handed in its depiction of man-woman relationships. It is more of a religious tribute to Lord Rama's divinity than a realistic retelling of the story itself.

In Ved Vyasa's version, the devices of ill-intentioned Manthara, misguided Kaikeyi and reprehensible Ravana are not the ultimate cause of Rama's misfortunes. In fact, it is not due to the asuras either. It is Brahma Himself, using the mortal avatar of Vishnu to cleanse the world of evil, as perpetuated by Ravana and his asuras, in order to maintain the eternal balance of good and evil.

My reasons for attempting this retelling were simple and intensely personal. As a child of an acutely unhappy broken marriage, a violently bitter failure of parents of two different cultures (Anglo-Indian Christian and Gujarati Hindu) to accept their differences and find common ground, I turned to literature for solace. My first readings were, by accident, in the realm of mythology. So inspired was I by the simple power and heroic victories of those ancient ur-tales, I decided to become a writer and tell stories of my own that would be as great, as inspiring to others. To attempt, if possible, to bridge cultures, and knit together disparate lives by showing the common struggle and strife and, ultimately, triumph of all human souls.

I was barely a boy then. Thirty-odd years of living and battling life later, albeit not as colourful as Valmiki's thieving and dacoit years, I was moved by a powerful inexplicable urge to read the Ramayana once more. Every version I read seemed to lack something, that vital something that I can only describe as the 'connection' to the work. In a troubled phase, battling with moral conundrums of my own, I set to writing my own version of the events. My mind exploded with images, scenes, entire conversations between characters. I saw, I heard, I felt... I wrote. Was I exhorted by Brahma Himself? Probably not! I had no reader in mind, except myself—and everyone. I changed as a person over the course of that writing. I found peace, or a kind of peace. I saw how people could devote their lives to worshipping Rama, or Krishna, or Devi for that matter, my own special 'Maa'. But I also felt that this story was beyond religion, beyond nationality, beyond race, colour, or creed.

Undertaking to retell a story as great and as precious as our classic adi-kavya is not an enterprise lightly attempted. The first thing I did was study every available edition of previous retellings to know what had been done before, the differences between various retellings, and attempt to understand why. I also spoke extensively to people, known and unknown, about their knowledge of the poem, in an attempt to trace how millennia of verbal retellings have altered the perception of the tale. One of the most striking things was that most people had never actually read the 'original' Valmiki Ramayana. Indeed, most people considered *Ramcharitmanas* by Tulsidas to be 'the Ramayana', and assumed it was an accurate reprise of the Sanskrit work. Nothing could be farther from the truth.

For instance, Valmiki's Ramayana depicts Dasaratha as having three hundred and fifty concubines in addition to his three titled wives. In keeping with the kingly practices of that age, the ageing raja's predilection for the fairer sex is depicted honestly and without any sense of misogyny. Valmiki neither comments on nor criticises Dasaratha's fondness for fleshly pleasures, he simply states it.

When Rama takes leave of his father before going into exile, he does so in the palace of concubines, and all of them weep copiously for the exiled son of their master. When Valmiki describes women, he does so by enumerating the virtues of each part of their anatomy.

There is no sense of embarrassment or male chauvinism evident here: he is simply extolling the beauty of the female characters, just as he does for the male characters like Rama and Hanuman and, yes, even Ravana. Even in Kamban's version, the women are depicted in such ripe, full-blown language, that a modern reader like myself blushes in embarrassment. Yet the writer exhibits no awkwardness or prurience in these passages—he is simply describing them as he perceived them in the garb and fashion of his time.

By the time we reach Tulsidas and later versions, Rama is no less than a god in human avatar. And in keeping with this foreknowledge, all related characters are depicted accordingly.

So Dasaratha's fleshly indulgences take a backseat, the women are portrayed fully clad and demure in appearance, and their beauty is ethereal rather than earthly.

How was I to approach my retelling? On one hand, the Ramayana was now regarded not as a Sanskrit epic of real events that occurred in ancient India, but as a moral fable of the actions of a human avatar of Vishnu. On the other hand, I felt the need to bring to life the ancient world of Epic India in all its glory and magnificence, to explore the human drama as well as the divinity that drove it, to show the nuances of word and action and choice rather than a black-and-white depiction of good versus evil. More importantly, what could I offer that was fresh and new, yet faithful to the spirit of the original story? How could I ensure that all events and characters were depicted respectfully yet realistically?

There was little point in simply repeating any version that had gone before—those already existed, and those who desired to read the Ramayana in any one of its various forms could simply pick up one of those previous versions.

But what had never been done before was a complete, or 'sampoorna', Ramayana, incorporating the various, often contradictory aspects of the various Indian retellers (I wasn't interested in foreign perspectives, frankly), while attempting to put us into the minds and hearts of the various characters. To go beyond a simple plot reprise and bring the whole story, the whole world of ancient India, alive. To do what every verbal reteller attempts, or any classical dancer does: make the story live again.

In order to do this, I chose a modern idiom. I simply used the way I speak, an amalgam of English–Hindi–Urdu–Sanskrit, and various other terms from Indian languages. I deliberately used anachronisms like the terms 'abs' or 'morph'. I based every section, every scene, every character's dialogues and actions on the previous Ramayanas, be it Valmiki, Kamban, Tulsidas, or Vyasa, and even the various Puranas. Everything you read here is based on actual research, or my interpretation of some detail noted in a previous work. The presentation, of course, is wholly original and my own.

Take the example of the scene of Sita entreating Rama to let her accompany him into exile. In my retelling, I sought to explore the relationship between Rama and Sita at a level that is beyond the physical or social plane. I believed that theirs was a love that was eternally destined, and that their bond surpassed all human ties. At one level, yes, I believed that they were Vishnu and Lakshmi. Yet, in the avatars they were currently in, they were Rama and Sita, two young people caught up in a time of great turmoil and strife, subjected to hard, difficult choices. Whatever their divine backgrounds and karma, here and now, they had to play out their parts one moment at a time, as real, flesh-and-blood people.

I adopted an approach that was realistic, putting myself (and thereby the reader) into the feelings and thoughts of both Rama and Sita at that moment of choice. I felt the intensity of their pain, the great sorrow and confusion, the frustration at events beyond their control, and also their ultimate acceptance of what was right, what must be done, of dharma. In my version, they argue as young couples will at such a time, they express their anger and mixed emotions, but in the end, it is not only through duty and dharma that she appeals to him. In the end, she appeals to him as a wife who is secure in the knowledge that her husband loves her sincerely, and that the bond that ties them is not merely one of duty or a formal social knot of matrimony, but of true love. After the tears, after all other avenues have been mutually discussed and discarded, she simply says his name and appeals to him, as a wife, a lover, and as his dearest friend:

'Rama,' she said. She raised her arms to him, asking, not pleading. 'Then let me go with you.'

And he agrees. Not as a god, an avatar, or even a prince. But as a man who loves her and respects her. And needs her.

In the Footsteps of Giants

Let me be clear.

This is not Valmiki's story. Nor Kamban's. Nor Tulsidas's.

Nor Vyasa's. Nor RK Narayan's. Nor Rajaji's charming, abridged children's version.

It is Rama's story. And Rama's story belongs to every one of us. Black, brown, white, or albino. Old or young. Male or female. Hindu, Christian, Muslim, or whatever faith you espouse. I was once asked at a press conference to comment on the Babri Masjid demolition and its relation to my Ramayana. My answer was that the Ramayana had stood for three thousand years, and would stand for all infinity. Ayodhya, in my opinion, is not just a place in north-central Uttar Pradesh. It is a place in our hearts. And in that most sacred of places, it will live forever, burnished and beautiful as no temple of consecrated bricks can ever be. When Rama himself heard Luv and Kush recite Valmiki's Ramayana for the first time, even he, the protagonist of the story, was flabbergasted by the sage's version of the events—after all, even he had not known what happened to Sita after her exile, nor the childhood of Luv and Kush, nor had he heard their mother's version of events narrated so eloquently until then. And in commanding Valmiki to compose the section about future events, Rama himself added his seal of authority to Valmiki, adding weight to Brahma's exhortation to recite the deeds of Rama that were already known 'as well as those that are not'.

And so the tradition of telling and retelling the Ramayana began. It is that tradition that Kamban, Tulsidas, Vyasa, and so many others were following. It is through the works of these bards through the ages that this great tale continues to exist among us. If it changes shape and structure, form and even content, it is because that is the nature of the story itself: it inspires the teller to bring fresh insights to each new version, bringing us ever closer to understanding Rama himself.

This is why it must be told, and retold, an infinite number of times.

By me.

By you.

By grandmothers to their grandchildren.

By people everywhere, regardless of their identity.

The first time I was told the Ramayana, it was on my grandfather's knee. He was excessively fond of chewing tambaku paan and his breath was redolent of its aroma. Because I loved lions, he infused any number of lions in his Ramayana retellings—Rama fought lions, Sita fought them, I think even Manthara was cowed down by one at one point! My grandfather's name, incidentally, was Ramchandra Banker. He died of throat cancer caused by his tobacco-chewing habit. But before his throat ceased working, he had passed on the tale to me.

And now, I pass it on to you. If you desire, and only if, then read this book. I believe if you are ready to read it, the tale will call out to you, as it did to me. If that happens, you are in for a great treat. Know that the version of the Ramayana retold within these pages is a living, breathing, newborn avatar of the tale itself. Told by a living author in a living idiom. It is my humble attempt to do for this great story what writers down the ages have done with it in their times.

Maazi Naroti

In closing, I'd like to quote briefly from two venerable authors who have walked similar paths.

The first is KM Munshi whose Krishnavatara Series remains a benchmark of the genre of modern retellings of ancient tales.

These lines are from Munshi's own Introduction to the Bharatiya Vidya Bhavan edition of 1972:

> In the course of this adventure, I had often to depart from legend and myth, for such a reconstruction by a modern author must necessarily involve the exercise of whatever little imagination he has. I trust He will forgive me for the liberty I am taking, but I must write of Him as I see Him in my imagination.

I could not have said it better.

Yuganta, Iravati Karve's landmark Sahitya Akademi Award-winning study of the Mahabharata, packs more valuable insights into its slender 220-page pocket-sized edition (Disha) than in any ten encyclopaedias. In arguably the finest essay of the book, 'Draupadi', she includes this footnote:

> The discussion up to this point is based on the critical edition of the Mahabharata. What follows is my naroti [naroti = a dry coconut shell, i.e. a worthless thing. The word 'naroti' was first used in this sense by the poet Eknath].

In the free musings of Karve's mind, we learn more about Vyasa's formidable epic than from most encyclopaedic theses. For only from free thought can come truly progressive ideas.

In that spirit, I urge readers to consider my dried coconut shell reworking of the Ramayana in the same spirit.

If anything in the following pages pleases you, thank those great forebears in whose giant footsteps I placed my own small feet.

If any parts displease you, then please blame them on my inadequate talents, not on the tale.

ASHOK K. BANKER
Andheri West, Mumbai
April 2011

PREFACE
Every End is a Beginning is an End is a Beginning

So here we are again in Ayodhya. The question is why. In late 2004, when I wrote the last pages of *King of Ayodhya*, I was sure I was done with the Ramayana Series. Two years later, when the book went to press, I wrote an Afterword that confidently stated that the series was over and even gave my reasons for not writing the part of the story that is known as Uttara Kaand in the Valmiki Ramayana. Next stop, Hastinapura, I said. And then went back to work on my Mba. No, not a business degree; that's just my personalised term for my retelling of The Mahabharata, a mammoth project by any standards, and equivalent to several degree courses! At a projected ten volumes of over 1000 pages in hardcover each, aiming to cover ALL the material in the original eighteen Sanskrit parvas, it was enough to occupy me (or several dozen other writers) for years if not decades. It should have been reason enough for me to wave goodbye to the Ramayana forever, hop on the slow train to Epic India and never look back.

But life has a way of deciding where and when to stop the train. And sometimes, looking back, most of the stops that really matter in the end, turn out to be unscheduled ones.

That's how it was with me and the tale of maryada purushottam.

The ending of *King of Ayodhya* left Rama and Sita and the others back home in Ayodhya. The war of Lanka was won. Sita recovered. The exile ended. Rama presumably crowned and ensconced on the sunwood throne. Sita pregnant with their children. And a world of possibilities ahead—all happy ones, we would assume.

Yet anyone who knows the basic story of Valmiki Ramayana—or even Tulsidas's commentary, which differs somewhat from the adi-kavya and adds a strong religious and revisionistic colouring to the original Vedic tale—would know that Rama's story certainly does not end there. In fact, one of the most dramatic events of the entire tale occurs after the return home to Ayodhya. Also one of the most controversial, and the reason most often cited by angry young Indians who still fume about what they feel was Rama's chauvinistic ill-treatment of Sita. Kamban chose to ignore that part of the tale—and so did I, at first, placing my small feet in the footsteps of the giants who went before. Because, as I said in my Afterword to *King of Ayodhya*, I couldn't reconcile my idea of Rama with the king who cruelly cast out his beloved life-companion. So it was with a clear mind that I put aside the Ramayana Series and went on to write about those amazing five brothers in that great ancient city.

But I was seeking to find answers to questions that had constantly plagued me (as it had plagued, and continues to plague countless Indians even today): Why did Rama act as he did? If dharma was his justification, then why did he have to be so cruel and heartless about it? Why not gently and regretfully banish Sita?

Because as anyone who puzzles over this age-old problem knows, the real issue is not just that Rama exiled Sita. We might swallow the difficult (near-impossible, in my honest opinion) argument about him abiding by dharma—I don't, but still. But how do we explain the extreme cruelty with which he treated her? Not in front of all Ayodhya, but in a private faceoff where only the two of them were present, and where he says things and addresses her in a fashion that is unlike the Rama of the preceding story. It's as if this is a completely different Rama now, one that is impossible to reconcile with the loving, gentle, equalitarian Rama whom Sita is able to speak harshly to, even slap, and otherwise act and behave on completely equal terms with throughout their earlier life. (This is one of the crucial differences between Valmiki Ramayana and Tulsidas and other recenscions, including Kamban to some extent: the egalitarianism of the sexes, and the clear evidence of womanly power in exchanges between men and women in those Vedic times, unlike the considerably diminished stature of women in sixteenth-century India during Tulsidas's lifetime.)

The problem I faced was a simple one: one, how to reconcile Rama's behaviour (not his actions, mind you, which can be justified, however absurdly, by the 'dharma' argument, but his behaviour towards his beloved wife) with the Rama we had known and shared mindspace and heartspace with for over 3000 pages in the preceding books.

And so my mind returned to Ayodhya, and as an idle mental exercise, began to follow the mindtrails and scent-trails of the imagination.

And then, I knew exactly how and why it had all happened. Or at least, my version of events. (Just as the previous books were my version of Valmiki and Kamban Ramayana.)

And so you now have this book in your hands.

And you're about to return with me back to Ayodhya. And to begin a journey that will seem both familiar and strange, I suppose, since that's how it seemed to me. And start down the wide, scented path that will lead you to a whole barrage of new questions that will answer some of the old ones, while raising completely new ones.

So in a way, every end is a beginning. Which itself is an end. And which in turn is a new beginning. And so on. After all, as they say, all stories are ultimately linked together. Just as all people are. All beings. All things. All matter. All universes.

And that's the last thing I have to tell you before we return to Ayodhya.

While *Sons of Sita* does conclusively end the Ramayana Series, it also begins a whole new tale. One that doesn't simply continue but also slips sideways and leaps forward in time to other linked stories.

In short, once you read this book, loyal reader, you run the risk of entering a maze of chambers. One leads to another to another and so on. Not endlessly. Because there is a definite end. But a long journey nevertheless. A journey that will take you through the entire mythology, itihasa, history and contemporary socio-political world of the Indian subcontinent (and to a lesser extent, the world at large).

Of course, you could still choose not to continue reading. In fact, it's quite possible that you may be so fed up of me and my work by the time you put this book down, that you may never read anything by me again. (Those who take extremist views for or against Rama may feel that way, since they most often have their own fixed notions of what they believe really happened, and are simply not interested in anyone else's point of view.) But since you're still here, still reading this long and possibly irrelevant foreword, I have a feeling you will go on.

And if you choose to do so, then I just want to remind you that I warned you. Right here. Right now. I warned you that reading this book will commit you to a very wide, very scented path that will lead on those dozens of other books, tens of thousands of pages, and a vast labyrinthine story that will take several years more to complete, publish, purchase and read, and will occupy a considerable portion of your waking hours and your book-buying budget.

Will it be worth it? You'll have to answer that one yourself. I think so. But then again, the engineer always enjoys riding the train. Just as the charioteer always loves leading the team of horses.

Why else would the charioteer be a charioteer otherwise? Or the train engineer a train engineer?

Ultimately, it will be up to you, constant reader, to decide whether this epic undertaking was worth the effort, time and investment.

And, in case, all the above seems like the insane dream of a bibliomaniac, well, one can dream, can't one? In any case, I'm only talking about writing the books. As was the case when I started writing my Ramayana Series, it's quite likely that no publisher will want to even look at the manuscripts, let alone publish them. It's equally possible that I won't live long enough to finish telling all the stories, or even most of them. But what the hey, I'm a 45-year old, balding, greying, paunchy father to a teenage daughter and an adult son, husband to a schoolteacher wife, care-giver to an adorable but stubborn basset hound, I live and work surrounded by books, family, some filmed entertainment and a few good friends, and that's pretty much it for me. A simple life, almost boring by Mumbai standards or any standard for that matter. So at the least, at the very very least, I can afford to dream big, and I'm damn well going to do so.

I have no idea whether or not I'll succeed, and whether you will feel at the end that it was all worth it. But I'm damn well going to give it an epic try.

I couldn't think of a better way to spend this lifetime.

And you're warmly invited to join me for the ride.

Chariots don't have seatbelts (neither do trains, curiously). So you're just going to have to hold on to my shoulder if you need some support. I'll try to coax the team to ride gentle, but at times we will have to ride fast and furious. And there may be bumps. And dips. And obstacles.

But at least we'll ride them together. And the journey is an amazing one.

That much, I can promise you.

prārambh

Sita...

Sweet whisper in her ear, myrtle breath upon her cheek. She startled awake with a lurch and a gasp. In the hut's impenetrable darkness, her hands sought out by instinct the looming mound of her belly. Her palms gently massaged the sweat-slicked pot, soothing both herself as well as her sleeping sons. Slowly, by degrees, the nightmarish visions of ten-headed rakshasas, moon-swords, and three-eyed devas faded away reluctantly, retreating, hissing and snapping to the far corners of the humble hut. She was too middle-heavy to sit up easily; instead, she leaned upon one elbow, head throbbing, throat hoarse from shouting forgotten prayers to uncaring gods. The darbha grass pallet was dampened by her own exudations. She listened idly, hearing only the absence of human sounds. The ashram was asleep around her. The night was peaceful, the forest quiet—or as quiet as a forest could be at night. The very music of the woods told her that all was well, no menace lurked in the dark recesses of the surrounding wilderness, no rakshasas approached stealthily, no mortal or un-mortal foes threatened. Within the centre of her being, the twin lives growing steadily—greedily, it seemed somedays—seemed barely to have stirred. She trusted their instincts more than her own now; for they seemed to sense better than she when true danger loomed. One kicked, the other kicked back instinctively, and she felt them both settling back into deep repose. The rhythmic cricketing of insects, droning of cicadas, and hooting of owls lulled her back to sleep. Darkness embraced her like a lover returned from a long war. She fell into sleep, and nothingness caught her and began to tug her insistently down into oblivion…

Sitey.

Her eyes opened, staring up into darkness. That name. Nobody called her by that name, in that tone. Her name, Sita, modified to the third-person plural, the tense used for royalty or formal addresses. Simultaneously affectionate as well as excessively formal. A name only a lover would use. Nay, not even a lover. Only a husband.

Janaki.

She swallowed, willing her heartbeat to slow, feeling a fresh bead of sweat coagulating upon her brow—she had always had a tendency to sweat a great deal from the crown of her scalp—and it took great restraint to stifle the urge she felt to speak out. Quiet and serene as the ashram was, its occupants were light sleepers, accustomed to living in woods populated by the fiercest predators. Rousing them would take little more than a raised voice, a tone of alarm, or even a strange sound that did not belong: Maharishi Valmiki would be up and ready in a trice, broadstaff in hand, a mantra on his lips. Then the devas help any intruder, human or otherwise. So she kept her voice stilled and emotions under control. There were also the twins to consider. At this advanced stage of her confinement, waking them would make sleep impossible the rest of the night, for they would be kicking and ready for action no less quicker than the Maharishi. The very fact that they still slept so soundly told her that whatever presence swirled around her this night, was not a force of evil that intended harm to her. Just as the Maharishi was sensitive to sound, the twins were sensitive to all else.

And that name and that tone. Janaki. Daughter of Janak. Again, an appellation used by one who cared about her.

Rama, she mouthed silently, her heart turning at the use of his name. *Is that you?*

Maithili.

This one was less intimate, more generic. Woman of Mithila. Yet coming as it did after the other familiar terms of endearment, it was more touching, not less, for its formal generality. She shuddered and covered her face with the crook of her arm, feeling hot tears spill carelessly down her cheeks. The appellation, uttered in the most affectionate of tones, caused her mind to resonate with a deep ringing that issued outwards in concentric waves, seeming to reach to the very ends of creation.

Vaidehi.

Woman of the Videha nation. This one was so generic, so formal, yet spoken in a tone so familiar, intimate, caressing, sincere, that it broke the last reserves of her endurance. The dam burst and she turned her head and cried into the straw, cut ends digging uncomfortably into her neck and arms and cheek; not caring. She heard her own sobs in the stillness and thought with a sense of wonder: *Who is that woman weeping so bitterly? Poor thing. She must have suffered some great loss.*

My love, forgive me. I did what I had to for our sakes. For the sake of our sons. For the sake of our future.

No! She cried silently in her mind's echoing chamber. *You did it for dharma. As you do everything. That's all you really care about. Nothing else matters so long as you fulfil your dharma. It's the way it has always been with you!*

A moment of silence, as if he did not debate her accusation. Then, gently, soothingly:

Yes. But you serve dharma too. In your own way. Surely you see that?

She raised her face at last and screamed into the darkness with the true voice of her heart, audible only to phantoms and miasmas: *I don't want to serve dharma. I don't want dharma. I just want you.*

She waited. But this time no reply came. Only the silent darkness pressing upon her from all sides like an invisible cage shrinking by degrees with every passing moment. She felt a sudden rush of remorse. Regret, at having spoken so harshly to her beloved—or to his phantom presence, or memory, or whatever it was that had come to her in the deep watches of the night.

Rama? She asked anxiously. *Are you there?*

But only the darkness remained. The darkness and the silence.

She lay awake the remaining hours to dawn, till the ashram stirred and the brahmacharyas rose and the daily round of chores and duties began anew. Within the swollen mound of her belly, the twins slept as peacefully as cubs in a den.

He never came to her again, that night, or any other night.

⟩⟩ KAAND 1 ⟨⟨

ONE

The heavily laden wagon-train trundled noisily through the woods. Sunlight fell in beams through the high leafy branches of the sala trees, some towering twenty yards or higher, illuminating the dust motes thrown up in the wake of the rattling wheels. The forest was rife with the colours of spring, bright bursts of saffron, vermilion, scarlet, russet, mustard, decorating the sloping hillsides across which the old trading path wound its way. Smaller animals paused in their foraging and raised slender necks or cocked furry heads to listen as the wagons rumbled past, then continued their nibbling unabated, accustomed to the passing of mortals through this neck of the woods. A leopard stretched out upon a high tree branch, snarled and bared her fangs silently as she paused in the act of sharpening her claws; long furrows of stripped bark and gouged slashes marked her chosen spot. After she had satisfied herself that the mortal noisemakers were only passing through, not stopping, she resumed her energetic grooming, purring with pleasure as the soft crumbly bark yielded to her razor-sharp tips. Below, and only a few dozen yards to the side, a mongoose ignored the sound and continued to burrow into a hollow trunk rich with the scent of cobra, disappointed to find only cracked egg shells and old sheaths discarded at the turn of the season. Suspended on the trunk of another tree, a wasp stuck in a drip of oozing sap struggled hopelessly one last time before succumbing to the treacly golden glue that sealed in its life. Cicadas kept rhythm as the forest went about its daily business of killing, eating, defecating, urinating, dying, and living. Higher up the sloping hillside, a tribe of langurs dozed in the shade, dopey in the late afternoon heat; from time to time, a squabble or mating duel provoked a babble which then quickly subsided. It was too hot to fight, mate, or do much except wait for the coolness of dusk and the night when the forest truly came alive.

The wagon wheel rims deepened the ruts in the oft-used path as they rolled along. Most of the occupants appeared to be coddled within the covered carts, sleeping or dozing. Even the drivers were still and silent, moving only the minimum they had to in order to keep the teams of horses in line. There were almost no arms in view, and those that were visible were tucked away in rust-rimmed sheaths and carelessly kept swaddles. At first glance, it appeared to be a traditional grama— literally, a travelling tribe, for a wagon-train was the traditional collective in which the Arya hunter-gatherer tribes of yore had moved from place to place before the relatively recent era of fixed townships and city-states. But the absence of any women, the complete lack of children, and the heavily laden carts, as evidenced from the exertion expended by the horses drawing the wagons, as well as the covered wagons and oddly quiet procession, suggested something else altogether. There were none of the usual entourage of brahmins trudging doggedly behind the wagons chanting their shlokas either, which ruled out a religious procession. Vaishya traders returning from Videha to Ayodhya, laden with the spoils of a good season of barter? Perhaps.

At one point, the path curved sharply, almost doubling upon itself as it skirted a jagged outcrop of rocks protruding from the hillside. At the same time, the trees at the bottom of this little outcrop drew back, providing a roughly semicircular clearing. At some time in the not-too-distant past, two old trees had somehow been uprooted and had fallen, cutting this clearing in half in a pattern that roughly resembled an arrow fitted to a curved bow. The trees were overgrown and rotting and intersected the original path in a manner which compelled all travellers to slow and manoeuvre their way in a zigzag fashion for a few dozen yards. Each wagon and horse rider had to slow down and turn left then right, then left again, go around the edge of the outcrop where a particularly enormous boulder jutted out like the fist of a bowman preparing to loose the arrow that was the fallen trees, and then turn inwards one last time, riding in the shade of a brief valley-like enclosure between the sharp rise of the hillside here to the left and the treeline to the right, before coming back upon the original path and settling back into familiar ruts. This slowed the entire train and necessitated some concentration of driverly resources, apart from separating each wagon from the one before and after for a moment or two at each turning point.

When the first wagon completed this minor obstacle course and turned the sharp final left, the driver's attention was immediately diverted to two figures standing upon the large boulder. The angle of the sun and the high positions taken by the two men made it impossible to look directly at them. They were little more than silhouetted male figures clad in simple dhotis, that much he could see. Both held bows loosely by their sides and bore quivers on their backs, each bristling with a goodly supply of fletched arrows. They wore no swords or other weapons that the wagon driver could make out, nor did they appear to have any other companions anywhere in sight. They stood together, facing outwards in an insolent casual posture that suggested they simply happened to be there on this fine spring day, enjoying the late afternoon sunshine, and the arrows fitted loosely to the bows held in the lowered arms were simply things they happened to be carrying.

The driver raised his eyebrows, but neither slowed nor sought to stop the wagon. For one thing, it was very heavily laden, overburdened in fact, and stopping and starting required far too much effort and energy. He did not see anything that occasioned risking it. The two figures standing upon the outcropping boulder appeared to be simply…standing. If not for their oddly intense faces, he would have raised a gnarled hand and hailed them pleasantly. But there was something in their curiously identical features and stillness that reminded him of a duo of young lionesses he had seen once in the Gir woods, in the moment before they had both pounced from diagonal points, converging upon a magnificent, but age-bowed, stag. This pair put him in mind of that same relaxed yet powerfully gathered predatory stance. He was an old PF whose ancient war injuries had proved too restrictive for him to continue active service. He had retired on the king's pension and now hired himself out to lead wagon-trains like this one to earn a little extra from time to time. Like all old soldiers who had seen violence explode, he knew how even the most innocuous gesture could sometimes seem provocative or hostile to a person of another culture. He lowered his half-raised hand and stilled his voice. Better to simply ride past and on. These were strange times and there were strange people afoot.

He clicked his tongue softly and completed the turn with deft ease, the wagon swinging around, rear wheels creaking noisily as it rounded the curve. The stallion on the fore right of the team, a healthy young brute in his prime who was given to covering every female in sight if given the chance, tossed his head and shortened his steps reluctantly to compensate for the sharpness of the curve, nudged and coerced expertly by the driver. The curve done, he lowered his head and pulled hard, drawing lows of protest from his companions who were in no particular hurry to reach Ayodhya. The young stud moved as if he had an appointment with a female waiting eagerly for him in the capitol, straining at the yoke. The old driver admired his strength and youth without envying him; he had been somewhat of a bull himself in his youth. In retrospect, he preferred the quiet wisdom of age and experience over the brash virility of youth any day. He was distracted for just a fraction of an instant by the young horse's antics—long enough for everything to change.

A movement on the boulder caught his eye. He glanced up just in time to see the two figures that had been standing still as statues, suddenly stir to action. Both bows were raised, cords taut, and the old wagon rider looked up to see the lethal metal points of two long arrows aimed directly at him. He had a brief instant to think of his great-grandchildren back in Ayodhya and of the toys he had bought for them from the toy mandi in Mithila. He had been looking forward to seeing their faces dance with delight as he drew each new treat out of the jute sack. Those little tykes were his greatest source of pleasure in these last years. But then again, he had seen his share of happy faces. He was not unafraid of dying, nor foolish enough to risk it just to save some rich vaishya trader's season's stock.

He clucked the team to a halt, yanking hard twice on the young stud's reins for emphasis—the fellow was thick-headed enough to ram into the outcrop if not corrected firmly—then dropped his hands, shaking his head to indicate he meant to take no aggressive action.

One of the figures standing upon the boulder spoke. And it was then that the driver had his first real surprise in a very long time. At his age, with his war record and lifetime of experience, he had been in any number of unusual situations. But it had been a long time since he had been genuinely surprised as he was now.

Because when the person on the boulder began to speak, he realised what he hadn't been able to see before due to the angle of the sunlight.

The two bowmen were just boys.

Little more than children.

TWO

Luv fixed a bead on the lead wagon driver and kept his aim steady. The man looked like he had seen violence before, judging from the scar running down the side of his head and neck, and the way he had yielded without argument. Another veteran, for sure. What did they call them, the fellows who dressed up in those funny purple and black dhotis and vastras?

'PF,' Kush said softly beside him. 'Tough old men willing to die rather than surrender. Keep your eye on that one. He looks like trouble.'

'I have him,' Luv replied. 'You do what you have to.'

Kush disappeared.

Luv was watching the wagon driver's eyes. They were looking downwards, at the ground, apparently not looking at anything in particular. Yet Luv clearly saw them widen as Kush vanished. Smart fellow, using his peripheral vision.

Yes, this one bore watching closely. Luv would have bet his straightest arrow on the grizzled old fellow being the head of the wagon-train's security force. An old ex-PF, retired, making a few cross-border trips like this one to keep busy and earn a little to keep up his sense of pride. There would be others in the remaining wagons, younger, stronger men, more eager and less sensible, but this one was the head. Cut off the head and the body would flail uselessly. Or so it went in theory. He watched the old driver without staring directly at him—a sure way to ruin your focus and tire your eyes quickly—and didn't miss the veteran's veiled glances back up the path.

He's expecting the next wagon to come around that curve any moment, hoping to use its appearance as a distraction to leap down to the right, roll quickly, and use the wagon to shield himself.

Luv resisted the urge to grin. The man probably thought he could move pretty fast, even at this age.

And he probably can. But not faster than an arrow. Watch out, old uncle.

But it told him the man was an honourable fellow, willing to risk life and limb to earn his coin. And that made him dangerous.

* * *

Kush stood in the centre of the path, directly in the way of the second wagon. Heavily laden like the first, it had taken a few moments to manoeuvre around the rock-strewn path. Two men rode in front of this one; an older man handling the reins, a younger one riding beside him with a shortbow laid on his lap. On catching sight of him, the younger man swore and raised the bow, fitting an arrow to the string. Then held it loosely in one hand, ready to shoot. Before he could draw, Kush's arrow knocked the bow out of his hands. It struck the wooden frame of the wagon, bounced off and fell under the rear wheel. Kush heard the sound of cured wood splintering. Waste of a good weapon.

The man swore again as he snatched up a javelin lying discreetly in a recessed groove beside his seat. He had the upper body bulk of a thrower and Kush had no doubt he had probably won many melas in his day.

He called out as the man raised the metal-tipped wooden pole to shoulder height: 'Drop the weapon. Keep your arm.'

The man showed his teeth and continued without so much as a sideward glance or hesitation. *Why do they never listen!* Kush sighed. The javelin clattered back onto the wagon's boards as the man stared uncomprehendingly at the arrow that had sprouted from his bicep, disabling his arm. To his credit, he didn't scream or cry out. *At least he's a professional.* He hated it when the vaishya traders, too cheap to hire good protectors, enlisted their own over-enthusiastic relatives to guard the trains. Someone always got badly hurt then.

Kush had already turned the bow back to point at the wagon driver, another arrow already strung and ready to be loosed. The older man didn't need to have the basics of life explained to him. He was already clucking and prodding and yanking frantically at the reins. With an effort he managed to stop the wagon barely inches from Kush. The breath of the lead horses puffed warmly on Kush's bare, hairless chest.

He bent his head forward and nuzzled the dripping snout of the lead horse, a roan stallion with a white leaf-shaped patch on his forehead, whispering a few words of endearment, while keeping the bow cocked and aimed at the wagon driver. If the man jerked the team forward at that moment, Kush would have to dance merrily to somersault out of the way of the pounding hooves in time. But he trusted horses more than men. The roan's eyes would flare the instant that happened, giving him the fraction of a second he needed to act.

He kissed the roan one last time. 'Someday, I'll own a herd of beauties just like you,' he said. The roan whinnied in approval as Kush walked away.

He jerked his head sideways at the wagon driver and the protector, indicating to them to get off. When both men were on the ground, the younger one glaring balefully at Kush, ignoring the arrow stuck in the meat of his arm, Kush pointed the arrow at each one in turn, making sure they looked into his eyes and saw he was serious. The younger one still looked rebellious, so Kush shot an arrow past his head, nicking his scalp with the fletch as it hissed past, just enough to open a cut that would bleed without actually harming the man. The man cursed again, tried to clap his injured hand to the head cut, slapped his own cheek instead, then got busy trying to keep the blood out of his eyes. Head wounds never stopped bleeding on their own, and the man would need patching and herbs to staunch the small but troublesome trickle.

That, along with the arrow still in his arm, would keep him distracted enough. The driver would give Kush no trouble: he could see it in the man's eyes. He probably had grandchildren in Ayodhya he wanted to get home to and fighting to protect some rich vaishya trader's summer's earning did not seem motivation enough to risk his life.

'Keep your arrows on them, brother,' Kush called out as he ran past them. 'I shall halt the rest of the grama.'

Their eyes flicked one way then another, attempting to seek out where Kush's companions might be placed. Kush grinned as he turned the corner. Good. That would keep them well-behaved till he returned.

He rounded the corner just as the rest of the wagon-train trundled into sight. He wondered what the Sanskrit high speech word was for a train carrying only produce and goods for barter and sale. A grama was, strictly speaking, a travelling clan or extended tribe. These wagon-trains that rolled through this neck of the woods were purely carrying loads of trade items guarded and ferried by hired hands from one market town to another. There were no families here, no kith or kin. Just male kshatriyas from every background possible, all armed to defend these goods. A vaishya-grama, it should be called, he thought scornfully. Not because there was anything wrong with the vaishya class, but because a grama so wholly devoted to naught but the pursuit of wealth and individual profit was unnatural, an abomination. Then again, these were city gramas, and cities were corrupt places, breeding grounds of venial vices. These men probably thought they were merely fulfilling their dharma; not that they even knew what dharma truly meant.

'Halt!' he shouted in a voice far greater than seemed possible for one of his small frame and slender torso. His voice carried the conviction of a man who would enforce his own command with the unleashing of weapons if need be. Never mind that he was less than ten years of age. It took more than years or kilos of muscle to make a man, a man.

The line of laden wagons continued to approach without slowing down. The riders had to have seen Kush but they were urging their teams on regardless, chins tucked low, eyes narrowed. From the hunched, tensed way they sat, Kush sensed that they had either expected something like this to happen, or were prepared for it. He also knew what they intended to do—ride over him. The foremost wagon rumbled at a steady pace towards him, just about twenty yards away now. He could see the colours of the eyes of the men riding on the rider's bench. They looked grizzled and tougher than the ones on the front two wagons. Grama-rakshaks. Luv and he had heard of them, kshatriyas who travelled with gramas like this one, guarding them for a fee. It was the first time he was facing one.

He raised his bow, aiming it at them. They seemed to hunch a little lower, but made no other move. The man beside the driver already had a bow in his hand with an arrow fitted to the string, stretched and pointed downwards. As Kush raised his bow, the grama-rakshak raised his own, both arrows ready to loose now. Other than that, there was no reaction to his shouted command.

He didn't entirely blame them. A single bowman barring their way, that too one of his physical appearance, probably seemed unworthy of any response.

He would just have to prove them wrong.

'Halt, or I shoot!' he called again. The wagon was barely fifteen yards away now.

In response, the man beside the driver loosed his own arrow. It was well aimed and Kush felt the heated wind of its passing tickle his chest as he swung his body just enough to make space for the arrow to go by. His arrow was already loosed before he swung around, a fraction of a second after the grama-rakshak's arrow.

The man cursed once, and stared down at the arrow sprouting from his muscled shoulder. It was not a serious wound but it rendered him incapable of using a bow for the time being, which was all Kush had intended.

The wagon driver cracked his whip and the team of horses lurched forward, breaking into a steady canter. The speed at which they moved startled Kush. It could only mean the wagon was not as heavily laden as

Luv and he had thought. They covered the remaining ten yards to him in a trice and he barely had time to sling his bow before the towering Kambhoja stallions thundered down on him, twice his height and each weighing a half ton. More than two tons of horse and wagon pounded over him relentlessly.

THREE

Luv knew Kush was in trouble even before he heard the whinnying of horses and shouting of hoarse voices from beyond the outcrop. He wasn't startled in the least, but the old PF with the scar probably assumed he would be and made his move. He leaped off the wagon with surprising speed and ought to have rolled to the right, behind the cover of the wagon; instead he rolled left, grabbing the team's rig, using the horses as a shield. Luv's first arrow whizzed harmlessly through the gap where he had expected the man to be and his second remained notched and ready but unloosed. Firing under the team's bellies would certainly startle them and with that lead the roan stallion already impatient and restless to be on his way again, that would only result in a runaway wagon. Not part of the plan. He didn't bother to call out to the man either: the fellow knew what he was doing and obviously still had a few tricks up his sleeve. Instead, Luv aimed at a new target, a slender leathery one, and fired off three quick arrows in succession. Then he grinned, pleased at the result, and loosed a fourth one directly behind the lead roan's rump, close enough that were he to go collect that arrow it would probably smell of horse's droppings!

The roan stallion snorted in response, kicked out once, then suddenly realised what had just happened. Somehow, by some miracle, he and his equestrian companions had been set free of their burdensome load.

Without further ado, he lowered his head like a charging bull and started down the path. Startled, the rest of the team had no choice but to follow, and with the burden of the wagon gone, they instantly broke into a canter that quickly turned into a cheerful gallop as they went around the last abutment and disappeared from sight.

In the trail of dust left by their passing, the ageing wagon driver lay sprawled on the ground, staring in dazed surprise after the fleeing horses. Before he could get back to his feet, Luv had leaped off the boulder, using a series of lesser stones to hop, skip, jump to the path. He aimed the bow at the man again, who started, convinced he was about to be killed.

'Easy,' Luv said. 'We never hurt anyone unless he tries to hurt us first.'

The man showed Luv his open palms. 'I'm not looking for a fight, yuvraj. Just an old wagon driver. I leave the fighting to the grama-rakshaks.' He jerked his head backwards, indicating the path behind the stranded wagon.

Almost on cue, a fresh burst of yells and horse sounds came to them from beyond the outcrop. Judging by the sounds, Luv estimated that it wasn't the second wagon Kush was having trouble with, but the rest of the grama. *I should go to him, there might be too many for him to handle.*

He saw the old driver watching him closely during the few moments it took him to think this and consider the options. *The old man may not want to fight, but he's still a shrewd one.*

'What's your name, oldun?' he asked.

The old driver frowned, his forehead wrinkling in a way that reminded Luv of the bed of the Sona River when it had dried up in last year's drought.

'Why do you need to know that?' The old driver asked.

Luv raised the arrow a fraction.

The man shrugged. 'All right. It's Bejoo. Used to be Captain Bejoo of the Vajra—'

Luv cut him off. 'Bejoo. I don't need your atmakatha. Listen carefully. I'm leaving you alone here for a moment. I could tell you that

I have companions watching you from the woods, but I won't do that because you seem like a sharp man. So I'm just going to ask you to stay here till I get back, and not run away. You do that and I'll let you walk away unharmed. Run and I won't. Clear?'

The man looked at him suddenly with a peculiar expression.

Luv raised the arrow another fraction. 'Clear?' He couldn't keep the tone of impatience out of his voice. Kush was definitely in trouble by now, or he would have been back.

The man swallowed, then nodded. 'Aye. Ayuh, youngun. Clear as the Sarayu in spring.'

Luv looked at him sharply. 'Remember. I know these woods like the back of my hand. Run and you die.'

The man nodded again.

Again that same peculiar look. *He looks like he's just recognised me and we were long-lost friends.* But Luv had never seen the man before in his life.

Luv turned and sprinted up the path.

'Kush!' he yelled as he went. 'I'm coming!'

* * *

Kush heard the men laughing even over the thundering of the horse's hooves and the racket of the wagon. *They mean to run me down!* By kshatriya code, that meant he was free to use mortal violence against them. When someone openly attempted to kill a warrior, he in turn was justified in killing the aggressors to defend his life. Even so, Kush scornfully discarded the idea: men who used a wagon to run down a solitary boy were not worthy adversaries. What was the phrase Maatr used? 'Don't soil your arrowheads with cowardly blood!' He grinned. Maatr was always saying things like that, Vishnu bless her.

He whispered affectionately to both the horses whose rigging he was clinging to, their warm breath on his neck and face tickling him and making him giggle involuntarily. He had been ridden over before and had learned at an early age how to let the horse take you rather than resist and fight the onward-rushing force. Flesh, sinew and bone could be destroyed by that onrushing weight as easily as a footfall would snap a twig. But if a kshatriya was trained and prepared, it was like a wayward puddle being collected by an onflowing stream of water and just as effortless. He had simply let the pounding horses bear down on him, crouched down at just the right angle, and grabbed hold of the rigging between the two lead horses at precisely the right moment—the warrior's moment, as he and Luv liked to call it. On the raj-marg, one either moved aside—often at breakneck speed to avoid some of those hot-riding royal contingents—or got crushed under thundering hooves and chariot or wagon wheels. Ever since they could remember, they had seen people killed thus, often old folk too weak or slow to move aside in time, poor unfortunate people carrying too heavy a load to toss aside in time and most heartrending of all, children as small as themselves, tiny bodies mangled from the hooves into a shapeless heap of shattered bones and oozing flesh. After viewing one particularly nasty aftermath of a visiting royal procession with an armed escort, Luv and he had begun to teach themselves how to survive such encounters without ending up as battered blood-mash. By the age of five, when they were tall enough to reach the rigging of the tall horses that thundered down the king's road, they had mastered the art of letting the horse take them. Now, it was easy as clinging to Maatr's breast.

He had begun working his way down the length of the rigging almost immediately after being picked up. Now he looked up between a crack in the floorboards of the driver's seat at the two men riding there. The one with the arrow in his shoulder was still cursing, but his indignation at his own pain was outweighed by his amusement at having run over the 'brigand'. They were tough grizzled old veterans, probably ex-PFs like the one in the lead wagon. Kush didn't waste more time on them. He was more interested in finding out what cargo they carried that had made them too nervous to halt. It was the work of only another moment to haul himself under the wagon itself, then up the side where he found enough space under the flap covering to slip into the vehicle without those in the following wagon seeing him.

Inside the wagon, the noise of the grama oddly muted by the heavy canvas covering, he stared around at the consignment for a long silent moment, stunned.

Of all the possible cargoes he had expected, this was not on the list.

Just then he heard the men shouting and the wagon slowing, and he knew that could only mean one thing: they had reached the stranded second wagon. And most likely, Luv as well.

Now, the fun would begin.

FOUR

When Luv came sprinting around the outcrop, two pairs of eyes instantly snapped around to stare at him. The two men on the second wagon looked startled to see him. *I know that look. They think I'm Kush and can't figure out how he could have run off in that direction and then appeared again from this direction.* He was used to that response. He yelled at them as he sprinted past: 'Stay where you are!' They looked too startled to try anything anyway.

Barely had he run past the wagon when he heard the sound of pounding hooves from ahead, around the next spur of rock. A few broken boulders lay on the path, their insides gleaming rusty red where they had broken open after falling in a minor landslide during the last monsoon. Others had been pushed over deliberately to block the path, for this was a popular ambush point on the raj-marg. The sound of hooves and rattling of wagon wheels was very loud by then and he knew better than to run around a blind turn. Instead he swerved and leaped up onto the largest broken boulder. He could smell the iron in the air here, so rich was the vein in the lohit stone. These hills were rife with minerals, good pure ore for making steel.

He stood in the relaxed archer position that Bearface had taught them, waiting.

Don't call your guru that name, Maatr's voice said in his mind's ear, *He is Gurudev to you, remember!*

Yes, Maa.

The position that Bearface had taught them, the lazy cobra, as their guru had called it, was now second nature. He waits, seemingly indolent, swaying lazily, but the instant threat appears, he strikes with lightning speed.

Luv didn't know if he moved at lightning speed, but the instant the wagon came into sight, he let fly. The first arrow hit its mark and the second was flying even before the wagon had rolled fully into view. A man shouted out with pain and tumbled off the wagon, with two arrows sprouting, one from each shoulder—the first had clearly been Kush's work. The driver screamed like a wounded horse and clutched at the arrow quivering in the meat of his thigh—the head must have struck the thighbone, hence the vibration and the extreme pain. Then the wagon rolled past and the next came into view, and still no sight of Kush.

Dammit, Luv thought, feeling the heat rise in his face, cheeks burning. *Where are you?*

The men on this wagon were better prepared and were better shots. Three well-aimed arrows came blurring at Luv and he had to somersault sideways to dodge both. Landing on his bare feet on the rubble of the lohit stone, he felt warmth on his waist where one had nicked the skin just enough to draw a bead or two. He loosed off two quick ones before the men could shoot the second volley, and both hit their marks. Both men dropped their own bows, one grunting, the other choosing the strong silent response.

Then the rest of the grama came into view, riding fast, faster than any grama ought to have been, especially on this twisting treacherous neck of the raj-marg. Everything began to move very quickly, so quickly that Luv felt his senses slowing to a crawl as they always did in a fight, the world popping into brilliant crystalline clarity and colour: the veins on every leaf visible, every knothole on the wooden slats of a wagon's side in view, hearing every grinding creak in a wheel, smelling the raw red odours of freshly spilled human blood mixed in with the pungent smell of horse sweat, man-sweat and the rusty tang of the lohit stone.

The flaps of the following wagons opened and revealed armed men. Burly, hirsute, armoured men in the familiar purple and black of Ayodhya's inner guard. PFs, or some new extension of the PF regiment—for PFs were meant to guard the inner city, not ride with trading gramas as hired escorts. Whatever they were, whomever they were, there were a lot of them, too many for Luv to simply disarm. He would have to fight them seriously to survive, kill some quite likely. And even then it would be touch and go.

The good warrior knows when to retreat, said his guru's gruff voice in his ear. The code of the kshatriya means nothing if there is no kshatriya left to fight!

Agreeing with Bearface—sorry, Gurudev—was his mother's voice in his other ear. *Run, Luv, run! You can't fight them all!*

Ji, Maatr, jaisi aagya, he said in his mind as he began the heavy task of fitting arrows to bow and aiming not to maim or disarm but to disable, possibly kill. *I would love to run. But not without my brother.*

'Dammit Kush, where the hell are you?' he said aloud as he began shooting.

* * *

Kush emerged from the wagon to see his twin brother standing on a pile of lohit stone landslide, the edges of the outcrop at his back, loosing arrows with concentrated ease. He appeared to be single-handedly battling what looked like at least five quads of armed PFs, even though PFs never ventured armed and uniformed outside the Ayodhya city limits. Clearly this grama was a notable exception to the usual rules.

Which makes sense, considering the cargo they're carrying, he thought as he sprinted away from Luv and to the other side of the raj-marg, unnoticed by either his brother or the men busy trying to kill him. In three deft leaps and grabs, he had climbed a tree and was standing on a near-horizontal branch twice as thick as his own thigh. It would have bent and drooped under a grown man's weight but it took his lithe form easily, and he steadied his left shoulder against the trunk, took aim at his first target and loosed. The man took the arrow in the meaty muscle joining shoulder to neck, and it popped out through his collarbone with a small spurt of blood. The man yelped like a pup and dropped the javelin he had been about to fling at Luv.

Without turning to look directly at Kush, Luv cried out with joy. 'Kush!' Then added in a disgruntled tone even as he continued loosing and dodging: 'Took your time, didn't you!'

'Had to make a short visit to the royal treasury,' Kush called back, grinning. He continued loosing, and saw his third target drop, roaring with frustration and fury as he tried to clutch at the arrow sprouting from his shoulder blade. *Hit the bone, hurts like blazes.* That voice was old Nakhudi's, who always seemed to know how to inflict maximum pain on the enemy without actually killing them. *Only male enemies,* as she liked to remind them, grinning to reveal her astonishingly white gleaming teeth in her buffalo-dark face.

The fight continued for another few moments, the PFs on and around the halted wagons trying with admirable skill to face an attack on two diagonally opposed fronts with diminishing success. Their leader, an efficient and intelligent-seeming fellow, tried to rally his men to use the wagons as shielding, while attempting to send a pair of quads around to outflank Kush—Luv was bolstered by the outcrop which would have taken hours to cut over and around—but the brothers had them at the deadliest cross-angle two bowmen could take, and the broken stones shielded Luv while the tree and foliage shielded Kush, and while many arrows and javelins were aimed at them, none came closer than a single wayward arrow that thunked into the tree branch between Kush's big toe and its neighbour.

Then, as fierce fights usually did, this one dissipated like a puddle evaporating under a midday sun, and suddenly the captain of the PFs was waving his arms in surrender.

Kush grinned and dropped down from his perch, making his way cautiously towards the halted wagons. He had his eye on some men at the back who might, if still feisty enough, try to fling a javelin or two as he approached. But every one of them and all the others as well had at least one arrow in their arm, leg or back, and one massively built chap who had refused to settle down with just two or even three arrows had four bristling from his extremities, lying on his back and cursing the sky roundly with a raised fist, turning the air blue with his choice of profanities. Kush grinned even wider, making a note of several for future reference. Living in an ashram community as they did, good curses were hard to come by!

Luv had leaped up to the tall broken lohit stone boulder, keeping his weapon trained on the PFs as his brother approached. Kush winked at him as he came and saw Luv shake his head in mock-disgust—complaining about the moments when Kush had disappeared from sight earlier. The PFs quietened as he reached them, holding down their moaning and grunting and cursing as they saw the 'men' who had bested them up close for the first time.

FIVE

'You should have seen their faces,' Kush said, slapping his thigh with delight. 'They looked like brahmins who had eaten ashubh bhojan by mistake and didn't know whether to spit it out rudely or swallow it and violate dharma!'

'And they had so many arrows sticking out of their arms and legs,' Luv said, 'if they stood close together in a bunch, they would have looked like a giant hedgehog!'

Both boys laughed in the high-pitched tone of young men whose voices had not been altered by maturity yet.

Nakhudi grunted non-committally, shaking her head wistfully. 'You boys. One of these days, you'll run up against someone who's a match for you two, and there will be hell to pay. How many gramas have you held up and robbed until now?'

'Nakhudi!' Luv said plaintively. 'We didn't rob anybody! We just took back a fair share of what Ayodhya takes from the people unlawfully, that's all.'

'That's right,' Kush said, equally outraged. 'Whatever we took from those gramas belonged to the people, and we took it to give it back to the people anyway. So it wasn't robbing!'

Nakhudi looked at their two young faces, identical chins turned up stubbornly to point at her, dusky cheeks flushed with their recent adventures and their present outrage. She shook her head slowly. She had been picking out berries from her thatched basket to offer them—the boys loved berries and she always kept some just for their visits. She put down the handful of choice berries she had picked out lovingly from the basket and stood. Her head almost bumped the roof of her little hut when she drew herself to her full height, for it was built low to withstand the sweeping monsoon winds that sometimes washed this hillock in the midst of the deep woods. She glared down at the boys. Standing to her full height, she topped their tousled heads by easily twice their height; she was taller than any woman they had ever seen, taller than most men they knew, and her scarred broad face, flat nose, shining dark eyes, and formidable bulk all combined to give her a fierce aspect. She used all of that as well as the hoarse voice that lent her an air of danger and made her seem angry even when she wasn't, to deliberately intimidate them.

'Listen to me, and listen well, for I'll only say this once,' she rasped, poking an outstretched finger into Luv's chest and then at Kush's chest. To the boys, strong as they were for their age, it felt like being struck by the blunt end of a thin staff or rod. She cracked her knuckles and stretched her hands, as if limbering up for more aggressive action, which only added to the air of threat. 'Ayodhya makes the laws in this part of the world. By Indra's hundred eyes, what am I saying? Ayodhya is the law. This jungle may seem unpopulated and a long way from any city, but it's still part of the Kosala nation. And by law, it falls under Ayodhyan jurisdiction and governance. That governance includes the right to tax the people as required from time to time. So don't call what they take unlawful.'

They glanced at each other doubtfully. Suddenly, the same two young bowmen who had stood up to an entire grama protected by armed warriors, had been reduced to just two startled young boys. It had taken only a change of tone and attitude on Nakhudi's part; the hermit woman always had that effect on them. Part of it was a result of the respect and awe they felt for her warrior skills and long-standing comradeship with their mother. But they were also scared of her. Nakhudi when angered was a fearsome thing to behold. For reasons they could not wholly fathom, she was clearly angered now. And they didn't like it one bit.

'Now, you boys may feel that after the droughts and famines and other ill winds that have harried the kingdom over the last several years, Ayodhya ought not to be taxing the people and I can't say I disagree with you. Kali Herself knows that times are hard enough as it is, and the tax is only one more back-breaking burden piled on top of too many others. But that's not for you or me to decide. That's Ayodhya's decision. And if Ayodhya chooses to levy the tax, then that makes it a lawful tax. You boys saw the suffering of a few people who reside in these remote parts and felt sorry for them. So you decided to hold up a grama or two—or is it three? How many is it anyway?'

She snapped her fingers right by Kush's ear, loud enough that it sounded like a twig snapping underfoot.

The boy didn't flinch but said sullenly, 'Three so far. But one was only—'

'Be quiet while your elders are talking.' She continued decisively, 'So you hold up three gramas in as many seasons, and take a wagonload from each one. And you distribute the contents of that wagonload to the poorest, most needy people you can find around here. And it's true, the few people who live here in this Durga-forsaken jungle are really poor and truly needy. And it's a great service you do them, by giving them those provisions. I don't deny that one whit. But make no mistake about this one truth: those wagonloads of goods you take by force don't belong to the people anymore. The minute Ayodhya's tax-collectors claim it, it belongs to Ayodhya. So you are robbing Ayodhya. I'm not saying it's not for a good cause; indeed, I agree that it's a very good cause. But that doesn't make it right, or just, or even lawful. So don't go fooling yourself about the rightness or lawfulness of what you're doing. Understand?'

Both boys glared at her with such identical expressions of righteous indignation on their handsome young faces, she was instantly reminded of someone else. A man's face, older, leaner, darker-complected. Much darker-complected, for they had inherited their mother's wheatish colouring and more than a smidgen of their grandfather's lightness of skin. But the features were the same. So much the same that looking at them now, with those defiant expressions on their young faces, it made her want to grin and burst out laughing. She restrained herself. She knew how much they respected and looked up to her and this was an important lesson she was giving them. Their mother had been right. 'Be a friend to them, Nakhu,' she had said quietly to her at the beginning, when she had first come to live here. It had been soon after she had rebuilt her old ties with her old friend and sometime mistress, and they had grown close enough to speak the heart's truth to one another again. 'Be the friend to them that I cannot be, because I am their mother. And as a friend, teach them the things that they will not heed if I try to teach them. For oftentimes, young boys and girls will heed the same advice when given by an outsider while they would shrug off a parent saying the same things.' And Vedavati, as she was now called, had smiled wistfully and shaken her head before going on with more than a trace of sadness: 'Because my boys are growing up already. And I fear they may be growing too fast.'

Nakhudi had taken these words to heart. She had wanted to give the twins this talk ever since they had burst into her hut last monsoon, flushed and bursting with pride from the thrill of having successfully waylaid the first grama and having taken an entire wagonload of grain from the tax collectors. But she had remembered their Maatr's words, gritted her teeth, and bided her time until now. She had even laughed with them and celebrated their 'success' at the time, although when they returned in the autumn to crow about waylaying the second grama, her smile had been forced and her joy a pretence. This time, she could not take anymore. It was time to stop being a friend and be something more. Perhaps even past time. A grama guarded by six or seven quads of Ayodhyan PFs? Parvati protect us all! Even allowing for some youthful exaggeration, they had still put their little heads into a tiger's jaws this time. It was one thing to hold up a tax grama or a trading grama and take away some grain or other provisions. This new shenanigan was in a different league altogether. She shuddered to think what would have happened had their little adventure gone awry. After all, for all their skill with the dhanush-baan, they were still just boys. Not yet adolescents. And if they continued on this path, not likely to achieve that stage of maturation. *Yes, Vedavati,* she said silently now, *your boys are indeed growing up too fast. And I think there is nothing anyone can do to slow or stop it.*

'But I can correct you at least,' she said aloud. They both frowned simultaneously, and where their frowns met in the centre of their foreheads, between their brows, two little diagonal crinkles appeared, like tiny crow's feet. Her heart leaped with emotion. Their father had the exact same crinkles on his forehead when he frowned. That little detail, more than all the similarities of face and body shape, and attitude, brought home to her once more just who and what they truly were. And why it was so important that they be bred right. She raised her palm, showing it to Kush, who was closest—and this time he did flinch, for she was close enough to slap him if she wanted, and an open-handed slap from her would hurt far more than just harsh words. But she only placed it on his left shoulder, firmly and quite gently, in fact.

In a much gentler tone, she said, 'I can correct you and show you when you're wrong. For that is what friends do for one another. And it is time you realised that you have gone too far. By taking on this grama today and injuring all those PFs, you've not just stolen another wagonload of provisions from the tax collector, you've challenged the military might and authority of Ayodhya herself. And that's not something you boast and laugh about, young men.' She patted Kush's shoulder affectionately, tempering her tirade with friendship now, before she lost their trust entirely. 'That's all I want you both to understand. As a friend who cares about your well-being,' she added, looking from one to the other slowly.

'They weren't provisions,' Luv said sullenly, looking down at the dung-packed floor of the little hut that had been home to Nakhudi these past two years.

'What was that?' she asked sharply.

'He said, they weren't provisions,' Kush replied. 'The wagonload we took today. It was something else. Something different.'

And he shot her a glance that was at once a defiant challenge as well as a triumphant comeback: *See? We're not just young children to be corrected and talked down to. We did something today that children could never do.*

Nakhudi swallowed. Something stirred deep inside her belly, some long-sleeping snake of forgotten fear.

'Show me,' she said shortly. And prayed to all the avatars of the Goddess she could name.

SIX

The ashram of Maharishi Valmiki was peaceful and quiet in the yellowing light of dusk. The red ochre robes of the rishis and senior brahmacharyas stood out in clear relief against the rich green darbha grass nourished by the recent rains, while the white dhotis of the younger acolytes caught the fading light and seemed to glow as if illuminated. The sky above the hermitage clearing was purple, broken by clusters of gold-tinged clouds that clung to the last light of the descended sun. Brahmins went about their evening chores, their clean faces and hands testifying to their recent completion of sandhyavandana in the nearby Tamasa River.

Most of the rishis and brahmacharyas deftly avoided crossing paths with, or coming face to face with, Nakhudi. Even though she too was clad in the faded yet still serviceable rust-brown garb of a sadhini, a female hermit on the same spiritual path as they, the ashramites still seemed to prefer to give her a wide berth. She barely noticed, striding across the centre of the ashram directly towards the thatched mud hut on the extreme north-eastern corner, set a sufficient distance away from the remaining structures to afford the ashramites a modicum of privacy from the only unattached female resident who inhabited it, yet close enough that the hut was not entirely separated from the ashram.

The soft questioning voices of the curious acolytes fell away behind Nakhudi as she turned down the short path that led to Vedavati's hut, nestled in a small cluster of sala trees. She did not need to turn to see if Luv and Kush followed her. This was their home. Where else would they go? Besides, it was Vedavati she had to speak to urgently. *Kali, grant there is still time to set this right*, she prayed silently, even as a sinking sensation in the pit of her belly told her that it was already too late. The damage was done, and quite likely the price would have to be paid when the time came. *But they're just boys*, she thought, *just boys doing what they thought was the right thing to do at the wrong time*. Surely they would not be punished too harshly for not realising what they might be getting themselves into? *Yes*, said the voice inside her head, *but you knew what they were doing and could have stopped them. It need never have come to this.*

She ground her teeth in frustration and stopped at the doorway of the hut. Like all huts in all ashrams, it had no door to speak of, merely a curtain of jute hanging across the open entranceway. She parted the curtain with her hand, swatting it aside, and peered inside. Nobody home. Well, Vedavati must be around somewhere. She would have been expecting the boys home in time for sandhyavandana. Nakhudi remembered belatedly that she had forgotten to stop and ensure that the boys underwent their evening ablutions as required by ashram rules. She had had bigger things in mind than rituals.

She looked around, uncertain. Where could Vedavati have gone at such a time?

'By the river,' Luv said from behind.

Nakhudi turned away from the entrance, allowing the jute cloth to fall back into place. She looked in the direction the twins were staring, and saw Vedavati coming up the path from the river, an earthen pot balanced on her hip. Looking at her erstwhile mistress's roughcloth robe, matted hair, and subdued aspect, not to mention the lines of age showing on her face, the charcoal-grey streaks in her hair, and the weariness in her eyes, Nakhudi felt a deep pang of sadness. Had she not known all that had transpired those ten long years ago, she might have been persuaded into believing that Sita was still in exile, the same exile in which she had been ten years before that, before the events that led her and then Rama to Lanka and altered their lives forever.

His exile ended, hers goes on. For how long, my Devi? Is this always a woman's lot? To suffer in silence while men live their lives in boisterous vitality? She carries a mud pot filled with water she drew herself from the river at dusk, back to a thatched hut where she sleeps on a straw pallet and eats falaahar the year round, while he sleeps and sits on satin sheets, is attended by thousands, and drinks the wine of the devas, precious soma, from golden goblets if it pleases his fancy? How can life be so unjust? Is this dharma? If so, it is man's dharma, not woman's dharma.

Vedavati was aware of their presence yet did not overly react. She approached quietly, greeting her sons with a knowing look, and Nakhudi with a wisp of a smile. 'Sister,' she said, before going into her humble domicile. Nakhudi decided to follow her inside, in an effort to keep their dialogue as private as possible for the moment. First she glanced sharply at the boys and pointed to the tiny patch of mud before the threshold. 'Sweep that,' she said, and went in.

Vedavati was carefully setting down the brimming pot in a shaded corner. She picked up a piece of the mineralised phitkari stone that every ashramite used, dipped it carefully into the water, stirring slowly for several moments, in widening circles. Nakhudi waited with growing impatience. The phitkari stone sterilised the water and separated any pollutants, dispersing them to the bottom of the vessel. Vedavati finished the sterilisation, put the stone carefully beside the pot, and covered the mouth of the pot with a fresh clean papaya leaf. Vedavati emptied, washed, and replenished the drinking water pot daily, replacing the leaf everyday as well. Nakhudi couldn't remember if she had done the same last week or last month! As always she was humbled and moved by how clean and sweet-smelling Vedavati managed to keep this humble domicile. Yet the simplicity of the dwelling shamed her, Nakhudi, who had herself occupied better quarters back when she had been Sita's bodyguard and captain of her personal queensguard in Mithila two-and-a-half decades ago. It was humiliating to see her former princess living here, like some common sadhini. No, not a princess anymore, she reminded herself, a queen! A queen-mother, no less. Maatr to the heirs of the greatest Arya nation.

Nakhudi shook her head once more in disgust and outrage: *Men!* At the same time, she felt pride at how well Sita upheld her dignity through this utterly simple yet immaculate existence. Truly, she was no less than a living embodiment of Devi herself. Even the name given to her by Maharishi Valmiki was an appropriate one: Vedavati. Nakhudi had heard it said around the ashram, always with a reverential awed tone, that Kush and Luv's Maatr was better versed in the Vedas than any other woman alive.

Dusk had turned to darkness by the time Vedavati was done with her evening chores. The boys had finished cleaning the outside threshold, aangan, and surroundings, and had even lit the house lamp that hung by the door of the hut, but they still remained outside. No doubt, to avoid chancing their mother's wrath as long as possible. The lamp's yellow glow provided sufficient light to illuminate Nakhudi and her longtime friend and mistress within the hut, though it also reminded her depressingly of the day-bright illumination that had lit up the glittering luxury and gleaming beauty of Maharaja Janak's palace in those days of yore. From light to darkness, they had come a long way from home, Nakhudi thought not without some bitterness. Her former mistress broke into her thoughts.

'What have they been up to this time?' Sita asked matter-of-factly, without preamble.

Nakhudi told her.

Even in the dim light and flickering reflections, she saw Sita blanch. She felt awful at bringing such news. But it was better than Sita not knowing.

'This will have consequences,' she finished at last, spreading her calloused palms on her meaty thighs. She waited for Sita's response.

The exiled queen of Ayodhya sighed. 'Ayodhya again.' She looked up at Nakhudi with a puzzled smile twisting her mouth. 'Did it have to be Ayodhya, of all places? Why not some other nation? Why only Ayodhya?'

Nakhudi shrugged, knowing better than to answer that one aloud. Silently, she thought: *Because your karma is eternally intertwined with his, that's why, my lady.*

SEVEN

Sita stood looking into the back of the wagon for a long time. So long that the boys grew nervous and fidgety and began shuffling from foot to foot, then hopping, then holding hands and doing a kind of jig, wholly involuntary and instinctive, until Nakhudi turned and gave them the full benefit of one of her formidable glares, which stopped them short. They stood with slumped shoulders then, though the overly beatific expressions on their faces suggested more than a touch of mock innocence. *What? We? Never!* She controlled the urge to cuff them on their backs, knowing it would only make them whoop and cough with pretended pain, while actually laughing. They were boys after all, though when watching them in a pitched fight, it was hard to remember that. She was certain their opponents didn't care, which only made their exploits that much more dangerous. *Only a matter of time,* she thought in dismay, *before they meet their match. Maate protect them both!*

Finally, Sita let the burlap flap drop and turned away. She put her fists on her hips and looked at the boys. Their innocent wide-eyed expressions deepened to the point of self-parody.

'Well,' Vedavati said at last. 'This time you've really gone and done it, you two.'

'We were just—'

'Shut up.'

'—taking back—'

'Be quiet.'

'—rightfully ours!'

'Hold your tongues!'

'We thought it was—'

'Silence, you scamps!'

'—another vaishya grama with grains—'

'I said—'

'—need food desperately, they're near-starvation and—'

'Enough!' Vedavati's voice cracked like a whip, making even Nakhudi wince.

The boys held their tongues this time.

Their mother moved closer, facing them directly, hands crossed firmly across her chest now. Nakhudi saw from the faint flush lightening Sita's neck and lower face that she was really upset this time. It took a lot to upset Sita. She swallowed, wishing she could slip away and leave mother and sons to sort out the matter on their own. She was dreading the moment when Vedavati would realise that Nakhudi had known about the boys' antics from the time of the very first waylaying. She glanced around, glad that the boys had been wise enough to hide the stolen wagon in this remote hollow deep in the woods, where there was nobody to see and hear. She had not even been able to bring herself to think about the consequences that awaited them once the survivors of the waylaying reached Ayodhya and reported to their superiors there. Sita brought up that very issue just then.

'Do you know what you have done?' Vedavati asked her sons, the colour rising in her face for the first time in weeks that Nakhudi had seen. 'You have transgressed against the authority of Ayodhya! Do you even understand what that means?'

The boys looked up at their Maatr, their big-eyed innocent expressions slowly fading as they saw just how angry she was, and how much effort she was putting into controlling that anger. They also saw what Nakhudi saw, that she had already flashed past her ire at the boys for their youthful waywardness to the larger issue at hand, and that observation deflated any further attempt to appeal to her maternal affections.

'Nakhudi explained it to us,' Kush said, looking down with his head tilted awkwardly, as young boys will do when they are discomfited. 'We broke the law, she says. But we didn't know that. We thought we were just taking back what was the people's. Honest, Maatr!'

'Yes, Maatr!' Luv chipped in, looking as disconcerted as his twin.

Vedavati glared at them both in turn, showing them what she thought of their understanding and misinterpretation of the law. But aloud she said: 'They won't let this rest. That's for sure.' She frowned, thinking. 'You say you waylaid this grama just this morning?'

Both nodded vigorously.

Sita looked up at the rock walls of the hollow, turning around slowly as she thought for a moment. The torch in Nakhudi's hand threw flickering yellow light up several yards, illuminating the overhanging broken rock walls that leaned together to produce the empty cave-like hollow where the boys had brought the wagon. The hollow was at the rear of the very outcrop near which the boys had stopped and robbed the wagon grama, although one had to know it was there or one would never find it easily, even though it was literally within stone's throw of the raj-marg itself. The choice of hiding place was as ingenious as everything else the twins ever did, but Nakhudi doubted whether that would help them much if what Sita feared came to pass.

'That means they ought to reach Ayodhya in three days, maybe even two if they travel fast.' She flashed them angry looks, the torchlight reflecting in her dark eyes and giving her an unmother-like aspect. 'But more likely they would have sent a rider ahead to give Ayodhya the news of the waylaying. In which case, he would reach Ayodhya before nightfall tomorrow.' She mumbled something incoherent that Nakhudi sure was a curse. 'Doesn't give us much time.'

'Much time for what, Maatr?' Luv asked in some puzzlement. Nakhudi glanced at them both, the torch sending their shadows fleeing as she turned it towards them. Both boys looked more concerned about their mother's stress than about any anger she might display towards them. *They still don't fully understand the implications of what they've done.*

Sita looked at them and shook her head in disgust as she came to the same conclusion. She sighed and said, 'To try to make amends.'

Kush looked at his brother. 'How, Maatr?'

Sita gestured at the wagon. 'Only one way that I can think of now. Unless you have a better idea?' This last she tossed at Nakhudi, who shrugged, then shook her head. Sita nodded, and raised her hands in the universal gesture of despair. 'Then, there's only one thing we can do to try and make amends. We have to give this back. At once. That means taking this wagon back to Ayodhya and delivering it to them with a full apology for your actions.'

Kush and Luv stared at their mother as if she had suddenly sprouted a second head and spoken in voices. 'What?' they said at exactly the same time, in the exact same tone of shocked outrage.

Sita looked at them both with her hands on her hips. 'Well, smarty boys, what would you have us do, then?'

Luv shrugged. Kush imitated him. 'Why not just keep it?'

Sita raised her eyebrows at them, then turned to Nakhudi. 'Of course! Why didn't I think of that, right, Nakhudi? Why not just…keep it!' She laughed a semi-hysterical laugh that echoed oddly in the enclosed rock hollow.

Nakhudi glanced around nervously. She didn't like being in a place like this, with only one ingress, in the jungle at night. Even the military gramas avoided passing through this neck of the woods at night. Panthers, boars, lions, wolf packs, snakes, you could take your pick of predators on the prowl. The Valmiki ashramites knew better than to venture even to the edges of the light-pools thrown by the ashram lanterns at night—and despite their extreme caution there were always incidents. She hoped Sita would keep her voice down to avoid attracting undue animal attention.

Sita shook her head in despair, walking several steps to and fro before turning to say to the boys: 'Do you know what you stole today? Do you even understand?' She went up to the back of the wagon, hopped up on the rear steps, and twitched the flap open with a single flick of her wrist, sending the flap over the top of the wagon where it fell with a heavy rustling sound. Nakhudi hefted the mashaal, raising it up to throw some light into the back of the wagon. Standing that way, her feet slightly apart, one arm raised with the torch in hand, reminded her vaguely of a statue she had seen somewhere in her many travels that was sculpted in an identical pose. For the life of her, she couldn't remember where or when. Then again, perhaps she was only wistfully wishing someone would sculpt her in this pose. Yes, sure, she thought sarcastically, the great lady with the upraised torch, casting light upon the ill-gotten gains of theft and brigandry!

'This,' Sita said, gesturing at the wagon filled with massive chests thrown open earlier by she herself when examining the contents, 'is a war wagon.' The treasure within the chests—for it was nothing less than a treasure—glittered, gleamed and shone as the gold ingots, silver bars, coins, gems, and other precious items caught and refracted the light from Nakhudi's torch. 'Tribute collected to finance Ayodhya's next war.'

Nakhudi nodded in agreement: she knew enough about the inner workings of a kingdom to recognise a war chest when she saw one. This was no mere tithe, lagaan, or other kind of tax; only a royal tribute could be this rich. And protected as it was by such a heavily armed contingent of PFs, Ayodhya's elite regiment of royal guards, a war wagon was the only likelihood that presented itself. Literally a wagonload of wealth to be used to pay for a major military offensive, which begged the questions: What war was Ayodhya planning to wage? Against whom? When? Nakhudi had no answers to such questions. Hell. She didn't even want to know the answers. She wished fervently now as she had that morning when the boys first brought her here to show her their rich pickings, that she had never laid eyes on that goddamned wagon.

Sita turned back to glare at her sons, black pupils flashing darkly in the torchlight. 'The penalty for stealing a war wagon belonging to Ayodhya is not mere imprisonment or a penalty. It is death to one's entire family, on grounds of treason.'

Nakhudi watched the boys' faces lose every last vestige of youthful brashness as the full implications of Sita's words sank in. She felt sorry for them in that moment. This time, they had truly bitten off more than they—or anyone else—could chew. They had just sentenced themselves and their Maatr to certain death. Now, no matter what any of them did next, their crime was beyond forgiving. Except…and Nakhudi drew in a deep breath, the arm holding the upraised mashaal shaking slightly… except by a king's pardon. And that, she thought, looking at the sons of Sita as they absorbed the crushing blow of the implications of their boyish transgression, was as unlikely as the moon lighting up the world with light as bright as sunshine.

EIGHT

For perhaps the first time in his long and wearying life, Bejoo felt no pleasure at seeing the familiar towers and skyline of Ayodhya appear on the horizon. As the grama topped the hilly rise that led up from Mithila Bridge before trundling down the raj-marg into the Sarayu Valley, he felt none of the relief and satisfaction that his fellow PFs felt in that moment. Their gruff voices, several shot through with more than a little anger at their painful wounds and abject humiliation, rang out in the still dawn air around him, lending the grama's last leg of travel a festive atmosphere. He did not share in it. All he felt right now was trepidation and gloom.

His mood had not altered by the time the grama rolled sonorously through the first gate and wound its way up Raghuvamsha Avenue to its destination, the royal quadrant. The high stone walls of the eighth gate only worsened his mood. Once, this had been a bustling intersection where citizens, merchants, and anyone and everyone had freely roved. A public space like all the rest of Ayodhya had been. It was hard to believe that was only a decade ago. Now, the forebodingly high stone wall that marked the end of the public sections of Ayodhya and the start of the highly restricted royal quadrant, was a symbol of the new Ayodhya, a city divided into two parts—one, the public prosperous trading and residential public city where almost a lakh of citizens of all castes, creeds, and persuasions still lived in cosmopolitan harmony as they profited, worked with, and traded with one another; two, the royal quadrant, where only a hundred or so royally favoured clans resided in luxuriant elegance, their lives, estates and activities separated from the hustle and bustle of the outer city—the Lower City as it had come to be called derisively of late—while they remained in the sheltered shadow of the Fortress.

For that was what the palatial complex had become now. A veritable fortress.

Bejoo looked up despondently as the grama entered through the trade gate of the royal quadrant—the front gate was only for royalty or the court-favoured clans—and felt even more depressed at the sight of the massively reinforced structures that had been erected a decade ago and added to considerably in the intervening years, altering the once-beautiful open architecture of the royal palace complex into an ugly forbidding military enclosure. He sighed. As a soldier, he ought to have appreciated the superior protection these architectural changes provided to the royal Suryavansha Ikshwaku dynasty which he was sworn to protect with his life. But as an Ayodhyan and Arya citizen, he felt more pity and sadness at what had been lost in order to gain this superior level of protection. Was it worth it in the end? He had never thought so, and today, feeling as despondent and morose as he did, he felt that the loss of the former beauty and sense of freedom and interconnectedness that the old layout had provided was too high a price to have paid for better defence. Much too high a price.

He put thoughts of architecture and security out of his head as he pulled up the team before the cantonment stables. Men rushed forward to take the weary horses and tend to them, moving with military efficiency. It was the work of moments for the vital contents of the wagons to be unloaded and carried to a suitably safe location indoors where they would be barred and sealed and guarded closely. And inventoried.

He sighed, stretching his travel-weary limbs and started towards the lockhouse with reluctant steps.

Pradhan Mantri Jabali was already waiting by the entrance of the lockhouse, along with his munshis. Bejoo didn't like the minister. He hadn't liked him when he had been just a minister, he had liked him even less when he became war minister and his notorious War Council was imbedded as a permanent fixture instead of the ad hoc committee it used to be; now, he actively disliked him as pradhan mantri. The chief of the ministers of the sabha, the assembly that administered the kingdom and its capital city under the guidance and oversight of the king, ought not to be a bigoted bad-tempered self-righteous and overly pious war-mongering old man. Especially when he had followed in the footsteps of Sumantra, perhaps the finest prime minister the Kosala nation had ever had.

Bejoo had never been high enough in the military chain of command to have been privy to the inner workings of Dasaratha's government, but he hadn't needed to be. The results were there for all to see, from the highest senapati to the lowest sipahi. Those in Dasaratha's army had been proud of the fact that the last Asura War had been twenty-two years ago and that peace had reigned supreme since then; a peace they took pride in being responsible for instituting and maintaining. Those in Rama's army—or, more accurately these days, Mantri Jabali's army—took pride in Ayodhya's military supremacy and how effectively intimidated even their closest allies were by that supremacy. Governance by cooperation versus governance by sword, Bejoo thought with more than a little bitterness. Like all old kshatriyas, he believed that the true purpose of the warrior class was not to wage war and inflict violence, but to help preserve a state where neither was necessary. He did not speak such thoughts aloud. These days, under this regime, such thinking was considered—

'Treason!' Jabali said sharply, pointing his forefinger—accusingly, it seemed to Bejoo—with the tip of the finger crooked, a result of the ageing minister's advanced arthritis. Bejoo archly noted the curious resemblance between the angle of the crooked finger and the mantri's hooked nose. 'Open treason that must be punished at once!'

Bejoo sighed inwardly. He had expected this very reception. Although he had hoped for a few moments of respite before the haranguing began in earnest. And perhaps, Shaneshwara willing, a brief audience with Rama himself, so that *I may try to put things in perspective before this old vulture twists it all out of recognition and embarks on another of his notorious demon-hunts.* He tried to put aside his weariness and despondency, and face the pradhan mantri squarely. 'Pradhan Mantri, allow me to explain what happened,' he began. 'The grama—'

'—was waylaid by a band of brigands!' the prime minister said loudly. 'Yes, yes, I already have the facts. Now it is time to take action. Such an open act of treason must be punished most severely and swiftly, before word of it spreads to our disgruntled allies and encourages further rebellion. We must crush the offenders with an iron fist!'

Whose fist? Bejoo wondered bitterly. *Not your own, I'm sure.* Indeed, the minister's right fist lay curled like a misshapen claw by his side, the result of what appeared to be a particularly bad arthritic day in this bracing autumn weather. 'Pradhan Mantri, if you will let me narrate the exact events—'

Jabali jerked his bent finger dismissively, 'Don't waste your breath, boy. My people have told me everything already. I got word last night itself and have already taken appropriate action.'

Bejoo's heart sank. *Boy? At sixty-eight years, still a boy?* 'Pradhan Mantri, if I may suggest a diplomatic course of action that will hopefully avoid needless bloodshed—'

'Needless?' The old minister laughed scornfully, his white brows twitching in his long face. 'Bloodshed is not merely needed, it is imperative! A kingdom is ruled by force, not by words. Diplomacy is irrelevant. Ayodhya does not negotiate with rebels. I already know which band of brigands was responsible for this latest act of treason.'

'You do?' Bejoo blinked rapidly. 'But it was no band, Pradhan Mantri. Merely two young boys up to some childish prank—'

Again the open-mouthed laughter burst in his face, the white brows twitching. He could smell the pradhan mantri's breath. Surprisingly, the man retained most of his teeth in pristine white condition even at his age. Even though he must surely have been a good decade and a half past Bejoo's own age. Then again, Jabali was notoriously given to extolling the virtues of fasting and self-deprivation and their beneficial effect on one's aatma and state of mind. When a man rarely ate, no wonder his teeth stayed as good as new!

'Come now, Grama-rakshak Bejoo. I hardly expected you to be taken in by that subterfuge. I have received a full report. The boys were merely placed in the path to confuse you and your men. The real bowmen were concealed in the rocks and the surrounding jungle. After all, you don't really think that two little striplings could outshoot and outfight an entire entourage of the finest Purana Wafadars in His Lord Rama's force, do you?'

Bejoo wanted to start by protesting that since the very term Purana Wafadar meant 'Old Faithfuls', it ought to have implied that the force was made of exactly that, loyal veterans of previous wars. Such as himself. The young untried army regulars who had been enrolled into the elite force these past few years did not deserve to be called Wafadars, being as they were untested and untried in actual war conditions, and they most certainly were not Purana, none being over thirty years of age! While they looked and trained well enough to dissuade most potential attackers, in a pinch they were hardly the elite fighting force they were supposed to be. The truth of the matter was that the 'two little striplings' had outshot and outfought the entire entourage. Despite the warning given by the boy who had so cleverly severed the horse riggings as Bejoo had attempted to break away, he had still followed the boy at a safe distance and arrived at the main length of the grama in time to watch the two young bowmen rout his men thoroughly in one of the most impressive displays of bowcraft he had ever witnessed. *Not just 'one of', it was the most impressive display, apart from just one other previous display I once had the privilege of witnessing, when a certain other pair of bowmen engaged in a far deadlier battle a long time ago in a jungle called Bhayanak-van, against a yaksi giant named Tataka.*

He kept all this to himself as he said aloud: 'Actually, Pradhan Mantri, I think—'

But Jabali was already waving his crooked hand at him dismissively. 'What you think is irrelevant. The culprits who did this must be roundly punished for this treasonous action. We must make sure that this entire colony of outlaws is dealt with once and for all.'

Colony? Surely he doesn't mean…

Jabali's left cheek curled to reveal a brilliant white eye-tooth. 'The so-called Maharishi Valmiki's colony of brigands and rogues masquerading as sadhus. They are behind the theft of the Maharaja's war wagon and this time they have gone too far. They must be entirely wiped out, down to the last man, woman and child, and I shall see to it that it is done.'

NINE

'Bhraatr,' Shatrughan said gently but urgently without preamble.
'I desire an immediate audience with Ayodhya-naresh.'

Lakshman looked at his twin impassively. The years had altered
their individual appearances so considerably, any onlooker viewing them
together for the first time could be forgiven for not recognising them to
be identical twins, or even brothers. Shatrughan's years of hard travel to
the farthermost reaches of the kingdom and beyond, the hard outdoor
living and fighting and endless waging of war had not been tempered
overmuch by his assuming the throne of Mathura these past several
years. If anything, the years of kingship had toughened him further,
tempering the unassailable steel of his character and will with greater
wisdom, insight, and moderation. No longer did he fly instantly into
rages or lose his patience at the slightest provocation when thwarted.
He had assumed a certain gravitas and dignity that he wore as well as the
robes of kingship. The sculpting away of his overly muscled physique
by the years of hard travel and warring had stripped him down to a
leathery wiry muscularity that lent him an almost pantherlike aspect
when he walked on the balls of his feet.

Lakshman glanced over his brother's shoulder. Shatrughan's
entourage remained several yards behind its king, alert but affable.

Whatever Shatrughan's crisis was, it appeared personal rather than nationalist in nature.

In contrast to his twin, Lakshman had changed too, but in wholly other ways. He had been lean and pantherlike when he had returned with Rama and Sita to Ayodhya in Pushpak ten years ago, skin burned, nut-dark from years of open living and hard fighting. But the last decade had seen him spend almost all his days within the newly raised walls of the palace complex, virtually Rama's personal guard and guide at all times. He had dealt with every daily crisis that cropped up—and at times, they did come thick and fast—from city riots to internal intrigues, with conspiracies and assassination plots, and the constant living under the air of stress and political intrigue had softened him outwardly to some extent, filling out his leanness, thickening his torso and face somewhat. Working out in the palace akhada had only expanded his muscles and bulk further, while he lacked the trimming and leaning effects of long travel or warring. At the same time, the stress had aged him quickly, the hair at his temples turning grey. Even his brows and the moustache he had taken to keeping, showed grey amidst the black now, Shatrughan saw this at close range. It was almost as if Lakshman had become an older, wearier-looking version of Shatrughan himself ten years ago. While Shatrughan had become an older, more dignified version of Lakshman from ten years ago! How ironic, how appropriate that they had both aged to resemble older versions of one another.

Lakshman regarded him with a measured glance. 'Well met Mathura-naresh. What business do you seek to discuss with Samrat Rama Chandra?'

Samrat? The last time Shatrughan had met his older brother, Rama had still been just a maharaja, a king of kings. Now he had dubbed himself emperor? Then, at least, some of the rumours were true after all. He ignored the title and focussed on the man, continuing to use the Sanskrit high speech term for brother, which both lent intimacy as well as carried respect: 'Bhraatr, my business is for Rama's ears alone.

I assure you it is most urgent. I request you kindly to announce me and permit me the pleasure of an audience with him at once.'

Lakshman folded his arms, his overdeveloped chest muscles bulging as he did so. Shatrughan recalled having exactly the same upper body bulk and felt relieved he didn't anymore. As one got older, it got harder to maintain muscle tone and an old wrestler soon began to sag like an old woman if he didn't watch himself. He thought it wise not to mention that to his twin. These days, Lakshman was rarely in the mood to listen to brotherly advice on anything, be it physical maintenance or anything else. 'In that case, you would have to wait. Someone is in the sabha hall with the Samrat. He cannot be disturbed until the conference is over.'

Shatrughan glanced at the barred doors behind Lakshman, guarded by six heavily armoured and armed sentries, all bigger built and tougher looking than Lakshman himself. He sighed and nodded, even as he said with a wistful smile: 'There used to be a time when the doors of the sabha hall were always left open, for anyone to walk into and out of, and almost all sessions were open to all, even the lowest sweeper on the streets. Now, I hear the doors are always barred when the sabha sits in session and the public audiences are only permitted to attend the four seasonal sessions.'

Lakshman shrugged. 'Times have changed. Ayodhya had to change with the times.'

Shatrughan shook his head. 'Not every change is for the best.'

He began to say something further, then thought better of it. Clearly, Lakshman was not interested in padapad talk, and he had no desire to get into another slanging debate as they had the last time. Brothers though they were—bhraatrey, to use the Sanskrit high speech—they seemed to be on opposite sides of the political fence more and more these days.

He walked back to his entourage, intending to stay in their company while he waited. He knew better than to try to pass the time bantering with his brother. That was one of the many changes he questioned and resented. Lakshman was no longer Lakshman. Nor was Rama. He leaned on the portal that overlooked the royal udyaan and was sad to see that it too had been walled-in like everything else in this part of the city. He stood there, musing on how much Ayodhya had changed since he had left, indeed, since their father's passing. In so many ways.

He glimpsed movement on the path below and saw a familiar pair of ageing feminine forms walking slowly together, heads bowed in conversation. He smiled to himself. There were two people who would not be as grim-faced and stern of tone as his twin brother. He paused to instruct his entourage to send for him at once the instant the sabha doors reopened, and then went down to the garden.

* * *

Sumitra was the first to see him. She smiled and slowed, placing a hand gently on Kausalya's arm to stop her as well. They both looked back up the path as Shatrughan came at a steady trot, his broad swarthy face open in a wide grin. He dropped before them, touching each of their feet with heartfelt sincerity.

'Maa, aashirwaad. Maa, aashirwaad,' he repeated, for though Sumitra was his womb-mother, in Arya families, Kausalya was no less his mother. In their turn, both greeted him with identical warmth and for an onlooker it would have been impossible to tell which was his biological mother. If anything, slight, small-built, delicately boned Sumitra seemed unlikely; while Kausalya, darker-complected but bigger-proportioned though no less feminine in form, seemed more likely. Both laid hands on his shoulders, Sumitra having to look up by an angle of more than two feet to her perpendicular. Looking at them both in that moment, Shatrughan thought to himself that the pride and pleasure on their faces could not be replicated in any official portrait, not even by the most accomplished artists in Aryavarta.

'Maatrey,' he said, and put his meaty arms around both women, enfolding them in a bear hug that drew gasps of surprised delight. Sumitra glanced at her companion over Shatrughan's bowed head and Kausalya's eyes twinkled back in response. Shatrughan saw this without actually needing to look at their faces, and his heart filled with the tenderness of a boy who still longed for the days when mothers had been the protectors of the universe and the world had extended only to their guru's kul and ashram and back, and the four of them had been as one being with four heads and a single mind. He bit back a tear as he released his mothers and clapped them on their shoulders hard enough to make them gasp with amusement.

'It is so good to see you,' he said. 'I missed you. I missed it all.' He gestured with a bend of his head, indicating the palace and the city, but what he really missed was the way things had been before it all changed, long long ago in a city far far away and yet right here, right now.

The two queens exchanged another glance and he saw that they knew all, understood everything. A great sadness fell upon him then, a profound sense of regret for all that had been, all that could have been, and that which would now almost certainly never come to be.

TEN

They found a shady spot to sit in beside the lotus pool. Kraunchyas stalked the far end of the pool, standing on one leg. Swans swam proudly in the still clear water, and below the calm surface Shatrughan glimpsed golden fish drawing lazy circles, their tails flashing as they caught the beam of sunlight falling on the water. A symphony of birdsong rose incessantly from all around the arbour and the scent of freshly blossoming marigolds came to him on a gentle wisp of wind. He sat between his mothers and wondered what would happen if he remained here all day, just sitting quietly between them, perhaps laying his head on one of their laps, sleeping away the quiet afternoon. The travails of the world seemed distant and remote here. The ascendancy politics of Mathura. The constant bickering and squabbling over river rights. The tribal feuds. The grama clashes. The daily sabha sessions where the complaints and issues raised always seemed too many for any single day, and had to be carried over to the next day, and the next, until people began complaining that they had been here for so many days, and others countered they had waited weeks, and some argued they had camped outside the city for months, and even after the bickering and hearing of both sides, and the endless arguments and counter-arguments, when he finally pronounced the final arbitration, invariably one side stalked off in a barely suppressed rage while even the winning side seemed oddly disgruntled and ingracious. The troubles of his wife with the other wives he had been required to take in order to entrench himself more staunchly into Yadava politics. The dandas that he had meted out in sabha, and which he was required by dharma to witness being executed: nothing like a few whippings, dismemberments and executions to make one's day.

How good it would be to simply doze here in this idyllic arbour, where all those problems and burdens of kingship might as well not exist. To regress to the boy he had once been, the son, the brother, the child.

A kraunchya bird immersed its head in the water with sudden force. Its dripping beak emerged with a thrashing fish scissored neatly. The other kraunchyas raised their wings, put their tucked feet down and raised their own beaks, calling out raucously. The bird with the fish pointed its long beak at the sky, opened the long tongs, jerked its head up once sharply, tossing the fish up, then caught it in mid-air and swallowed it neatly. The fish thrashed once in a last act of desperate futility, its silver scales glittering gaudily in the sunlight, then was imbedded in the kraunchya's long throat.

He came out of his reverie to find his birth mother looking at him with that sad sure expression that he knew so well.

'Is it the raiders?' she asked quietly.

She was referring to the cattle and horse thieves that had been plaguing the border gramas the past season. Shatrughan had learned at the very outset that the thieves were renegades and outlaws from the Andhaka tribes who resented the sharing of river rights with the Suras; they took the stolen heads upcountry and sold them to unscrupulous traders who then cleverly sold them in other neighbouring kingdoms, many turning up in Ayodhyan markets, their brands marking their origin quite clearly. Despite his efforts, he had been unable to procure the cooperation of the Ayodhyan authorities in ending the trade and resale of these stolen beasts. All Ayodhya had to do was issue a proclamation prohibiting any trade or sale of beasts marked with Sura brands. With their most lucrative market gone, the thieves would soon find the effort of evading

Shatrughan's diligent marshals and the risk of transporting the animals to other more remote points of sale uneconomical, guaranteeing a natural end to the thievery. But despite three visits, Shatrughan had been unable to get the sabha here to reach a decision. True, the tangled web of Arya politics complicated the matter, especially since Ayodhya could not be seen favouring Mathura merely because it was ruled by a son of Ayodhya and a brother of Rama: that might cause further resentment among the Andhakas who had been spoiling for a war ever since Shatrughan had brokered the recent hard-won truce between the two major Yadava tribes over the long-standing issue of river rights. War always had more supporters and vested interests than peace. There was no profit in peace. The very essence of trade was exploitation, whether fair or excessive, and war ensured the highest exploitative profits possible. It took every ounce of his strength and will to maintain the truce, making kingship a task so onerous that he rarely had time to himself.

He shook his head. 'It's everything,' he said. 'This.' Again the all-encompassing gesture. Except that this time he meant Ayodhya in its current state. Not the idyllic Ayodhya of his childhood but the fortress-city-state of today, perpetually in a state of war-preparedness, every decision governed by military interests and strategy. And military interests were not always human interests; in fact, they rarely were.

Sumitra sighed and looked down at her open hands resting upon her lap. Her silks rustled, her jewellery tinkled lightly, counterpointing the chirruping of a pair of songbirds on the tree immediately above the marbled nook on which the three of them were ensconced. Like her sister Queen Kausalya, she had always chosen to adorn herself as simply and elegantly as possible, ignoring the customary Arya excesses designed to draw envy and admiration from the masses. He admired that in her and in Kausalya-maa. They were women with their own minds, the kind of women who had built Aryavarta into the great civilisation it was today. Women such as they had founded the Bharata nation and nursed it through a thousand generations, until it had spread and flourished throughout the known world. The days of the matriarchs had long passed and for one reason or another, men were now as likely to rule and dominate the grama as women—perhaps more likely—but in women such as Kausalya and Sumitra, that ancient strength of character and will could still be seen. Women such as they were the pillars upon which all Arya civilisation stood today. And to see Kausalya-maa, First Queen and Queen Mother, and his own maatr, so close in friendship and companionship with his womb-mother Sumitra, was heart-warming to him. Sumitra truly lived up to her name which literally meant 'good friend' in high speech. Aryavarta in general and Ayodhya in particular had far greater need of women such as these two than of warrior-queens like Kaikeyi, he thought not without a trace of bitterness. Even though as a kshatriya, it was his dharma to accept the need for violent action and the consequences of that action, as he grew older there were times he questioned whether violence was the only means a kshatriya should use to achieve his goals and fulfil his dharma. In his experience, violent action often worsened the situation rather than resolved it. And even when it did resolve certain situations, the solution was ephemeral, while the deep wounds and emotional scars of that violence lingered for much, much longer.

'Yes,' she said simply. 'Ayodhya is not what it once was. Nor is Rama.' As she spoke the latter statement, she sought out Kausalya. 'Excuse me, Kausalya.'

The First Queen nodded, her proud aquiline profile hardened by time, the once glossy long hair peppered with streaks of silver, the grooves bracketing her mouth deepened by decades of sharing that beautiful smile.

'You are as much his mother as I, Sumitra,' she said, her voice throatier than Shatrughan remembered it. He recalled her mentioning a persistent cough. Possibly that had hoarsened her speech. 'And what you speak is true. Whether Rama has changed Ayodhya or Ayodhya has changed Rama, even I cannot say. What is indisputable is that they have both changed, and,' she sighed softly, lowering her eyes, 'all change is not for the better.'

Shatrughan hesitated before speaking. He was unaccustomed to this kind of candid conversation with Kausalya-maa. For one thing, the past years had altered his own perception of himself considerably. From a younger prince—the youngest, if only by mere moments—he was now a king in his own right. That demanded an alteration of both self-perception and outward bearing. Yet he felt that if there were two persons he could trust to weigh his words fairly and advise him wisely, he could find no better than his two maatrey.

'Is the rumour true then?' he asked them, careful to keep his voice low, too low for even the kraunchyas fighting over fish in the pool to hear, not because he thought they might be spied upon—no spasas could find ingress into this innermost sanctum of the Kosala nation's capital—but because he felt saddened that he had to pose such a query to his mothers rather than to his bhraatr in order to be certain of an honest and direct response. 'Is Ayodhya preparing to go to war with its neighbours?'

Both queens were silent for a moment. A strange lull fell over the garden as if even the fauna paused in its singing and squabbling and daily business of living for a moment in order to hear their answer.

Finally, Sumitra raised her eyes to Kausalya, communicating some wordless request.

Kausalya drew in a deep breath, let it out, and said matter-of-factly:

'Not just its neighbours. Ayodhya is preparing to go to war with the entire world.'

ELEVEN

Bharat slid off his horse, tossing the reins to one of several stable boys who had come running up eagerly. They fought briefly over the right to groom the steed of Ayodhya's eldest prince and the winner triumphantly led the tired mount away, snorting and steaming faintly in the cool autumn air. Bharat stood for a moment, enjoying the sensation of being on solid ground and instinctively slapped down his garments to rid himself of some of the dust of the road that had accumulated over the long ride. As he was turning, he spied a trough nearby that looked as if it had just been mucked out and refilled, and went over to it. The water felt deliciously cool and refreshing and the faint scent of horse it carried did not bother him in the least. He had drunk from pools that smelt worse than this trough, and he had no patience to go to a private chamber and wait for serving girls to bring him the scented jars of heated Sarayu water to bathe in. Bathing and washing were necessities and not the luxuries some men made them out to be, and Bharat was happy to get them out of the way so he could get on with the real business at hand. And the business at hand today was grave business indeed.

He had just finished washing the grime from behind his neck when he saw a reflection appear in the water of the trough. Distorted and distended as it was by the lapping water and angle, he could tell at once that it was a man who carried himself in the familiar wide-stepping manner of a kshatriya. He kept his head down and eyes averted, pretending to finish up his toilet as he watched the figure approach, ready for any eventuality. After all, this was Ayodhya and he was a natural target. But rather than make any sudden attempts to attack, the man stopped short, put his hands on his hips, and chuckled softly.

'Well, well, bhraatr, are the scented baths of the palace too good for you? Or have you decided to give up princehood and take up sarathi work now?'

Bharat smiled grimly as he turned to face the oncomer. 'It's kingship, in case you hadn't heard, bhraatr mine. Ever since I managed to put down that pesky rebellion among the Gandharas, I've had my own kingdom. You may even have heard tell of it. The capital city is named Takshashila.'

Shatrughan pretended to make a face of mock disbelief. 'What? That little arid patch in the Ghandara ranges? I thought it was named for your son, little Taksha!'

Bharat chuckled at Shatrughan's disparagement. 'It is, actually. Just as Puskalavati is named for my daughter, little Pushkala. They're just two cities in my kingdom, which comprises the entire Gandhara nation now that I've subdued the rebels.'

Shatrughan twisted his brows into a mock expression of amazement. 'Impressive. Those Gandharas can be really tough to chase down and kill, especially with all those hilly ranges and caves to hide in. Why, they're even said to be related to the Nagas, the snake-like asuras, because of how quickly they vanish into the ground and take refuge in the tiniest crevices.'

Bharat nodded, clapping a hand on Shatrughan's shoulder, and squeezing his brother's deltoid muscle hard enough to draw an involuntary twitch of the lips. 'That's why I didn't make the mistake of wasting years and men trying to hunt them down as greater generals before me have done in the past. I simply built the most beautiful city ever known to the region, filled it with the finest artists, musicians, dancers, performers, and personally made sure it flourished and grew more prosperous than any Gandhara nation ever before.'

Shatrughan put his own hand on Bharat's shoulder, squeezing his deltoid muscle and drawing a similar involuntary grimace from his elder brother. 'And as everyone knows, though the Gandharas are the fiercest hill-range warriors in the world, they are also great lovers of fine music, art, dancing, and cannot resist the lure of such things. So sooner or later, they could not help but come to Takshashila to see if a firangee had indeed outdone them at their own artistic pursuits. And when they saw how magnificently you had built the city and how prosperous and artistically accomplished its denizens were, why, they all but threw down their weapons at your feet and asked to be allowed to serve you till the end of time!'

Bharat threw his head back and laughed, giving Shatrughan a brief but clear view of his pink uvula, quivering with his mirth. 'Not quite so simply, bhraatr! Not quite so simply. There was much fighting, and several dozen battles to boot, some quite nasty and ugly.' He shook his head, sighing. 'Those hilly bastards can be tougher and sneakier than snakes, as you rightly said. And with their long beards and deftness with blades, and vajra-like fleetness with unsaddled horse cavalry, they harried my troops to an inch of extinction. But your information is right in one respect. It was through my patronage of their arts and culture that I eventually won them over. The fact that your own nephew and niece—and your sister-in-law and cousin Mandavi—undertook to learn their arts from the finest gurus of the Gandhara school of music and dance and grew to become expert practitioners of the same, impressed them no small whit. Yes, I must admit that in the end, they turned out to be as passionate as friends and allies as they can be enemies and rivals.'

Both brothers looked at one another with enduring fondness. It had been a long time since they had met casually thus with no pressing political, or military issue to deal with, and it was with brotherly curiosity and interest that each examined the other from head to toe, noting all changes that age and hard living and warring had wrought in the intervening time. And once the initial gruff banter and masculine was dealt with, Shatrughan cleared his throat. 'So thanks to your self-aggrandising exaggerations and fanciful account, I deduce that my bhraatrjaya Mandavi—who also happens to be my cousin on account of her being my wife's sister—my niece Pushkala and nephew Taksha are all doing well. And how are you, bhraatr dear? Apart from having put on a little weight and let yourself go to seed, I mean?'

Bharat ignored the patently absurd remarks at the end: while it was true he had filled out a little over the years, coming to resemble their late father Dasaratha in a startling manner, he was by no means overweight, nor could his muscled bulk be said to justify the description 'gone to seed'. He replied amicably and with evident emotion: 'First tell me, how is my bhraatrjaya and cousin Shruta Kirti and your sons Subahu and Shrutasena?'

Shatrughan inclined his head in a half-nod. 'They are well. Mathura has been good to all of us. It is home now, I suppose. Although she never lets a moon-phase pass or a festival go by without berating me for keeping her apart from her precious sisters! As if we men deliberately create wars and political upheaval just to be able to avoid family gatherings!'

Bharat laughed. 'Well, I don't know about you, bhraatr. But I'm not past drumming up a skirmish or two, or even a brief war, just to avoid having to sit through a week of festivities and rituals. The moment those blessed brahmins begin to chant their mantras—'

'—I feel like running miles away, and continuing to run until I reach the ends of the Earth!' Shatrughan finished. It was an oft-repeated refrain among kshatriyas in general and they had repeated it often during their childhood years. It was a good-natured way of grumbling about the intense patience and serious aspect required by temperamentally restless action-oriented kshatriyas during the seemingly endless yajnas and brahmanical rituals.

They laughed together. And with that laugh, the years apart were gone, snapped off by the wind, as if they had never been apart a day, or an hour, let alone three whole years.

Later, over drink and refreshment, Shatrughan told Bharat of the long talk he had had with their mothers in the royal garden. Even though they were never sodara, children of the same womb, it was Bharat and Shatrughan who had formed the closest bond during the early years, just as Rama and Shatrughan's twin Lakshman had formed an equally firm bond in the same period. Just as Rama's and Lakshman's bond had deepened during the fourteen long years of exile, and the ten years since their return to Ayodhya, so also Bharat and Shatrughan's fourteen years together in Ayodhya, battling the political and emotional consequences of Rama's exile and Bharat's mother Kaikeyi's perceived betrayal, had brought them closer together than ever before. The fact that the past ten years had seen them spend more time apart than together, as well as the burdens of kingship and family responsibilities, made no difference. Their kinship was stronger than time could bend or other relationships alter. They were, brothers in soul.

TWELVE

'A war against the entire world,' Bharat repeated softly, careful to keep his tone low and expressions guarded.

They were seated in a temple in the sudra quarter of the city that they had been fond of frequenting ever since they were both young yuvrajas—princes in waiting—back in the day when hunting and training had seemed to occupy the bulk of their days. The temple was kept by a sudra artisan turned pundit who distilled his own soma and offered it to a select few on the condition that it be consumed only within the temple precinct and that no drinker should arrive or depart so intoxicated that he or she should lose control of basic faculties. To this end, each new arrival and person departing was required to hit a target set up by the temple entrance at least once out of three tries with a training arrow. Those who failed had to leave without consuming any of the famous concoction, and those who were unable to hit the target at least once on departure were never permitted entrance again. It was a strange method of ensuring temperance, but an effective one. After a few incidents when Bharat and Shatrughan had gotten too drunk and too much in trouble in their adolescent years, the then Pradhan Mantri Sumantra had guided them to this establishment. Bharat always suspected that it had been his father who had instructed Sumantra to do so, but he had never been able to find out for certain. Now, of course, he would never know whose idea it had been. Either way, the method had succeeded. Both Bharat and Shatrughan had learned to control their drinking and long after they had stopped coming to the temple, they had maintained safe drinking habits. It was more than most Arya kings—or kshatriyas—could claim.

'What does that mean?' Bharat wondered aloud. 'Does he mean to invade our neighbours unprovoked? To resurrect the old asura bogey to justify expansion? What exactly?'

Shatrughan shrugged. 'Maatr Kausalya and Maatr Sumitra didn't know for sure. But they are quite sure that Rama and his War Council have been massing a war treasury for some time now, and using it to hire and train a prodigious number of new akshohinis, not just in Ayodhyan military precincts but across the entire kingdom.'

Bharat nodded sombrely. 'Aye, that's true enough. I've contributed my share of war wagons.'

'As have I,' Shatrughan admitted.

'But what does Rama intend to do with this much mobilisation? Who does he intend to invade? The last of the asuras are gone. The rakshasas that remain are all converts to Sanatan Dharma, thanks to King Vibhisena of Lanka. They're as devout bhaktas of the devas and practitioners of our Vedic rituals as the Mithilans, I've heard said.'

'You heard the truth.' Shatrughan took a sip from his earthen mug. Chandra's soma was pure nectar as always. The very taste brought back boyish memories that took an effort to push away. 'It's troubled me as well as my allies. Even Maharaja Janak and Maharaja Kusadhwaja met me to speak on this very matter, along with several dozen other troubled grama-lords.'

Bharat nodded, quaffing his soma like water. 'Mandavi told me so. She had word from Shruta Kirti. It was that very missive that prompted me to call a meeting of my local chiefs and that's what brought me here today.'

While Rama and Lakshman were married to Sita and Urmila, daughters of Maharaja Janak of Mithila, king of the Videha nation, their brothers Bharat and Shatrughan were married to Mandavi and Shruta Kirti respectively, named sisters of Sita and Urmila, adopted daughters of Janak, but in fact they were the daughters of Janak's brother Kusadhwaja, king of Sankasya, a pura in the Videha kingdom fed by the river Ikshumati. At the time of their wedding and several years earlier, Kusadhwaja's ongoing feud with several other clans of the Sankasya pura region made it too dangerous for him to keep his daughters by his side, let alone arrange their marriages. So Janak had adopted his nieces and raised them as his own. To most people, the girls were regarded as 'Janak's four corners', the pillars of his household. It was only inevitable that they would all be married together—and pure good fortune that the eldest among them, Sita, happened to find a soulmate who had three eminently suitable brothers. In the years since, Kusadhwaja had not only succeeded in weeding out the hostile elements in his pura, he had united the clans and knitted together a veritable minor kingdom of his own, one that had begun showing signs of prosperity, thanks to the rich fertile fields fed by the Ikshumati. Both brothers regarded the marriage of their daughters to the sons of Dasaratha as being responsible for their change of fortunes. Which was why they were so concerned to hear of Ayodhya's inexplicable amassing of a war treasury and build-up of forces along the Kosala-Videha border. As the Kosala nation's neighbouring kingdom, Videha stood to lose the most if Ayodhya went to war. Not because they feared Ayodhya would invade them, but because they feared being forced to ally with their powerful war-mongering neighbours and relatives and get dragged into yet another long and painful campaign. Over time, the Chandravanshis had grown far more fond of spiritual triumphs than martial victories, and if they were called upon to support the Suryavanshis in a new war campaign, it would be with the utmost reluctance.

As sons of Ayodhya as well as sons-in-law of Mithila and Sankasya,

Bharat and Shatrughan had the doubly complex task of finding out where their family's political ambition was leading them while remaining considerate of their fathers-in-law and their desire for continued peace. Add to that their own recently built kingdoms with their own individual mixtures of political complexities and complications, and it was shaping up to be quite a tangled web.

Bharat voiced his anxiety again. 'By Indra's yoni-covered face, what does Rama intend to do with a force that size? Invade swargaloka and narakaloka as well as the mortal realm?'

'That's what I've been trying to find out. But none of my entourage seems to be able to get anyone to talk. There's a danda on any Ayodhyan caught or overheard speaking about military matters to any outsider. The danda, by the way, is execution on the spot by the PFs.'

Bharat stared at him. 'Outsiders? Us?'

Shatrughan indicated towards Bharat's insignia, now hidden discreetly beneath the cloak he had thrown on for their incognito visit to their old drinking spot, then his own mark of kingship, also concealed beneath his robes. 'You're king of Gandahar. I'm king of Mathura. Face it, big bhraatr. We're not Ayodhyans anymore.'

Bharat finished his mug with a vehement flourish that barely masked his anger. 'I'm not sure I'd want to be called an Ayodhyan anymore. Not in these times.'

Shatrughan grinned. Bharat had always had a tendency to overreact at times, especially when he drank. 'You don't mean that. No matter how many cities you build and name after your children or yourself, you'll always be an Ayodhyan through and through. Let's face it. So will I. Once an Ayodhyavaasi…'

'…always an Ayodhyavaasi.' Bharat finished with just a twinge of bitterness in his tone. He sighed and grinned back at his brother. 'What can I say? I'm not a perfect master of dharma, like Rama. I lose my patience at times.'

He held up the empty mug and waved it in the air for a moment.

Shatrughan, who was facing into the temple precinct, saw Chandra's eyes rise from his scroll, then drop again. The pundit would fetch them refills, but only after a fair wait. Yet another of his efficient methods to enforce 'safe drinking' as he put it.

Shatrughan offered Bharat his own mug. It was still half-full and he was really just drinking to pass the time. These days, he rarely felt safe enough in Ayodhya to truly surrender his senses. It was partly the reason why he had insisted on leaving Shruta Kirti and his sons home. What did it say about his homeland when he did not consider it safe enough to bring his own family here any more frequently than was absolutely necessary? Nothing good, he concluded morosely.

'It's not just you,' he admitted with a deep sigh. 'Everyone feels the change. Just that they don't have the luxury to remark on it for fear of their heads. Jabali runs a tight house. His spasas are everywhere.' Shatrughan glanced around. 'I'd even advise you not to speak your heart too openly, bhraatr. The way things are going, one never knows.'

Bharat didn't respond to that. He was looking off to one side with a speculative expression. Shatrughan glanced back over his shoulder to see what had attracted his attention. 'Who is that? Someone you know?'

Bharat nodded slowly. 'Someone you know as well. Remember Captain Bejoo of the king's vajra?'

Shatrughan did a double take. 'That's Captain Bejoo?'

Bharat nodded. 'Not anymore. He's a PF now, I think. But knowing his calibre, I'd bet he's still pretty high up in the inner circle. I'm going to have a few words with him.'

Shatrughan put a hand on Bharat's shoulder as his elder brother started to rise. 'Careful, bhraatr. These are dangerous times.'

Bharat retorted, 'That's why information is precious.'

Shatrughan watched him walk over to the spot beneath a pillar where the former vajra captain sat nursing his own mug of soma. He had to admit Bharat was right: there were a great many things he would like to know as well. He just hoped Bharat remembered that the danda on Ayodhyans speaking to outsiders also applied to the outsiders who received the information. And with Rama's dogged adherence to the law, it was possible that even his own brothers might not be considered exceptions to the rule. If they were caught or overheard discussing Ayodhya's internal matters with a ranking officer of the PF, the danda would be on-the-spot execution for all three of them.

THIRTEEN

Bejoo was surprised when he recognised the man walking towards him. Yuvraj Bharat? Well, technically, he was Gandahar-naresh now, ruler of the new territories up north beyond the Himalayas, a legend in his own time for having achieved what he had in that brutally rough country. But to Bejoo, he would always be that strapping young prince of Ayodhya who had stolen his best chariot and horse from right under his sarathi's nose one festival day to run a race with his three brothers down the length of the raj-marg. Bejoo had been livid that day, but of course, he could hardly berate or punish a prince of Ayodhya. So he had punished the sarathi instead. He winced inwardly now as he recalled how hard he had come down on that poor fellow. *Ah, but I used to be a hardass in those times, damn my battered soul.*

The man who now sat beside him on the cool stone floor was much leaner and harder looking than the puffed up young prince of that day, almost thirty long years ago and he had discreetly clad himself so no evidence of his kingly status was outwardly visible. But it was prince Bharat, no question about it. And the man who had been sitting with him across the way and was now rising too to come over and join them, why, that was prince Shatrughan, for certain, now Mathura-naresh.

'You were hard on that poor sarathi,' Bharat said in a conversational tone, taking Bejoo by surprise.

Bejoo started. 'I cannot believe you still recall that incident, master Bharat. It has been a fair while since the days of your youthful excesses.'

'True. But the older one gets, the more fondly one seems to remember those youthful excesses, don't you agree?' Bharat glanced at him sideways, waiting for a response.

Bejoo nodded. Then grinned. 'You were quite the hell raiser back then. Must make for some good memories now!'

Bharat nodded, grinning too. 'Except that I always felt bad for the poor sarathi and how hard you came down on him that day.'

'Well, young master. As I recall, it was you who were responsible for his plight, not I. 'It was his job to guard the rath. He ought not to have been swayed by your sweet princely tongue.'

Bharat spread his hands in a what-to-do gesture. 'True, true. But my words to him were compelling. Did he tell you what I said to him that day to make him hand over his reins to me so readily?'

Bejoo thought back a moment, then shook his head. 'Nay, that he did not.'

Shatrughan came over, flashed a smile of greeting, and sat down beside his brother.

Bejoo took the cue and simply nodded back in return, understanding that they wished to remain incognito for some reason. He continued: 'In point of truth, young master, I did not let him explain. It was the principle of the thing, I told him, if I recall correctly. A sarathi never surrendered his chariot on pain of death. It was his dharma.'

Bharat shook his head regretfully. 'Not if his prince told him that another prince, Yuvraj Rama Chandra, lay injured and bleeding and he needed to commandeer the chariot to rush to his aid at once.'

Bejoo's face lost any trace of a smile. He stared bluntly at Bharat. 'You told him that?'

Bharat nodded. 'I was a young fool then. Used to getting my way. And I so wanted to win that race. Right, Shatrughan?'

Shatrughan nodded. 'Surely. You always had to prove you were better than Rama, even when you weren't.'

Bejoo shook his head slowly, remembering how harshly he had penalised the sarathi. 'Poor man. Had I known that then…'

'You would probably have still punished him anyway,' Bharat said. 'You were a tough old bastard back then, Captain Bejoo. No offence.'

Bejoo nodded. 'None taken.'

'That's why our father put you in charge of his personal vajra. He took great pride in the way you ran that outfit. He was always using you as an example when trying to discipline us, wasn't he, Shatrughan?'

Shatrughan grunted, smiling ruefully: 'He did. I can vouch for that as well as the danda we got while he berated us for not being more like Captain Bejoo.'

Bharat glanced at the old man. 'I have to admit, that was part of the reason why I stole your rath in particular, and not one of the others.'

'Oh yes, sir, he came down that raj-marg yelling, "I'm Captain Bejoo, make way, make way!"' Shatrughan laughed, and Bharat laughed with him. With barely a pause, Bejoo joined in as well. The other drinkers in the temple precinct turned their heads to look at them curiously. Chandra Pujari continued fanning himself slowly, frowning as if wondering whether he had served too many mugs of soma to this particular group.

Finally, Bejoo stopped laughing, sighed deeply and looked down at the rough stone floor on which he sat. 'Sometimes, I wonder if it was worth it. Being as tough a bastard as I was back then.'

Bharat glanced up at him quizzically. 'What do you mean?'

Bejoo shrugged. 'Well, as time tempers one's mettle, it also leads to introspection. I do not deny that a warrior's countenance is part of a kshatriya's dharma and all that. But sometimes I wonder. Is not a kshatriya also a man? A human being? A husband, a father, a brother? We are not just machines of war, surely?'

Bharat looked at him for a long moment. Elsewhere in the temple compound, a man raised his voice, demanding more soma harshly. The voice cut off abruptly as the drunken fool felt the blunt end of Chandra Pujari's staff.

'That is a very insightful thing you just said, Captain Bejoo,' Bharat said at last. 'A very very insightful thing indeed.'

Bejoo made a throaty sound. 'It's not Captain Bejoo anymore, boys. Hasn't been for a very long time. I'm Grama-rakshak Bejoo now. Although I suppose I'm technically some kind of ranking officer in the PF hierarchy, but don't ask me where I figure in relation to all the rest in the organisation. It changes every day these days, it would seem.'

He noticed Bharat and Shatrughan exchange a quick glance. Shatrughan seemed to nod briefly as if saying yes, go ahead, to his brother. Bharat turned back to Bejoo with an expectant look on his face.

'Actually, we'd like very much to speak with you about exactly that,' he said quietly. 'About the changes.'

Shatrughan added: 'That is, if you don't mind speaking about such things with us privately.'

Bejoo drank the last of his soma, literally licking his lips and tips of his upper moustache. Ah, that Chandra Pujari really had a deva's touch. 'Of course, young princes. The day when an old veteran and two princes of Ayodhya can't speak freely, if privately, about their own city hasn't come yet.' He lowered the mug and flashed them a broad smile and a wink. 'Not as far as I'm concerned, at least!'

He was pleased to see them both return beaming smiles. He raised his mug, requesting the pujari for more soma. And was surprised when the pujari actually fetched them refills.

* * *

Pradhan Mantri Jabali continued to stare fixedly at the far end of the chamber as he listened to the spasa kneeling beside him. The man whispered in tones that only the pradhan mantri could catch. Not even the artist standing before the canvas across the chamber, attempting to capture the prime minister's dignified pose in all its hawk-nosed grimness, could have caught more than a susurration. Finally, the spasa finished and waited for his master's command. Jabali remained staring at the same spot as before, for the benefit of the portrait which after all, he had commissioned. But two tiny spots of colour began to appear on his high protruding cheekbones, and in a moment, he looked as if he had painted daubs of crimson on them. Except for those two telltale signs, and the intensity with which his eyes bored into the pre-arranged spot across the chamber—a marble bust of Raja Harishchandra, one of Rama's most illustrious ancestors—there were no other indications of just how upset the ageing minister had become after hearing his spasa's message.

But the spasa saw and read these signs correctly. And later, after he was dismissed and back in the security unit in the dungeon below the palace complex, he shuddered and told a colleague over their evening meal: 'I wouldn't want to be the next person to cross the old hawk.'

'What did you tell him that made him so upset?' asked his companion, less interested in the actual information than in knowing what, of the several dozen things he already knew of, had triggered the pradhan mantri's anger. Slow as it was to trigger, that anger was a terrible thing to behold once fully stoked. He was more interested in knowing the trigger from the point of view of self-preservation. Jabali had been known to kill the messenger more than once, if the rumours were to be believed. It would be useful to bear in mind that such-and-such a report might be the one to set off his formidable ire.

The spasa shrugged, stripping off a hunk of goat-meat from a marrow bone which he then sucked dry before tossing to the dogs who fought over it raucously. 'Just that I saw yuvrajas Bharat and Shatrughan drinking soma with an old PF at the sudra's temple.'

The other spasa frowned. 'That's it? What were they talking about?'

'Don't know. Couldn't get close enough to hear without arousing suspicion. Couldn't have been anything very important, it seemed to me. They were laughing and drinking.'

The other spasa shrugged. 'Politics.'

They enjoyed their goat meat and soon forgot the incident.

The pradhan mantri, on the other hand, most definitely did not.

FOURTEEN

Old Somasra watched as the young soldier leaned over the top of the first wall, peering down its length. 'I see it, Soma sir, I see it right there!'

Somasra resisted the urge to knock his lance against the youngun's backside. Had there not been sharp-toothed things swimming about in that moat down there, he'd have knocked the fellow over without a second thought. He was sick and tired of these greenhorns they sent him these days, blustering young fools who couldn't throw a spear twenty yards and hit a whole wagon. In his youth, duty at the first gatewatch had been a posting of immeasurable pride. A young soldier could have his pleasure of any number of women over the first several weeks just on the back of that simple statement: 'I'm first-gate-watch.'

He had been the youngest ever to pass the rigorous tests they set back then and his entire akshohini had been damn proud of the fact. 'One of ours!' He sighed and shook his head in disgust as the young soldier continued to lean dangerously over the wall. *Sure. I was the youngest then and now I'm the oldest gatewatch still on active duty. So what does it mean? Have I gotten too old for the job? Or has Ayodhya changed from under me? Probably a bit of both.*

Either way, it stank like the moat in the days before refilling time—when the mulch and dead carcasses and other rotting stuff grew too dank and noxious, and the dam-gates connecting the moats to a small diversion of the Sarayu had to be knocked open to let the water be refreshed, the mesh-screens ensuring that while fresh water came in and filthy water went out, the denizens themselves remained in their watery enclosure as their predecessors had for the past centuries since Ayodhya had been built. And later, hauling up those mesh screens when they grew too clogged with gunk, and replacing them with fresh ones. Now that had been a task in itself. He had helped out a few times, because back in those days, everyone did everything, not like it was today with even hairless younguns dodging work saying, 'It's not my varna,' or 'Below my varna to do that'. Besides, he had wanted to see what it was like. The way those jaws and slick snouts emerged and snapped and thrashed and rolled madly in the water the moment human hands or feet came remotely within chomping range…it churned his stomach even now to think of it. Especially since he had seen what those gnashing jaws and razor teeth could do to a living creature—on more occasions than he cared to count in fact, Shiva take his blessed soul.

'I got it, Soma! I got it!' cried the youngun now, leaning so far over the top of the wall, that his lower garment was pulled up high above his thighs, exposing his fuzzy rear end.

Somasra cursed, reached out with one hairy knuckled fist, grabbed hold of the young soldier's langot by its waist knot, yanked on it hard to get a grip—the youngun yelped once as his crown jewels were squished more than a little—and hauled the fellow back and down, thumping him on the hardwood platform again. He turned around, the errant pennant that had fallen off and gotten stuck a yard down on a convenient splinter was clutched in his hand, face red with effort. 'What did you do that for?'

Without a word, Somasra snatched the nearest mashaal off its iron sconce, leaned over the wall and pointed down. The youngun's curiosity made him look over once again, and Somasra held the torch low enough that they could both see the dimpling dark surface of the moat below. Somasra hawked and spat a gob. The instant it splotched into the water, a dozen twisting writhing shapes thrashed and fought and lunged.

Finding nothing for their efforts, yet still able to smell human product in the water, they fought one another, gharial versus shark versus crocodile versus piranha versus watersnake versus…well, versus whatever else was down there. He drew back the arm with the mashaal, plunging the moat below into the shadowy darkness again, fitted the torch back into its sconce and turned to see the young fellow standing stupefied, eyes round with shock.

'Holy Shiva,' the man said slowly. 'If I'd fallen over into that…'

Somasra grunted. '…you'd have saved the moat-keepers having to drop tomorrow morning's load of meat, is all. Mayhaps not even that.' He pinched the young man's bicep, barely as thick as Somasra's wrist. 'Mayhaps just a treat for our fellows below.'

'Fellows?'

'Ayuh. They's gatewatchers same as we are. More effective even. Intruders might get past us somehow. But them?' Somasra chuckled and shook his head. 'How would anyone even know for sure what was down there and how many and how to fight them in the water? Even old Sankarshan, Captain of Moats, probably doesn't know for sure anymore—them creatures have been breeding in the moats since before great Raghu was a little babe running around without a dhoti. Who knows what exactly is in there now and how many they might be?'

The young PF shuddered as he realised how close he had come to finding out exactly what and how many were down there in the moat. Hoarsely, he thanked Somasra for yanking him back in time and then went off to a corner where Somasra suspected he would soon hurl the contents of his stomach out. *Young fools. Too stupid to avoid danger, too scared to deal with it after the fact. What they all need is a good knock on the head with the end of my lance.*

Not long after, he saw a light winking on the opposite side of the gate, went over to the lantern and turned it to face a different side, causing it to wink as well and show a different coloured side. The gatewatchers used that system of coloured faces on their wall-lanterns to indicate the changing of the watch. This change meant that it was the end of Somasra's shift. The next shift guards were already here and he surrendered charge to them and climbed down the wooden ladder to street-level. A man was standing there, apparently waiting for him, clad in the officious purple, black, and green outfit that indicated he was a PF-provost, one of those new-fangled titles that they handed out like roasted treats these days even to kshatriyas untested in combat. *Munshis is all they really are*, he thought, trying not to let his disgust show. *Glorified clerks dressed up in soldier guises.*

'Gate-watch Somasra, father's name Uchasravas?' asked the man.

'First-gate-watch Somasra,' he answered. 'Ayuh.'

The man blinked, not seeming to see the difference between a simple gate-watch guard and a first-gate-watch, the latter being the best of the best, one of a very select few chosen and entrusted with the vital task of manning the very first gate, the first boundary of defence of the entire city. *Another young fool who doesn't know his itihasa or sanskriti*, Somasra thought. *They're growing on trees like rotten fruit these days.*

'Somasra Uchasravas, you are commended for your service. Ayodhya thanks you. You may now enjoy the fruits of your long and honourable service. You are hereby retired from active duty. Congratulations.'

And the man turned to go. Done. Finished. Just like that.

Somasra's hand shot out and grasped hold of the man's shoulder, pinning him. 'Hold your rabid horses in check, youngun,' Somasra said, more than a little angry. 'What are you saying here?'

The man glanced at him curiously, and a bit nervously, probably feeling the strength of the hand on his shoulder. 'You are relieved from your duty. Retired. You don't need to show up for work here at the gate anymore.'

Somasra stared at him so intently and silently, the man actually writhed, trying to wriggle out from the stone-hard grip. Finally, Somasra relented and released him. The man scuttled away nervously, glancing back once before scurrying up the raj-marg the way he had come—back to the governance quadrant.

Somasra looked around, at the towering structure of the first gate of Ayodhya, pride of the Arya world, looking quite proud and magnificent in the light of the mashaals at dusk. Ayodhya the Unconquerable. A large part of that legendary reputation was because of the efficiency with which these seven gates were manned and monitored. And he, Somasra, the oldest surviving first-gate-watch still on duty, was now informed that his service to the state was over and done with. Thank you. Congratulations. Commendations. As easily as that, he had been cast off like an old coat.

So that was it? The end? Of his career? And his career was his life. For he had lost his wife and son in the last Asura War, in a particularly brutal skirmish in a hamlet not far from here, on the north bank of the Sarayu, back when asuras had prowled this land like beetles in a dank dungeon. Pishachas had done it, and had gotten away clean with it too. By the time Somasra had arrived, nothing but their ravaged barely recognisable carcasses remained. He had never remarried, never took children. The first-gate-watch had been his pride and his life. Doing his bit to ensure that his fellow Ayodhyans never fell prey to the fate that befell his own loved ones. That task had given him succour and strength for forty-two years, not counting the twenty-four years before that when he had been in active military service; a total of seventy-six years out of his ninety-one years upon this earth. What was he to do now? Take up Vanaprasth Ashram? Kshatriyas rarely lived long enough to even consider the second ashram, let alone the third. He was old enough to take up Sanyas Ashram directly now, yet he didn't know the first thing about spirituality and meditation. He had spent his life serving with strength, and the use of weapons and force of mind was all he knew.

Slowly, he began the walk back to his quarters in the military quadrant. Probably he would now have to vacate that tiny room as well, with whatever meagre possessions he owned, to make way for the young and the new. He watched a squad of new recruits in their spiffy new PF uniforms march past in perfect step. None of them was more than a quarter of his age, none had probably seen combat in his life or known anyone who had seen combat. They spent their days drilling and marching to perfection, but were they good for much more besides that? It bothered him to know that they were now in charge of the defence of his homeland.

What does it matter either way, Somasra? Your time is done now. You are an old bull being put out to pasture. Go gracefully and go with strength. The old must pass to make way for the new. This too is your dharma.

He straightened his shoulders and walked the raj-marg, going the opposite way from the lines of marching recruits. One last march. A solitary figure, gnarled and white-haired and grizzled with the ravages of age and old wounds and shattered bones and long hard living. Yet he cut a no less impressive figure than the dozens of straight young bodies marching the other way. As they passed each other, the old man just walking home and the young men marching to show off their youth and their strength, it was hard to say who walked the more impressive walk. A few of them who knew who he was—a living legend among gate-watchers—muttered to each other and glanced back as he passed by. Somasra neither returned their glances nor looked back. He walked on and passed into the annals of obscurity.

FIFTEEN

Bharat sprang to his feet. His sword was in his hands, and he was ready to fight the instant the intruders entered his chambers. But as they swarmed the night-darkened chamber with silent deadly efficiency, surrounding him on all sides in less time than it took him to alter his position from a front-pointing to a raised hacking posture, he realised he had no desire to fight these warriors. He lowered his sword slowly, reluctantly, and watched as they crouched, perched, squatted, crept, and otherwise filled his chamber with such a mass of furry simian force that any attempt to fight would have resulted in the tastefully white chamber being redecorated in lifeblood crimson. Several of them swarmed up the twin pillars that flanked his bed, squatting comfortably, eyes gleaming in that reflective way animal eyes gleamed in darkness. There was little moonlight from the verandah and open windows but it was enough for him to see that none of the vanars was armed nor seemed to be offering any threat. They merely seemed to be observing him, holding him hostage, and waiting.

He sheathed the sword, sat on the edge of his own bed, and waited with them. The chamber was rank with their odour. To Bharat, used to travelling on long campaigns with horses and dogs and fellow humans who seldom had the opportunity to bathe, it was not an entirely unpleasant odour. He could grow accustomed to it.

A short while later, a familiar figure entered the chamber, walking taller and straighter than any other vanar, his leonine head shot through with much more grey than Bharat recalled at their last meeting. God, but he cut a proud figure even at his age, which in vanar years Bharat assumed would be the equivalent of over sixty mortal years. Few human kshatriyas could look so fit and strong at sixty. The strength of his belief in Rama makes it possible, just as it makes all his extraordinary powers possible.

Hanuman bowed, joining his palms with his customary sincerity. 'Forgive the sudden intrusion, Lord Bharat, but I felt it more becoming your stature than the manner in which Pradhan Mantri Jabali desired to have you apprehended.' He indicated the chamber full of vanars. 'As you can see, none of my warriors has made any attempt to threaten or harm you, and that will not change so long as you heed my words and accompany me graciously.'

Without replying, Bharat held up his sheathed sword on both his open palms, showing that he had no intention of using it. Hanuman nodded. Bharat kissed the sword, placed it lovingly on the bed, and rose to his feet. 'Lead the way.'

The vanars parted like water before a ship's prow.

Shatrughan joined them in the corridor outside the sabha hall, accompanied by his own contingent of vanars, none of whose furry heads came to higher than his chest. He seemed in good spirits as if being rousted out of bed in his private chambers by half a hundred vanars was something that happened every second night. 'Bhraatr,' he said by way of greeting, a faint tone of irony in his tone.

The palace was quiet and still at this late hour. Yet in the distance, Bharat caught the sounds of shouted commands, marching feet, hooves and wheels. Something was afoot in Ayodhya. Something very substantial. Yet he felt a sense of disapproval at any military exercise or campaign being conducted in these hours. The kshatriya code existed for a reason: warriors deserved their rest and leisure hours. To mobilise troops in the middle of the night could only lead to tired soldiers, come daylight. What could be so urgent that it required mobilisation by night? What national emergency could not wait until dawn at least, which was after all only a few short hours away, less than half a watch.

Their silent progress through the winding corridors led down two flights of marbled stairs and past the Hall of Ancestors. Bharat saw the vanars peep curiously into the great museum-like chamber where gentle lighting remained lit at all hours, to honour the illustrious Suryavanshi Ikshwaku forebears. It was testimony to their discipline that none lagged behind or dropped back to take a quick tour, even though their intense fascination was palpable. These artefacts must be unseen in their cities. He had never had the pleasure of visiting Kiskindha, the capital of the vanar nation deep in the redmist mountain ranges beyond the north-easternmost boundaries of the Aryavarta empire, but he had heard enough accounts of its wonders to know that stone and canvas were not the usual media used by vanar to commemorate their famous dead. They believed in honouring their ancestors through their deeds rather than through carved marble busts and painted art. The artistic wonders that greeted them at every turn were unlike anything they had seen or heard of in their rustic vanar lives.

They reached their destination, the rajya sabha hall, and the contingent came to a halt.

Hanuman stopped before the closed sabha doors. Rama was evidently inside and some manner of official meeting was clearly in session, as was obvious from the presence of the guards diligently guarding the corridors and doorway.

Bharat half-expected to see Lakshman there as well, in his usual place. But his brother was conspicuous by his absence from his familiar spot. The sentries opened the doors to Hanuman who went inside the sabha hall and returned moments later, indicating that they should follow him inside.

The vanars remained outside, the vaulting doors groaning shut behind Bharat and Shatrughan. Bharat glanced around as they followed Hanuman up the long central walkway between the endless rows of pillars. The hall was almost empty, and lay mostly in darkness. The only people present were gathered around the throne dais, where a pair of mashaals crackled quietly, illuminating the dozen odd faces that Bharat recognised easily as the War Council. The only ministers present were Pradhan Mantri Jabali and Mantri Ashok. Another face he recognised unhappily was that of Bhadra, scion of a noble family of Ayodhya and a friend and sporting rival to Rama as a boy. He had himself seen Bhadra's friendship to Rama grow considerably in the past ten years and had heard growing rumours of just how much power and influence that friendship had earned Bhadra. He was also the chancellor of the War Council and the governor of the city now, Bharat had heard. His name had been one among a few that had cropped up several times during his talk with Shatrughan and Bejoo last evening.

Bhadra must have sensed Bharat's intense scrutiny because he looked up just then, canny knowing grey eyes flashing straight at Bharat. His handsome, fair features betrayed no trace of his feelings as he returned Bharat's gaze with a cool appraise of his own. If anything, he looked a capable, upstanding man, and an able administrator. *Then why do I feel that he has grown too close to Rama too soon?*

Hanuman announced them. 'Samrat Rama Chandra, as you instructed, I have chaperoned Mathura-naresh Raja Shatrughan and Gandahar-naresh Raja Bharat to your presence.'

Rama glanced at Bharat and Shatrughan before replying. 'Yes, thank you, Anjaneya. That will be all.'

Hanuman remained standing.

Rama looked at the vanar. 'You may leave now, Maruti. Your chore is done.'

Hanuman cleared his throat gruffly in the vanar manner, a cross between a nervous cough and a plaintive sound. 'I beg your pardon, sire.

But I also wished to inform you that the troops you requested have arrived. I received word when I was on my way to fulfil this errand.'

Rama nodded, looking pleased. 'That is excellent. Have they entered the city?'

Hanuman shook his head once. 'I sensed that would be unadvisable if not difficult, given their numbers, sire. But they await your inspection within sight of the city. If you will trouble yourself to ride out with me just a yojana or two…'

Rama waved a hand dismissively. 'Out of the question. We are about to sit in council now. I can't leave here.'

Hanuman bowed his snout humbly. 'As you say, sire.'

Rama frowned, crooking a finger. 'However, I can use the Seer's Eye to look over them from afar. Yes, I believe I shall do just that. Arrange for them to be in view of the tower and I shall be able to look over them briefly. How soon do you think you can arrange them?'

Hanuman scratched the sparse silvering fur on the back of his head, thinking. The ability to tell time, especially in the tiny increments mortals divided it into, was a feat that generally defeated the vanar intellect. But in this, as in so many other things, Hanuman was an exception to his race. 'Within the hour, sire. I shall fly out myself and organise them.'

Rama nodded. 'Good. Do that then. Go now. Call me only when they are ready to be viewed.'

Hanuman left the chamber—but instead of going back towards the doorway, he went the other way, towards the window. Bharat watched as the vanar moved easily from a brisk walk to a quick sprint to build up momentum, then launched himself out the window into the black of night. One last glimpse of his tail flicking as his powerful legs launched him skywards, then he was gone.

Bharat turned his attention back to Rama.

He was a little discomfited by the intensity of Rama's gaze. Not a gaze, it was more a glare.

'Gandahar-naresh Bharat,' Rama said with stiff formality, 'it appears you have committed a grave transgression against Ayodhya. I have summoned you and Mathura-naresh Shatrughan here in order to give you an opportunity to defend yourselves before I pronounce the sentence on you and impose the applicable danda for your violation of our laws.'

SIXTEEN

Bharat exchanged a glance with Shatrughan before looking up at Rama. 'Ayodhya-naresh, Kosala-narad,' he said formally, yet in as friendly a tone as possible, 'I believe I speak for both Shatrughan and myself when I assert that Mathura and Gandahar are both sworn allies to Ayodhya. The question of transgression does not arise. We have nothing but goodwill towards the Kosala nation and its capital city. Not to mention the fact that we are both loyal sons of Ayodhya and patriots to the core.'

Even as he spoke he was aware of the hostile looks directed at both himself and Shatrughan, as well as the presence of swords and daggers among the members of the War Council. But weapons were forbidden by law in the sabha hall! It had been so since the days of Manu and the Ignoble Uprising. The event that had precipitated the imposition of the law had occurred during the reign of Manu the Lawmaker, an illustrious ancestor of theirs who was legendary for his creation of the famous Laws of Manu, a code of conduct that did not find favour with all who served under him, particularly those whom the Laws sought to muzzle, constrain, or otherwise restrain. That had led to an uprising of the court nobles on one occasion, and a bloody fight in the sabha hall—this very sabha hall—and the subsequent imposition of the rule that weapons would henceforth be forbidden within the sabha hall, an offence punishable by immediate and lifelong banishment from all court affairs. The event came to be called the Ignoble Uprising and the rule had stuck. Until now. Bharat wondered grimly how many other changes Rama and his War Council and state advisors had brought about, and which other time-honoured traditions had been overthrown as summarily as this one.

Rama accepted a goblet of some manner of drink from a serving man—a serving man, not girl, which was another unusual change, Bharat noted. He seriously doubted the use of men in place of women to serve the liege had anything to do with equalitarianism. More likely it was for other more military reasons; the fact that the serving man had the body and manner of a trained soldier and carried a discreetly worn shortsword did not escape him either.

Rama sipped briefly from the goblet before speaking. 'Your past actions have no relevance. All that matters is your present transgression against the state. Do you accept or deny that you have acted against the best interests of Ayodhya?'

Bharat frowned while still trying to keep his voice polite and expression friendly. 'My Lord Rama, how can past actions have no relevance? They have every bearing upon a man's motives and present actions. Every living breath expended by either of us has been in the service of Ayodhya. Besides, we have not even been informed what these allegations against us may be. How can we accept or deny them then?'

Rather than reply, Rama continued to sip his drink while his eyes remained on Bharat. Instead it was Bhadra who spoke up in the irritatingly laconic tone that had always sounded to Bharat as if he was sneering at everything and everyone.

'You are impudent to even question the sunwood throne thus. The rajya sabha has already heard the charges against you and found them meritorious. There is no obligation to inform you of the details. In fact, the only reason why Lord Rama is permitting you this appearance is on account of your past services to Ayodhya. The Council itself has already found its verdict and the vote is against you. All that remains now is to announce the danda imposed on you two.'

Years of kingship and numerous diplomatic parleys and negotiations with a variety of other powerful people had tempered Bharat's youthful temper considerably. While he might never become legendary as a diplomat or politician, he was justifiably proud of the fact that unlike most Arya kings and lords, he had learned to wield his tongue rather than his sword to convince those who disagreed with him. But hearing Bhadra speak now, completely out of turn and against all protocol, that too in a tone that dripped with irony and utter disrespect for Bharat's lineage, made him want to cry to hell with diplomacy and fling himself at the hefty advisor. *Who in the name of Ravana's butt is this fool anyway? When we were kids, and he tried to tag along with us, Rama was the one who used to have the least sympathy for him. A spoilt snot-nosed rich noble's brat who inherited too much family fortune and power at too young an age. And now he sits by Rama's right hand and speaks for him? Outrageous!*

He felt Shatrughan's calloused palm on his shoulder and warm breath on the side of his neck. 'Sabar, bhraatr,' whispered his brother. Patience, brother.

The watchful eyes and alert hands poised over pommels and hilt-guards surrounding them underscored the merit of Shatrughan's advice. Besides, he had no desire to start a blood-battle with the administrators of his own family throne, no matter how strongly he might disagree with their methods.

It still took an effort for him to reply in a level tone. 'With due respect, Lord Bhadra, I believe my brother and I have every right to know the allegations made against us and to be given a fair chance to speak for ourselves. Where I do agree with you is that the sabha is not obliged to inform us of these allegations. The accuser must personally face us in open court,' he gestured at the virtually deserted hall to indicate that it, by no means, satisfied the definition of an open court, 'and speak his accusations in our presence. The question of the Council finding a verdict against us does not arise, since the process of justice has not yet been carried out under Ayodhyan law, let alone Arya law.' Again, he emphasised 'Ayodhyan' to highlight the fact that while Arya law might be interpreted variously by different tribes and nations, Ayodhya was legendary for its justice and fairness—if Bhadra, whose lineage came from a particularly brutal bloodstained grama with a history of resorting to violence in order to amass its lands and wealth, regarded that emphasis as a reminder that his own family did not have the best record for abiding by the law, well so be it. He was rewarded by seeing the man's eyes narrow at that emphasis.

Bhadra moved his mouth as if to speak, but Bharat held up his hand and continued: 'Besides, it was my impression that Lord Rama had addressed me. Is it now acceptable protocol for a mere nobleman to interrupt when kings are in formal dialogue?'

That one struck home hard. Bharat saw Bhadra's eyes widen, and his nostrils flare along with his anger. Bhadra's own temper was notorious. Even as a boy he had been in the ugly habit of beating his dogs and horses to death when they did not obey his commands to the letter. Bharat now saw a flash of that same boyhood cruelty rise to the fore as the advisor took a step forward, hand reaching for the hilt of his sword. *Come on then, make a move against me, and we'll see who gets the danda then.*

Rama's hand rose. Bhadra stopped short, although his eyes burned now with a hot rage that Bharat had seen too often before to mistake for anything less than a death-wish. He marked in his mind as a reminder of the exact moment when the advisor had first become his mortal enemy.

'Enough.' Rama placed the goblet on a tray beside the sunwood throne. 'This is a waste of valuable time. The Council has far more vital matters to discuss today.'

He looked at someone beyond the edge of the circle of counsellors and ministers and made a gesture that Bharat could not catch. Someone flitted away into the shadows in response, off to do Rama's bidding. Rama turned his eyes back to Bharat, a faint trace of a smile evident now.

'Lord Bharat, your concern for Ayodhya law—as against Arya law,' he said, showing that he had caught the nuance as well as the implied insult to Bhadra's own family background, 'is commendable. However, you are not facing a lok sabha. This is a rajya sabha. Hence there is no requirement of an open public court. We are in a time of war. This is a War Council seated here today. We operate under rule of martial law now, and all decisions and judgements are summary and immediate and not subject to the usual process of public hearings and trials.'

Bharat's heart sank as he realised what this meant and what Rama was leading up to. Rama read his reaction and smiled coldly before continuing.

'I see you follow my meaning now. Under martial law, the War Council in conjunction with the rajya sabha,' Rama indicated both the circle of counsellors as well as the usual roster of ministers, 'is empowered to consider any act of transgression or treason against the state in private and arrive at private judgement. Only the danda need be announced publicly, and it is that part of the process for which you are summoned here today.'

Rama gestured again and Bharat glanced back to see a group of figures coming forward from the shadows, apparently just brought into the sabha hall on Rama's summons. He was more than a little shocked to see the Queens Kausalya and Sumitra, as well as a few other elder statesmen and stateswomen of the court. From the puzzled faces, he knew that the 'witnesses' had not been told anything either.

Rama gestured to the small group who were now standing in the light of the mashaals, blinking and looking curiously at Bharat and Shatrughan as they tried to understand what was going on. 'Here are the witnesses as required by law, and in their presence I shall now pronounce your danda. Bharat and Shatrughan. For transgressions against the state of Kosala and the throne of Ayodhya, you are both stripped of your kingships and all other possessions and placed under house arrest within the bounds of the Royal Palace with immediate effect and for an indefinite period of time. This sentence is now pronounced by me,

Rama Chandra of Ayodhya, under the auspices of Ayodhyan martial law. I ask that the War Council second it.'

'So seconded,' said Bhadra eagerly, his teeth glinting whitely in the light of a mashaal. He locked eyes with Bharat, lip curling in that familiar sneer of triumph.

'The Sabha of Ministers confirms it,' Pradhan Mantri Jabali said aloud.

Rama nodded. 'The motion is carried. Have the accused taken into custody at once.'

SEVENTEEN

'Wait!' cried a woman's voice.

Had it been anyone else, Shatrughan knew the plea would have fallen on deaf ears. But it was Kausalya-maa who cried out. First Queen of Ayodhya by Dasaratha's side, then Queen Regent during those long years of exile, and now Queen Mother to the seated king. For the past ten years, she had played no active role in the administration and governance of Ayodhya—had, in fact, been relieved and happy to surrender all responsibility to Rama—but the knowledge of her power and stature remained, as did the overwhelming affection the people, the court, even the armed forces felt towards her. Many considered her an avatar of the goddess, and while associations of royalty with divinity were common across Aryavarta, in Kausalya-maa's case, they were believed more fervently and by greater numbers than was usual.

The soldiers who had encircled Bharat and him in a ring of spears and were about to shepherd them out the sabha hall halted at once. Shatrughan saw them glance at each other uneasily. That single uneasy glance told him more than an hour of questioning would have revealed. *They know things are not right here. They don't like it. But they have no choice but to follow orders.*

He saw his clan-mother step forward, out of the group that had been summoned at this unearthly hour to serve as witnesses in this sorry excuse for a trial. She walked through the circle of seated ministers and counsellors, towards the royal dais itself. Pradhan Mantri Jabali stood in her way, looking down his hawk nose at her imperiously. She met his hawk gaze with an eagle stare of her own, and he visibly blanched and shuffled aside. Like most politicians who advocated war and invasion and signed the death warrants of countless young bodies sent out to do violence on unseen enemies in distant lands, Jabali was a coward at heart. Shatrughan bitterly wished Sumantra were still in charge, with his quiet grace and wisdom. But this was what they had to work with, the likes of Jabali and Bhadra. This was Ayodhya today.

Bhadra made a move as if to block Kausalya's path too, and from the insolent expression on his face, Shatrughan knew he would not cow down as easily as Jabali had done. The advisor was no coward, he was something far worse: a man who took pleasure in harming others through brute violence, but clever enough to disguise it as a warrior's willingness for combat. Shatrughan would not put it past him to lay a hand on Kausalya too.

But Rama spoke then, in a voice so quiet, it was clearly intended only for Bhadra. 'She may speak.'

Bhadra hesitated, then stepped back to his position to the right of the throne. He folded his arms across his muscled chest, biceps bulging and anga-vastra tightening around them, as he watched Kausalya approach.

She walked to the foot of the dais, up the steps, and right up to the sunwood throne itself. Shatrughan saw several counsellors and ministers turn their heads to speak with one another, without taking their eyes off her for an instant. It was against protocol to approach a sitting liege thus, without being expressly ordered or given permission. But Rama had said 'She may speak', and he seemed unperturbed by her approach.

She stopped one step below the throne, maintaining a little more than a sword's length distance between Rama and herself—though of course, she wore no sword at all—and remained over two heads lower than his eyeline. Thus, she maintained the decorum of the court and

throne, still looking up to her liege and keeping safe distance, yet using
the unusual position to assert her own stature and power. Now that is
a brilliant politician, Shatrughan thought, resisting the urge to flash
a grin. And not one playing to advance her career either; everything
that Kausalya-maa did, she did for the common good. Nothing more
or less. Nobody else in the whole world would dare to approach the
King of Ayodhya thusly, yet after all, nobody else in the whole world
could claim to have borne the King of Ayodhya for nine months in her
own womb either. For all its recent emphasis on masculine muscle, Arya
civilisation was after all, a matriarchal civilisation. For as the cheeky old
commonspeak saying went: 'Lineage is father's privilege. But only the
mother can say who is truly whose!'

Kausalya spoke words to Rama then. She did so quietly enough and
rapidly enough that nobody, least of all those standing as far away as
Shatrughan and Bharat were, could catch her words. No doubt Bhadra
could hear her quite well, being as close to Rama as he was, and it was
by watching his face as well as Rama's own features, that Shatrughan
had some semblance of understanding what Kausalya might have said.

Bhadra's face turned white with anger almost at once, then red with
frustration as she continued speaking and Rama continued listening
without reaction or response, then finally it turned purple with impotent
rage by the time she finished, reached out, laid a hand gentle on Rama's
knees, stretching out to touch it, then stepped back, dismounting the
steps as gracefully as she had mounted them and without once needing
to glance down or backwards. She reached the foot of the dais, adjusted
her garment to ensure her head was properly covered as court protocol
required, and waited quietly.

Bhadra stepped towards the throne, his adam's apple bobbing
furiously in his throat. He opened his mouth to speak, but before he
could get a word out, Rama raised a hand, causing Bhadra to stop, and
gestured him back with a faintly admonishing gesture. Bhadra stepped
back and stayed quiet, but it was evident that the amount of self-control
those two simple acts required cost the advisor dearly. He knew better

than to glare at Kausalya the way he had glared at Bharat earlier: hot-headed as he might be, Bhadra was shrewd enough to display enough outward control to have reached this far. *But he's not going to take this lying down either*, Shatrughan thought grimly. *Whatever Kausalya-maa said to Rama, it must have been really effective.*

As if agreeing, Rama lowered the same hand he had raised to stop Bhadra and pointed it at Bharat and Shatrughan.

'Release them.'

Pradhan Mantri Jabali sputtered in protest: 'My Lord!'

Rama gestured Jabali to silence. 'Queen Mother Kausalya, in her capacity as Elder Maatr of the dynasty, has proposed an alternative danda for the two transgressors. As Samrat of the assembly, I have considered her proposal and deemed it acceptable. Therefore, instead of placing Lords Bharat and Shatrughan under house arrest, I am entrusting them with a task. If they oversee the completion of the task successfully, they shall be deemed to have proven their fealty to the Kosala nation and the sunwood throne beyond doubt. But should they fail in this task or waver in any manner, their danda shall be increased to the maximum penalty under law. Namely, summary execution.'

Shatrughan swallowed. What in the name of Devi had just happened? Was this supposed to be a reprieve or an escalation? He glanced at Bharat and saw the same thought reflected in his eyes: Two princes of Ayodhya, threatened with execution for transgressions against Ayodhya? Surely their father—nay, all their ancestors—must be fuming in the afterlife!

But then he looked at Kausalya and saw something very different in her face. She looked grim too, but she also looked relieved, as if she had achieved her goal. Their eyes met and she inclined her head very slightly, just enough to reassure him.

Without wholly understanding what had just happened and what lay ahead, Shatrughan nevertheless felt better than he had just moments earlier. He trusted Kausalya-maa. With his life if need be. Whatever she had wrought for his and Bharat's sake, it would be right.

Before anyone else could say another word, a familiar furred shape flew in through the same window through which it had exited not long before. Hanuman walked up to the foot of the dais, bowed deeply and said, 'My Lord Rama, they are arrayed as you commanded. Awaiting your inspection.'

Rama nodded and rose from the throne. At once, everyone present who was seated rose as well. Rama walked down the steps of the dais. Following in his wake, the rest of the entourage went with him, Bharat and Shatrughan as well.

EIGHTEEN

From the lofty height of the Seer's Eye, the distant horizon already held the promise of dawn. The sky in the east was marginally lighter than the inky blackness of the rest of the world. The mashaals and lanterns of Ayodhya lay far below the 1008-foot stone tower, illuminating the city in pockets. Beyond its walls, crow-black darkness claimed the land. Seen thus at this hour of ghor suvah, it was possible to understand why the Aryas of the Satya Yuga had chosen this location. Bounded by the river on one side, straddling it, in fact, with the rugged mountain ranges at its back, the foothills of the Himalayas, and facing the wild jungles of the Southwoods that had long marked the great patch of central aranya wilderness dividing the southern Arya nations from the northern ones, the city was ideally situated for defence. Beyond that great southern sprawl of tumultuous forest wilderness, the great and splendid tribes of the southern part of the subcontinent flourished in no lesser grandeur than Ayodhya. But that central forest had long marked a natural border in the spread of Arya civilisation; a boundary not of mortal making but of nature herself. And nestled within its sprawling largesse, many minor kingdoms had grown and flourished independently. Some, like the Gangetic fisher tribe, the Nisadas under Guha, were friendly to Ayodhyans and Aryas. Others were openly hostile. Seen from this height, it was like viewing an ocean of darkness untouched by the mashaals of Arya knowledge and Vedic wisdom.

'Extinguish the lights,' Rama commanded as he took up a position at the south-east side of the circular promontory. The wind up here was too wanton for mashaals. The PFs accompanying the royal entourage had carried lanterns. They extinguished them now at Rama's command.

Bharat looked around as the light faded from the last of these, marvelling at the sheer number assembled here. There were no less than thirty people on the main promontory, with a few at the back where he stood, by the half-platform at the head of the winding stairs that afforded climbers a space to catch their breath. He had never seen so many here together at one time before. Why was it necessary to bring the entire War Council, the counsellors, the advisor, their mandatory PF guards, and even the Queens Sumitra and Kausalya? Whatever Rama intended to show them, it must be quite extraordinary to require their presence. He had hoped to have a moment alone with Rama to speak in private and discuss matters in a more brotherly fashion, rather than the absurd formality of the hearing—if it could be called that—to which they had just been subjected back in the sabha hall. But that seemed unlikely now.

Bharat wistfully recalled coming up here with his brothers in happier days of yore—with Rama as well, though what a different Rama he had been back then; he remembered this one thing they had all loved to do, even though it was expressly forbidden to them. They would each take turns standing in the centre of the promontory, arms held out, head flung back then turning round and round as fast as they could manage, pinwheeling, until the pillars bounding the chamber seemed to vanish, leaving one with the illusion of a completely clear view all around. It had been remarkable—and more than a little frightening, at that age. And once, when he had lost his balance and gone rolling across the stone floor, it had been Rama who had caught him, just a yard short of the unbounded edge. He had clasped his brother's shoulders and hugged him warmly. And Rama had hugged him back.

Now he remembered those days with sadness and regret. What had changed? Why had it changed? Why did it have to change at all? He would give anything to have those days, that brotherly love, that sense of utter closeness and completeness, back again, if only for a day, an hour, a moment.

As the last light of the last lantern faded out slowly, and Bharat saw the faces of those nearest to him fade into obscurity, he realised why Rama had asked for the lights to be extinguished. The answer came in the form of a collective intake of breath from those standing at the fore, looking out between the pillars that were the only thing between themselves and the darkness beyond the tower.

Due to the prescient design of the tower, every one of those gathered here on the promontory was afforded a view of the lands that lay beyond the Sarayu Valley. Despite the thick forestation of those parts, it was possible to see what Rama had brought them here to witness.

Visible between the gaps in the trees, and in front of the treeline, their fur contrasting sufficiently with the verdant flora to make them stand out, was an army of vanars so immense that Bharat had no words to describe it. Mammoth? Huge? Enormous? All these seemed weak choices to describe the sheer profusion that carpeted the land to the east of Ayodhya, stretching for yojanas in that direction. A moving, stirring, sea of vanars, their fur rippling like grass on an open plain. Bharat felt his own breath catch in his throat. There must be lakhs of the creatures. A crore even. Two crore? Possibly.

A small shape hovered above the gathered vanar armies, floating in mid-air. Even without the silhouette of that familiar leonine head and the bushy tipped enormously long tail curled upwards, Bharat could not have mistaken Hanuman. As he watched, the vanar expanded himself in size until he grew large and tall enough for his feet to touch the ground—a hummock of earth dissolved beneath his heel, crumbling to dust—and his head stood at the same height as the Seer's Eye itself. He put his palms together and bowed towards the tower, towards Rama, speaking in a great rumbling tone that reached the gathering on the promontory like a great wind redolent of vanar fur and sweat. 'By your grace, Lord Rama, I present to you the vanar armies assembled and awaiting your command.'

Rama raised his hand which, Bharat noted, now held the gleaming raj-taru of the Suryavanshi Ikshwaku dynasty. 'Thank you, my loyal friend. Once again, you have lived up to your word and done me a great service.'

Hanuman bowed deeply, shrinking as he did so. In another moment, he had resumed his normal size and flew back towards the vanar ranks, descending to ground level before them.

Several excited voices began to speak in the gathering. Rama cut them all off by turning and raising his hand again, the royal sceptre commanding instant obedience.

'If we shall all turn to look north and west now, we shall see what Lakshman has to show us as well.'

The gathering turned at once in the direction specified. Bharat turned with them, his eyes meeting Shatrughan's as his brother turned too. He saw the simulacrum of his own astonishment reflected in Shatrughan's eyes. What is Rama up to? What does he intend to do with a vanar army of that magnitude? Invade Lanka again? Surely not! There was nothing in Lanka worth taking, he knew. Which meant Rama had other territories in mind. But which ones? And why? Ayodhya had no more natural enemies left, now that Ravana and his great asura and rakshasa hordes were gone. Yet he would not have called for Hanuman to assemble the vanar multitudes just for a parade!

Then he saw what lay to the north-west and all thought, all logic drained from his mind. When the gathering gasped collectively this time, he opened his mouth as well. Although no sound emerged, he felt no less stunned.

On the northwestern plains above Ayodhya, cleared generations ago to accommodate the city-state's great standing army and provide space for its military manoeuvres and training, there now stood a force of mortal soldiers on foot, on chariot, on horseback, and on elephant-back.

It was the army of Ayodhya, but Bharat knew the size and extent of Ayodhyan forces. This assemblage far exceeded their normal standing numbers. Where Ayodhya's regular standing army had perhaps four akshohinis or battalions, this force was far, far greater in size.

His practised eye scanned the neat rectangular formations arrayed out in impressive order on the practice plains and beyond. The dawn was just breaking, and as the assembly on the promontory gazed out at this astonishing spectacle, spreading tentacles of light crept across the landscape, catching and reflecting off the gleaming polished armour and weaponry of the assembled ranks. Bharat estimated that no less than six akshohinis were assembled, perhaps even seven or eight if those shadows at the mouth of Ikshwaku's Canyon were also soldiers. Eight akshohinis? It was staggering. Twice the size of Ayodhya's army! And this was in addition to the vanar hordes!

Rama said: 'Behold, the greatest army ever raised in the history of the world. A force of mortals and vanars together comprising greater numbers than all the other armies of the Arya nations combined. With this great force we shall perform the Ashwamedha yajna and go forth today to challenge all the nations of the known world.'

And he raised the raj-taru, catching the slanting first light of day and setting it aglow.

'Ayodhya Anashya!' he cried.

Three dozen voices answered him from the promontory: 'Ayodhya Anashya!'

And from the vanar hordes behind them and the mortal army before them, a great and terrible cry resounded, filling the world with a rumbling no less than thunder:

'AYODHYA ANASHYA!'

NINETEEN

Bejoo heard the thundering roar of the armies and shuddered. Between the vanars on one side and the Ayodhyan army on the other, as well as the PF forces assembled here on the main royal avenues, the sound was deafening, like a thunder crack directly above. As the echoes faded away into the silent dawn, he glanced up at the Seer's Eye morosely. The slanting first light highlighted the raj-taru held up by Maharaja Rama Chandra—nay, it's Samrat Rama Chandra now, remember—and limned it in dull golden light. A cheer rose from the throats of the PFs around him and he raised his hand unhappily, pretending to join in. One never knew who was watching these days, and after witnessing what happened to those who seemed less than enthusiastic about displaying support for the emperor, he had decided to keep his objections private and his displays public. He even shouted the ubiquitous chant 'Samrat Rama Chandra ki jai!!' along with the rest, almost fumbling over the first word, which had been 'Siyavar' for so long rather than the recent 'Samrat' that he had yet to grow accustomed to saying. It tripped awkwardly off his tongue. Emperor Rama Chandra in place of Sita's Husband Rama Chandra. That amendment of the customary cheer pretty much summed up the change in Rama over the past ten years and described all that he considered to have gone wrong with Ayodhya in the same decade.

From his position in the midst of a large regiment of similarly attired grama-rakshaks, Bejoo could not see what the distant figures on the lofty tower were presently viewing. But he had heard the awed descriptions of the sheer size of the vanar forces, and he had personally borne witness to the growing ranks of Ayodhyan regulars over the past year, and he could imagine the mind-numbing size of the two armies that now flanked Ayodhya. Those thundering cries had been like nothing he had ever heard before. An old senapati had once said when Bejoo was but a young novice soldier, that while men stood and walked alone, they still counted as men. But the moment they banded together, they grew into a kind of beast. The greater the number of men together, the less human and more bestial they became. Until finally, when it became the size of a national army, its individual humanity was all but lost in the hive-mind of the great majority. As the old craggy general had summed it up, *an army has its own sense of morality, and that sense has very little to do with what you or I call dharma.*

Now, the greatest beast ever created stood outside the walls of Ayodhya. Roaring a challenge.

And the fact that it was on their side rather than some external enemy's side offered little comfort to Bejoo. Once awakened, the beast must be fed. It will be fed. And if it cannot find sufficient nourishment outside, it will eat its own home, family, and finally, itself. For such is the nature of the beast, that slouching shambling monster that men become when they go to war. It needs no reason, for war itself is against all reason. It merely needs to be unleashed. And then the massacre begins. The old veteran's words still rumbled in the caverns of memory.

Bejoo shuddered again.

A little while later, after the assembly was over and the samrat and the others from the Seer's Eye had descended once again into the bowels of the palace, during the brief respite before the yajna itself was scheduled to start, Bejoo was standing by his wagon, checking that all was in readiness. The task of the grama-rakshaks was to bring up the flanks and rear, providing an unbroken supply chain that led back from the frontlines all the way to Ayodhya. To this end, his grama was sparsely manned, just the minimum number required to drive the wagons and load and unload. They were all over-the-hill old or partially incapacitated PFs deemed unfit to fight or march or ride along with the regular army. And they carried only supplies. In Bejoo's case, that meant mostly weapons of all kinds. Two wagons were filled with only arrows, some so freshly fletched and leaded he could smell the birdshit on the feathers and the smelting on the irontips. The other wagons carried an assortment of every kind of device or tool that could accomplish the brutal business of killing and sundering human beings. He supposed it was better than having to carry food provisions, like old Nachiketa's grama, or vaids to administer to the wounded on the field like Jagannath's grama. He sighed as he resecured a loose binding and flicked the flap of the wagon down again, hooking it deftly to prevent it flapping up as they rode. It was hard to believe that these weapons and tools of war would be used against fellow Aryas—against fellow humans, for that matter. All their lives, old soldiers like Bejoo had prayed to their chosen amsas or avatars of the One God, in his case that had been Shaneshwara, his family's patron deity, that someday they would annihilate the asura races from the mortal realm, restore peace and usher in a new era of contentment and prosperity.

And look at us now, he thought as he walked around the large dusty field where dozens of other gramas were similarly awaiting the order to move out. We annihilated the asura races at last. Restored peace. We even achieved the prosperity part of the bargain. But then, instead of being content with that, we're about to start the whole vicious cycle of violence all over again. Except that this time, since we don't have a common non-human enemy to fight, we're just going to make do, and slaughter one another. It made him sick to the stomach to even think of the countless men and women who had died over the decades, centuries even, so that the Arya civilisation could attain its present level of stability and prosperity. Was it all for this? This miserable sodding relaunch of the same old madness all over again? What the bloody hell for?

Angry and impotent, he kicked a loose stone and winced as it narrowly missed hitting the foot of another grama-rakshak. The man glared at him as if he was insane, and Bejoo raised a hand in sheepish apology. The mood across Ayodhya was taut as a bow pulled to its maximum stretch, as it usually was before any campaign, and the last thing he needed was to get into a brawl. The other grama-rakshaks regarded him with barely disguised hostility, not the least because of his earlier high office and closeness to the late King Dasaratha as well as his fame as a vajra captain, hero of many legendary exploits. They knew he was too good for this post and resented his presence among them. And they were justified in their resentment. After all, he wasn't here because he enjoyed inhaling the 'dust of the road and watching the hindquarters of a team of horses twitching tails for fifty yojanas every day. He was here because he had been kicked down here to this position, courtesy of Pradhan Mantri Jabali and his cronies. Not just he, much the same fate had befallen most of those old vets who had enjoyed the trust of the late Maharaja. Dasaratha had tolerated Jabali because of his efficiency and his old ties to Kosala nobility; he had never made a secret of his personal dislike of the man and his personal habits and beliefs. After Dasaratha, and more importantly, after Pradhan Mantri Sumantra's resignation 'on grounds of dharma', War Minister Jabali had swept the royal house clean of all those who had been in the late king's favour—replacing them with his own cohorts. It was typical transition politics and Bejoo understood it well. What he didn't understand, and found increasingly difficult to tolerate, was the growing hawkishness of Jabali's administration. And Rama's growing espousal of that hawkishness.

And today, all his fears had been proven true.

He stopped and looked around listlessly. He had reached the end of his grama, and everything that could be checked had been checked twice or thrice; there was nothing left to do except wait for the order to roll out. He was bitterly unhappy about having to participate in the coming campaign. *This is not what I signed up for, forty gloamyears ago. And this is not what Ayodhya is supposed to use its power and military might for. Shaneshwara curse that hawk-nosed fool and his cronies. I warrant they're the ones who poisoned Rama's ear until he finally agreed to this madness.*

He suddenly felt defiant.

What if he simply refused to take the grama out? If he just resigned his commission and walked away?

But then again, what good would that do? It would make no difference to this massive war machine that had already been set into motion. The only one it would affect was old Bejoo himself. Military service was now compulsory in Ayodhya. Refusal or resignation— or going absent without leave—was tantamount to treason, under the new interpretation of Manu's Laws. And the danda for such an act of defiance was execution. He would be arrested for treason and probably be executed summarily, like the handful of other protestors or dissenters who had found the Ashwamedha campaign beyond their limits of tolerance. His body would still be warm as the other gramas trundled out onto the raj-marg, and he could almost imagine the other grama-rakshaks sneering or even spitting on his cooling corpse as they passed by. He sighed and rubbed his chest. No. A futile protest was no good to anyone. He may as well go along, do his duty, serve his time. At least he was not expected to participate directly in the brutality.

He leaned morosely against the side of his lead wagon, mulling over the unfairness of it all. So distracted was he by his own thoughts that he failed to raise his head even when he heard a wagon approach. He hardly noticed even when the wagon stopped close by and the horses snickered quietly.

A voice spoke from the wagon. A voice he had not heard in Shaneshwara knew how many years—decades? A voice from a distant, happier past.

'So tell me, Vajra Captain Bejoo, have you danced with any vetaals lately?'

TWENTY

As the soft gloam of first light gradually illuminated the promontory of the Seer's Eye, Shatrughan sought out Bharat and saw his own worst fears reflected in his brother's face. Bharat was clearly as shaken as he himself felt after viewing the extraordinary display.

Ayodhya Anashya indeed. This isn't what our forebears intended when they first roared that slogan in battle. Ayodhya stands for defensibility, for making a stand against injustice and the madness of conquest and invasion, not for them!

The mood of exhilaration remained even after the spectacular formal viewing of the armies was over and the elite gathering had begun to disperse. Shatrughan had never felt so out of place in his own homeland before in his life, so severely pitted against the tide of public opinion. Even though the Seer's Eye was so high above the city, their father, the late king Dasaratha, had always believed that immense spiritual power with which the tower was infused enabled a king of Ayodhya to read the mood of the city from up here. He often came here during times of trouble, or when a difficult decision had to be made, and now as Shatrughan stood there with head reeling and senses shaken, he understood why. It was as if the tower acted as a kind of emotional listening post. He thought he could actually hear and feel what people were feeling across the great expanse of the capital city. After all, this tower and its sister structure, the Sage's Brow in neighbouring Mithila, were said to have been erected not by mortal architects but by the saptarishis—the seven legendary brahmarishis of yore—using only brahman shakti. Even as a young boy, Shatrughan had always been awed by the sense of power and intimate connection to the people that standing here evoked in him. He felt it again now, as a thrumming living vibration that was drawn in from the city by the tower like a beacon, passed up through the very spine of the structure, and through those stones on which he now stood, transmuted into energy and emotion that rippled through his body and mind, giving him a vivid image of what Ayodhya felt and thought at this moment in time.

There were no surprises there.

All across Ayodhya, the mood was overwhelmingly one of excitement and anticipation. A sense of power. Of eagerness to go forth and conquer. It was the mood of a people embarking on a great venture, naively unaware of the long-term consequences and repercussions.

He felt frustrated and more than a little angered. What was Rama thinking? This was no time to put on such a display of military might. And to embark on the Ashwamedha yajna now? This could well be the act that tipped the delicate balance of inter-nation politics and precipitated a war between the Arya kingdoms. Unless of course…he realised with a sinking sensation…unless that was what Rama and his advisors wanted to achieve.

Up here, he needed no spiritual infusion to read the mood. The sombre wizened old mantris and counsellors were infected with war fever. Even now they murmured excitedly amongst themselves as they shuffled towards the narrow egress, starting the descent down the narrow spiral stairwell which was designed, like most Arya stairwells, to stifle the progress of men clad in armour bearing arms and make the use of those weapons all but impossible. Shatrughan estimated that it would take several more moments for them all to descend and deliberately hung back, indicating with a brief nod of his head to Bharat to do the same. He wished to have words with Bharat in as much privacy as was possible under the circumstances.

Rama, Jabali, Bhadra and a pair of other senior ministers seemed in no hurry to descend either; they remained standing at the far edge of the promontory, talking. Shatrughan noted with a discreet glance that Bharat and he were virtually unguarded; the handful of PFs present were more intent on maintaining the suraksha chakra—the perpetual 'circle of safety' they were required to maintain at all times around the person of the king—than in watching the erstwhile offenders. They were aware of Shatrughan as he moved closer to Bharat but did not object by word or gesture. After all, despite their 'offences', they were still royal sons of Ayodhya and that counted for something with most. Though not with Rama, apparently, he noted with a tinge of bitter regret.

Finally, he found his moment when the counsellors standing nearby moved towards the egress to take their turn to begin the long descent. He shuffled close enough to Bharat to speak without being heard by anyone else.

'Bhraatr, the situation is beyond control. Something must be done.'

'Aye. We must speak with Rama.'

Shatrughan glanced at the group across the promontory and was not surprised to see Bhadra's light grey eyes glinting sharply as they flicked in this direction. He avoided meeting the counsellor's eyes, pretending to look down morosely as if lost in contemplation. After a moment or two, when he saw Bhadra engaged in conversation once more, he spoke again, keeping his face averted so his moving lips could not be seen.

'We must speak with him alone. Away from the long ears of those two bheriyas.'

He didn't have to spell out who the jackals were. Bharat made a soft sound of assent. They were quiet again for a long moment as the remaining two ministers also came closer, awaiting their turn to descend the narrow mouth of the stairwell. Finally, they had passed out of easy hearing. Shatrughan shot another discreet glance and saw that only Bhadra, Jabali, and Rama now remained. Both war minister and prime minister seemed to be talking at once, eyes glinting in the gaining light as they spewed more madness and poison into Rama's ears.

Finally, Bhadra finished speaking and gestured to one of the PFs. When the soldier approached him, the war minister spoke quickly and brusquely, and gestured with his raised chin at Bharat and Shatrughan. The PF came over with quick efficient steps towards them.

'Move along, now, my Lords. Samrat Rama has instructed that you be taken to your stations.'

Bharat stood his ground silently. Shatrughan followed his example.

The PF frowned. In a somewhat gentler tone with a modicum of respect, he said, 'Come now, Yuvrajas. My orders are to escort you down. Kindly do me the courtesy of moving.'

Bharat raised his head a fraction, just enough to meet the PF's eyes, but not enough that Bhadra could see his face or know if he spoke. 'If you value our position as princes of Ayodhya, you'll leave us be. We wish to have words with our bhraatr.'

The PF looked unhappy. 'My Lord, I served under you briefly in the battle of Ahichatra, during the Panchala campaign…I have no wish to use harsh words or actions against you.'

'Indeed you did serve under me, Surasena, and you served well, particularly in the action on the hill where the Mlecchas were rooted in. That was where you took the wound in your side, did you not?'

The soldier's eyes flashed with bright pride. 'You remember, sire? It was a long time ago and a small affair in a foreign land.'

'Yet no effort is too small nor any man insignificant if he risks life and limb in the struggle for freedom,' Bharat replied, still using the PF's body to conceal his face. Shatrughan saw Bhadra watching them openly now, contempt distorting his otherwise handsome features. 'You fought bravely and when your wound prevented you from returning to active service, I recommended you for an officer's posting in the Purana Wafadars. I see you have done well for yourself. King's guard, no less.'

'Thank you, sire,' the man said, clearly delighted now and seemed about to snap off a salute. Then he remembered where he was and what duty he had been assigned and his face slackened. 'I apologise again, sire, but my orders—'

Bharat nodded. 'You have fulfilled your orders. You have informed us quite clearly and unequivocally that we are to move out. But as your superior and senior, I countermand that order and ask you to step aside now. We intend to stay. Not to do anyone harm. Simply to speak peaceably. Stand down, soldier.'

The man named Surasena hesitated, swallowed, then came to a decision. He stepped back three paces, resuming his former position on the rim of the suraksha chakra. Then he fixed his gaze in that distant ten-yojana stare that the PFs were famous for on parade grounds. They were trained to stand that way for hours if need be. Shatrughan resisted the urge to grin.

'Well handled, bhraatr,' he said, touching his brother's shoulder.

Bharat said grimly, 'Don't be too quick to praise me, bhraatr. I have a feeling those two won't be as easy to convince. But we still have to try. For Ayodhya's sake.'

And he moved towards Rama, even as the ring of PFs came to full alert and raised their weapons at once, protecting their king from the offender.

Shatrughan prayed that Bharat would be able to talk Rama out of this madness before it was too late, and without provoking further bad blood between them.

But in his heart, he had a feeling that it might already be too late.

TWENTY-ONE

Nakhudi had travelled all of one full night and day, reaching within sight of Ayodhya by the previous night. New gate-watch rules required that all those unable to pass through before nightfall had to wait until dawn to be admitted. She had spent the night outside the first gate, not sleeping, but walking among the many other travellers who had failed to make it through before nightfall, talking and exchanging gossip, news, tidbits of information, with people from as far away as Kalinga. It had been a very useful night and by the time she finally returned to the wagon to bed down, she had gleaned more insight into the state of the kingdom than even the king possessed. She had no fear of thieves here: under the new laws, the danda for even an attempt at theft was the severance of a limb at best, and execution at worst. After all, the contents of the wagon were not really hers, they belonged to Ayodhya. Had she impressed that fact upon the gate-watch, she had no doubt they would have relented and permitted her passage. But she had her reasons for wanting to wait another night. She wished to be here in the morning. If all that she had learned was accurate in fact, then the morning would be a momentous one for Ayodhya.

Not just Ayodhya, for the whole wide world, she thought now as she looked down from the wagon's seat at the old PF. For this is the day Ayodhya lays claim to all prithviloka.

The old vet stared up at her in bemused confusion, and she smiled beneath the shawl covering the lower half of her face as she imagined how much more befuddled he would look when he recognised her.

'Who—' he began, then stopped as she reached up and undid the shawl to show him her face. Dawning recognition spread across his lined and weathered features. His eyes and mouth crinkled in a smile. He never used to have those lines, she thought. Looks like Captain Bejoo of the King's Vajra finally learned how to smile—a lot! Though he hadn't looked like he had much to smile about as she had approached. In fact, he looked like a man awaiting a death sentence.

'Nakhudi?' he said tentatively, then more confidently, 'it is you, isn't it?'

She grinned as she bent over to secure the reins, then leaped down from the wagon. The ground, churned by the wheels of hundreds of gramas, was as loose as an over-ploughed field and a sod gave way beneath her not inconsiderable weight, causing her to stumble. Bejoo caught her instinctively, and she felt his hands on her waist and her left breast, gripping tightly, and felt a flash of heat. She saw his eyes widen and his throat working. Well, at least he's still got his virility, the old dog. Then he retracted his hands like a man who had just touched scalding steel, and she laughed openly, throwing back her head to the dusty sky.

'Well, maybe it's women I should have asked about instead,' she said, when she was able to stop guffawing. 'Looks like you haven't… danced…with one in a fair while!'

Bejoo glanced around. 'Keep your voice down, you brainless hussy! Do you want everyone to hear?' He indicated her shawl. 'And cover your face up again. It's a bad day to be on the wrong side of the law in Ayodhya.'

She chuckled as she hitched the end of the shawl over her ear again, concealing her mouth. 'What makes you think I'm on the wrong side? I could be a grama-rakshak same as you, couldn't I?'

He issued a short unamused barking laugh at that. 'Yes, of course. Because Ayodhya is so short of old fogeys that it has to resort to calling up the women reserves. Besides, you aren't an Ayodhyan. Quite the opposite, remember?'

She shrugged good-naturedly, unperturbed by his hostility—pleased by it, in fact, because it was obviously a feeble attempt to cover up that moment of shocked lust she had glimpsed in his eyes—and patted down her team to preserve the illusion of their being just two grama-rakshaks having a conversation. 'You mean the fact that my nation happens to be one of the many that are opposed to Ayodhya's military arrogance? Well, truth be told, Captain Bejoo, I don't know how loyal I am to my nation anymore, seeing as I've been away for almost two decades and the last time I took up my sword in her service was even farther back than that!'

He snorted. 'We king's warriors had an old saying…"His backside may be in Lanka, but his heart will always be in Ayodhya".'

She snorted a horse-like laugh. 'How quaint. What does it mean?'

'That it doesn't matter where you stay now or how far you've wandered from home, Nakhudi, when it comes to the pinch, you will gladly lay down your life for your homeland.'

Her dark eyes glittered playfully. 'It is nice to see you again, Vajra Captain Bejoo. You know, the last time we met, I had a great urge to get to know you better. But there was so little time and so much to do.'

He grunted, not sure if she was pulling his leg or being serious. It was hard to say. He wasn't that young anymore, although back then… he sighed. She could almost read his thoughts with that sigh: *Those days are gone, old fool. Put the past behind you. There is only today and today's tomorrows.* 'I'm no longer Captain. The Vajra was disbanded a long time ago. Now they have something else called a Trishul.'

'Makes sense. A vajra is Lord Indra's weapon, the thunderbolt from heaven. A trishul is Lord Shiva's weapon, the celestial trident.' She glanced around at the wagon train he was manning. 'So surely a vajra veteran like yourself would be the logical choice to captain this Trishul, whatever it may be?'

He looked at her sharply and she instantly realised she had touched a sore spot. 'The Trishul was Lord Bhadra's brainchild. He personally captains it in battle. He and his brothers. He reports directly to Pradhan Mantri Jabali.' He seemed to be about to speak further, then stopped himself and looked down, staring murderously at a chariot wheel. For good measure, he kicked the wheel hard enough to make the lead horse of that particular wagon's team snort in surprise. The canvas rigging shook. *Old mule still packs a mean kick*, she thought.

The very mention of Bhadra and Jabali worked a change on him, and she could tell that the men, whomever they might be, had played some part in the disbanding of Bejoo's Vajra and his subsequent demotion to grama-rakshak. Politicians, no doubt.

She sensed the change in him and was quiet for a moment. Across the field, a grama-rakshak grew impatient with a horse and flicked the end of a switch. The horse whinnied in pain.

Bejoo grimaced. He started to say something, stopped, then spoke after all. 'Back when I ran the vajra, we took as good care of our animals as of ourselves. "We are all soldiers," I used to tell my men, "some of us happen to be four-footed, others two-footed".'

Nakhudi nodded in approval. 'They ride with us, carry us into battle, bleed with us, die with us. They are warriors too. They deserve to be treated as such.'

He looked at her with a strange look and she found his scrutiny curiously intense. After a moment, she turned her head away.

He went on quietly.

'The way I see animals treated in Ayodhya now makes me want to take a whip to some of the fools meting out the abuse, if only to ask them how they liked to be treated that way themselves.'

'Ayodhya has changed,' she said and her foreign accent made even that simple statement seem like an accusation.

He nodded, turned his head, and spat in disgust. Part of a grama-rakshak's qualification was being able to imbibe and withstand copious quantities of dust, she guessed. She had eaten more than her stomach's fill on the ride here.

'More than we Ayodhyans would like,' he said.

'We thought you might have issues with the changes. That was why I came straight to you. It wasn't too hard to find you, once I heard your name from the boys and realised you were a grama-rakshak now.' She gestured at the field.

'We?' he asked. There was a glint of interest in his eyes.

She glanced around to make sure nobody was within hearing range. Then she leaned closer, close enough to smell the sweat and man-odour of his body. It was not an altogether unpleasant odour. 'My Lady Vedavati and I.'

He looked at her. The glint of interest had hardened to something else: hope? Perhaps. 'Lady Vedavati,' he repeated slowly.

She nodded. 'Lady Vedavati. You met her sons a few days ago.'

A new light gleamed in his eyes. 'The boys who held up the grama...?' he asked softly.

She nodded a third time.

He stared up at the sky. No, not at the sky, but at the tall stone tower that loomed above the city. She glanced at it as well and saw figures standing there at the top, too shadowed by the still not-quite-daylight flush of dawn. 'Then that makes them...princes.'

'Aye,' she said. 'Princes of Ayodhya.'

He stared intently at the top of the stone tower for a long time. She wondered who was up there. Then the rose-tinted dawn luminescence caught something bright and shining held by one of the figures up on the tower, something golden, and she caught her breath. Of course. *He* was up there.

'His sons and heirs,' Bejoo said at last.

'Yes,' she said in barely a whisper. 'Although there are many who might disagree with that description.'

'Not I,' said Bejoo. He had a faraway thoughtful look. 'I knew there was something familiar about those boys. And their audacity in holding up my grama!' He shook his head, chortling gruffly. 'Outrageous!'

Nakhudi laughed with him. 'Yes. Well. They're boys. And boys will get up to such antics at times.'

He glanced at her. 'Antics? Do you know the danda for highway robbery? Let alone stealing away royal Ayodhyan property? Attacking the king's men?'

She sighed, rubbing the back of her head through the scarf. Even looking away, she saw the way his eyes cut to her raised elbows and what lay beneath them. *Well, well,* she thought, glad that the shawl concealed her smile, *Vajra Captain Bejoo isn't that old after all, it seems.*

'I have some notion,' she said. 'I can't undo what's done. But I thought perhaps some form of reparation might prevent the wrath of Ayodhya from coming down on them too harshly.'

Bejoo frowned. 'What did you have in mind? And what makes you think you can bargain with these people? You have no idea how ruthless Ayodhyan jurisprudence has now become, Nakhudi. It isn't panchayat or grama justice anymore. This is—'

He broke off. She had walked over to the back of the wagon she had brought and now she flung open the rear flap, revealing its contents.

'Would this go some small way in appeasing them?' she asked.

TWENTY-TWO

Bharat was careful to keep his movements slow and unthreatening. The king's guard kept their spears pointed at him, maintaining the protective ring around Rama. Over the tips of the spears, Jabali and Bhadra glared at him with deep suspicion. Even Rama was standing with arms folded across his chest, eyes narrowed.

'Rama, I only wish to say a few words,' Bharat said.

Bhadra stepped forward with his hand on the hilt of his sword. 'Lord Rama, I told you it was a mistake to bring them here. They will try to impede and obstruct every chance they get. That is their plan.'

'It is part of the conspiracy to keep Ayodhya from realising its full potential,' Jabali barked in his stentorian manner. 'These two should be given the severest danda under law to set an example.'

Rama raised a hand, commanding silence from both flanks. 'We have already ruled upon this matter. Let us not waste time rehashing it.' He looked at Bharat directly. 'You were made to understand your position. It is extremely delicate. My advice to you,' he flicked his eyes to include Shatrughan, 'is to hold your silence and do as instructed. Anything else will only worsen matters for both of you.'

'Rama,' Bharat said in as placative a tone as he could muster, 'it would only take a moment of your time.'

Rama looked at him. Bharat looked back and tried to appeal to Rama personally. But all he saw in Rama's dark eyes was a resoluteness that he knew too well. Once Rama got that look in his eyes, nothing could steer him off the course he had embarked on. Not for nothing did the kusalavya bards call him Maryada Purshottam Rama. Rama Who Does As He Says.

'My time belongs to Ayodhya,' Rama said. 'And Ayodhya cannot spare the moment.'

And he turned his back on Bharat, turning to face the eastern sky where daylight had broken and the first tentatively probing rays of the imminent sun were turning the sky above Ayodhya golden. Some of that golden hue fell upon Rama's silhouette as he turned and somehow, despite the beauty of the illumination, it lent him a dark, terrible aspect. Samrat Rama Chandra. Emperor of Ayodhya, lord and master of all Aryavarta, the civilised world, prithviloka, the mortal realm.

All this, Bharat realised in a flash of insight even as the king's guard PFs moved forward, jabbing their spears at him and Shatrughan. One point pricked his side, piercing the skin, drawing a trickle of blood. He did not feel it. Nor did he care about the harsh mocking tones of Bhadra and Jabali who ordered the guards to escort Shatrughan and him from the tower and see that they were secured and that they were not permitted to come into the king's presence again. That last image of Rama staring out at the rising sun, cold-hearted and resolute, stayed with him. It was the rock against which the surging tide of his emotions pounded and broke unrequited.

* * *

The sun had risen by the time Bejoo had a chance to speak with the prime minister. He waited as Yuvrajas Bharat and Shatrughan were escorted under armed guard from the tower and taken to the palace. His eyes met Bharat's as he passed by, and Bejoo was saddened to see the look on Bharat's face. It was the face of a man facing a death sentence. He knew that was not the case, because the news of how First Queen

Mother Kausalya had intervened and had Bharat's and Shatrughan's dandas transmuted was all over the city, but apparently to Bharat and Shatrughan, even the alternative was no less a punishment.

His fist tightened in anger on the pommel of his shortsword as he considered the injustice of it all. Princes of Ayodhya, sons of the Suryavansha Ikshwaku line, patriots of the Kosala nation, Rama's own brothers! Being treated like criminals! It was beyond tolerance. What he failed to understand was why he too had not been arrested. From what he had heard, Bharat and Shatrughan's only crime had been to discuss and question the king's new martial policies, which under the new law could be construed as treason. Yet it was he, Bejoo, with whom they had discussed and questioned those policies. So then, why was he not being interrogated, arrested, or somehow reprimanded for the same? There was only one possible answer: the spasa or spasas whose reports had resulted in their being arrested had not been able to provide any concrete details. Because had they provided concrete details, it was inconceivable that Bejoo would not be arrested by now. Which meant that they had been arrested on mere suspicion.

No, not mere suspicion. As a preventive measure.

Bejoo knew enough about politics to understand that this was the likely answer. It hardly mattered if Bharat and Shatrughan had been overheard voicing treasonous opinions or merely taking a stroll on the north bank of Sarayu. They would have been arrested under any pretext, however flimsy. The whole point was not to actually charge them, merely to prevent them from interfering in any way with Rama's plans.

No, not Rama's plans—Jabali's plans. Bhadra's plans. All those war-mongering political power factions that stood to profit from Ayodhya going to war.

Yes, that made perfect sense.

He watched as the man he had been waiting for finally emerged from the lane that led to the Seer's Eye tower, escorted as always by his retinue of thuggish-looking guards. Bejoo knew that each one of those so-called bodyguards was responsible for as many murders, assaults, and other dark deeds carried out in the shadows of night than most condemned criminals in the dungeons of Ayodhya. But of course, all their crimes had been committed in the name of national security and in the service of Ayodhya, so they commanded respect rather than dandas. Such was politics. So would it always be.

'Pradhan Mantri? A word, if you please?'

Jabali frowned down his long nose. His thugs glared at Bejoo, waiting for a single word or gesture to crack his skull. The man closest to Bejoo, a menacing hulk of a fellow with tiny rat eyes, looked almost disappointed when the prime minister gestured them aside and deigned to step a foot or two closer to hear what he had to say.

'Quickly, man, this is the most important day in Ayodhya's history and I have a great deal of work to do,' snapped Jabali.

Yes, of course, such as barking orders at the men who will actually go forth and fight and die for Ayodhya while you recline on the silken cushions of your royal palkhi and sip soma.

'Aye, my Lord,' Bejoo said apologetically, 'but I thought this merited your immediate attention.' He gestured at the wagon standing a few yards away on Suryavansha Avenue. 'I have succeeded in recovering the king's property.'

Jabali frowned. 'What rubbish are you blabbering abou—' He broke off as the sight of the wagon refreshed his memory. 'Surely you don't mean...' He shoved Bejoo aside roughly and strode to the wagon. A barked order and his henchmen raised the rear covering for him to peer inside, his bright eyes glinting with greedy delight as he viewed the contents.

He turned to Bejoo. 'You? You recovered the stolen war wagon?'

Bejoo bowed his head in humility. 'Aye, my Lord. I had my men on the trail ever since the unfortunate incident, and they were able to track it down and return it safely.' He gestured towards the wagon. 'Not one thing is missing. The complete inventory is present. You may have it checked.'

'I certainly will,' Jabali said sharply. 'But what of the miscreants who held up the grama and wounded so many? Where are they?' He looked around as if expecting to see the culprits standing nearby, trussed in ropes and chains. Bejoo had no doubt that if that had indeed been the case, Jabali might well have given the order to have them executed right there and then.

No. What he would have done was to parade them and claim credit for their capture, and then have them executed. That was his way.

'They were dealt with most severely,' Bejoo said.

Jabali clicked his tongue impatiently. 'Yes, of course they were, or how else could you have recovered the property. But where are they now? Or...their bodies?'

Bejoo shook his head. 'Lions.'

Jabali stared at him. 'Lions?'

'Aye, my Lord. During the fight to recover the wagon, they were wounded and retreated deeper into the woods. Unknowingly, they strayed near a den. The pride tore them to shreds. They were in no state to bring here. There was virtually nothing left to bring, in fact.'

Jabali's eyes gleamed briefly as he contemplated this ultimate penalty meted out by nature in her mystical wisdom. '...tore them to shreds, you say.' He sighed. 'Oh well. They were given their danda, that's what counts.' The disappointment was palpable in his tone—he would have loved to have meted out those dandas himself, no doubt. But still and all, he had Valmiki's colony to satiate this desire. He glanced again at Bejoo. 'Quite impressive, Grama-rakshak...?'

Bejoo, 'Sire, you commissioned me yourself.'

Demoted me, actually. But let's not get prissy. You damn well know who I am, and who I was.

'Yes, of course, Bejoo,' Jabali crooked a long finger. The way the skin creased on the bone reminded Bejoo of the claw of a starved fowl. 'Well, you seem to have surpassed yourself, Grama-rakshak Bejoo. I shall have to see to it that you are given a suitable reward for your exemplary service to the king.' He began to move away even before he finished speaking.

Bejoo cleared his throat cautiously. Now came the tricky part. 'Actually, sire, I desire no reward at all. No pecuniary reward, that is. Rather, I desire an opportunity to serve the king further, if he so wills it, and by your grace, of course.'

Jabali stopped and looked impatiently at Bejoo. 'What did you have in mind, soldier? Be quick, I have much to do.'

Bejoo told him.

TWENTY-THREE

The armies of Ayodhya were mobile before the sun had risen more than a double hand's breadth above the eastern horizon. It was an awe-inspiring display of planning, coordination, and precision. Queens Kausalya and Sumitra watched from the highest balcony in their palace as the akshohini wheeled in enormous crescents in order to maintain their formation while navigating their way out of the city precincts.

A dust cloud the size of a mountain rose up high above. Panicked flocks of birds crisscrossed the skies, alarmed by the great and unusual gathering of mortals below; their scavenging brethren began to collect overhead and follow the procession, knowing that such large gatherings of mortals usually meant fresh meat to be had, if not right away, then soon. Mortals rarely collected together in such vast numbers without great violence and numerous casualties resulting; it was an enduring trait of humankind. The exodus itself was an awe-inspiring sight, the immaculate uninterrupted movement of procession after procession belying the enormous drilling and discipline that made such efficiently coordinated movement possible.

The great contingents took all day to exit the city, the supply trains bringing up the rear departing only in the late afternoon. This long tail would link the armies to the city across their campaign trail, providing the vital sustenance that enabled an army to fight abroad. More wagons would be added as required. Ayodhya was capable of supplying, feeding and maintaining a warring force till as far away as three hundred yojanas. This impressive capacity made the city-state a force to reckon with even in the most far flung corners of Aryavarta, and beyond. Unlike other nations, Ayodhya did not rely on its own surrounding towns and villages to fulfil its needs; it was entirely self-sufficient. The original reason for this self-sufficiency had been to enable it to withstand a prolonged invasion and multiple sieges. Today, that same self-sufficiency was being used for the exact opposite purpose: to enable Ayodhya to supply and maintain a force that ventured outwards aggressively.

'A system created for defence perverted and used to perpetrate offence,' Kausalya said sadly. 'I wonder what Dasa would say if he were here to see this.'

Sumitra put her hand reassuringly on the Queen Mother's shoulder. 'Dasaratha might not have been as averse to it as we are, Kausalya. Remember, he was a man of war. He believed in resolute action.'

Kausalya sighed. 'You are right. That's why it's pointless to speculate on what the dead would have said or felt with regard to things now. But I can say this with certainty: I do not approve of what is happening today in Ayodhya. I do not approve at all.'

Sumitra nodded. 'Neither do I. It is a monstrosity. A terrible misuse of power. If only we could speak to our sons and try to make them see how wrong this is…'

'Words cannot resolve every problem, Sumitra. For too long now, I have begun to feel as if everything I say to Rama has been falling on deaf ears. Or blocked ears, at least. It is as if he sees my point of view perfectly, knows exactly what I mean to say, but does not feel it is even worth the effort to debate it with me. He simply accepts it silently and discards it later like a garment that does not fit. If only he would argue at least, debate the issues at stake, I believe he would be compelled to see reason. But when a man turns himself to stone as Rama has done, he feels no need to bother with intellectual debate. He simply does as he pleases and nothing can sway him.'

Sumitra looked at her, concerned at the intensity in Kausalya's tone and face. 'You make him sound like a tyrant.'

Kausalya shook her head. 'Not a tyrant, no...but yes, if a king, however powerful, does not use his power to serve, to build, to create, and starts to use the power instead to destroy, attack, bring down, then what difference between that king and a tyrant? I fear that Rama could well become one if he continues uninterrupted upon this present path. You know how quickly and easily absolute power corrupts even the most idealistic mind. For all his fine qualities, Rama today is not the Rama he was ten years ago when he returned from Lanka, or the Rama who left us fourteen years before that. He has changed so much.'

'Or has been changed.'

Kausalya nodded, turning away from the bird's eye view of the endless rows of infantry, chariot regiments, elephant regiments, cavalry, and other units wheeling and proceeding out the gates of Ayodhya. Already the sun was risen high and the dust cloud churned up by the departing army had all but obscured the southern sky, as vast and wide as a mountain range that must surely be visible across most of the Kosala nation. 'Or has been changed. By time. By experience. By the inevitable alterations that age and circumstances impose on us all. But also, I fear, by bad advisors. That is what concerns me most of all. The fact that Rama may be falling prey to the war-mongering hawks who seek only one way forward for Ayodhya, for all Aryavarta. What is that term they use now, Sumitra?'

'Republicans. After the idea of forming a republican nation that will be self-governed by the people through a democratic process.'

'Yes, Republicans. A fine ideal. A lofty purpose. But often a murderer will pretend to be a patriot in order to justify his killing spree. Some thieves will proclaim themselves levellers of wealth and friends of the poor to gain sympathy for his cause. So also a war-thirsty group of tyrants who seek only their own aggrandisation and self-benefit will pose as benefactors of society in order to go about their selfish business with the full approval and consent of the very people they exploit and abuse. Republicans. Supporters of democracy. Peacemakers. They come in many guises but always with the same purpose: to enrich, empower and aggrandise the few at the expense of the many. Beware the king who cries out that he only serves his people while secretly taxing them to death and filling his private coffers with gold and public dungeons with dissenters. I would much rather have a king who was less rich, less powerful, less feared, but greatly loved, with a richer public, happier citizenry.'

Sumitra gestured at the wheeling hordes below. The sound of the armies moving out was so loud, it sounded as if they were in this very balcony, tramping and marching and yelling orders. 'And you believe this is what Rama's advisors are up to? Why they convinced him to undertake this Ashwamedha yajna?'

'Yes and no. The Ashwamedha yajna in itself is a ritual every Arya king undertakes from time to time. It is a ceremonial, symbolic act. Dasaratha conducted it once, and I, as his queen at the time, performed the yajna. But this,' she waved a hand in disgust, 'this is no ceremony or ritual. This is a war campaign. A carefully planned, orchestrated, mounted, financed, and managed campaign to spread Ayodhyan rule from one corner of the sub-continent to the other. No king ever sent forth an army of this size after the black horse. There is only supposed to be a symbolic force of riders following the horse, ensuring that none captures it and thereby symbolically challenges the authority of the king. But an army of this size?' She shook her head. 'An army of this size can only be intended to crush, trample, roll over the countryside, leave a swathe of death and destruction in its wake. This is akin to what the Asura hordes sent forth when they began their invasion and attempted conquest of prithviloka.'

Sumitra frowned. 'And one argument raised by the likes of Jabali and Bhadra is exactly that. They say that not long ago the asura hordes led by Ravana sought to cut a swathe of death through the mortal realm. Now, it is time we mortals put on a show of strength so great that no other force would ever dare to attempt such audacity again.'

Kausalya made a sound of exasperation. 'They are wrong. Invaders invade because they desire to take lands by force, to rape and pillage and destroy. To conquer. It is the most vile act of mankind, the lowest ebb of human behaviour. It is one thing to defend oneself against such invaders. But to imitate them? To emulate their example and send forth our own forces to do the very thing...? What sense does that make? For one thing, where are we sending these forces? Through our own lands! To subjugate our own people, and our neighbours and allies!'

'And a few hostile nations who are neither neighbours nor allies,' Sumitra added thoughtfully.

'Yes, but who are not enemies either! And by doing this, we are certain to force them to become our enemies. For the sheer size of our forces will compel them to band together and unite against us, and so, we shall have created a new, more powerful enemy than actually existed. Besides which, what gives us the right to do all these things?'

Sumitra shrugged. 'They say we must do it because we are Ayodhya. We are the land of freedom and courage. The nation that the world looks to for protection, for hope. They say it is our responsibility. Our dharma!'

'Dharma!' Kausalya laughed bitterly. 'They do not know the meaning of the word. Dharma does not mean going to war when there is no threat to oneself! Dharma is not raising a force great enough to conquer all the known worlds and then use it to do just that. Dharma is not pretending to conduct a symbolic horse sacrifice and using it as a cover for a full-scale invasion—of one's own land! It is not dharma that drives them. It is greed, pure and simple. Lust for power. Arrogance. And because it is couched as dharma, presented with pretty words and fancy ideas like republicanism, democracy, a people's kingdom, duty, responsibility, protection, necessity...because of this devilish subterfuge, it verges on tyranny. It is tyranny.'

'Yet Rama is no tyrant,' Sumitra said firmly. 'On that we are agreed.' She might be the mother of a different son, but she could hear no ill spoken of Rama without debating it hotly.

Kausalya touched Sumitra's shoulder affectionately. 'No, he is not. That is why it pains me so much to see him caught up in this manipulative politicking and vile rhetoric.'

They watched the processions for a while. The sun drifted overhead and passed into the afternoon, dipping lower and lower towards the western horizon. And still the regiments wheeled and turned and wound their way up the avenues and out the gates and up the raj-marg. It seemed as if they would go on thus forever.

'What shall we do then, Kausalya?' Sumitra asked a while later. 'We must do something. Otherwise there will be terrible bloodshed and once that occurs, the chain of violence will be set into motion yet again.'

Kausalya nodded. She knew what Sumitra meant. United by the last Asura War, mortal nations had fought largely together, putting aside their own territorial ambitions and other differences to fight a common, far more powerful invading foe. But now that there were no asuras left to fight, all those petty differences and ambitions had begun rising once again to the fore, needing but a catalyst to set the pile blazing into a bonfire of crisscrossing clashes that could only lead inevitably, eventually, to a great internecine war. There was far more than just Ayodhya's future at stake here, or Rama's reputation as a king. It was the future of all Aryavarta that hung on the outcome of this so-called Ashwamedha yajna.

'Yes, we must do something and we must do it before those armies cross our borders and cross swords with our neighbours and allies, let alone other hostile ones. Once begun, this will lead to a war among the Bharata nations such as has never been seen before.' Kausalya was referring to the original 'bharata' tribe governed by the legendary Vedic king Sudas, who had fought and won the historic Dasarajna war, defeating ten powerful kings to claim this sub-continent for the bharatas. Today, all Aryas residing in this part of the world were descendants of that great bharata king Sudas and his original tribe. Indeed, while the term Aryavarta described their civilisation and culture, the correct name by which the sub-continent was known was Bharat, or Land of the Bharatas.

'A Maha Bharata,' said Sumitra, using the Sanskrit word, wherein the word 'war' was implied contextually. 'A great war of the bharata nations.'

'Yes,' Kausalya said, 'A Maha Bharata. And once that happens, then it will be not just a great war but the greatest war of all time. That is why we must do whatever we can to ensure that this yajna goes no further than the borders of our Kosala nation.' Which was as it was supposed to be as per the Vedic ritual of the Ashwamedha: the horse was not expected to rove the entire mortal realm after all, nor was the king sponsoring the sacrifice expected to conquer the whole of prithviloka. Merely his bordering kingdoms and regions.

'Yes, Kausalya,' Sumitra said, agreeing whole-heartedly. 'But what can we do? How can we stop it? How can anyone stop it? More importantly, who can stop it now?'

Kausalya shook her head sadly. 'I do not know, Sumitra. All I know is someone must.'

They sat in silence then, watching the last of the army regiments exit the city gates. And Sumitra thought to herself how much of Rama's strength, his resoluteness, his determination came from this woman, his mother. Now that Rama was older, approaching middle age, she could even see the similar line of their features clearly. The spiritual likeness was even more striking.

If there is a way to set things right, she thought, *then surely Kausalya will find it. If he is now an emperor, then she is the emperor's mother.*

⟨⟨KAAND 2⟩⟩

ONE

Kush smelled the strangers long before they appeared.

He had been roving with Sarama and her pack since morning, pretending to be one of her cubs. It was a game Luv and he had played ever since they could keep up with the lovable mongrel. Now, of course, she was old and greying, the dark whiskers around her muzzle turned completely white, and she often trailed behind the pack. Kukur, the alpha male of her first litter, now a mature but still robust fellow, led them, and he set a hard pace. But he never chastised the others when they straggled or came back to check on Sarama who was often left heaving far behind. In that sense, he was a kind son and not prone to the instinctive cruelty that animals resorted to in packs. Kush corrected himself—Maharishi Valmiki always cautioned them that it was not 'cruelty' no matter how harsh such behaviour may seem at times; animals too, like humans, or birds, or insects, or even the rocks and trees and water and earth, were simply aspects of brahman in different forms. And all forms of brahman were subject to the law of dharma.

The thought made Kush smile now as he loped along in a crouching stance, imitating Sarama who panted heavily as she jogged beside him. The sounds of the pack were several dozen yards ahead but they were still quiet, so that meant they had not yet found their prey. He smiled because he sometimes found Gurudev's pronouncements amusing after the fact. When listening to Gurudev's pravachans, Luv and he were always intent and rapt, hanging on to every word, particularly the Vedic shlokas which were full of such wonderful stories. But afterwards, when discussing what they had learned at gurukul that morning, usually with Maatr, they sometimes found something quite amusing in retrospect. The thought of dogs adhering to dharma was one of these. How could dogs have dharma! It was too much to comprehend. Their mother had laughed as well, her eyes crinkling in that way he loved to see, and he had exchanged a glance with Luv, for it was not often that Vedavati laughed, and rarer still that she smiled.

Others smiled much more often. Rishi Dumma for instance, probably the fattest rishi he had ever known and also the jolliest, seemed to laugh or smile all the time. He often had to be admonished for it by Maharishi Valmiki, especially when other rishis were visiting or when they went travelling to other ashrams or to the occasional sammelan in the big city. Maatr never came with them on those trips, particularly the visits to Mithila city, which was a shame, because both Luv and he loved visiting Mithila. They loved everything about the city, and the palace was a thing to marvel at for days. But most of all, Maharaja Janak was such a fine king; 'the finest who had ever lived', Maharishi Valmiki always said, putting a hand on each of their shoulders when he said it, his face turning skywards and that familiar expression of infinite sadness coming over him.

'The finest king who ever lived, and a wonderful father as well,' he would usually add, which always mystified both of them because what did Janak's relationship with his children have to do with anything? Even stranger was the fact that Maatr also grew as sad as Maharishi Valmiki when they tried to tell her about Mithila, about the marketplace and the streets and the buildings and palaces, and all the wonderful sights, and the grand feast that Maharaja Janak had laid out for the visiting brahmins and scholars from all the Bharata nations, and how his daughters and their husbands and children once came especially to join in and to feed the brahmins personally.

At this last recounting, Maatr had suddenly produced a choking sound, risen from the floor and left the hut. Gurudev had stopped them from going after her, pacifying them with the explanation that it was a womanly matter and she would recover in time. He then suggested, gently, that perhaps they should speak less of Mithila and tell her about the other wonderful things they had seen on the trip. Of course, nothing had been as wonderful as Mithila, but both Luv and he were smart enough to get the point and they had changed the topic when Maatr returned, her eyes pink-cornered as if she had been weeping.

Now, he paused, resting on his bunched fists and forefeet to imitate the elderly mongrel beside him, raised his head, and sniffed curiously. At once, Sarama stopped and did the same. From her reactions he deduced that he was not alone in detecting a strange odour among the normal earthy smells of the forest.

She suddenly issued a growl, and he saw her hackles rise, and then he was sure. That was unwashed uksan he smelled on the downwind, and unwashed human too, if he was not mistaken. And even if he was mistaken, Sarama was not. She would only growl if there was a creature that posed physical danger to her or her pack—which of course included Luv and himself—not just a deer or other docile creature of the woods. As he and his brother knew so well by now, the deadliest of all predators were those that walked on two legs.

Sarama suddenly released a volley of barks. Kush wanted to shush her but knew better than to try. She was simply alerting her pack. They responded at once. Kush recognised Kukur's distinctive mournful howl, followed by a chorus of excited yaps and barks. In moments, the pack was racing back to join their matriarch. Luv was with them, bounding along in the same bent-over position as Kush. He woofed once at Kush who woofed back and they slapped 'paws' together in a playful imitation of sibling pups before turning their attention to the approaching threat.

Sarama crouched in a low stance, teeth bared, snarling. She was pointing her muzzle upwind. Luv and Kush cut back a few yards, slipping behind a thick sala tree; the trunk was big enough for both their slender forms to stand behind and there was still room on either side. The pack remained with Sarama, Kukur standing wither-to-withers beside her, howling long and low. Elsewhere in the woods, birds took off in flight, monkeys chittered, and other creatures issued sounds that most humans would not even notice, spreading the word that a predator was present in this neck of the forest.

Luv knew the pack well enough to be able to tell what kind of predator they had scented. If it was a bear, they usually reacted with snarls and low growls but retreated without barking or howling. There was no point barking at a bear—the rksaa was apt to get mad and come chasing after them, and a bear on all fours was a beast no dog ever wanted to take on! If it was a big cat—there were lions in this part of the woods and a few other felines, though no tigers—then they howled and barked and got riled up, but still retreated. The scent of cat brought out the dog in them to the utmost, but they still knew better than to go head to head with it. They took what satisfaction they could from warning off any prey the cat might be hunting and then running away themselves! If very hungry, they waited till the cat had killed and eaten, then harried it from a safe distance till the cat retreated in disgust, leaving the pickings to them.

But when it came to man, they stood their ground, howled long and hard to alert the whole forest, and were prepared to fight to death if necessary. The great dog packs that dominated the forests around this region had no fear of men at all. It was men who feared them—and for good reason. With their low height, ability to see in the dark, powerful jaws, and fearlessness in battle, only a very foolish man would dare oppose them in their own terrain. The thick vegetation camouflaged and obscured dogs perfectly, while leaving humans woefully exposed. Even a dozen armed men could be taken down by a dozen dogs, at best leaving every man severely wounded, and at worst, slaughtering every last man and feasting on the remains. Luv and Kush had seen it happen on one grisly occasion when a gang of bear-hunters had come by to visit some old friend they claimed lived in this region. Maharishi Valmiki had tried to prevent Luv and Kush from seeing the terrible scene but as already expert trackers they had been able to retrace most of the encounter afterwards.

Other packs that lived closer to human habitation, such as this one, had an uneasy relationship with men. They could be tamed individually, but when roving in packs and living wild and free for generations as this pack had done, they distrusted armed men in groups and often attacked if provoked. The reason, of course, was that armed men—such as the bear-killers—were the only creatures on earth who killed for no discernible reason at all. Not all men, and not always, but often enough that a wild dog's initial reaction was one of distrust and fear. And with a wild beast, fear always manifested itself as hostility.

There were exceptions, of course. Luv and Kush had proved that by befriending Sarama when she was still a pup, the solitary survivor of a litter that had been killed by unknown means in a ravine near the ashram. As young boys, they had dearly wanted to keep her in their hut as a pet, the way they had seen other men do sometimes, tying a dog to their wagon or horse with a rope on their travels or keeping the animal tied to a pillar or post outside their homes.

But their Maatr had explained to them that it was cruel to treat any living creature thus. 'Would it be all right if someone were to tie a rope around our necks and keep us tied to a post?' she asked gently.

They admitted it would not be all right.

'Just because they are a different species from us does not make them inferior in any way. We have no right to control them or treat them harshly, no more than we have the right to treat other humans badly. We were all born free, and none of us have the right to take away that gift of freedom.'

So they had set Sarama free. And she had roved the woods nearby and visited them often, almost daily, but retained her freedom. Once or twice she had come back with a companion dog or two—a stray separated from its pack or a runaway. That had given them the idea of seeking out travellers with dogs in tow and secretly slipping the animals loose! That was one of the many little mischiefs that Maatr as well as Gurudev didn't know about. Thus, Sarama's pack had been assembled, a motley bunch of creatures, some of such vastly different appearance from her own that the twins had taken to comparing each one with a different animal or creature. So there was Monkeytail, because her tail curled like a monkey's; Wagh, because his fur was a beautiful golden hue and his eyes a mesmerising yellow too; Vaman, because though a third the size of most full-grown dogs, he was compact and powerfully muscled. Over time, Sarama had mated and birthed her own, and now the majority of the pack was her children or grand-children, but the motley mutts still stood out and the pack itself had grown expert in finding and setting free other imprisoned dogs on their own. At present, the pack was thirty-strong and growing constantly.

Luv exchanged a glance with Kush as they listened to Kukur's deep booming bark echoed by the varied howls and barks of the others. They shared a deep love for the pack; these wild dogs were not pets to the twins, they were playmates and friends. And they were proud of their friends. The usual behaviour of the pack would have been to charge towards the approaching threat; the only reason they were waiting here was because Luv and Kush had requested them to do so.

Now, both grinned and winked at each other as they strung their bows and fixed arrows. The increasing intensity of the pack's barking told them that the stranger or strangers were closer now. Both boys pointed their arrows around the trunk of the sala tree, aimed in the general direction at which the pack was barking, and waited for the enemy to show itself.

TWO

There was a darkness in Rama's heart that would not dissipate. Lakshman knew this just as he knew everything else that lay in Rama's heart and mind. Twins were supposed to be joined thus in emotion and thought but somehow, by some quirk of karma or kismat, it had turned out that he shared such a connection not with his own twin Shatrughan, but with Rama. The pairing had happened soon after they were able to move on their own volition, and after that, Rama and he were inseparable. When Bharat and Shatrughan partnered up as well, it was obvious it was because they wished to emulate Rama and Lakshman. Although they shared a close brotherhood too, it was not like the one shared by Rama and him. Somehow, Lakshman had always been like the mirror to Rama's face, the leaf to his branch, the river to his rain. He could not claim to actually feel everything that Rama felt, or think his thoughts, or know what he was about to say before he said it. But he knew these things. He knew them well enough to be able to know what Rama was feeling at any time, or thinking, or was likely to say. And he was rarely wrong. He might not like knowing what he knew, or agree with Rama's thoughts and feelings and pronouncements on many things, but he rarely erred in the facts of those matters.

Just as he knew now that the darkness that lay upon Rama's heart was one that would result in grave consequences. It was a darkness vast and dense enough that if unleashed it could easily cover the entire world. Like a fog that would pass across the land and envelope every living creature in its cold clammy embrace.

Everything Rama did was epic. His epic love, his epic tragedy, his epic war, his epic life itself. And now, if he unleashed the darkness within his soul, it would be an epic tragedy not only for him and all those around him, but for the world entire. This war itself was the final stage in that unleashing, and Lakshman worried that it might engender the very rebellion it sought to suppress.

Lakshman was not afraid of war itself. Or of dying in one. It was a greatly desirable end for any kshatriya. He wanted to die fighting, not old and sickly and wasting away in his bedchamber in the palace, tended by Urmila and her maids and the royal vaids, a pale shadow of his own self. What else was death by natural causes if not a kind of war as well? A war against disease, old age, chronic debilitation or injury, old wounds and new ailments? If he must die fighting, he would rather fight foes he could face with a sword and a bow, rather than those invisible demons of the flesh and physic that slaughtered you piece by piece without ever showing themselves or abiding by the kshatriya code of battle. Phshaw! That was no death for any warrior, male or female, mortal or otherwise. He would rather be fighting this way from now until the end of his days, whether that end came today or a hundred years hence.

But, if there was one thing he did fear, it was a needless war. Violence without purpose or necessity. Like any kshatriya who had been bloodied in battle on myriad occasions, Lakshman loathed violence. Contradictory as that might seem, he knew that it was the very essence of the warrior code. A warrior's dharma was not to fight or kill or maim for the sake of doing so. It was to do so when all other means to communicate failed and one's enemy threatened one's life, one's loved ones, and one's homeland with certain death and destruction. Violence and war were the final steps in a human tragedy. The kusalavya bards might sing their songs from city to city and extol the praises of epic warriors—such as Rama himself and even he, Lakshman—from now till the end of time; it would not change the fact that war was a brutal terrible tragedy, nothing more nothing less. The only victor in a war was death itself. Only Lord Yama could walk into a battlefield after the conflict ended and claim to have won. Any other claim of victory was a sham.

And yet, one went to war when one had to, when there was no other way to survive, to protect one's own, to defend one's land.

Was this campaign they were embarking upon, this grand Ashwamedha yajna, a necessary one? Would it serve its stated purpose and unite all the various factions of the Kosala nation and neighbouring principalities as well, or would it simply be seen as a naked act of aggression. An open declaration of war to serve Rama's intentions of building an empire? Might it not be misconstrued to be the very opposite of what it was intended to be, as things often were in this world? And what then? Total war with all Aryavarta? With their own fellow Aryas, Bharatas, call them whatever one desired? Unite them at the point of a sword? Compel them to bow symbolically to the magnificent black horse—and, by implication, to Samrat Rama Chandra as well? Or, if they refused to acknowledge the horse and to let it pass freely to rove across their lands, symbolising Rama's claim over those territories, then what? Round them up like stray kine and force them to bow?

Lakshman's bond with Rama was such that it far exceeded any normal mortal standard of loyalty. He would do every single thing he was told or expected to do, regardless of the consequences. But he was deeply concerned about some of Rama's recent decisions; particularly those that he felt might have adverse effects on Rama's own well-being.

In particular, this Ashwamedha campaign troubled him greatly. It was too loud a statement of imperial might and power, too provocative a display. He feared it might well stoke the fires of disagreement and churlishness into a full-blown rebellion. He was glad that the horse had chosen to head south at the outset rather than north. Had the stallion gone the other way, the pahadi tribes and the rugged Himalayan clans would have taken it as an outright taunt and come roaring down to do battle. Blood would have been shed before the horse could go more than a few dozen yojanas. Thankfully, the nations to the immediate south of Ayodhya were less belligerent and might be more prudent in their response to the yajna. At least, he hoped so.

He was also deeply uncomfortable with the deviation from the ritual. As per Vedic ritual, the Ashwamedha yajna had to be initiated by the Queen Consort in order to be fruitful. That meant Sita, of course, because Rama had no other wives or concubines. Lakshman knew for a fact that Rama had not so much as laid hands on another woman with that intent since Sita's departure. Since only the king's own consort could undertake the ritual, that left a void. The purohits had urged Rama not to undertake the yajna as it would be inauspicious to do so in the queen's absence. One or two bold pundits had even suggested—timidly and with appropriate deference—that perhaps Rama might choose to take a wife in order to fulfil the ritual requirement. After all, Arya kings were required by dharma to produce progeny, especially heirs, and Rama had none.

Rama would not hear of it, of course. Instead, he had ordered that a life-size effigy be made of Sita, carved from jet black lohit stone—the famed ironwood of the Sarayu Valley—and fixed upon a one-horse chariot. The statue had been used as a stand-in for the ritual, despite the disapproving protests of the purohits, and it was that same statue that now followed close behind the unbridled horse at the head of the great procession winding its way out of Ayodhya.

Lakshman twisted in his saddle to look back at the endless rows of foot-soldiers stretching out along the raj-marg as far as the eye could see, over the rise of Seventh Hill, and down to the Sarayu Valley, stretching yojanas back towards Ayodhya—and yojanas up ahead as well. The chariots and horse regiments had already gone on ahead and the elephants were being taken by a different route to avoid congesting the raj-marg further. The sheer logistics of the campaign were mind-boggling and if not for the rote obedience of Ayodhya's troops, this undertaking would have been impossible. As it was, there would be a line of grama-trains following behind the army, stretching back all the way to Ayodhya, in order to keep this enormous fauj supplied and fed.

He spurred his horse into a canter, moving up the rise and beyond the Sarayu Valley in moments. Ahead lay the mist-shrouded silhouette of Mithila Bridge. The spray produced by the impact of the roaring white waters striking the rocks below cast a perpetual mist-shroud over the bridge. Seen now at this angle, with the rising sun peeping over the eastern horizon, the infinite droplets of water suspended in mid-air caught the sunlight and refracted it, turning the air around the bridge into a glittering veil of diamonds, rubies, emeralds, and sapphires. It was a sight to behold. After being shown this same sight as young boys, Rama and he had taken to riding out here to view the sunrise over Mithila Bridge every day for a week, even though they had been forbidden at the time to go outside the Sarayu Valley. That was before they had achieved the age of seven and turned old enough to go to Guru Vashishta's gurukul for formal education. Lakshman leaned on his pommel and smiled at the thought: those had been some of the best years of his life. The world had been filled with infinite wonder and hope, the impossible had seemed possible, the sky had loomed larger and bluer, the river's cool water an elixir of youth, and they had been princes of the earth and all upon it. Princes of Ayodhya.

The smile faded slowly as he remembered who and where he was, and the many duties, chores and obligations of his post returned to clamour for his attention and time. He was still a prince, and Rama now the emperor, not just a king. But nothing was the same again. Even the mesmerising beauty of the sunlight refracting through the mist over Mithila Bridge seemed like a tawdry effect produced by a travelling theatre troupe for an hour's entertainment. Those two boys who had sat thus upon this very ridge, chins resting on their palms, elbows on their pommels, gazing at this very sight with ecstatic rapture…those boys were long gone. And with them, all that they felt and hoped and dreamed was gone as well.

Lakshman shook his head to clear it of foolish fancies and childhood memories. Twisting his horse's bit a little harder than was needed, he rode down the raj-marg past the endless lines of soldiers, picking up pace as he went. Some sipahis raised their wooden shields instinctively to avoid being struck across the face by the pebbles and stray stones kicked up by his horse as he passed, one of the routine hazards of foot travel on the king's highway. The majority didn't even bother with the shields and trudged on in the infinitely plodding way of all foot soldiers.

By the time he reached Mithila Bridge, he had forgotten all about those childhood mornings spent watching this magical sight from the ridge. Like the ridge itself, those idyllic childhood days were behind him now. He rode onwards, leaving them both behind.

The head of the procession had reached the junction where the raj-marg forked in three directions: one road went on over the hilly ranges to Mithila, another went west, and the third went east. The chariot with the black statue was almost at the crossroads as Lakshman came riding up at a brisk canter. The sarathi driving it was none other than the old Pradhan Mantri Sumantra, his straggly white hair tied behind his head, his large bald spot shiny with perspiration. He glanced back as Lakshman came up beside him, then jerked his head, pointing.

Lakshman looked in that direction and saw the black stallion stopped by the side of the crossroads, head lowered, munching kusa grass. He looked like any wild horse ranging freely, stopping where he pleased, foraging when he desired. And he was free. The great army following behind him was none of his concern after all. The whole point of the Ashwamedha yajna was that the horse represented Rama and that Rama was free to go where he pleased. It was only when he was stayed by any man's hand that it represented a challenge to Ayodhya's sovereignty and could be regarded as tantamount to a declaration of war.

Lakshman fervently hoped that no man would be foolish or rebellious enough to stay the stallion. Declaring war against Ayodhya was one thing; challenging the might of this great army was suicide. This was no mere token force symbolising the sovereignty of Ayodhya, as the horse ritual customarily required; it was the entire fighting strength of the nation! There had rarely been a precedent for such a massive display of military might, if only because most chieftains and tribal leaders might rightly view it as exceeding the requirements of the Vedic rite and amounting to imperialistic aggression. Which, Lakshman admitted regretfully, it was indeed.

He glanced back at the winding line, stretching back across the gently undulating dips and rises of the raj-marg, like a great serpent snaking its way across the land. Like the serpent it resembled, its sole intention was to swallow the independent nations and tribes of the Bharata world alive.

'If we stand here, the line will have to stop,' he said to Sumantra, leaning over the rim of the chariot. 'And if the line stops…'

Sumantra nodded. A veteran of more logistical operations than Lakshman had year-notches on his life-stick, he was well aware of the problems that would arise if such a large juggernaut had to stop and stand for even a few minutes. The resulting congestion and confusion would snarl up the raj-marg for hours. The best thing for such a huge force was to keep it moving, constantly moving, stopping only when they reached one of the designated overnight campsites. The old face turned eastwards, catching the sunlight which unkindly limned every one of the myriad lines and creases of the aged statesman's features. In his own quiet unassuming way, Sumantra was part of the unselfishly dedicated system that had kept Ayodhya functioning through every crisis, war and outbreak. Men and women like him were the backbone of the nation and of Arya civilisation itself. The basic tenet of Vedic philosophy: to do one's duty without concern or desire for the fruits of one's labours, was rarely better exemplified than in men like Sumantra.

'Lord Bhadra has given instructions that if the horse should stop, it is to be encouraged,' he said quietly to Lakshman. Even though there was nobody within hearing distance—the first row of cavalry was several yards behind them—it was evident that he was speaking the words for Lakshman's ears only.

Lakshman glanced at him curiously. They were not supposed to lead or guide the horse, merely to follow it. But Sumantra already knew that better than he: he had presided over the Ashwamedha yajnas performed by Lakshman's own father Dasaratha decades ago. What did this odd instruction from Bhadra mean?

'Encouraged…?' Lakshman asked, nonplussed.

Sumantra nodded, his ragged white eyebrows almost concealing his dark brown eyes, but said nothing further.

Lakshman glanced back at the stallion. The animal took hold of a fresh clump of green kusa grass with his teeth, yanking it out slowly, then threw his head back and began munching on it happily. Frothy cud dripped from the sides of his mouth. He looked like he could stay there in that little patch of meadow beside the crossroads all day long. His tail twitched rhythmically, shooing off a swarm of midges and mites.

Lakshman considered the location where the stallion had chosen to partake of its impromptu repast. If the animal were to go eastwards as the raj-marg itself led, it would end up in Videha territory, the sister nation to Kosala. That would mean a direct challenge to Mithila, sister city of Ayodhya, seat of the moonwood throne of the Chandravanshi dynasty and ancient ally to Ayodhya, seat of the sunwood throne of the Suryavansha dynasty. Maharaja Janak of Mithila was the very opposite of an aggressive king; he had disbanded his army years ago, employing only a reserve guard and relying on a citizen's militia that adored their liege and his kind paternal regime so fiercely that they acted as a better deterrent than any salaried army. Not a soul in the Videha nation would raise so much as a finger of aggression against Ayodhya, or attempt to captivate the sacred stallion on its ritual course; but in the unlikely event that there were to be an incident on Videha land, it would lead to terrible, undesirable consequences. Maharaja Janak was not merely the kindest, most spiritually enlightened and humanitarian Arya king in all Aryavarta, he was also Lakshman's and his brothers' father-in-law, for all four sons of Dasaratha were married to Janak's daughters or adoptive daughters.

Including my banished sister-in-law, he thought with a twinge of sadness even after all these years.

For the stallion to tread on Videha land, or so much as turn its head toward Mithila, could well bode disaster.

On the other hand, were the beast to head south and west, it would then pass through the great Naimisha-van forest, bordering the great central aranya—the Arya term for uncivilised and unsettled wilderness—and would transgress no borders or boundaries.

Lakshman knew the old pradhan mantri well enough to understand when he was attempting to communicate much more than he was able to say aloud. Sumantra was telling him that Bhadra—and no doubt the rest of the War Council—*wanted* the horse to stray into friendly territory, to provoke an incident and justify annexure. It was a heart-stopping thought but, he realised with a sinking heart, also the logical corollary of the yajna itself. The Ashwamedha yajna was not conducted merely to remind existing vassals of the king's dominance; it was intended as a campaign of expansion and consolidation. His heart raced as he considered the horror of invoking outright war with his wife's homeland. Unthinkable! Yet not for Bhadra, Jabali, and those other war-mongers. He had heard them speak lasciviously of Videha's considerable wealth as well as its lack of a standing armed force. Clearly, this was the first phase of their plans of empirical 'expansion'. If they could give instructions for the horse to be 'encouraged' into Videha lands, they could as easily arrange for a few mercenaries to captivate the horse and justify Ayodhya's declaration of war against the Videha nation for that transgression. In the horror that followed, it would hardly matter whether or not the men who stopped the horse had been Videha citizens or Kosala citizens or neither—their dead bodies would be all the evidence needed to inflame Videha's passions and cause their citizen militia to take up arms in their own defence.

On the other hand, if a horse could be encouraged to go in one direction, it could as easily be encouraged to go in another.

Lakshman smiled.

He glanced at Sumantra who looked at him with interest. Lakshman knew that the old statesman was sharp enough to have followed a similar line of thought, even if he might not see Lakshman's solution to the problem. But Sumantra said nothing.

In turn, Lakshman himself dared not speak his thoughts aloud: he knew the efficacy of Rama's spasas too well to risk being caught saying the wrong thing himself. As the Enforcer of the law, it would not do for him to be caught subverting the imperial diktat. And Bhadra's word was no less than Rama's word.

Lakshman unslung his bow, put an arrow to the string and aimed at a rotting tree trunk lying at the edge of a thicket. It was just beyond the patch where the stallion grazed, the line of fire passing just behind the sacred horse itself. With a single motion, he loosed the arrow, sending it flying just behind the rump of the sacred stallion. The horse was never in danger: Lakshman was a master bowman. The arrow missed the beast by a clear inch or three, passing through the small cloud of midges around the stallion's rear, but the wind and violence of its passing were enough for the sensitive creature to instantly lurch forward, its grazing forgotten.

A clump of half-chewed kusa grass fell from its open jaws as it neighed softly in dismay, then, with the inevitable skittishness of the equine species, it neighed twice more, sidling nervously, then picked up its heels in a brisk trot, heading in a south-westerly direction. Precisely the opposite direction from the arrow that had grazed its rump. Towards the great central aranya of Naimisha-van and the Southwoods that lay beside and below it. No-man's land. And certainly, no king's.

Lakshman looked back at Sumantra. The old minister smiled approvingly, then dropped one bushy-browed lid in a loud wink.

Lakshman winked back, then rode on after the horse, into the woods.

Ayodhya followed.

THREE

Nakhudi and Bejoo made their way carefully through the woods on horseback, Nakhudi leading the way as she knew these forests and he did not. That is to say, he knew the paths and the raj-marg well enough, but they had left those behind a long way back. They were now in uncharted terrain and if not for Nakhudi, Bejoo had no doubt that he and his band could be wandering in these woods for weeks without being able to find their way.

Bejoo glanced back from time to time at the riders following them. The forest floor was littered with leaves that had been dampened by a shower or two that morning and the mulch formed a carpet that muffled their hoofbeats. Apart from the occasional snicker or whinny of a horse, there was almost no sound to indicate that almost a hundred men were making their way through the woods on horseback. Had they been young brash recruits like the ones he had commanded on that last grama-train, he had no doubt they would be drinking and laughing and bantering loudly enough to wake up the entire forest for miles around and alert anyone who might be ahead that they were coming.

But these were Purana Wafadars in truth, not merely in name like those new upstarts who wore the purple-and-black without having earned the colours. Every single man here was known personally to Bejoo, several older than he, veterans of war before he was so much as a suckling babe on his Maatr's arm. All had seen battle numerous times and suffered injuries ranging from grievous to maiming, forcing them to retire from active duty and enter the PF regiments. Many had had the pleasure of serving directly under Saprem Senapati Dheeraj Kumar during the heyday of the PFs. Now, Dheeraj Kumar was long gone, en route to his ancestors, and it was his son Drishti Kumar who was now Saprem Senapati, two of his grandsons captains of the King's Guard, a grand-daughter a captain of the Queen's Guard, and numerous other grandsons and grand-daughters serving their nation in other martial capacities. At least three men in the group following Bejoo now had served under Maharaja Dasaratha himself in the last Asura War, which made them old enough to be Bejoo's grandfather.

He knew one closely: old veteran Somasra had not had much to do with his days since being retired from his charge as gatekeeper of the First Gate, no less, and Bejoo's duties as grama-rakshak had involved much downtime between trips. They had both spent many pleasant hours together faffing over mugs of various beverages. When he had gone to Somasra and asked him if he wanted an opportunity to do more than just faff, the old veteran had glanced at him without a word, risen to his feet, grunting briefly as he wrested something wrapped in an old dust-layered length of cloth off a high shelf, then unwrapped it slowly and carefully to reveal a pike of a design Bejoo had never seen before. The seal of the Suryavansha Ikshwakus was unmistakable, melded into the base of the pole, and Somasra had flipped the weapon over with an expert, heart-stopping ease to show it to him.

Bejoo had raised his eyebrows in response, knowing a royal prize when he saw one, knowing also that such prizes had been handed out last by Maharaja Dasaratha during the last Asura War and then only to those who distinguished themselves in battle. He felt his throat thicken as he realised what that meant. If there was a higher honour for any kshatriya serving in Ayodhya's armed forces now or in the past three-quarters of a century, he did not know of it.

He glanced back and saw Somasra, two men behind him and to his right at a diagonal. The old gatekeeper dipped his grizzled jaw at him, and Bejoo nodded back. He made out the long length of the pike rising behind the man, sheathed behind the old PFs saddle and ready for use. He wondered if he would get to see Somasra use the weapon and hoped not.

In fact, when he had asked Jabali to commission him the task of wiping off Maharishi Valmiki and his sadhus, his masked intention was to prevent violence, not to perpetrate it. He hoped this entire exercise would pass off peaceably.

After what seemed to be another yojana or so of slow manoeuvring through thickly growing woods—it was difficult to judge how far one had travelled in such deep forest—Nakhudi finally held up her hand. Bejoo imitated her gesture, glancing back to make sure the others had seen his action. They had already reined in their mounts. He felt a flicker of pride. Ayodhya's veterans were still sharp of eye and clear of mind and undoubtedly wise. Almost as a counterpoint he thought: if only her youth were even half as wise. He knew that the exercise they were about to undertake might well save lives; but he also knew that if things turned bad, these hundred lives and his own would be the least of the fatalities in the days to come.

Nakhudi beckoned him forward. Since she had dismounted, he dismounted as well and walked his horse to where she waited. He looked over her shoulder but could see nothing ahead except endless rows of trees and shrubbery, identical to the yojanas of forest they had travelled through already.

'Something is wrong,' she said. 'There is someone in the camp.'

'Someone?' he asked, puzzled. 'What do you mean, someone?'

She glanced at him with a look of unmasked irritation. 'If I knew, I would have said who it was, wouldn't I?'

He bit his lip. It had been a long time since a woman had snapped at him. It reminded him of his long-dead wife, who died in a fever epidemic almost fifteen years ago. She had been the only woman to roundly berate him on a regular basis, especially when he demonstrated one of his habitual flaws, which, he had to admit, he had several. It had been how she expressed her love for him mingled with the exasperation of a very long marital relationship—they had been together over fifty years when she died.

He said nothing, waiting for Nakhudi to go on.

When she spoke again, she sounded gruffly contrite. 'I didn't mean to cut your throat. I just don't like this whole situation. There is too much at stake. I care about these people. They are the only family, clan, nation, call them what you will, that I have left.'

'Grama,' he said.

She looked at him.

'Grama,' he explained. 'The original grouping of families linked by blood, marriage and comradeship. They travelled from place to place, living off the land, joining together to fend for themselves and one another. An extended family. It was the basis of early Arya society. The gramas went travelling across such vast distances, to this date, nobody knows for certain where they started from. The poets argue even now whether they originated here in Bharata-varsha and then later migrated north-westwards, or originated in those far northern lands and then travelled here.'

She looked taken aback at this unsolicited information, raising her eyebrows. 'Were there arrowposts?'

He frowned. 'Arrowposts?'

'Arrows, shot into tree trunks by the roadside to show which way to go next, an old traveller's trick to help those following stay on the trail.'

'I don't understand.'

She waved in exasperation. 'The poets can argue all they want. As far as I know, unless someone posted arrows directing everyone to go only this way or that, people go where they please when they please. In my culture, we don't call that migration; we call it wandering the land in search of greener pastures.'

He thought about that for a moment. 'Interesting. But—'

She held up one large dark palm and for a moment he thought she was about to smack him in the mouth. 'Do you mind? We can debate itihasa later. Right now, I wish to make sure my people are all safe and well.' She paused. 'My grama, as you so eloquently put it. I shall go ahead through there,' she pointed, 'and I need you to split the group into two and circle around through there and there,' pointing twice more, 'and then wait for my wolf-whistle before showing yourselves. Clear?'

He nodded. She flashed a dark grin at him and slipped away, moving with surprising ease and stealth for a woman her size. He wondered again how much of that considerable height and bulk was muscle and sinew, and how much...well, womanly splendour would be the polite term.

He thought he might not mind having a chance to find out.

* * *

The strangers did not appear slashing swords and loosing arrows as Luv had feared. That itself was something of a shock.

When Kush had called him back to alert the pack and him to the arrival of strangers, he had assumed it was one of those nauseating bearkiller gangs come around these parts again. He intensely disliked those people and could not understand for the life of him why Maharishi Valmiki permitted them to visit. Somehow, Gurudev always seemed tense and uncomfortable when they were around, but after they left, his mood lightened considerably and he would even display a rare smile at times.

Once, when Rishi Dumma, who was prone to opening his mouth before he had thought his words through, had commented archly, 'Mlechhas!' as the bearkillers left the camp, grinning lewdly and speaking raucously in the vulgar way they had. Several of the other rishis had sniffed in agreement and the brahmacharyas had bobbed their bald heads, their little chottis wagging.

Even the twins knew the word was the most derogatory one any Arya could use, meaning barbarians or uncivilised people. And if Dumma was justified in using it to describe anyone, the bearkillers certainly qualified. But to their surprise, and everyone else's, Maharishi Valmiki had swatted Dumma lightly across his shoulder, and said gruffly, 'There but for the grace of Brahma, go you and I.' Then he walked away, retiring to his hut. But he had been in an exceptionally good mood for days afterwards and had even given the twins a holiday from their kavya practice.

Nobody quite knew what to make of that comment. Did Maharishi Valmiki mean that anyone might become a bearkiller? That was impossible! Why would a brahmin, sworn to a life of yogic ritual fasting, penance, meditation and the pursuit of learning, suddenly take up the tools of violence and start killing the innocent animals of the forest? Brahmins had no use for earning, and were content to beg for their needs if unable to provide for themselves—or to starve. In any case, their calling exalted fasting and starvation. And even if they changed varnas, as some brahmins did, to take up tradecraft or statecraft or even the use of weapons, surely they would pursue more honourable occupations than merely animal slaughter? It was unfathomable. Yet nobody dared question the guru or even discuss the matter behind his back. So, after several perplexed looks were cast around by all present, the ashramites returned to their respective chores—there were always chores to be done in an ashram—and thought no more of it.

But Kush and Luv had never forgotten that day or that statement, and had known instinctively that it had a deeper significance than anyone else realised.

Now, he saw the first of the strangers come into view even as the dogs flew into a frenzy, leaping and jumping and rolling in the air with the foamy jaws and gaping snarls of a pack ready to fight to death if need be. And with a grim heart, he saw that they were indeed bearkillers. Those ragged clothes, stained deeply crimson-black with the blood of countless slaughtered animals, those rusting axes and long barbed-point spears they favoured, and those filthy faces with broken yellow teeth flashing in grinning mouths, the plaited hair plastered with tree sap in a mockery of Shaivite tapasvi sadhus…yes, they were bearkillers, all right. Luv even recognised a face or two as having been part of that same troupe that had visited the ashram some moons earlier, especially that one, a tall lanky man with a horribly scarred face but surprisingly clean and perfect teeth that flashed brightly against his dark face. He plaited his hair in a particular way that reminded Luv of a procession of tantric sadhus he had seen once, passing by as Kush and he waited for a grama-train. The man had seemed to be the leader of the bearkillers, from his bearing and manner on their last visit. It was he who had gone in with Gurudev into his hut for a private talk—although what Maharishi Valmiki and a bearkiller could have to talk about, nobody in the ashram could guess at, not even Rishi Dumma who was usually quite adept at coming up with outlandish explanations for anything under the sun that he didn't understand.

Luv kept his arrow pointed at that ugly face, tightening his draw, ready to drop the man on the spot. The dogs were going crazy and he had no doubt they could take give as good as they got, but he knew that men who were capable of hunting and slaying bears were not likely to be brought down easily by a mere pack of wild dogs. And he would not stand by and let his friends be chopped down brutally by these...these Mlecchas!

He sensed Kush coming to the same conclusion and tightening his draw as well. He also knew that Kush was aiming at the other man, the one to the right of the scar-faced one. That was one of the gifts Kush and he had always possessed, the ability to instinctively know what the other would be thinking, saying or even doing at any point in time. Even taking into account the usual conjoined consciousness of twins—the typical explanation everyone used to explain away their extraordinary feats of coordination—what they had was beyond explanation.

The splitting of targets was a much simpler trick: the scar-faced bearkiller was on the left, as was Luv while the other man was on the right, as was Kush. Even without looking back at Kush's position, Luv could map his possible lines of fire mentally, just as Kush could map his own lines of fire. It just made more sense to split the targets in that manner. As more targets came into view and the choices grew more complex, the decisions to split them grew more complex as well, but they were still based on the time-honoured practice of lines of fire that Arya bowmen had been trained to work with since deva knew how many millennia.

He was itching to loose and put an arrow through that grotesquely mauled scarred face. *Just raise your axe to one of Sarama's brood*, he thought, *and it will be the last time you raise that hand!*

But the hand never rose, nor was the axe removed from its sheath on the bearkiller's waist. Instead, the man did a shockingly unexpected thing.

He bent down and allowed the snarling leaping pack of dogs to jump upon him and have at his throat and face, without offering any resistance.

FOUR

The lady Vedavati was playing the veena.

As she picked out the variation on Raga Bhairav, making the melancholy raag sound even more disconsolate and doleful than usual, she felt the peculiar mixture of grief and transcendence that only music could unleash from the depths of the human soul.

The stringed instrument seemed to express her feelings more eloquently than words ever could. Then again, even if words could express what she truly felt, and even if she could find the perfect words to achieve that task, to whom would she address those?

To Maharishi Valmiki? He was a mentor, a father figure, a guide, and guru. There were some things one could not say to such a figure— things one would not want to say.

To the other women of the ashram? Certainly not! They were all wives of devout brahmins, each so pious and absorbed in the daily rituals and chores of ashram life that they were wives and mothers only in the most literal sense. At night, instead of lullabies, they sang mantras to their newborn babes. The life of a kshatriya woman—a warrior princess no less—would be incomprehensible to their religious sensibilities, if not outright offensive. She had to conceal even the fact of her prowess with weapons and intimacy with violence from them, for fear of inviting shock and dismay on a daily basis. While she shared a common gender with the other women of the ashram, she knew that they were completely different kinds of women, almost a different gender altogether and would never be wholly alike.

To Nakhudi? She was a friend, yes, and there had been times when she had cried and pressed her face into Nakhudi's meaty shoulder and had found comfort in her former bodyguard's strength and presence, by the knowledge that she had known her back when she was simply Sita Janaki, the only person apart from Valmiki himself who knew her entire story. But that very intimacy and long-standing relationship also caused her some embarrassment. She enjoyed Nakhudi's company as a friend and equal now, the one woman she could talk to freely and without fear of censure or criticism, the one woman who lived within the general environs of the ashram yet had not renounced life and society altogether. She needed Nakhudi as a companion and friend, and to break down completely and express her heart's deepest, darkest feelings and thoughts would put too great a burden upon that relationship, force Nakhudi to become protective and maternal. As it was, the former bodyguard had a tendency to play the old role again too easily, even slipping and addressing her as 'Janaki Devi' or 'Princess' at times. Were Sita to yield to these impulses and treat Nakhudi like a confidante of her most intimate fears and sorrows, Nakhudi would certainly feel compelled to take action and address her former mistress's plight, perhaps even do something that would draw undue attention to them all.

And if there was one thing that Sita did not desire, it was attention. Especially the attention of Ayodhya. Cut off though they were in this isolated forest hermitage, deep in the Naimisha-van forest, she was nevertheless reasonably well informed. The constant traffic of brahmins and acolytes to and from various other ashrams and cities, distant as well as near, ensured a never-ending supply of news and updates. She had followed the growing hardening of Ayodhya's political position this past decade with growing dismay. And now, when it was believed that the sunwood throne was about to embark on its most ambitious programme of political expansion and consolidation, the last thing she wanted was to draw the scrutiny of that powerful juggernaut upon her tiny community.

She had long ago given up any hope of reconciliation.

For one thing, the very absence of any attempt on his part—she refused to take his name even in her thoughts—to find out where she was, how she was, and more importantly, how their sons were faring, had long ago convinced her that he had hardened his heart and mind and blinded his senses and memory to her very existence. To *their* very existence. Herself and her sons. What father ignored his wife and sons for ten whole years? What husband turned his back on the woman he had once claimed to love more than life itself so remorselessly? What dharma impelled a grihasta to abandon his family for some obscure ideal of philosophical ethics?

Had Rama cared one whit for them, he would have come to the ashram long ago. Or sent someone at least. The fact that he had not done so was more chilling than the circumstances of her exile itself. Mere abandonment might occur in a moment of extreme anger or rage. But after the anger had cooled, after the rage had dwindled, surely a loving heart would feel some regret, some curiosity, some doubt? If not to admit its own fault—for which man liked to admit he was at fault?—then at least to question if the separation had been warranted. Even a condemned criminal was condemned for a certain length of time. How long was her sentence to be? And what crime had their sons committed even before birth that they were forced to grow up thus, deprived of their birthright, their social status, their dynastic heritage, their community, their home, their father?

These were the unspeakable sorrows she expressed through her playing. Not the pain of being abandoned, exiled, forgotten—that pain had struck her ten years ago like a sword point piercing her heart, as she had watched Lakshman ride away in the chariot, back to Ayodhya, leaving her in the aranya, the wilderness of Rama's abandonment. The sorrow of continued punishment, the danda of being deprived continually, every moment and every day, of her rightful place, upon the throne beside him, in his life, his house, his family, and most of all, within his heart. It was that unspeakable grief that she cried out through the straining instrument, turning heartache into music and music into the voice of womanhood wronged. As the veena softly wept, she smiled in woeful ecstasy, her eyes shut tightly, not a single tear leaving her dark lashes or staining her wheat-brown cheeks. For the veena cried for them both, herself and Rama, for their lost decade, for their lost love, for their lost destiny.

'Milady!'

The voice cut through her playing.

It was one of the ashram women, the wife of Dumma, judging by the sharp, high-pitched voice. The voice was a familiar one, cutting through the daily hustle and bustle of the ashram and the padapad rote chanting of the brahmacharyas on the occasions when Dumma was berated by his spouse for some new buffoonery or other, which, Dumma being Dumma, was almost every other day. But this time her voice was raised not in wifely irritation but in sheer panic. It was that sound of a woman terrified that cut through Sita's desolate mood and brought her back to reality in a thumping instant.

'Milady, soldiers!' cried the voice, with rising terror. 'They—'

And then the horrible yet unmistakable sound of a javelin punching through breastbone and flesh, and the wet splatter of bodily content out the other side, followed a moment later by the dull sound of a body falling to the ground.

Sita dropped the veena and sprang to her feet, racing for the back of the hut, reaching for the discreet hole in the ground artfully concealed with straw and covered by a tribal shawl, where she kept her weapons. For she had known that someday this moment would come. She had not expected it to be today. But if it was to be so, then she was prepared for it.

* * *

Kush watched in irritated amazement as Sarama and her brood, rather than viciously mauling and attacking the bearkillers, greeted them with adulation and joy instead. They ran from one to the other, wagging their tails, barking and yapping loudly. Sarama herself stood up on her hind legs and actually licked the face of the leader of the gang, who in turn rubbed her shaggy head and back affectionately and whispered sweet words to her. This went on for a few moments as Luv and he watched with growing pique and frustration. He wanted to send an arrow or three through the greasy hands patting the dogs and send the lot of them fleeing for their lives, but there was no call to do so. He loosened the pressure on the bow-string, lowering the bow but keeping the arrow still in place, and glanced over at his brother. Luv rolled his eyes and shook his head in disgust, clearly as irritated as he was. They would both be having a word with Sarama about whom she lavished her affections on. Of all the aranya outlaws to befriend, she had to wag her tail at bearkillers!

The leader of the gang had crouched down to greet the pack. Now that their initial excitement had subsided, he rose slowly to his feet and spoke. He pitched the words in Kush's direction with surprising accuracy.

'I see you,' he said in a voice loud enough to be heard by both twins, but not loud enough to carry much further. 'Do not be afraid, we mean you no harm. We are friends of your Guru Ratnakaran.'

Ratnakaran? Kush glanced at Luv again. Luv shrugged but raised his bow slowly, cocking an eyebrow to let Luv know that they were not to trust these fellows so easily.

'Our guru's name is Valmiki,' Kush called back in as insolent a tone as he could muster. 'And bearkillers can never be friends of ours.'

The man chuckled, revealing two blackened teeth in the top row. He glanced back at his gang. 'You hear that, people? We can never be their friends!'

There were titters of laughter from the group.

Kush sent an arrow past the man's face, close enough to snip off a tiny lock of his hair and let him feel the wind of the sharpened iron blade whistle past his temple. It went home in the trunk of a teak tree with a dull thwack.

The bearkiller lost his smile. His hand clapped to the side of his head, he said, much louder now: 'Stop that! We said we're friends, didn't we?'

'Go tell that to all the bears you've killed,' Kush replied. Luv had left his spot and was circling around behind the gang. After all, they had spotted Kush somehow and his position was confirmed by his speaking, but they might not still know where Luv was. 'Especially all the little cubs, and the mothers protecting them. Tell them you were just trying to be friends.'

'We haven't killed any bears,' said another voice. A woman came forward. She had a face marred by heavily pockmarked cheeks and there was something odd about her singlet and the way she held her bow that Kush could not make out right away. 'We're not really bearkillers. We're outlaws.'

Kush laughed. 'That makes me feel much better now. You only murder men, women, and children, not bears, is that right?'

'We don't kill anybody!' said the first bearkiller, the leader. 'Unless they come around trying to kill us first!'

'Yes, well, we have the same policy. So if you'll take your weapons and move on, we don't want any trouble here, if you please.' Kush considered snipping an errant lock of hair on the man's right side, to balance the one snipped on the left, then decided against it. He was keeping them occupied while giving Luv time to circle to their rear, not aiming to provoke an all-out fight. He wasn't scared of facing this bunch, he just didn't think they were worth the arrows.

'Listen, you snotty-nosed little fellow—' started the leader, then stopped as the pockmarked woman raised a hand and said something in his ear. 'All right, Ragini, you give it a try.' He settled for glowering in the direction where Kush's voice was coming from.

The woman he had called Ragini raised both her hands to show her open palms. She took several steps forward, causing Kush to immediately take aim at her: 'Please, believe me. We are not bearkillers or brigands in the sense that you mean. We do not murder people to steal their belongings. We are outlaws banished a long time ago to the aranya for various offenses—some unjustly laid accusations, and some genuine crimes as well. But none of that matters now. We are here to warn you and assist you. And we must move quickly as time is scarce.'

Kush suddenly realised what was odd about the woman's singlet and the way she held her bow. Her chest was bumpy only on one side— it was flat on the other side, the side on which lay the arm with which she pulled her bow-string. He had heard about this from Nakhudi and seen women archers on the raj-marg who had sliced off one side of their chests in a similar fashion. It was the unmistakable sign of a true archer, one who had sacrificed a part of her own flesh in order to be able to hold and pull a bow-string as perfectly as possible. It gave him a little more respect for her.

But he still kept the arrow pointed.

'Whoever you are,' he called out, 'we don't need your warning or your help. Move on. This is your last warning.'

A bird call joined the various sounds of the forest, sustained just a little longer than the gurung liked to call. That meant Luv was in position and they were ready to take on the bearkillers in a two-way crossfire. Kush's finger ached to release the arrow, not because holding the string taut for so long was hard, which it was, but because he was suspicious of the motives of these ruffians.

Pockmarked Ragini shook her head. 'No, you don't understand. We are the only ones who can help you now. It was Maharishi Valmiki's last wish that we should take charge of you and raise you as best as we could in case anything should happen to him. And your mother wanted the same. Will you not heed the last words of your own mother and guru?'

Last words? A chill blade slashed through Kush's nether regions, forcing him to lower the bow and loosen his hold on the string. If there was anything the bearkillers could possibly say that would cause him to lower his guard, that was it. What did she mean? Surely she didn't mean that Gurudev and Maatr were…?

'THEY LIE, KUSH! Do not fall for their trick! Attack now!'

The voice was Luv's and it came from the rear of the bearkillers. Kush had never known his brother to give away his position before—nor had he himself ever done so—but he also knew from the way he felt after hearing the woman Ragini's words that Luv was hugely upset, and angry. And that, like him, he had come to the natural conclusion: wretched bearkillers attacked the ashram and killed everyone!

He raised his bow again, pulling the arrow tighter than before, taking aim not on the pockmarked woman's shoulder as he had earlier but at her throat now. One more incensing word from her and she would be dead before the air left her lungs.

But before he could let it loose, a sound came to them from across the treetops. A sound that he knew well, for Luv and he had often produced that same sound too, practising it until Maharishi Valmiki was satisfied that they could do so even under duress and at a sufficiently loud volume to be heard miles away from the ashram.

It was the sound of a conch shell trumpet, issuing the call that signalled the ashram was in mortal distress.

FIVE

Nakhudi fought the rising sense of outrage and fury that threatened to engulf her as she walked through the settlement. The rational part of her mind reminded her that she ought to have been more circumspect and circled the village first, making sure that none of the attackers were still around. But once she had seen and smelled the horror that was all that remained of her people, all rational thought had fled her mind.

And if they were still around, she would dearly love to meet them face to face! And to do more than simply ask them how and why they could massacre an entire settlement—her grama, as Bejoo had aptly called it—of impoverished forest-dwelling people, the majority of whom were women, children and elderly. Barely a fourth of them had been men of fighting age and fitness, and even those had been no match for the strength and weaponry of trained Ayodhyan soldiers. The hundred-odd people with whom she had resided here in this little clearing, sharing food, clothing, shelter, resources as readily as members of one large extended family, had been outcasts—some literally outcastes, forced out from Ayodhya itself following the rise of the subtle but increasingly belligerent bias against lower castes and mixed castes that had begun in recent years, others criminals and outlaws with broken bodies and battered minds who had been released from the dungeons and prisons of the great shining capital city in some generous fit of amnesty, yet were unemployable due to the years or decades of disease, privation, and abuse endured in their incarceration.

The irony of the system of justice meted out by the current regime was that while the hardened criminals stayed on in the city to pursue illicit trades, those who had had their bellyful of crime and punishment, and were therefore rehabilitated in the truest sense of the term, preferred to leave the city that had been so harsh to them and retreated into self-imposed exile from the glories of Arya civilisation. Each year, more and more severely punished people, some brutalised for the most minor of offences, ended up in ashrams or settlements such as this one. Sometimes, a few found companionship, camaraderie, even love and kinship over time, and slowly, painfully, the wounds of their own past misdemeanours and the terrible dandas initiated, enforced, and inflicted under the iron rule of the King of Dharma, healed partially. They were hardly people in the proud 'Arya' sense of the word, but they had been people once, and they were human still. And most of all, alive. Or at least they had been until a few days ago, when she had left this settlement, filling the crisp forest air with the spicy aroma of their cookfires, their laughter and rough talk. These had been simple people, broken people even, bent down and battered by the might and power of Rama's rigid interpretations of dharma and the consequences of straying from that hard path, but still people.

Now, they were just corpses. Food for the vermin and the worms.

She walked through the smoking, scorched, broken, cracked, and battered ruins of the score of humble thatch-and-mud huts that had served as the domiciles of those dregs of society. Each reluctant step took her past a new horror: children lying in one another's arms or their mother's embrace, eyes open and filled with blood, faces splattered with the effluents of their own or loved ones' gaping wounds, severed limbs, speared bodies, butchered corpses…Tears slipped past her iron veil of self-control and spilled from her eyes as she recognised faces, profiles, or, in some awful cases, limbs, and tattered garments. From the way the bodies were strewn and cut down, it was obvious that the attack had been sudden, brutal and swift. Many of the fatal cuts had been inflicted on the backs of the heads and torsos of the victims, suggesting that they had been turning away or running from the attackers. Around her, the looming trees and lush forest seemed to echo with the memories of screams and pitiful cries that must have rung out only hours earlier. She could almost hear familiar voices, crying out in anguish and mortal terror.

She paused when she saw a living figure up ahead, her sword already out and ready, rising to deal out the vengeance she ached to deliver, but realised at once that it was only Bejoo. The vajra captain looked sallow-faced and as grim as she felt, his grizzled jaw tight with his own anger. His eyes met hers then cut away at once in shame. She might not think of herself as Ayodhyan, or even as 'Arya' in the purest sense of the term, but he did, and she could see that it pained him greatly to witness such dishonourable butchery committed by fellow Aryas, let alone fellow Ayodhyans.

He had circled around as instructed by her—she could see the other men holding back in the trees, probably on his orders—and was examining a dozen-odd corpses laying in a ragged line on the ground. This was the rough pathway that led eventually to the raj-marg, or Mithila Road, as it was called by her people, and it was the direction from which the attackers had surely come.

He crouched down beside one body, which she recognised with a small shock as having been Nandu, the white-haired elder who functioned as a kind of roughshod chief of the little community. He was examining the footmarks on the ground and reading the trail. She crouched beside him, steeling herself to ignore the stench of the corpses, left out in the open for at least a day and already ripening, and read the signs as well.

'There were a great many of them,' she said, 'at least a hundred healthy, heavily armed men on horseback.'

She rose and walked further up the winding trail that led through natural gaps in the trees. Forest folk followed an unwritten covenant not to cut down healthy trees merely to make way for themselves; they respected the forest too much for that. As it was, the forest made way for them to live in it and supported their existence. The least they could do was protect and serve it as best as possible. This meant that the trail was a long winding one that did not follow any of the usual geometrical patterns of man-made roads. It also made riding along it on horseback a challenge—unless one knew the way intimately.

'They came down the trail, riding quickly without stopping.' She glanced at Bejoo as she spoke, walking quickly as she continued to read the signs on the trees and ground—snapped branches, cracked twigs, hoofprints embedded in mulch, chipped bark on a tree trunk where the edge of a sheathed weapon had nicked it accidentally while passing, a hundred other indicators that she could read as clearly as a brahmin could interpret Sanskrit neatly printed on a scroll.

Bejoo nodded to show he understood: for such a large group, so heavily burdened, to have come through this winding forest 'path' on horseback at such a speed, meant that they had a guide who knew the way. Her grama had been betrayed. By whom? And why?

'They were here for one reason only, to slaughter,' she said, for it was evident that the attackers had left as soon as they were done killing every last man, woman, and child in the settlement. 'The men of the grama tried to mount a resistance, to draw the attackers away from their families, but were encircled in a chakravyuh and slaughtered to the last man.'

Bejoo nodded. As a veteran ex-military man, he knew that a chakravyuh—a complex encircling attack technique—was unique to Arya military forces. It confirmed that the attackers were not merely some armed gang of bandits or marauders passing by, but heavily armed and healthy soldiers on well-fed mounts come here for the express purpose of murdering the entire village.

Nakhudi's trail-reading had taken the better part of an hour and led her on a winding route around and to the south-west of the settlement. She was aware of Bejoo's men following them discreetly, spread out through a wide swathe of forest, the better to ensure that they were not encircled and trapped or ambushed by the same attackers. She was glad for his presence and his military acumen, for right now, her entire consciousness and being were filled with only the raging desire for vengeance.

'And once their butchery was done,' she said, pausing beside a tree with a low-hanging branch on which several twigs had been snapped and lay freshly broken and trampled by horse hooves on the beaten ground below, 'they did not go back the way they came. Instead, they took this route, towards...'

She broke off, her eyes widening, heart racing. Her sword hand rose, fist tightening on the pommel. She sensed Bejoo react, turning to look at her in evident alarm.

'What?' he asked. 'Speak, woman!'

'Guru Valmiki's ashram,' she said. 'They are headed for the ashram!'

And then she began running.

* * *

Sita knew better than to go running out of her hut—straight into the waiting blades of the enemy. For no matter who or why they were there, the screams and unmistakable sounds of weaponry and slaughter from outside clearly announced that enemies were in the ashram. She had faced violent opposition frequently and regularly enough in her life not to waste time questioning the how, why and wherefore of it, but to merely act in a manner designed to ensure her own survival and the survival of those she loved.

Which was why she did not run across the threshold of her hut.

Instead, she kicked aside the earthen pot of water she used for drinking and cleaning hands and faces, shattering it with one expert blow, and pushed at the thatched panel at the bottom of the back wall. It rose up on a hinge made from two sections of half-bamboo ingeniously interlocked to allow just so much movement in one direction, opening an exit just large enough for her to crawl through—more than sufficient for her sons to slip through.

She went through with practised ease, her slender form in better physical condition than it had ever been in her life. Not quite the hard, overworked lithely muscular form of her days in Janasthana or Chitrakut, but nevertheless slim, fit, and strong enough to fight to save her own life and the lives of her sons if they needed saving.

Or the lives of others.

The back of the hut looked out upon a steep fall-off that in turn overlooked a narrow winding path that led down to the river Sona. She had built her hut in this location for this precise reason: isolated from the rest of the ashram, discretely tucked away just behind a line of trees, its natural materials and the artful construction made it appear to be a part of the hillside rather than a man-made structure. Even if the enemy knew where to look and found it, they could only approach it from the front. The steep fall-off at the back was unclimbable because of the soft yielding earth, dampened by rain part of the year and deliberately dampened by Sita herself in the dry seasons.

She glanced out over the edge, careful not to step too close to the mushy rim, and was relieved to see no armed soldiers rushing up the path from the river. That suggested that the attack was not directed at her or her sons. That was good, that was very good. No matter how artful or expert she might be in the ways of survival, there was no true way to defend oneself from direct, sustained assault. Especially not when one was genuinely a penniless penitent living in a hermitage in the forest.

That meant that this was some random attack by brigands or dacoits. Or unknown forces with an unknown agenda.

She had torn off the lower part of her modestly flowing garment to free her legs for quicker movement. Now, she unwrapped the tribal blanket and extracted its treasures. In the aranya, weapons were more precious than gold or jewels. One could use weapons to ensure one's survival, or to hunt and feed, which was the same thing; however, there was nothing here to buy even if one possessed all the gold and precious gems in the world!

She slung the rig, packed tight with carefully crafted arrows, made by herself, Nakhudi and the twins and replenished weekly after their training sessions. Each of them had their own cache, although Nakhudi and the boys took theirs around openly, while she kept hers stored secretly and only brought it out for her daily practice sessions.

She strung the bow with quick expert actions, slinging it over the same left shoulder as the rig. Then she unsheathed the sword and the short iron pike with the specially designed grip-guards that doubled as shortblades, and she was ready.

But she took a moment to listen and orient herself to what was going on, or at least what she could discern by way of hearing. Once she went around the hut and exposed herself, she might be fighting for her life, and it was worth taking a moment or two to learn as much as she could about whom she was fighting and what they might want.

The entire process until now—from reacting to Dumma's wife's screams to this moment of total readiness—had taken only a few moments. The shouts and yells and sounds of men and metal and horses had continued unabated. The ashram housed over four dozen inhabitants, and there was a party of another two dozen just arrived from Thiruvananthapuram. And if there was one thing brahmins were well-versed to doing, it was raising their voices. All those years of chanting and reciting nonstop all day long had conditioned them to be able to raise a great hue and cry in this time of crisis. The sheer sound level from across the ashram suggested a few hundred people rather than merely six dozen. From what she could make out, all that noise and uproar was not merely screams and crying out; many of the brahmins, particularly the senior rishis and maharishis, were not men or women to fear kshatriyas and their violence. They were berating the attackers loudly and unequivocally, several issuing shraaps and eternal curses in the names of various deities. It was a bold and godless dacoit who could withstand such an onslaught of priestly curses, she knew, and the fact that she could still hear sounds of violence and screams of agony punctuating the cacophony meant that whoever these men were, they were dangerous, deadly men come here with the express intention of committing the crime of brahmin-hatya. Priest-killing was not something most kshatriyas did lightly and it meant that the men were most likely mercenaries working for coin, and with no scruples or attachment to any nation, liege or other loyalties. That was not good, not good at all.

She wished Nakhudi and the twins were with her right now, or at the very least, were in some place far away, secure and isolated. The canyon. She must get them to the canyon. That was a defensible position. There, they could hold off even a small army if need be, or at least defend themselves until they ran out of arrows and replenishment.

But they were not here, and she was. And she was the only person in the ashram capable of fighting back against these intruders, whomever they might be. Those were her daily companions dying out there, and she could not simply run away and leave them to their fate. Moreover, there was Maharishi Valmiki himself. After all he had done for her and the boys, she could hardly abandon him to such a fate. The boys were wherever they were, and until she knew where, it made most sense for her to go out there and fight. If the odds were overwhelming—which seemed likely—then she would extricate herself and escape into the forest. The boys and Nakhudi were smart enough to know something was wrong and would not simply blunder into the ashram. She could count on them joining her eventually at the canyon, their agreed-upon refuge in the event of such a calamity.

Her mind made up, she took a deep breath, then slipped around the side of the hut and went running down the path to the main ashram grounds, bow-string pulled taut, first arrow notched and ready to loose. The row of sala trees blurred past and then she was out in the open and in the thick of the fray.

SIX

Somasra found himself unable to control his anger as he raced along, following former Vajra Captain Bejoo and the ex-rani-rakshak Nakhudi. He had seen the bodies of the slaughtered villagers and was thoroughly disgusted. How could Ayodhyans have stooped to such a heinous deed? These people might not be Arya anymore, if Arya meant one had to be literally pure and noble and superior in behaviour, thought and deed, since they had committed crimes at some point and fallen from that status of nobility of character. But they had been punished for their crimes and had additionally chosen to take themselves into exile from Arya society, which was further punishment. From the looks of their humble habitation and their ascetic lifestyles, it was evident they had not prospered through ill-gotten gains nor continued upon the path of crime—which was more than could be said for many people who still remained within the auspices of so-called Arya society.

And yet they had been slaughtered mercilessly by a heavily armed company of cavalry without warning or cause or even opportunity to arm and defend themselves. There were certain rules for combat among Aryas, and this not only violated that kshatriya code of conduct, it was an affront to any warrior. He had known that the murky politics of Ayodhya had taken a bad turn these past years—he had seen the steady decline himself among the PFs, the common soldiery and the city itself. But this was unacceptable.

He was aware of the other men, all senior PFs recently retired from active duty, at the edges of his vision. He was proud to see that they were all able to keep pace with the much younger woman, as was the ageing Captain Bejoo. Even though none of them had seen active combat for decades, there was enough activity on gatewatch—small skirmishes, sudden violent outbreaks, encounters with brash youngsters, minor riots, communal clashes—to have kept them all fighting fit. Besides, each and everyone in this handpicked band of white-haired retirees spent one full day each week at the training camp. He had even seen Captain Bejoo there, even though as a grama-rakshak now, he didn't have to adhere to such high standards of fitness. The training camps were no mere formality. Run by veterans like himself and held to the same high standards as they had been since the time of Manu the Lawmaker, they were a gruelling day's routine of drills, exercises, mock combat, war games and tactical briefings and discussions that kept the mind sharp and the body on the cutting edge of fitness. They might all be over seventy-five here in this band, in fact several were a decade older and at least two were in their tenth decade of life, but they were nonetheless able to hold their own.

As he sprinted at a demanding but sustainable pace through the forest, negotiating the overhanging branches, mulch-carpeted and snake-holed ground, and bushes and stones and other flora expertly, he felt as if he was not retired, but rejuvenated. This was why these men were so fit and strong even at their age: because they loved the demands and challenges of combat. It was when they were put out to pasture and told to go home and spend the rest of their days staring at sunsets and snowfall that they grew fat around the waist and the brain. Right now, he was confident that he and his band of octogenarians and nonagenarians could take on that company of cavalry and come out on top. They might not survive it—not all of them, for sure—but they would take as good as they got and still triumph. He was sure of it.

He had seen the way the younger, new PF troops drilled and trained at the camps in the cantonment north of Ayodhya, and he and his mates had laughed at the absurdity of it. Then again, what could one expect of men and women who had never known first-hand the terrors of a pishacha ambush or gone hand to hand with a rakshasa, or faced a swarm of nagas? Warfare today was only about mortals versus mortals, and after one had faced asuras, mortals just didn't seem as dangerous.

But these mortals made him angry. This was murder, nothing less. They had no right to come here to these people's grama and slaughter them thusly. And if what he had heard Nakhudi say to Bejoo was right, and they were attacking an ashram now, then these mortal soldiers did not deserve to be called Aryas, let alone Ayodhyans. They were no less than rakshasas and deserved to be killed like rakshasas.

He looked forward to coming face to face with them and showing them how real kshatriyas fought.

* * *

Bejoo sensed the anger in Nakhudi. Twenty-five years ago, when he had first met Nakhudi, he had been impressed by the young woman's fierce dedication to her duty and her fearless fighting attitude. At the time, he had been in charge of the vajra force assigned by Maharaja Dasaratha himself to follow and protect Princes Rama Chandra and Lakshman on their journey to Bhayanak-van with Brahmarishi Vishwamitra. They had encountered Nakhudi and Princess Sita Janaki after the Bhayanak-van mission, while on their way to Mithila. Nakhudi and her mistress had disguised themselves as men at the time, to make it easier to move incognito across the land as well as deflect the excessive attention that a princess would naturally have drawn.

He had been very impressed by Nakhudi's fighting skills as well as her fierce loyalty to Sita, and when he had learned that the rani-rakshak was, in fact, a woman herself, he had been doubly impressed. Not because he had not expected a woman to fight that well or be that skilful:

Arya society was a matriarchal society, and Bejoo had met and seen women kshatriyas who would put most men to shame in battle, and who chose to undertake the challenges of motherhood and family-raising just as efficaciously. No, he had been impressed because Nakhudi was impressive, just for who she was, and how she worked and the lengths she was willing to go to in order to fulfil her duties. He had felt more than a little attracted to her then. But he had been happily married and the question of betraying his wife, even for a brief encounter, had been untenable morally.

Now, two-and-a-half decades later, she was still impressive, and he found himself still admiring her fierce devotion to her mistress, her fearless decisiveness, and yes, he still desired her. He was not as young as he had been back then, but then again, neither was she now. The age difference of almost two decades between them hardly mattered. All that mattered was that he had finally found a woman he cared about, even though just days earlier he would have thought such a thing to be impossible, and whom he now believed he could come to love as deeply and strongly—if very differently—than he had loved his long-standing companion and belated wife. And he thought that she too cared about him, which mattered most of all.

He followed her through the woods, admiring the ease with which she negotiated the treacherous obstacle course of the deep forest as if it were a city avenue. He admired also the way she displayed anger but kept it banked, using the energy from that anger instead to fuel her forward movement and pace, even after having just found her entire community slaughtered to the last woman, elder and child. He could hardly imagine what fortitude it took to overcome that shock, and the inevitable outrage and fury that must be bubbling up inside her as a result. Yet he could see no wavering of hand or eye, no clumsiness of footing or rashness of action. Her breathing remained even, if short, and her aspect contained and measured. It reminded him of the great commanders and leaders he had followed into battle in his younger days; Nakhudi was no less a leader of warriors than they had been.

He smiled despite the circumstances, shaking his head once as he ran through the sun-dappled shadows, and thought that even if she did not consider herself 'Arya' and mayhap she might not be Arya in the strictest sense of the term, yet she was, in fact, the very epitome of the epithet. Pure of soul, noble of purpose, elevated in deed and thought. Yes, she was Arya to the core.

He decided then that if they survived this hare-brained adventure, unlikely as it was, he would ask her to marry him, and live the rest of his days with her by his side. *If she would have him, of course, which was another question altogether.*

He heard the shouts and screams, and metallic sounds of weapons a fraction of a moment before she stopped and raised her hand. Behind and around them the rest of the vajra stopped as well. He realised it was odd to call a band of old retired PFs on foot a 'vajra'. How could this group of old fogeys possibly strike forays and retreat with the swiftness of the mythical lightning bolts of Lord Indra? The very analogy was absurd. Yet, he would call it a vajra. For in their own way, in these circumstances and this environment and under this leadership, they would strike and retreat as swiftly as lightning. He would see to that. He had promised Nakhudi he would.

And she had tried to smile coquettishly—which only made her expansive dark face look menacing—and said, 'I know you will. That's why I came to you.'

Now, she ducked down to a crouch and crept forward for the last hundred yards. He could see the smoke from the ashram cookfires curling above the rooftops up ahead, but due to the denseness of the woods, he did not see the ashram itself until they were barely twenty yards away.

He frowned.

The ravagers could hardly have stumbled across two such cleverly hidden settlements accidentally. They had good directions, or a guide. Which meant this entire sordid operation had been planned down to the last detail.

That made him angrier. Bad enough that these vermin were slaughtering unarmed and innocent women, children and elders—and now brahmins as well. But it was infinitely worse to know that someone had plotted and planned these massacres and executed them with such ruthless cruelty.

He put aside the romantic notions that had been filling his senses for the past few moments and focussed on the task at hand. The man in him yielded to the kshatriya in him, and he pursed his lips grimly and passed the hilt of his blade across his unshaven stubble, producing a rasping sound that only he could hear and which helped him sink into the mental state required for complete concentration during a battle or fight. The scenes of violence and abuse unfolding before them needed no explanation or argument. It was quite obvious who were the aggressors and who the victims and what needed to be done.

'Attack at will,' Nakhudi said from ahead, her voice cold and deadly.

He raised his hand and gave the signal to his vajra.

Then he led them into battle, following after Nakhudi.

* * *

Luv feared the worst. At the sound of the trumpet call, Kush and he had begun racing back to the ashram, followed closely by Sarama and her pack—and the bearkillers. He knew the bearkillers must have something to do with the alarm being raised, but explanations could come later. All he cared about was getting back to the hermitage as fast as possible. Fortunately, they were only a few miles away. Even so, the race through the forest seemed to take forever and the thought of what might lie ahead was unbearable. His greatest anxiety was for Maatr.

Prithvi-maa, protect her.

But a part of him knew that his mother was no ordinary sadhini. Ever since his brother and he had been old enough to understand such things, she had explained to them, calmly and without transferring any sense of fear or emotion, that it was imperative that they maintain a certain discipline about some things, such as their daily weapons and physical training, and that they follow certain pre-arranged codes and signals in the event of a calamity. What form the calamity might take was never quite clear, but they had come to understand that it would most likely take the shape of a group of attackers and that Ayodhya would have something to do with it. That was more than enough. So they drilled and trained and practised and prepared for the event of an unexpected attack by armed Ayodhyans. Today, that training was about to be tested, it seemed.

Because Kush had been at the far side of the group, he was a fairways behind. But the pockmarked-face woman named Ragini kept good pace with Luv as he ran. She even managed to speak, though the last thing he wanted to do was talk. 'This is what we came to warn you about—they had already slaughtered Nakhudi's village and we tracked them moving towards Valmiki ashram. We hoped to reach you two and warn you before you blundered into the thick of it.'

Luv kept running, moving his arms and legs efficiently, breathing rhythmically, as he had learned to do. He did not bother to waste breath on a response.

'Your mother could be dead already. You know that she gave specific orders for how to act in such an event. You are not to return to the ashram. You are to go to the pre-arranged meeting point and wait there.'

This time he could not resist. Rather than ask the most expected question—*How do you know what we had pre-arranged?*—he asked the next most relevant one.

'Wait there for what?' he demanded, not slowing his pace. 'If she is indeed dead as you claim—which I don't accept—then what are we to wait for?'

'For us,' said Ragini, turning her head to look at him.

He glanced at her briefly as they ran and saw the earnestness in her light brown eyes. She was telling the truth. The forest blurred behind her.

He felt a small flutter of shock: these were the 'friends' that Maatr had spoken of? The ones who would come to help them in the event of a calamity? Impossible! They were bearkillers. Scum of the forest!

'Our association with your father and mother goes back a long way, Luv,' she said.

He was not impressed by her being able to tell his brother and him apart, since he had yelled out Kush's name earlier. But he believed her when she said that she had known his mother. Maatr had spoken of old friends of their father and her. Everything this woman, this bearkiller, was saying rang true. He swallowed, feeling a twinge of emotion even as he sprinted. That meant the bearkillers had known their father. And to think that Kush and he had regarded them with scorn and derision, often making jokes about their appearance or derogatory comments about their hygiene and sense of dharma. Even Rishi Dumma had often participated in these jocular insults, coming up with real gems. Dumma did have a sense of humour, that and a great appetite.

'Turn away now,' Ragini said, bringing him back to the moment. 'Follow your mother's orders. Turn away and come with us. We shall protect you and care for you. We are sworn to do so until our dying breath. Do not go back to the ashram.'

He hesitated mentally, even though his feet continued pumping and his arms swung to and fro and the breath chugged in and out of his lungs in the rhythmic pattern that he could maintain all day and for twenty yojanas if need be. Then the sounds of screaming rose again from ahead, very close now, barely a mile or so, and he shook his head grimly, lowered his chin and increased his pace.

Ragini had to strain now to catch up. Whatever else the bearkillers might be, they were not long-distance runners—or perhaps they were burdened by their heavier metal weapons. Kush and he only carried bows and rigs, which made a difference. Someday, they would graduate to metal blades, and in a pinch, they could use them just as well up close, but at his and Kush's age and size, the weight of swords and blades far outweighed their usefulness.

Besides, Maatr had always preferred that they use bows. *So that we could fight from a distance and be safer. She always tried to keep us safe.* He fought back the emotion that was threatening to engulf him and sucked in two sharp, shallow breaths, regaining control.

Because he had not replied, Ragini reached out and touched his shoulder lightly, a gesture of affection. 'I see you will not heed my warning. Very well then. Whatever happens now, in the ashram,' she said, 'you must not risk your lives unduly. Remember that your brother and you have a far larger purpose to fulfil. It is not your destiny to die at the hands of those mercenaries today. Leave the fighting to us. Stay with your brother. Stay back. It was your mother's wish.'

And then, surprising him, she shot out a foot and deftly tripped him, sending him sprawling in a pile of wild grass, winded but unhurt.

'Stay back and let us fight!' she shouted, then was gone, sprinting up ahead.

The rest of her gang raced past him, the scarred man glancing down briefly as he passed to make sure that he was all right. Then the dogs were there, also loping past, long muzzles dripping froth, Sarama whimpering as she ran past as if to apologise for running with her pack rather than stopping to help him. Her tail flicked his nose as she whipped past.

Luv sat up and rubbed his head, wondering at how neatly the half-chested outlaw woman had tripped him. He was not harmed or injured in any way, but it had effectively stopped him, if only for a moment or two. That was all the advantage she had needed, clever woman!

He was on his feet and picking up pace again just as Kush caught up with him. Luv glanced sideways at his brother who grinned back at him, displaying a fleck of grass between his upper front teeth. From the blades of grass and leaf or two pasted to Kush's face and arms, Luv guessed that he too had been similarly delayed by the bearkillers. They exchanged a glance and it was all he needed to let him know that his brother had had a similar exchange with one of the gang members,

probably the scarred man, and that they both knew all that was needed
to be known.

Except what happened to Maatr and Gurudev Valmiki.

Shoulder to shoulder now, they ran the last few hundred yards to the
ashram. Up ahead, they could already hear the sounds of the bearkillers
roaring and calling out in their vulgar way and the dogs growling and
snarling with the low-toned ferocity of animals at war as the new arrivals
clashed with the attackers in the ashram.

Moments later, Kush and he burst into the clearing and joined them.

SEVEN

Even though Sita saw what she had expected to see, it was still a shock.

The large rectangular central courtyard of the ashram, lined by huts on either side, with the ashram's largest domicile at the head, was a melee of flailing bodies, human, and equestrian. Rishis and their wives, all dressed alike in red-ochre dhotis and anga-vastras, with their junior acolytes clad in white, ran about everywhere in confusion and fear. Riding among them were the attackers, armed and armoured horsemen wielding longspears, swords, axes and pikes. The attackers were randomly chasing down and slaughtering the ashramites without cause or provocation. It was a massacre.

Sita watched as a frail dark woman whom she recognised as the wife of Rishi Divakara attempted to run down the alleyspace between two huts and was checked by a spear flung by a horseman. The spear struck her in the back, severing her spine, and she fell, instantly dead, her eyes still open and staring blankly.

She saw the ageing Rishi Kanwa, a visitor from the south-eastern kingdom of Kalinga, standing with his hands clasped together in silent appeal, as he was hacked down by two separate horsemen, one from the front cutting through his clasped hands with a sword, the other chopping at the juncture of his neck and torso with an axe. He fell into a spreading pool of his own blood, half-severed limbs dangling grotesquely, lips still parted in recitation of a shloka of forgiveness. Bodies lay sprawled everywhere, blood splatters staining the white robes, the red-ochre robes concealing the brutality meted out to the bodies they clothed. The air of the ashram, usually so pristine and clear and crisp, was sullied by the stench of death and the odour of bodily effluents spilled out into the dust.

It had been a long time since Sita had seen such brutality, the brutality of unbridled human arrogance unleashed for its own selfish pleasures—male arrogance, to put a fine point on it—and she had forgotten how cruel men could be, kshatriya men in particular, when embarked upon a mission they were convinced was their dharma to execute. Forest living was harsh; the animal kingdom was ruthless; life itself was never easy, and nature herself posed as many relentless challenges to existence as she provided succour and nourishment. But this, this was naked male arrogance, the madness of muscle and virility unchecked, the naked lust for violence that some men insisted was a natural part of all humankind, but was, in fact, only an ailment of their own twisted psyches, perpetrated by them through generations in order to justify their own violent urges and lustful indulgences. Only an evil man spoke of good versus evil; and those who spoke of good versus evil always insisted they were on the side of good. In fact, as any sane, rational person knew, there were no good or evil people or beings, only people who did things to serve their own ends—whether those things were adjudged good or evil depended on the perception of others.

Yet, if she were to start believing in evil, this was as good a time as any. For what was being perpetrated here, under whatever guise or excuse, was an evil, abhorrent act.

She had watched the horrific slaughter for only a few moments, the bare minimum time needed to orient herself to the sheer ruthlessness of the attackers and the shameless manner in which they pursued their given task. She witnessed only three actual deaths, although many other victims were already dying or about to be attacked when she appeared on the scene. And she could hear the sounds and screams from beyond the huts and within the huts as well. But it was all she needed to see and hear. There was no point in appealing to such men. Any kshatriya who would ride into a peaceful camp, ignore the sacred appeal of a man of the cloth, and murder him as brutally as they had just murdered Rishi Kanwa, were not men at all. They were monsters driven by a misguided madness, a fanatical devotion to an aberrant sense of dharma, soldiers who had the power to mete out life and death and were abusing it to slaughter rather than save, to murder rather than protect. They were exterminators driven by a distorted interpretation of dharma. Dharmanators, to coin a term. And there was no arguing or speaking to such dharmanators. They could only be stopped in one way—by killing them as quickly and efficiently as possible.

She aimed at a helmed face with its mouth open wide in laughter, raising a sword high as it prepared to strike down a young rishi who had been ordained only days earlier, his face wet and shiny from copious weeping.

She loosed, and watched the arrow punch into the open mouth and through the back of the head, the arrowhead striking the inside of the helm with a metallic clanging impact. The rider toppled backwards off his horse, his sword striking the rump of another horse nearby and sending it bolting, knocking that rider off his aim as he was about to throw a spear at another woman running away in shrieking panic.

The young rishi blinked through his tears, saw the arrow sticking out of the gaping mouth of the man lying on the ground, the man who had been about to kill him only a moment ago, and stared upwards uncomprehendingly. Unfamiliar with war and its methods, he could not fathom that the arrow had been shot by a mortal hand. He assumed that his soldier had been struck down by the devas.

Sita turned her attention to another target.

A soldier on horseback was about to hack down a kneeling rishi with his parasu. The kneeling rishi was Rishi Angira, an old and venerated man known for his ascetic habits and ever-joyous temperament.

The younger acolytes always joked that Rishi Angira had never lost his temper or said a word in anger all his life, so when he did turn angry, it would surely be an epic temper tantrum! Looking at him now, calmly cradling the head of a fellow brahmin—Rishi Ashita, she saw, with a horrible disfiguring wound to his face and neck—as he sat on the stoop of his own hut, Sita thought that if he was not losing his temper now, he never would. To have such self-restraint and single-minded conviction in his vows was beyond admirable, it was proof to her yet again of the inherent goodness and desire for peaceful co-existence that pervaded all creatures of the universe. That face, calm and self-assured even in the face of a hideous violent death, was proof that the natural state of all beings was peaceful existence.

The face beyond the tip of her poised arrow displayed the exact opposite of that natural calm. It was a face distorted by its own anger and lustful energies, nostrils flaring as the man snarled in evident delight at his brutal task, swinging the parasu at a diagonal angle intended to lope Rishi Ashita's head from his body. To see a man use an axe for such an act was itself a reminder why the legendary Parasurama, Rama of the Axe, had taken up the weapon, intended for chopping trees and wood, and used it to eliminate the kshatriyas of the mortal realm seven times over in order to teach them humility and respect for their own preceptors. Clearly, this kshatriya had not heeded that lesson.

She loosed and saw her arrow strike the man in the slim gap between his helm and his chest armour. It took him in the neck, passing through the soft liquid-filled stalk and punching through the other side in a small explosion of blood and gristle. His snarling turned to a liquid gurgling, and the parasu fell useless from his muscled hands as he grasped at his mortally wounded throat. He fell, thrashing in his death throes, singing a different tune from the cry of victory he had been snarling a moment earlier.

She loosed three more arrows in quick succession, saw three more men fall. Two of them were mortally wounded and died in moments, but one was forewarned by the fall of the soldier next to him, and swung away just as she loosed, the arrow gouging open a bloody track on his upper thigh but missing all vital organs. He screamed in pain and outrage and turned to point at her position, having already watched her two earlier arrows strike home and placing her with accuracy.

That brought the attention of the others to her and a half dozen riders galloped towards her at once, roaring with pleasure.

'It's her!' shouted one to the others, swinging his sword overhead as he came. 'Remember the reward, men!'

She took him down with an arrow in the throat, wincing as his feet and hands tightened instinctively, bringing down his horse in a fetter-snapping fall. The horse screamed out the agony that he could not express and she loosed again, and again, and again, bringing down another, and a third, and wounding a fourth. But there were still three riders coming at her, and she was out of time. She had known she ought to have stopped after the first or second shot, circled around to a new position and then fired again, but she had been unable to let more innocents die as they would have if she had taken the extra time, so she had continued standing her ground and loosing arrows, and now it was too late to get away. So much for her plan of self-extrication!

She leaped over the dead tree trunk that marked the northern boundary of the main ashram grounds, ducked behind an ancient banyan tree, and ran through the thickest part of the woods to make it harder for her followers. But there were more riders coming at her from the other side and there were too many of them, and the same obstacles that made it harder from them to follow also made it harder for her to shoot while running with any degree of accuracy. She knew they would catch her in a moment and when they did, she would be dead, so she made a decision in an instant.

She leaped up on the Y-shaped cradle of an ageing tree, swinging around and letting her back strike the trunk hard, bracing herself, then raising her bow and preparing to shoot the first horseman who came into sight. That eliminated their height advantage of being on horseback.

There was no way for her to escape this alive now, but she would take with her as many of them as possible before dying.

* * *

Nakhudi cried out with outrage.

She had emerged from the forest into the gurukul. This was a large clearing just north of the main ashram, used mainly for children's games, morning and evening group exercises, and rote chanting by brahmacharyas—the youngest acolytes of the ashram. Unlike the more permanent denizens of the hermitage who were all brahmin by vocation if not by birth, these young acolytes could be from any varna. They were children sent here to be schooled in the guru-shishya parampara, also known as Upanishad, or learning-by-the-side-of-the-guru, and they ranged from the age of seven to fourteen.

From the looks of it, they were the ones who had been here at the time of the attack, drilling in martial training exercises as they did everyday, under the supervision of the rishis. The red-ochre garb of the half dozen rishis who had been supervising today stood out across the clearing, laying where they had been standing at the time of the attack. They were overwhelmed by the three dozen other, much smaller bodies clad in white that lay sprawled around the clearing. Many of these smaller corpses lay in postures and attitudes that suggested they had tried to use their meagre training weapons against the intruders. But wooden swords, lathis and ropes were hardly a match for steel blades and iron spears.

She passed around the clearing with rage boiling in her belly. How could anyone do this to little children? Mere boys, these were. What had they done to deserve such a fate?

But after all, it was not about what anyone had done or not done, simply about who they were.

In a world of haves and have-nots, the man in armour upon horseback with a sword felt he was entitled to run down and slaughter even innocent young boys—because they were not 'Arya', not noble-born, city-living, high and mighty citizens here, just shishyas in a forest gurukul. And in a world where power and wealth and citizenship were what made you superior to your fellow man, if you were out here in some remote forest, you were not human in the same sense that those superior beings were human; you were no less than animals, and as such, fit only for slaughter.

Not a single intruder's corpse lay in the clearing, testifying to the shock and overwhelming odds of the attack. These boys and their teachers had never stood a chance, nor been given one. It went against the very spirit and rule of the kshatriya code, but after the massacre in her village, she already knew that these intruders were not kshatriyas, merely vendors of death, come to ply their business in exchange for coin paid by the highest bidder. No king, no minister, no Arya court of justice would find them guilty of any crime or wrongdoing. Theirs is the sword, therefore, theirs is the power and the glory.

Well, she thought, hefting the specially weighted blade she carried to suit her larger form and heavier carrying strength, *I have a sword too, and unlike those poor brahmacharyas and brahmins, I know how to use it and will do so!*

The sounds of butchery and terror were loudest up ahead, past the vegetable gardens where the ashramites grew their own food. Horse hooves had tramped through the gardens as well, she saw, for when one did not respect life, then why would they respect the things that sustained life? She circled around the crushed pods and yams and then, she was running past a line of sheds that smelled of cow. She was relieved to hear the panicked mooing and looing of the milk-giving beasts and thanked Durga Maa that the attackers had not slaughtered the animals as well. Then she realised it was not out of compassion or even out of reverence for Go-Maata, the sacred Mother Cow, sustainer of life and nourishment, but simply out of expedience that they had spared the cows—they would probably be back later, to finish them off, once they had killed their main targets, the human residents.

She came around a cow shed just in time to see a woman in saffron-coloured sadhini's garb come shrieking from the direction of the main ashram complex. Three horsemen followed the poor woman, swinging bloody swords and pikes, and a fourth was following belatedly, hefting what looked like an elephant mace—the kind used to club war elephants in battle and crush their brains within their skulls. The faces of the men were glowing with excitement and lust, the lust for blood and slaughter that she had seen too often before. It was a face she too had worn, but never as a mask against the slaughter of innocents or the unarmed. And in response to those leering expressions of lurid lustfulness, she put on her own face of terrible justice.

The woman ran past her without even registering who she was, simply stumbling on in panic. She was already bleeding from a deep gash on her back where a sword had chopped a chunk of flesh out, and her eyes were dilated and wild with terror. For a woman who had spent years, perhaps her entire life, in silent contemplation, meditation and prayer, the onslaught of armed horsemen seeking to slaughter her for no reason at all, was a shocking violation of her worldview. She was half-mad with terror.

Nakhudi let her go by, standing in the path of the men following her.

They too had eyes only for the task at hand, hunter to her hunted, and whooped and called out obscene words as they cantered down with the audaciousness of men who had no fear of anything and would do as they pleased to whomever they pleased.

They were about to receive an object lesson in what they should not do.

Nakhudi raised her sword and waved it at the first horseman, who was a good ten yards ahead of the others.

'You,' she called out, 'Try me instead. I'm more fun to play with.'

He blinked and grinned, noticing her for the first time. She realised that even the sword in her hand had not caused him any concern. As far as he was concerned, he was king of the world and every living thing was his to command. He was wrong, and was about to find out just how wrong—the hard way.

He swung his sword in a loping action as he rode up, not slowing a whit. His intention was to cut her down and ride on after the sadhini. She didn't try to deflect his sword. Defence was not her goal. Instead, she swung higher, raising herself up at just the right moment, and hacked viciously hard at the junction of his shoulder and arm.

Her sword, weighted one-and-a-half times as much as most longswords, was strengthened by the rider's own forward motion. The blade sliced through the man's shoulder, severing armour, bone and muscle easily, and lopped off the entire arm. The arm, still clutching the useless sword, fell to the ground, and the man rode on, the fist-sized hole in his torso gushing deep crimson heart's blood over the crushed vegetables. He made a sound like that of a child wailing, the kind of sound the youngest brahmacharyas might have made when they had been cut down mercilessly by his associates and himself. She heard him fall off his horse behind her but did not bother to turn to look. She was busy greeting the other riders.

The second one tried to skewer her throat with his iron pike. There were gobs of flesh stuck to the point and she could smell the reek of something awful as the weapon shot out at her with deadly efficiency.

She dodged the point, feeling it scrape the edge of her collar, and plunged her swordblade upwards, into the gap between his armour and his belt. It stabbed deep into the region of his liver, and beyond, into his vitals, and he screamed much louder than the first man, sounding more like an animal than a human, and fell sideways onto her. She had been prepared for that possibility and hurled him over, sending him sprawling on the ground with a sickly cracking of bones and more animal screaming, freeing her sword with practised effort.

The third man shouted with anger. He had not expected to see his friends die before him, killed by a woman he probably assumed to be another sadhini from the ashram, and was furious. He was the one with the elephant mace and he came at her with a speed and ferocity that almost undid her.

She rolled in the nick of time—across the path of his horse—and narrowly missed having her skull stoved in by the pounding hooves. But then she was up and swinging, and he yelled with outrage as her sword hacked through his leather garments, severing his thigh. He swung the horse around for another pass, but she had slipped a throwing dagger into her palm from a belt at her waist, and she flung it at his throat where it stuck and cut off any further sounds of protest he might wish to produce.

She turned just in time to see the last rider—he was, in fact, the third rider but he had hung back after watching her cut down the first man—raise a spear. There was no time to turn or dodge before he threw the yard-long length of wood and iron.

EIGHT

Luv and Kush arrived at the ashram's south side to see the bearkillers
clashing with at least two dozen armoured mounted soldiers.
The dogs ran amuck, snapping at the horse's legs, panicking them into
kicking and jumping, which threw the riders off their aim as they tried
to hack and cut and spear the new arrivals.

They took in the number of white-clad and ochre-clad corpses lying
about with growing dismay, trying to spot the familiar long, black-haired
and red-clad form of their Maatr among the dead. Both finished the
scan of the visible area and shook their heads at the exact same time,
knowing it did not mean that she was not dead, merely that they could
not see her body.

In their hearts, they could not bring themselves to believe she could
be slain. Not her. Not Maatr. They had watched her spar with Nakhudi
any number of times and both secretly thought that she was the greatest
warrior that had ever lived. Only their guru's epic poem which they had
been taught to recite daily ever since they could pronounce Sanskrit,
filled as it was with tales of derring-do and incredible battles, described a
warrior that could match the great Vedavati's prowess at arms. And that
was the man who was both the subject of the poem as well as the architect
of its greatest tragedy, Raja Rama Chandra. They felt certain that even

if the legendary Rama Chandra of the poem were to face Maatr, it was she who would carry the day.

But that did not stop them from worrying.

They watched briefly as the bearkillers held their own against the superior arms and number of attackers, but then began to lose ground almost at once. More and more horsemen kept coming from around the ashram, called by their comrades to join the fight, and their sheer numbers and superior arms and mounts made them impossible to defeat. They knew that they ought to leave the bearkillers to the fight and go to the canyon as they had been instructed. But they had still not seen Maatr, dead or alive, and those were their daily companions and friends and gurus lying dead there on the ground.

With one motion, both slung their bows, notched arrows and drew together.

They glanced sideways at each other, winked with the closest eye, and let fly. As before, their almost preternatural ability to know one another's thoughts and actions enabled them to pick different targets.

Two horsemen about to converge on the scar-faced bearkiller from behind suddenly sprouted arrows from their throats and fell screaming and thrashing off their horses. The dogs were at their faces and feet at once, snarling and ripping and tearing viciously, showing the fallen attackers as little mercy as they had shown their victims.

Scar-face did not have time to turn and look in their direction, but he waved two fingers pressed close together in a sketch of a half-salute and they understood that he was acknowledging their help. Then he was back in the fray and so were they.

For the next several moments, they picked out targets and took them down, each time with a single arrow. Only once did it take more than one arrow and that was because the man in question turned aside at the last instant and Kush's arrow was deflected by the jutting metal of his helm. It clanged off and the man turned to glare at the place where the boys stood. He shouted to his comrades who shouted at each other in turn. The fight was turning swiftly. Luv and Kush alone had brought down over a dozen riders and the bearkillers and dogs had managed as many. The attackers had likely not expected such resistance and were unwilling to take such losses. Already, some of them were turning the heads of their horses and riding away.

Luv and Kush both drew together and with concerted coordination, shot the man that Kush's first arrow had missed. Both their arrows took him in the open mouth, silencing his angry instructions. He gurgled, blood pouring from his mouth and fell, shuddering violently, onto his head on the ground. Even the dogs gave him a wide berth as he crashed, already dead.

After that, the spine of the attack was broken and the remaining horsemen retreated. But they were not to get away that easily.

Even as Kush and Luv whooped loudly and watched the last of the intruders riding away, the sound of yells and weapons rose from the north side of the ashram.

Again, moving as if with one body and mind, they slung their bows and ran.

They ran past the bearkillers, who shouted at them. Ragini tried to grab at Luv as he went past, but he dodged and slipped away easily, and he heard her curse herself as he flew by. Kush and he went around the corner of the largest hut and beyond the main ashram courtyard to the north side, where the vegetable gardens and training grounds were located.

They saw a rider about to fling a spear at a woman whom they recognised at once as Nakhudi, from her stance and the way she held her sword. She had been caught unawares and the spear would hit her squarely in the chest—or in the side if she tried to turn away.

But another spear came shooting out of the thicket beyond the vegetable garden and struck the rider low in the belly, just as his own spear left his hand. The other spear struck just a fraction of a moment before he released his weapon, just enough to cause his aim to go awry. The spear passed within an inch of Nakhudi's side, ripping a tear in her garment noisily as it flew past. A little blood spurted from the spot but

Nakhudi didn't even bother to react or clap a hand to it as anyone else might have done. Instead, she ran straight towards the main ashram, the expression on her face like nothing Luv and Kush had ever seen before.

They ran out in front of her, blocking her way and for an instant, Luv thought that she would run straight at them, cutting them both down with a single stroke of her sword. Then something changed in her eyes as she registered and recognised them, and she blinked and lowered her sword, slowing her pace.

She stopped before them, the terrible mask slipping from her face and another more familiar face replacing it. This Nakhudi they knew well. This Nakhudi clasped their shoulders with great relief.

'You are well! Kali be blessed. Where is your Maatr?'

They shook their heads.

'Not dead,' Luv said for both of them. 'We haven't seen her body anywhere. The bearkillers said she might be dead already but we would have seen her by now.'

'Quickly, then,' she said, 'she might be somewhere in the ashram precinct still. We must find her before they do!'

They needed no further urging.

'Luv and I will search the eastern side,' Kush said. 'You take the main complex. But be careful, there are soldiers there still.'

'That's all right,' she said grimly. 'I have soldiers too.'

She beckoned and the man who had flung the spear that saved her life came jogging through the vegetable garden, looking apologetic as he trod the last of the pumpkins to a pulp. Behind him came a swarm of other men similar to him, white-haired and thick with age. They ran past, following Nakhudi.

Kush and he looked at one another in puzzlement. 'Old soldiers? What can they do to help?'

The brothers shook their heads as they sprinted to the east perimeter to search for their mother.

* * *

Sarama was not an old dog, but she was ailing. Constant birthing had taken its toll on her and she had produced more litters than dogs twice her age had did. She was very proud of that and of the size of her brood and their robust health and strength. But being a Maatr was not easy and it had drained her resources considerably. As a result, she had grown as frail as most dogs twice or thrice her age. Nature had a way of balancing things out in the end. She could no longer run, jump, bark or fight even half as well as she once did.

But there was one thing she could do as well if not better than ever. Scent.

Even as the rest of her body and senses shrivelled away and weakened, her sense of smell remained strong. In fact, due to her eyesight fading and her other senses failing, she had come to rely almost entirely on that sense of smell, and used it to great advantage. Where other dogs would use a combination of sight, hearing and smell to make decisions, choose directions and otherwise pursue various courses of actions, Sarama relied mainly on her nose to lead her through the last remaining months, perhaps years, of her life. Dogs that grow blind or deaf will often do the same, coming to rely on the one sense their kind trusted the most. For eyes could be deceived by illusions, sounds could resemble one another or be mistaken, but smells were pure and perfect. No scent was quite like another, and even groups of scents, while sharing an affinity and similarity, were easily discernible from one another. To a dog, the world was a world of smells, each to its own. Not a black and white world but a universe where each and every scent was a unique, distinct shade of colour. Sarama often confused men with one another, or even with trees and horses, and she would puzzle over sounds for hours sometimes, unable to fathom their meaning, such as the nasal repetitive sounds recited over and over by the little humans in the ashram each day, but she never confused smells. Smells were sacred. Thus had the great creator of dogkind made all her followers in Her image. Go forth and scent the world, it is yours to sniff and snuffle to your nose's content.

It was this sense of smell that told her that the good Maatr was in trouble.

She milled about at the edges of the fight in the ashram grounds, barking mostly and snarling and nipping a little, but mostly keeping away from the flailing limbs and hooves and nasty metal cutting things that humans used to harm one another. Her brood was doing admirably well, participating and assisting their human friends with great enthusiasm and success. She was very proud of them. But she knew better than to try to fight as they fought, for if she received so much as a cut to her vital organs or a hard blow, she knew she would not survive it. The last litter or two had taken a heavy toll on her. Three of her pups had been still-born and of the remaining four, only two survived beyond the first year, and even those two were relatively frail and prone to illness.

Also, there was a constant pain in her birthing chamber that only worsened as time went by, and she sensed that this pain was caused by some inner canker that would ultimately be the death of her. She knew this and accepted it with the equanimity of all animalkind, for life and death were one and the same thing, and this world or the next, they all belonged to Pashupati, lord of animals. Not understanding names or the human words by which they called to their own kind as well as her kind, she did not know that she had been named after the great Sarama herself, matrix of all dogkind. But even so, she knew that all dogs, good or nasty, smelly or sweet, toothless or sharp-fanged, must lie down someday, never to rise again. So it was to be with her, and so it would be with every living creature.

But there was nothing wrong with her sense of smell. On the contrary. And as a downwind from the east brought a fresh batch of scents to her keen black nostrils, she became aware that the Good Maatr, the one who lived in a kennel apart from the others, with her two little pups, all three of whom were exceedingly kind and generous to Sarama as well as to her brood, and who had nursed her and many of her offspring through many ailments and injuries, that good matriarch was in trouble. She could smell the scent of her blood and her sweat, ripe with fear and anger, the peculiar mixture of the two that exuded from a being when it was on the verge of death. She knew that scent well, she knew she would smell it on herself someday soon. And it was not right that Maatr should be exuding that scent.

Barking loudly, she tried to attract the attention of some of her brood. But some of them were busy finishing off the metal-furred men who had fallen off the backs of their horses, and the rest were chasing after the ones who were trying to ride away. The humans she and the other dogs had accompanied here were busy fighting and chasing too, and paid her no heed. She was, after all, just one of thirty dogs barking and running around!

So she turned and made away on her own.

She did not have far to go. In moments, she found the spot from where the wind had carried the Maatr's scent to her. It was a little enclave set off from the main ashram, and as such not directly visible from there.

The scenario was bad, worse than she had expected.

There were several of the horse-riding bad men here, waving those horrible metal things that cut and hurt terribly and that dogs must avoid being struck by at all costs, on pain of death. A few of the men lay dead or mortally wounded on the ground, their horses milling about or slipping away into the woods to try and find their fellow equines. But a pack of more than one paw's worth and less than two paws' worth still surrounded the tree before which the Maatr stood, defending herself with her own metal thing.

It was good that Maatr had a metal thing to defend herself. But Sarama sensed that Maatr had been up on the tree not long before, and from that position had shot those flying wooden missiles that hurt from afar. That was how she had killed so many of her attackers already. But apparently she had run out of wooden things to shoot and had been forced to use the metal thing and now she was at a grave disadvantage. For there were many of the men and only one of her, and they were clad in that iron-scented metal fur which no dog could bite through for fear of breaking the teeth, and they were very vicious, snarling brutes who seemed to want nothing more than to tear her throat up and rip out her guts.

Sarama did not wish to see Maatr lay down there and end her life. She loved Maatr and her young cubs.

She milled about restlessly for a moment, fretting and worrying. Finally, she realised there was nothing else left to do. She was the only one here who could help Maatr. Either she risked her life to do so, or Maatr would die.

She had no choice really.

She shook herself vigorously, waking up her ailing body as best as she could. She felt a sharp arrow of pain in her nether regions and yelped, but then forced herself to ignore the pain. There was no time to think of her pain now, it was Maatr who was in grave danger. And Maatr must be helped.

Turning in the opposite direction she took a running length, then turned around sharply and launched herself at the men in metal fur, her yellowed fangs bared in a snarl.

Luv and Kush heard the sounds of a dog in distress and knew at once it was Sarama. She had a distinctive yelp when in trouble or pain which they had heard often over the years. Being the oldest dog they knew, and one they had been intimately friendly with almost since birth, her voice was as recognisable to them as any human's. They sprinted in the direction her yelps had come from, separating and taking opposite, converging routes to go around the thicket. When they came around into view of the banyan tree and the violent scene before it, both had arrows notched and ready to loose.

It was a heartbreaking scene, underscored by a cacophony of tired barks, punctuated by the sound of steel on steel.

Maatr stood with her back to the old tree, defending herself valiantly with a sword in her left hand against three of the attackers. She was bleeding from a dozen nicks and cuts, her right arm hung limply by her side, her right thigh bled profusely from a gash, and there was blood on her chin and chest from what appeared to be a copious nose bleed. Kush guessed that a sword hilt had been pummelled into her face, breaking her nose. Luv thought that her arm was dislocated and that the fact that her bow lay broken on the Y-juncture of the tree trunk, just above and behind her, indicated that she had been up there, firing arrows from her vantage point, when one of the riders had flung something, a spear perhaps, or even an axe, and in avoiding the weapon, she had lost the bow and dislocated her shoulder. She seemed otherwise all right, but her strength was clearly failing her and the sword work was tiring her out. The attackers knew this and were deliberately forcing her to keep her guard up and keep swinging this way then that, exhausting her good arm, until the moment came when she let the sword drop for an instant, and they could plunge through.

A few more minutes and that moment would have come and they would both have been orphaned; it was a miracle she was managing as well as she was at all. From the looks of it, she had killed seven attackers with the bow and another three with the sword already. It was unlikely she would take any more down, but just the fact that she had cost them so heavily had earned her a grudging respect from her opponents, which was why they had opted for this slower, but more effective method of tiring her out.

The dog stood with Maatr, barking and leaping about, trying to avoid the deadly sword points and blade edges, but more concerned with keeping the attackers at bay. From the looks of it, at least two of the fallen men had their throats torn out, which was obviously Sarama's handiwork. That itself was impressive. More impressive—and heartbreaking—were the many slashes, cuts and jabs on the ageing matriarch-dog's body, bleeding profusely from a dozen wounds, any of which were probably enough to end her days. The very fact that she continued to bark and snap so valiantly, with nothing to protect her from the lethal steel swinging to and fro, testified to her loyalty and courage.

Both boys felt lumps in their throats at the sight.

Time to end this now.

Luv whistled sharply.

Maatr was smart enough not to look in their direction. She had already seen them in her peripheral vision and restrained herself from showing any reaction. She continued swinging her blade to and fro in the defensive movement, blocking and parrying the regular thrusts and cuts of the three men. She had trained her boys herself in the art of seeing without turning to look. Taking one's eyes off one's opponent might be the last time one turned to look at anything, she had warned them.

The others were not as smart.

Two of the men turned at once, expecting deva knew what. The instant their faces looked towards Luv and Kush, their swords turning away from Maatr, both brothers loosed as one. The arrows sped as one bolt, striking at the exact same instant, producing a combined chunking sound as the points went home into the exposed sides of the necks of the men. Both men dropped their swords, clutched identically at their necks, and fell to the ground, quivering in their death throes. They resembled dancers in some grotesque palace performance, mirroring the same dance steps.

Sarama wheeled as well and saw them. She leaped up into the air, barking with renewed vigour and joy. She even performed a complete somersault, something they hadn't seen her do since they were five and she almost as young. She was that thrilled to see them.

Sadly, as Maatr had rightly warned, that was the worst thing any person could do when the enemy was at your throat. That somersault and the sight of her young masters were the last things the poor old dog ever did or saw.

The third soldier, nearest to Sarama, had probably been waiting for an opportunity. The raw wounds on his right arm and foot suggested that she had already mauled and savaged him more than once during the fight and he had been waiting to pay her back. He turned his sword, plunging it into the breastbone, and into the furry body beneath.

The boys gasped as they saw most of the length of the sword slide into their beloved Sarama's body.

She collapsed, falling with a sickening thump to the ground.

The attacker laughed with satisfaction as he yanked the blade out of the dying dog, pressing the heel of his boot against her snout to brace himself. Even in that moment of ultimate surrender, she still attempted to nip at his ankle, the heel snapping off her canine tooth as it came down hard on her face. Any sound she made was lost in the gruff laughter of the man. Blood spurted from her mouth, and she collapsed, lolled her tongue, and died.

The man's laughter was abruptly cut off by the sensation of a sword piercing his guts. Maatr plunged the blade in hard enough for the point to emerge from his back, very low. He bent over, grunting mournfully. She put her boot to his face, kicking him away and freeing her blade in the same motion. He toppled backwards and fell, not dying immediately but rolling in agony, beyond help and unable to rise and do more harm.

The instant he was clear of Maatr and Sarama's body, the boys put an arrow each into him. The bolts thumped home, stilling his groans. They wanted to keep shooting arrows into his body but knew better than to waste good bolts on a dead enemy.

Maatr looked over their shoulders, then around, checking the fallen attackers and keeping a wary eye out.

They ran to her. She stilled them with an upraised hand, still holding the sword, as she continued her check.

'The rest are dead or fled,' Kush said. 'Maatr, are you all right?'

She turned to them. 'Are you sure?'

Luv slung his bow over his shoulder. 'Maatr, are you wounded badly?'

'Are you sure?' she repeated urgently, still holding the sword up defensively.

Both boys nodded in unison, eyes wet with tears.

She looked around, then back at them, saw the tears in their eyes, and finally relented. 'All right,' she said wearily, 'all right.' She lowered the sword, pushing the point of the blade into the soft earth and resting on the hilt. 'If you're sure it's over, we're safe…?'

'The bearkillers are here, and Nakhudi has friends,' Luv offered, resisting the urge to run to her and hug her tightly.

'If you like, we can check for ourselves,' Kush offered, though he did not want to do anything of the sort; all he wanted to do was run to his mother and bury his face in her belly and cry.

She looked around one last time, leaning hard on the sword, her eyes filming over with exhaustion and relief. 'Good, good. I mean, no. Don't go to check. I'm sure Nakhudi will take care of it. And the bearkillers. Good.'

She looked at them and her expression changed. Both of them saw her eyes soften and dampen instantly, as she finally permitted herself to be just their mother again. 'I am so pleased to see you both, my sons. Alive and well. So pleased.'

She toppled backwards, fell on her rear end on the ground, then fell back unconscious. The sword remained stuck where she had put it, swaying slowly.

They rushed to her.

* * *

It was a very subdued and oddly mixed group that assembled in the ashram courtyard some time later. The corpses of the dead—friend and foe alike—had been carried over to the north clearing and lined up there, awaiting last rites and cremation. Maharishi Valmiki himself sat with his head and arm bound with whatever clean cloth was available. He had been caught unawares early in the attack and struck down hard by a mace blow when he emerged from his hut to see what the commotion was about. Somehow, he had survived with only a bruised skull and broken arm. He looked sombre and sad. Every face was grim, several still stained by tear streaks, some still in pain, with injuries minor or major, and more than a few were angry, even on the verge of rage. The double rows of little bodies were responsible for invoking that last emotion. Even the most peaceable of brahmins or sadhinis could not overcome the revulsion and rage that rose unbidden at the thought of those little innocents being hacked down so mercilessly. There had already been several tirades and angry words, and it had taken a while and some words from Maharishi Valmiki before they calmed down sufficiently to sit silently.

Sita herself felt that same rage, but coupled with it was a great sense of relief that her sons had survived. She knew that was only because of the training she had imparted unto them, and the fortuitous fact that they had not been present at the time of the attack, so were not caught unawares in the thick of the melee. But had the bearkillers not been alerted to the approach of the attackers by the assault on Nakhudi's village earlier, and had Nakhudi herself not arrived when she had, with a whole company of ageing, but nevertheless fit and armed, ex-soldiers, then the entire ashram would certainly have been wiped out, down to the last living creature. One attacker had been about to start killing the milch cows when Captain Bejoo and his men came upon him and his companions—had they come even moments later, the cows would have been hacked down where they stood. And the children! Oh, the children. What monsters could do such things?

She forced her own emotions under control and listened as Maharishi Valmiki began to speak. The guru sat on the raised mud stoop of his own hut, as he did everyday during his daily pravachan. But never before had he addressed such a motley gathering: before him the remnant ashram inhabitants sat cross-legged as they always did, barely two dozen-odd brahmins and sadhinis who had survived from almost twice that number, most of them injured physically, every last one grievously soul-struck and psychologically shocked. To his right sat the bearkillers, crouched down on their haunches, weapons laid behind them out of consideration for the Maharishi, yet close enough at hand just in case. They had lost only two of their number and suffered a few minor injuries, while causing over a dozen casualties. To the guru's left sat Bejoo and the retired PFs. They had suffered no losses at all, just three minor injuries. By the time they had appeared on the scene, the attackers had already been in retreat and apart from the attempted cow-killer and three or four of his associates, they had caused no further casualties in the enemy ranks either. Nakhudi, Luv, and Kush sat close beside her.

She listened with only half her mind as the guru spoke deep glowing words of reassurance, drawing on his deep knowledge of the Vedas, the sacred repository of all knowledge in the mortal world, and providing explanations that threw light on the events of the day.

They were wonderful, healing words and she felt their efficacy in calming her spirit and acting as a balm to her emotional wounds. But she could not help thinking through the details and reasons of today's assault.

In all, about forty of the attackers had died during the ashram attack and its aftermath, almost half of that number killed by Sita herself and her sons. That was an inherent advantage of arrowcraft, of course, but it was more than that. It was the difference between armed and trained kshatriyas in a state of preparedness and innocent unarmed brahmins caught unawares. Sita had long since thought that if only she and a few of the other acolytes could form a permanent sentry watch of the ashram, they could have ensured a better defence in the event of such an attack. But Maharishi Valmiki had forbidden that outright each time she suggested it, and moreover, while many ashrams encouraged the bearing of weapons and even the use of them in training on a daily basis, Valmiki Ashram emphasised ahimsa, peaceful existence, as a way of life. Even the young brahmacharyas who trained in warcraft were only permitted to use wooden training weapons—their final year of weapons training was conducted at Vashishta Ashram north of Ayodhya. While many maharishis spoke of non-violence and peaceful co-existence fervently, Valmiki made it an integral aspect of everyday living.

But that was not the reason this had happened. Living in peace was not the reason for so many having died violently today. Armed mercenaries as well-equipped, trained and experienced as these had been did not simply come rampaging through ashrams. Rakshasas had once attacked outposts, ashrams and travellers in just such vicious fashion, and there was no doubt that these men had behaved like rakshasas in their brutal assault. But rakshasas attacked because their kind and mortalkind were engaged in an internecine struggle for dominance of the mortal realm. These mercenaries had no racial or species survival motivation for their actions. They were quite obviously following orders and getting paid exceedingly well for doing so. Purses had been found on every single one, identical purses filled with goldcoins. The coin was Ayodhyan, struck with the king's seal, no less. And the number had been the same in every case: thirty gold coins. A small fortune, sufficient to enable each one of them to live comfortably for years, buy his way into a good position at any Arya court, or provide capital to set up his own trade or business. Retirement funds. That explained the brutal vigour with which they had pursued their mission. But it didn't explain why the persons who had paid them had ordered them to attack these particular targets. It was possible that even they did not know or care. Their job was to ride here and kill everyone, and they had tried to do that as best and as quickly as possible.

She also thought that they were not likely to return. The losses they had suffered had been considerable, almost half of their total number. They could not have expected such heavy casualties on such a mission. It must have come as a great shock to those who survived and got away. They would likely not care to return to their employers, who might well get upset with them for having left any survivors, and might even demand that they return forthwith and complete their given task. *Fulfil your dharma, kshatriya,* as the phrase went. Which they would not want to do, when faced with such superior opposition. So they would probably just ride out and keep riding and enjoy their ill-gotten gains. She understood their type well enough to be certain that was what they would do.

Which meant the ashram was safe enough. For now.

But sooner or later, the people who had sent this attack force here would learn of their survival. And once they learned that some of them still lived, they would send more mercenaries. Again. And again. Until they accomplished their task.

They must act before that happened.

Her mind made up, she waited for a suitable break in the pravachan, then stood and waited until Maharishi Valmiki acknowledged her.

He did so very soon. His drawn face and deeply set eyes reflected his own inner sorrow as he nodded, permitting her to speak.

'Gurudev,' she said in a voice loud enough to be heard across the courtyard, yet sombrely enough to reflect the grim mood of the occasion, 'A terrible thing has happened here today. Someone from Ayodhya has ordered our extermination.'

Valmiki sighed and looked down for a moment, as if she had said the very thing he had been dreading she would say. 'It is a terrible thing indeed. Yet we cannot know who caused it or what their reasons were. Let us not make hasty assumptions.'

She shook her head, disagreeing gently but firmly. 'Not assumptions, Gurudev. Conclusions. The evidence we have found points to only one source for this heinous assault. Ayodhya.'

There were murmurs of agreement from both sides, as bearkillers and veterans agreed alike with her conclusion. Even the wan and pale ashramites listened with morbid interest. She saw her sons exchange a glance and saw that Nakhudi observed that glance with a peculiar expression, and felt her heart ache with a familiar pain. *And I even know his name but cannot speak it aloud, for he is the father of my children.*

'Even if we cannot name the ultimate perpetrator responsible, there is no doubt about Ayodhya's involvement.' She held her hand down to Nakhudi who understood what she meant and passed up one of the purses to her. Sita held it up, removing a coin and holding it up so it caught the evening light and gleamed coldly, viciously. 'This is the king's seal. These coin purses were not given to ordinary men for any ordinary task. These were men personally hired and instructed by the king himself or someone close to him. Former Vajra Captain Bejoo can confirm this. He received similar purses from the late Maharaja Dasaratha during his reign and the present liege, King Rama Chandra.'

She held a hand out in Bejoo's direction, the same hand that held the purse. The other hand had been reset by Nakhudi but still ached terribly and would be unusable for a few days. Bejoo stood and looked around, nodding sadly, almost shamefully.

'It is true. That is a maharaja's purse, given only to those following his explicit orders on private missions. These men were working for none other than the king of Ayodhya.'

This provoked an outburst of murmurs which Sita quelled with another gesture.

'Given this evidence, I say we act at once and ensure that such an attack does not happen again.'

Many heads bobbed, nodding in agreement. But there was one whose opinion counted more than the others. She turned to look at Maharishi Valmiki, joining her hands together in supplication. It hurt to move the injured hand even by that much but she held the namaskaram out of respect for her guru and protector for all these years.

'Gurudev,' she said. 'We ask your aashirwaad to go forth and attempt to resolve this situation. Pray, grant us your sacred blessings that we may ensure the survival of the inhabitants of this ashram and the continuance of your great work here.'

Maharishi Valmiki looked at her with troubled dark eyes. His once-jet black beard sprouted several curls of white and his face was lined and drawn with the pain of the day's events.

'Lady Vedavati,' he said, 'You feel this is our only recourse? Cannot we simply put this incident behind us and continue with our lives as before?'

She shook her head slowly, using her good arm to point north, towards the northern clearing, where all the bodies lay awaiting their final unction. 'Can we? Truly?'

He lowered his head, acknowledging the truth of what she said. Several heads bowed with his as well, sharing his sorrow. Sita felt his pain at seeing this day come to pass and resented the man who had brutalised the peaceful environment of the Maharishi's ashram and brought things to such a pass.

Yet she knew that they must act, if only to survive. And taking action meant doing whatever was necessary.

What other choice do we have now?

What choice has Rama left us?

TEN

Shatrughan and Bharat rode silently at the head of the long column. Glancing back, it seemed as if the line went on forever, to the horizon and beyond, endlessly. *And these are only our own forces. The vanar armies are on a separate route, moving across woodland and hinterland, eastwards.* The thought of an army of this size—two armies, to be precise—was mind-numbing. This was no Ashwamedha yajna, it was a campaign of empirical conquest and expansion. And every maharaja, raja, clan chief, tribe chief, and grama chief across Aryavarta would see it as such.

Bharat could not believe that such a day could come to pass when Ayodhya, the great emblem of democracy and kingly virtue, would send forth an army to conquer its own neighbours, allies and friends in this manner. There was nothing this yajna would achieve that could not be achieved simply by calling a Grand Council, a Maha-Sabha of all the leaders of all the forces that governed the diverse nations and communities of the sub-continent and outlands.

Such a Maha-Sabha had been called before, by the great Manu when he proposed a uniform code of kshatriya conduct and recommended a similar code be drawn up by the heads of each varna and adhered to throughout the civilised world. Many other great things had been proposed and ratified at that same Maha-sabha. The shelves in the king's Library of Ayodhya were heavy with the scroll records of its achievements. Guru Vashishta had made them spend several dusty days studying the original scrolls themselves as young men, to see for themselves what their ancestors had wrought through diplomacy, wisdom and through Arya dharma—the noblest form of dharma possible.

And today, what good were all the scrolls in that great library, all those annals, all those treaties and writs and declarations and codes and lawbooks? In one fell swoop, the war-hawks had driven Rama to build an army the likes of which had never even been imagined before and which was certainly not required, and his hawkish advisors and ministers had convinced him to send forth the army on this travesty of a ritual. There was no need for an Ashwamedha yajna. Ayodhya was already acknowledged as the supreme power in the Arya world. A king did not need a ceremony to remind people that he was still king. And even if such a ceremony was called for, it certainly did not require the sending forth of an armed force of this strength and magnitude to ensure that nobody disagreed with the king's authority. Only a tyrant deployed such an iron hand. A great king needed only a firm voice to command obedience.

Bharat knew Rama was a great king. Ram Rajya, his reign was rightly called. And he had done a great deal of good for the kingdom and the capital city. But at what cost? Dharma, his catchphrase, his unofficial slogan, his motto for all occasions, was all well and good. But this was not dharma, this was beyond dharma or anything akin to it. This was simply war-mongering. And he did not believe Rama was a war-monger. As Dasaratha's son, as the heir to the sunwood throne, protector of the Arya world and inheritor of the burden of responsibility of caring for the welfare of the civilised world, he knew better. But those years in exile, the things he had undergone, the atrocities and wars and struggles, perhaps they had changed Rama more deeply than even he, Bharat, had suspected at first.

Or perhaps it was the loss of Sita.

Yes.

That was what his heart believed. The true cause at the centre of Rama's change of personality and outlook.

Banishing Sita had altered Rama forever. From within and without. He was no longer the man who had left for exile as a young married prince in love with his new bride, nor was he the man who had returned from that long and punishing exile, marked by the scars of a thousand violent encounters and a terrible war. This man was someone else. Someone Bharat did not entirely understand. All he knew was that the day Rama had banished Sita, he had begun to change. And today, this travesty that was being passed off as a yajna—this was only the culmination of that long process of change.

The sound of a conch shell trumpet startled him out of his reverie. He looked up, trying to discern the source of the alarm.

Shatrughan pointed up ahead, over the hill that obscured their view. 'Up ahead from the front of the line. That sounds like...' He broke off, glancing at Bharat with a grim expression. 'I hope it isn't what I think it is.'

Bharat cursed softly under his breath. 'Let's go.'

They broke away from their line and rode along the shoulder of the raj-marg. The lines of foot-soldiers, marching six-abreast in full battle kit, blurred past as they broke into a full-out gallop. The conch shell alarm was taken up by their own trumpeter, followed thereafter by the one at the head of the next column and so on down the line. With the sheer number of columns and regiments in the procession, he thought it would probably take an hour or more for the alarm to finally reach Rama himself, for based on the distance Shatrughan and he had come and their relative position to the royal regiment, Rama was probably only just departing the First Gate now, on the evening of the day the great yajna had begun.

They crested the hill and saw that it was indeed what they had feared. From the ranks of cavalry riding at a brisk canter a yojana ahead—they could make this out from the shape and movement of the dust cloud raised by the horses—they estimated that the incident had occurred just west of the Videha border. Bharat felt a surge of alarm mixed with uncertain emotions. Surely Videhans were not involved! He couldn't bear to even think of the possibility of going to war against his own in-laws! What would Mandavi think? And Taksha and Pushkala were in Mithila as well, along with their mother, for one of their grandfather's frequent peace ceremonies. The thought of this mighty force going up against the voluntary reserve militia of Videha made his blood run cold.

'Come on,' he said grimly, spurring his horse downhill. Shatrughan needed no urging; the same thoughts were surely passing through his mind as well. After all, they had the same in-laws.

* * *

Lakshman pointed an accusing finger at the man at the head of the mercenary force. 'What do you mean, someone took the horse? The only ones I see here are you fellows!'

The man stared arrogantly back at Lakshman. He and the sixty-odd soldiers behind him were all mounted on handsome horses, fully armoured and well-equipped. While Lakshman didn't recognise him or any of the men he commanded, he recognised the equipment well enough. It was king's issue, given out only to those on missions for the maharaja himself. *I mean missions for the samrat,* he thought acidly. That and the fact that the man had known the proper Sanskrit codes that pronounced him as one of their own was scant reassurance to him. His gut told him something was wrong and he trusted his gut over any number of codes or authorisations.

For one thing, he knew that these men had no business being here. Nobody was supposed to be ahead of the sacred stallion. Sumantra and he were the frontrunners, the only ones permitted to watch the animal from close quarters. Everyone else was expected to follow.

Yet these men had appeared from nowhere, cutting across his and Sumantra's path, almost startling the horses drawing the old prime minister's chariot, and had just made the astonishing claim that the horse had been taken.

How? When?

Only moments before, Lakshman had been watching the rear end of the horse with his own eyes. Tail twitching rhythmically, the beast had been cantering leisurely along the wooded path, heading deeper into the woods and farther away from any recognised human settlement, which suited him perfectly.

Then, suddenly something had startled the beast and he had seen it lurch, whinny in panic, then break into a gallop, racing off the path and into the woods. He had coaxed his horse to speed up and was about to follow the sacred stallion when suddenly, this band of armed horsemen had burst out of the woods, blocking his way effectively and shouting that the royal horse had been captured and a challenge issued. He had ordered them out of the way so he could follow the horse. He was certain that it could not possibly have been taken in the few moments since he had seen it bolt into the woods, and even if it had, how could these men have seen that happen, and ridden out to intercept him, all within a moment or two? It was impossible. Yet this man provided the pre-arranged code which identified him as one of the maharaja's regiment, and insisted on this absurd claim.

'We are the emperor's men,' said the man leading the band. 'It is our sworn duty to protect and serve our liege and his interests. We tell you, the horse has been taken and the challenge issued. Sound the alarm, ex-pradhan mantri. You know the protocol.'

Lakshman had glanced back at Sumantra. The old man's bushy brows were knitted together suspiciously as he stared at the newcomer.

'Do as you are told, oldun,' said the man harshly. 'Or you will be reported to Lord Bhadra and Pradhan Mantri Jabali and dealt with severely!'

Sumantra's eyes narrowed and he held the man's gaze for a moment. 'I will issue the alarm, not because I fear reprimand, but because you are right, it is the protocol.' To Lakshman he said in a kinder, almost apologetic tone, 'If we lose sight of the stallion for even as long as this much time, it is our duty to sound the alarm and inform the king.'

'Emperor,' the horseman corrected harshly.

Sumantra glared at him, but said nothing. Instead, he picked up a red flag on a pole from the floor of the chariot, hefted it up as high as he could manage and waved it to and fro several times until it was seen by the next contingent behind them. The flagman of that contingent responded by waving a similar flag back at him, then turned and instructed the trumpeter beside him on that chariot. The man immediately took up his conch shell trumpet and sounded the clear booming tones that carried across the landscape loudly enough to be heard miles behind. The instant his conch shell fell silent, the next one in the procession a mile or so behind them sounded, and in this manner the alarm was taken up and followed down the line, all the way back to Ayodhya where it would be heard finally by the king. *Sorry…emperor.*

Lakshman pushed his horse a yard forward, taking it almost snout to snout with the newcomer's horse. 'What name do you go by, soldier?' he asked roughly.

'Why?' asked the man with a sly grin. 'Do you wish to suggest me for a commendation?'

Lakshman resisted the urge to draw his sword and slice the insolent grin off the man's face. Instead, he said, 'Your name.'

The man shrugged. 'Aarohan.'

Lakshman stared at him a moment longer, then snapped his reins, urging his horse forward. He rode straight at the rest of the gang milling about, blocking his path. He saw their eyes flick to their leader, over his shoulder, as he approached. He also saw several of them reach for the hilts of their swords and other weapons, as if prepared to fight him rather than let him pass.

He did not turn to look back, but from the relaxing of their expressions and the fact that they moved their horses aside with brisk tugs of their reins, he understood that they had asked and received permission visually from their leader to let him pass.

That galled him no end. What right did they have to decide whether or not he passed! Who were these men anyway and why were they permitted—or ordered, as they claimed—to ride ahead of the horse itself in violation of the ritual's rules? And what was this game they were playing? Besides, he could see bloodstains, tears and rents, and other indications that this group had been in a fight very recently. What did that mean? The horse had been in his view until only moments ago. There had been nobody to fight. So whom had these men been fighting and where and why?

He had no answers to these questions, and it was possible they did not matter. His only concern right now was the horse and what had happened to it. That was his sole responsibility. He would never have lost sight of it had these buffoons not come riding out and blocked his path as they had done—quite deliberately, he knew, although he also knew that it would not sound logical were he to explain the same to Rama or to anyone else, because they would in turn claim that they had only been riding to warn him.

But he knew damn well the horse had not been taken or challenged until they had appeared.

And he would prove that in another moment or two, once he followed its trail and found it.

He rode past the last of the men, clearly nursing a broken or badly injured arm in a makeshift sling, and then went past them and into the forest, praying he could pick up the trail of the horse and locate it before it grew too dark to read signs. He didn't think it would be possible. Already, the sun was low in the western sky and long shadows were drawing across the forest. And while the men might be louts and arrogant asses, he did not think they were lying altogether. Someone must have taken the horse, even if that someone turned out to be one of Aarohan's own men or associates.

The question was why.

He intended to find that out.

* * *

Shatrughan exclaimed in a low voice. Bharat and he were galloping down the raj-marg, just passing the head of the first column. The officers saluted both of them as they rode past. Bharat didn't waste time saluting or slowing. He had seen the same thing Shatrughan had and didn't like the looks of it.

They were still a good four or five hundred yards from the frontrunner's chariot. He knew that was manned by the former pradhan mantri Sumantra, with Lakshman riding alongside on point to keep a watch for any challengers or threats to the sacred horse. That was the custom. Strictly speaking, the king or chieftain for whose good fortunes the yajna was being performed usually rode the chariot, with the queen's foremost champion riding alongside as protection. But since Rama was now an emperor and presumably too important to be riding a bumpy old single chariot by himself, he had delegated the task to Sumantra. Although why an ex-prime minister should be handling the chore rather than the incumbent prime minister, Jabali, who at least filled an official capacity in the government of the nation, Bharat could not fathom. Like most of Rama's operations and decisions, his motives were inscrutable to all but the most intimate of his advisors. For that matter, Bhadra, as the declared champion at the last mela, ought to be the one riding alongside the chariot, but Bhadra being Bhadra, was way back there with Rama.

And now, if he was seeing correctly ahead, Bharat thought he might guess at the reason why protocol had been conveniently sidestepped.

He saw what looked like a violent scuffle up ahead. A band of armoured and heavily armed horseriders—the setting sun flashed off their armour and reflected off their weapons as they swung them— seemed to be attacking a lone man in the frontrunner chariot. That would be Sumantra. Where was Lakshman then? Bharat had no idea. But he would certainly find out very quickly. He didn't know who those men were or why they were attacking the ageing pradhan mantri who had been acknowledged as one of the finest diplomats ever to grace Arya governance, and one of the greatest peacekeepers as well, but he knew that it could not be because Sumantra had wanted or invited violence.

If Sumantra was engaged in a violent clash with an entire company of armed cavalry as it seemed, then the horsemen were the ones attacking without provocation.

He urged his horse to gallop faster, pushing the mare to her limit. He was glad that protocol required at least a third of the marg to be kept clear for riders and chariots on urgent missions to be able to move quickly, and that his ancestors had built such fine kings-roads and maintained them so well all these centuries.

Even so, all that fine planning and maintenance and a powerful Bhoja mare between his legs could not carry him to the aid of Sumantra in time.

He was still a hundred yards away, Shatrughan neck to neck with him, when they saw one of the horsemen ride around the chariot and throw a pike at Sumantra's back. The pike struck home—and stuck. The old man twisted, freezing in mid-air, and that pause was all his attackers needed—they moved in, chopping and hacking and pounding at will, five or six of them at once, the cowards, and even as Bharat came within shouting distance, he saw the old diplomat fall upon the railing of his own chariot, collapsing with a sickening finality.

'COWARDS! Leave him be!' Bharat roared, feeling the frustration and impotence of the past several days explode in a burst of righteous rage.

Beside him, Shatrughan had unslung his bow and now loosed three arrows in quick succession. All three found their mark in the torso and neck of the coward who had struck at Sumantra from behind. The man clutched at his throat as he fell off his horse, his death rattle audible even as the brothers bore down on the armed murderers. The other men continued to hack and poke at Sumantra with their weapons.

'COWARDS!' Bharat shouted.

At the sound of his voice, they broke away from the chariot, shot nervous glances back at the approaching horses, and spurred their own mounts into a fitful gallop, riding for the treeline.

'STAND AND FIGHT, YOU CRAVEN!' Bharat yelled.

But the horsemen had the advantage of being close to one of the densest forests in all Aryavarta, the fabled Southwoods. Even as Bharat and Shatrughan came abreast of the chariot, the horsemen were disappearing into the shadowy depths of the forest.

Bharat would have ridden past the chariot and given chase, but he saw Sumantra move and slowed his horse to a reluctant halt.

'Go on!' Bharat yelled at Shatrughan, who thundered past him, loosing arrows as he went. 'I'll catch up. Don't let them get away!'

He paused beside Sumantra, his horse snorting and shaking her head. Bharat reached out and grasped hold of the old statesman's hand. He was sickened by the number of wounds on the man's torso, head and neck. *The butchers! What kind of soldiers were these to attack a solitary old man?*

'Who were they?' he asked, squeezing Sumantra's hand gently.

Sumantra coughed up a mouthful of blood, spitting it over the side of the chariot. His eyes were rheumy and filled with blood streaming down from a gash on his skull. An axe wound. He kept blinking, but could not see Bharat. Still, he recognised his voice.

'Yuvraj Bharat,' he said, as he had said so many thousands of times before, through Bharat's growing years when he had been both father's friend and father figure to all four brothers.

'Treachery within…' Sumantra said, then coughed up a burst of blood, much of which spattered on Bharat's tunic.

Bharat held on to the old man's hand without flinching or turning away: he had seen his share of blood spilled, and had spilled his share as well. He listened and waited for more, but the wrinkled hand had lost all life and the eyes had shut, sticky with blood, and the old balding head full of white hair dyed crimson had fallen forward on the railing of the chariot, lifeless.

ELEVEN

Nakhudi held up her hand, cocking her head. Maatr passed on the instruction, emphasising it with a downward chop of her hand.

At once, all those following froze in place. Nakhudi had spent several minutes reminding the group that she would be in charge and they must follow her lead in all actions. The twins knew that even though she had seemed to say this to the entire group, it was actually the two of them she was addressing. They had sighed impatiently and nodded reluctantly. And had almost immediately after regretted doing so, because Nakhudi set such a slow pace. But, they had agreed, and while they sometimes did things that displeased Nakhudi, Maatr, or even Guru Valmiki on occasion, they never blatantly disregarded or disobeyed a direct instruction. It just so happened that they seemed to always find some loophole in interpreting it, so they took advantage of that!

Right now, though, with Nakhudi leading the way, and Maatr on the second point just behind Nakhudi, they could hardly just race ahead, even though they knew they could make five times the pace she was making. Besides, that old fogey Bejoo and the rest of the retired soldiers were right behind them, and despite their age, they were pretty sharp and savvy; so Luv and Kush were behaving themselves and trotting respectfully behind Nakhudi and Maatr as instructed.

There was a grim mood upon the group. The massacre at the ashram and the village had shaken everybody. The surviving rishis and brahmins of the ashram had been the worst affected, of course, being men and women of Vedic learning and quiet meditation all their lives. The kshatriyas had recovered sooner, but were no less injured emotionally by the experience. Such things were not supposed to happen. Not in the reign of the great Rama Chandra of Ayodhya. Then again, as Luv and Kush knew quite well because of their daily recitation lessons taught by Gurudev himself, Rama Chandra was not entirely the great exalted being that he was often made out to be; he had feet of clay that were painfully brittle. The long epic poem that had formed the main body of their instruction by the Maharishi ever since they were old enough to recite and memorise long Sanskrit passages, told a quite unflattering version of the itihasa of the great king of Ayodhya's life and adventures. Even the name seemed ironic to them now: Rama-yana, literally, 'the travels of Rama'.

Well, it seemed that the great Rama was on the move once again, and the slaughter had resumed. Why was it, they wondered—and had often asked Gurudev after their daily rote recitation lessons—that Rama's tale was so replete with blood-letting and violence? Maharishi Valmiki had been silent for a moment, as he almost always was after being asked a question, then he had said that they must examine the poem he had composed and which they now knew well enough to recite by heart from start to finish, for themselves, and come to their own conclusions. It was important, he added, that one consider the actual verses and interpret them oneself, without an intermediary involved, even one as learned as himself, the creator of the work! There might be commentaries written about his Rama-yana in ages to come, and perhaps once the wisdom of Treta Yuga dimmed to give way to the lesser self-awareness and thirst for knowledge of later yugas, people would pay less attention to the original shlokas he had composed and give more weightage to its recensions, retellings, and commentaries instead, but for now, there was only the original text itself, and it would have to suffice.

'A life must speak for itself, on its own terms, in its own words,' he had said gravely, looking at each one of them in turn with that penetrating yet deeply empathetic and benign gaze he had, making each of them feel as if he could see right through to the depths of their souls. 'It is a mistake to listen to interpretations and versions of any fact and assume that they too are fact. Only truth itself is truth. Anything that refers, references, or even repeats it, is but a version. For no repetition can be perfect and exact in every detail. A man is a man. A portrait of a man, no matter how accurate, is not the man himself, merely a portrait. Similarly, a story of a man, merely a story. My Ramayana is already a version of itihasa, not itihasa itself. To know that truth, one would have to live and observe those events oneself—not merely as a bystander, or even a participant—but as Rama himself! Until you can walk in his paduka and be Rama, you can never truly know what he was and why he did what he did, you can only offer individual interpretations—and when it comes to interpretations, each one is as valid as any other. So be careful of judging him. For by doing so, you are judging only an ephemeron.'

He had gestured to the moths flying around the oil lamp that hung from the pole of the stoop. 'Like an insect that lives only a short time, any poem, portrait or description of a man is simply a moth. Hold it close to the agni of truth and that version burns to ash and disappears. Only the flame itself is truth. And who can enter into the heart of agni and live to report that truth?'

Now, they each wondered grimly if Rama Chandra had indeed sent those vicious murderers to massacre their friends and neighbours so brutally. If they could not judge his past itihasa, they could certainly judge his present actions. They dearly wished to know how a man hailed by the world as the king of dharma could be responsible for such undharmic deeds. This was not a debatable act such as the killing of Vali or the invasion of Lanka, both of which were contentious, but justifiable in some way. This was pure and simple murder of innocents without cause, provocation or justification. Surely Rama could not be so hypocritical to have sent those men himself to do this unforgivable deed? There must be a better explanation—and as shishyas of the great Maharishi Valmiki, they would suspend judgement until they knew what that explanation might be. But it had better come soon and it had better clear all their doubts.

They waited impatiently, but with absolute discipline as Nakhudi and Maatr went up ahead to investigate something.

Finally, Luv sighed. Kush glanced at him, reading him as easily as he could read the thoughts of his own mind.

Luv looked at him in a certain way. To anyone watching the twins, it would have seemed just a look, with no particular meaning or inflection. But to Kush, it spoke as eloquently as words themselves.

Luv was asking him if they should go forward just a bit, to take a small peek.

Kush looked back at him with the faintest twinkle in his eyes. Again, that careful observer might not have seen any change of expression in the boy's face, but somehow, Kush conveyed his response:

Yes!

Moving as one, both twins left their place behind a papaya tree and slipped ahead, following the direction their mother and Nakhudi had taken.

* * *

Bejoo watched the boys go and knew they ought to be waiting patiently until Nakhudi or Vedavati returned and gave the order to push forward again. But he didn't judge them. He had no problem following Nakhudi's lead, she was as effective a leader as many fine commanders he had served under, and far better than many juniors he himself had commanded. But this was not a military operation, fought under the kshatriya code and in the usual battle circumstances. This was something else altogether; he did not know what it was exactly and that troubled him. It troubled him more than the actual massacre. Death and slaughter disturbed him as much as it did the peaceful denizens of Valmiki Ashram, but unlike them, he could think and act beyond the shock of those events. That was his job, and the essence of his varna. It was the reason why varna existed in the first place: so that enough individuals in any Arya community or kingdom were capable of doing their vital given task even under the most challenging circumstances and conditions. Such as a soldier capable of withstanding the horrors of violence and continuing to fulfil his dharma as a warrior. Or a house builder capable of building houses even while a war raged, because that was his dharma. Bejoo's life had prepared him for violence and for acting despite the net of confusion and madness that violence inevitably cast upon those affected by it. But the massacre in the forest had shaken even that sense of kshatriya fortitude, not because of the horror of the deaths, for he had seen far worse, but because of the possibility that the marauders might have been on a king's mission, as the discovery of the purses and their accoutrements seemed to prove. He was determined to find out the truth behind the attacks. And like the boys, he was as impatient to keep moving and get answers quickly.

He was also troubled by Nakhudi and Lady Vedavati taking so long. A moment or two to check if someone lurked ahead—that was fine. But they had been absent several moments and that was not fine.

As the leader of his company, he decided that the prolonged absence of his commanding officer entitled him to disregard that commander's last order and move ahead.

He raised his hand, gesturing forward, and began moving ahead himself. The PFs would follow like shadows.

He was not surprised to see that the twins were already out of sight and hearing. Those two boys moved like arrows on a backwind. He only hoped that their very speed would not propel them into the arms of trouble too quickly.

* * *

Sita knew something was wrong the instant she saw the horse. It was a magnificent black stallion, a great one, and it was adorned with the marks and signs of a yajna. This was no ordinary horse and it was not here by accident. She was well aware of the Ashwamedha ceremony being performed by Rama and the epic army accompanying the horse on what was clearly a campaign of empirical conquest and expansion. Seeing this stallion, she knew at once that this was the horse being used in the sacrifice.

But what is it doing here? And why is it unaccompanied?

The first question could be answered easily: the horse could have wandered into this neck of the woods. It was only a stone's throw from the raj-marg after all, which was why Nakhudi and she had been heading this way, the quicker to reach their destination.

But the second question was a disturbing one. It was not conceivable that the horse could be allowed to stray on its own into the woods, out of sight of its followers. That defeated the whole purpose of the Ashwamedha yajna. It was imperative to follow the horse closely and watch where it went at all times.

She exchanged a glance with Nakhudi who shook her head doubtfully. This was not right.

They watched the horse for a few more moments. It was wandering aimlessly, nuzzling a patch of grass here, then snorting and moving on to find a more appetising patch elsewhere. It came towards Sita and she blanched, backing away to keep a distance. Even being seen near the horse could be misconstrued. Her heart beat faster as she looked over the animal's rump. But there was nobody there, nobody in sight, just the forest. She listened and heard bird sounds from about a mile or two further up, just about where the raj-marg ought to pass by this section of the forest. This part of the woods was dead silent, which meant there were no other intruders here.

Even so, she kept her distance from the beast. It flicked its ears to and fro as his keen senses smelled her out and Nakhudi too, but as they did not move or do anything that seemed alarming, he continued around the shrubbery behind which they crouched, trotting slowly past them, moving deeper into the forest.

Nakhudi came closer to whisper to her, 'You know what that is?'

Sita nodded grimly. 'It's no coincidence.'

'No, it isn't. I don't like the smell of this.'

'What should we do?' Sita asked. 'If we let it stray further that way, sooner or later they will follow.' She jerked her head backwards to indicate the direction the horse was heading. Valmiki Ashram lay that way.

Nakhudi rubbed her forehead slowly, as she often did when she was trying to think her way through an especially knotty dilemma. 'We cannot stop it. Even touching it or being seen near it might be misunderstood.' She glanced in the direction of the raj-marg with uncharacteristic anxiety. 'We should not even be this close to it.'

'But what else can we do?' Sita asked.

Nakhudi thought for a moment. 'Scare it away.'

'What?'

'Startle it into turning tail and heading back the way it came. And we should do it quickly, before the Ayodhyans come as they surely will.'

Sita nodded approvingly. 'Very nice. After all, it is a horse.'

Nakhudi nodded. 'Let's go get it before it loses itself in the woods.'

They turned and were about to start back when suddenly the sound of neighing came to them clearly.

They exchanged a startled glance. Then started running.

* * *

Luv grasped the mane of the stallion and patted his side reassuringly. 'Easy there, big fellow. We won't harm you. We're just wondering what a fine beast like you is doing here in these forests!'

'He's a beautiful horse, isn't he?' Kush said, patting the horse's rump and admiring the sleek muscles beneath the glossy coat. 'I've never seen anything like him before.'

The horse snickered again nervously, but didn't rear up or neigh as loudly as it had when the boys came sprinting up and startled it. He even let Luv put his hand around his neck and bury his face in his soft, furry side.

'Maybe we can keep him for ourselves,' Luv asked eagerly. 'We'll ask Maatr.'

'She'll say no,' Kush grumbled. 'Look at those marks. He must be part of some kind of yajna or something.'

'So? Maybe Gurudev can complete the yajna and we can keep him afterwards.'

Kush shrugged doubtfully, stroking the horse's side. 'I don't know. Let's ask Maatr first and see.'

The stallion settled down, whinnying one last time but very half-heartedly, as if reminding them that he could bolt at any time. He seemed to be enjoying the attention lavished on him by the twins and stood still as they massaged and rubbed and generally fussed over him.

'Luv! Kush!'

Maatr's voice was distinctive even from a distance.

Both brothers exchanged a wearily knowing look. 'Uh oh,' said Luv. 'Here she comes.'

'I told you!' Kush said. 'Let's go back to our position, and pretend we never moved an inch. It worked that last time.'

Luv shook his head. 'No, maybe she's not upset with us. Maybe she's in trouble and needs our help.'

Kush shrugged, but didn't argue.

A few moments later, Maatr came sprinting through the woods, Nakhudi close behind. They stopped dead in their tracks when they saw the horse. Maatr's eyes grew big and round and she stared in horror at her sons.

'Boys,' she said in an exaggerated whisper. 'Get away from that horse.'

'He was just wandering around on his own in the woods,' Luv said. 'Can we keep him? Please, Maatr!'

'Luv! Kush! Both of you! Move away from the horse at once. Do as I say!'

They sighed and released the horse. They took several steps away, shoulders slumped in a defeated gesture.

They stopped and turned around.

Maatr was still staring at them, only this time her hand was clapped across her mouth in an expression of abject dismay. 'No!' she said. 'No!' Luv felt a rush of warm air on his left shoulder and frowned.

Kush turned to see the horse right behind them. He nuzzled Kush's chin affectionately. His bright black eyes glittered mischievously beneath his fringe of coal-black mane. He snickered softly.

'Look! He likes us, Maatr!'

'He wants to be our friend,' Luv added. 'Please, can we keep him?'

Nakhudi came towards them, clapping her hands loudly. 'Shoo!' she said, waving urgently at the horse. 'Get away, you! Go from here! Leave us!'

The stallion snorted and stepped backwards in dismay, upset by Nakhudi's voice and tone and the sound of her clapping.

Luv held the horse's mane, comforting him. Kush shot Nakhudi a dirty look. 'You're scaring him!' he said.

'Boys!' Maatr said, even more urgently. 'I said get away from that horse! Leave him! Right now!'

Nakhudi waved her arms vigorously before the stallion, startling him into rearing back.

Instinctively, Kush caught hold of his mane and tried to calm him down.

'GO AWAY!' Nakhudi shouted. 'Get lost!'

At that moment, Bejoo and the PF company came running up, stopping short at the sight of the Ashwamedha horse, and Luv and Kush holding on to him even as Nakhudi and Sita tried to shoo him away.

'Jai Shri Shaneshwara aid us in our moment of need,' Bejoo said mechanically, the colour draining from his face as he read the situation.

'Boys!' Maatr said loudly, 'please leave that horse! We're not supposed to touch him!'

Luv and Kush released the horse's mane reluctantly, obeying their mother's instructions. But the stallion seemed to think they were his protectors and stayed beside them, following even when they tried to move away. Or perhaps he was only trying to get away from the large woman who was yelling and waving her arms at him violently.

'GO!' Nakhudi shouted. 'Go before you get us all into trouble, you stupid horse!'

Just then birds began to call out and fly from the treetops above and the familiar rumbling sounds of horses approaching became audible to all present.

Luv and Kush saw their Maatr turn and stare at Nakhudi with a look of abject terror.

'Too late,' their mother said hoarsely. 'Trouble has arrived.'

TWELVE

Fourteen years of forest warfare had made Lakshman an expert in reading signs and tracks. He knew at once that the gang of riders he had met on the raj-marg had come from the direction of the forest. That itself was suspicious. What business had they in the Southwoods? There was nothing in this vast wilderness that would be of interest to Ayodhyan troops, let alone the king's guard as they had claimed to be, apart from a few ashrams and communities of outcastes and outlaws, which didn't count.

Also, on entering the treeline, he had immediately found signs that indicated they had waited here, within sight of the raj-marg. A closer inspection confirmed that they had been loitering here for several hours, perhaps the better part of the day, awaiting…what? The arrival of the sacred stallion and the procession, of course. And the instant they had set eyes on the horse, they had ridden out, blocking its way and forcing it off the raj-marg and into the forest, even as the larger part of their party had continued up the raj-marg, blocking Lakshman's way and line of sight, and delaying him until the horse had been coerced successfully into going into the woods.

The question was: why.

He didn't mind the horse going this way. He himself had urged it in this direction, rather than towards Mithila, to avoid a confrontation.

Was that their intention too? If so, they had certainly chosen a strange way to go about it! He had also actively disliked the arrogant manner and bearing of their leader Aarohan as well as the way they had all looked at him, as if he was just another rival kshatriya they would have no compunctions in cutting down in a moment. He had fought enough fights and battles to recognise the killing lust in another kshatriya's eyes—Devi knew he had often harboured that same lust in his own eyes, in the heat of battle or when faced with impossible odds—but to see it reflected in the eyes of men who were in the employ of Ayodhya, of Rama no less, was deeply disturbing. Yet he had not been mistaken: those horsemen had been willing to fight him at a moment's notice and would perhaps even have welcomed an opportunity. He knew kshatriyas well enough to recognise those signs as well.

Again, the question was why. Why challenge the brother of the king...of the *emperor*? Why divert the sacred stallion and delay him and Sumantra long enough for the animal to lose itself in the woods? There was some larger game afoot here and he meant to find out what it was.

The tracking and reading of signs had slowed him down. He had dismounted and remounted half a dozen times already, the better to read the ground and shrubbery and lower trunks of trees. He was certain of what he had read in the tracks. But the process had also cost him time. He was not worried about the horse itself—he had found its trail most easily of all, and the animal's leisurely pace meant that he could catch up with it in a few ticks. But as he bent one last time to read a snapped twig and a hoof print, he felt the familiar vibration of the ground that indicated several riders were approaching fast, from the direction of the raj-marg.

How interesting. So the gang was now following him into the woods? Why not just ride with him at the same time? Why let him go ahead and then follow?

He weighed his options quickly: the horse was in no great danger. It was sensible enough not to go too far into the deep woods. In fact, left to itself, it would probably find its way back to the raj-marg in a little while.

The only reason it had ventured into the woods was because it had been forced into them.

On the other hand, he was very curious to see why the horseriders were following him into the forest.

His decision made, he slipped behind a tree trunk, remounting his horse as he did so. With the instinct that had seen him through a hundred battles and any number of smaller encounters, he unslung his bow and notched an arrow. Then he waited.

Moments later, the gang came into sight, riding at a steady pace, clearly following the same tracks he had been following. He expected them to be following his trail as well, but they went right past him without stopping. He kept the point of the arrow on the neck of the surly leader, Aarohan, watching the man as he rode past with a broad leer on his face. Aarohan was quite pleased about something. He wondered what that might be. In a moment, they were out of sight, swallowed instantly by the dense forest.

As the thunder of their hooves faded away, he lowered the arrow, frowning.

What was going on here? If they were following the horse, they could have done so earlier, instead of waiting on the raj-marg and blocking his path and wasting time. Yet they were clearly not following him, since his trail ended here and they hadn't bothered to stop or check if he was around. They had simply gone straight on, keeping to the trail of the stallion—which meant they had chased the horse in here earlier, prevented Sumantra and him from seeing where it went, and were now following it. *What did they expect would happen in the short while that the horse was out of view? And why were they following it now?*

Before he could come up with any answers, or even theories, he heard the sound of another horse, a single rider coming fast.

He raised the bow again.

A moment later, the rider came into view. He was surprised to see it was his own twin brother.

'Shatrughan!' he called out softly, issuing a low whistle as he did so.

Shatrughan glanced up, as surprised to see him, and slowed to a halt. He looked angry.

'Lakshman?' He looked around suspiciously. 'What are you doing here, bhraatr? What the devil is going on here? What game are those ruffians playing at?'

Lakshman raised his eyebrows. 'So you met Aarohan and his nasty bunch too, I see. I don't quite know, but they seem to be chasing the sacred stallion which got away somehow. What's your excuse?'

Shatrughan glared at him. Lakshman felt a twinge of guilt at the distance that had grown between them these past years, particularly in the most recent months. 'I want to see the bastards who murdered Sumantra punished, that's what. How can you tolerate such things? I know that Rama calls himself 'emperor' now and wants to conquer the entire known world, but is this the way to—'

Lakshman held up a hand in protest. 'Hold on. What did you say? *Murdered Sumantra?* What do you mean?'

Shatrughan almost spat the words out in anger. 'Them!' He pointed in the direction the riders had gone. 'Bharat and I heard the alarm sound and raced to the frontline. We saw those brutes attacking Sumantra. They saw us coming and fled in here. Bharat said to follow, he would be close behind.'

As if on cue, the sound of another horse approaching reached Lakshman's ears. He was still reeling from the news of Sumantra. Was this some ruse on Shatrughan and Bharat's part? He couldn't believe his brothers would do such a dastardly thing.

The new arrival was indeed Bharat. If Shatrughan had seemed angry, Bharat was clearly furious. He reacted violently when he saw Lakshman, wrenching his mount to a standstill and pointing an angry accusing finger.

'This is what your great emperor brother condones? Murder in broad daylight? Sumantra died in my arms moments ago.'

He held out his hands. Lakshman was shocked to see that there was indeed blood splashed on his arms and his garments. But he forced himself to remain calm. A part of his mind even whispered: *He could have murdered Sumantra himself, that could be how he got that blood on his person.* He immediately felt ashamed for thinking that his own brother could do such a thing. But ten years in the corridors of Suryavanshi Palace had taught him that power and politics corrupted everybody sooner or later.

He concealed his discomfiture by taking issue with Bharat's accusation of Rama. 'Rama has nothing to do with this,' he protested. 'Don't drag his name into everything that happens.'

'Of course, he's responsible,' Bharat said, 'those men are king's guard, they as good as said so to my face, the swine. If they had waited a moment longer, I would have shown them what I thought of them and their cowardly methods! They slaughtered poor Sumantra and then fled into the forest.'

Lakshman tried to keep his voice calm. 'I will get to the bottom of this,' he said, 'but you have no authority to go about challenging or fighting our own soldiers. If they indeed assaulted Sumantra as you say, then I shall see to it they are brought to book. But until I gather all the facts in this matter—'

'If?' Bharat shouted, red in the face. 'You dare to say "if" to me? Your own brother? There is no "if". Sumantra was murdered and the men who killed him fled into these woods like craven jackals. *If* you are our father's son, then come with us and let us punish them right now for what they did! The sons of Ayodhya need no authority to mete out justice when they see injustice done!'

Lakshman was about to reply when suddenly the sound of violent cries and shouts erupted. The clamour came from deeper inside the woods, but was not very far away.

Bharat turned the head of his horse at once. 'There! You see? They are up to some game here and if you were not so enamoured of our bhraatr, the emperor, you would see it as well.'

Lakshman controlled his urge to shout back at his brother. 'Very well, we shall ride together then and investigate further. But there will be no drawing of weapons or engaging of hostilities unless I say so. Remember. You are both under a danda, and disobedience will not be tolerated!'

Bharat snorted and spoke aside to Shatrughan: 'Neither will murder. Those cowards killed Sumantra by attacking from behind. I saw this man ride around the chariot and throw a pike into his back! The man wore a beard clipped in that eastern style, with some of his cheek shaved clean, and his chin full of hair and he was a big fellow, even bigger than me by at least half a foot. I would recognise him anywhere. He will answer to me personally, danda be damned.'

Lakshman realised with a start that Bharat had just described Aarohan, the leader of the horseriders. He set his mouth grimly and turned his horse. He could not admit it to his brothers, but he too had his suspicions about that gang and that was why it was important that he approached this matter with caution and intelligence. There was a great game afoot here, no doubt about it, and evidently it was important enough to the players to sacrifice an ex-prime minister and even a prince or two to achieve victory.

'Let's go,' he said curtly and rode into the forest, his brothers close beside him.

* * *

Bejoo arrived on the scene just in time to see Luv and Kush clinging to a sleek black horse that could be no other than the sacred Ashwamedha stallion. Their mother was urging them to release the horse even as Nakhudi tried to shoo it away. The horse itself seemed nervous and he distinctly saw it nuzzle one of the boys, as if seeking his protection.

Then the sound of pounding hooves alerted him and he instantly reacted, gesturing orders to his men. He saw Somasra, who was acting as his second-in-command, nod and pass on the instructions to the others. At once, they melded into the forest, keeping out of sight for the time being. Bejoo had seen just enough to know something was desperately wrong with the scene before his eyes. The sacred stallion could not have simply wandered into the forest unaccompanied. And he had been only moments behind Luv and Kush, so he knew quite well that the boys had not gone out of their way to seek out and capture the horse. Somehow, the horse had come to them and they were only trying to comfort and calm it down. He had been a boy once and had loved horses then with a passion that had never faded since; he understood the protectiveness the boys felt. Besides, from the looks of it, they had no idea it was forbidden to touch the horse, nor were they aware of the consequences of doing so.

But he was. And he had a feeling that all heaven and hell were about to come crashing down on their heads now. And those two innocent young boys were going to need all the help they could get.

So he hid behind a tree and waited to see what happened next.

He did not have to wait long. Moments later, a large company of horseriders appeared, riding hard and fast. He felt a surge of anger as he recognised them as the same brigands who had committed the slaughter in the village and the ashram. The brutes had the gumption to come back? But, of course! This must be part of the plan! He was no politician or statesman, but he knew enough of the dirty tricks those people played to see that this whole day had been scripted from morn to dusk, and that this scene unfolding now was a crucial part of the whole play.

He saw the man at the head of the company haul up his horse. He was a big fellow, brutish looking and powerfully built, with the kind of musculature that came from exercising with elephants. Bejoo had been a vajra commander once and elephants had been an integral part of his vajra. He had known men who had trained with elephants to build their muscle strength to extents that could not be achieved merely by lifting weighted objects or boulders. Elephants did not lie still like rocks or weights, they pulled and pushed and bore down in unexpected ways. Training with them could leave a man with crushed limbs or worse very quickly, but if he survived and persisted, he would achieve a body bulk that few others could. This man leading the horse gang was clearly an elephant wrestler judging by those bulging neck muscles, shoulders, arms, biceps—just about every part of his body, in fact. Bejoo suspected the man also took some of the forbidden herbs known for increasing a man's strength albeit at the cost of his senses and wits.

The man had a distinctive way of wearing his beard, shaving away the sides to bare his cheeks, leaving a bristly chin. That suggested vanity, which went with the naked arrogance he displayed.

The man spoke in loud commanding tones, clearly delivering a carefully rehearsed speech: 'YOU THERE! You have violated the sanctity of the Ashwamedha ritual and challenged the supremacy of Samrat Rama Chandra of Ayodhya! The penalty is instant execution. Surrender yourself to our mercy or die now!'

There was an instant of shocked silence. Into this brief pause, Bejoo heard Luv's voice—or perhaps it was Kush's voice, he could not tell the two apart—say in his boyish way but with a cold steely edge that was far more mature than most ten-year olds, 'Those are the men who attacked our home this morning.'

And he heard the other boy reply just as grimly: 'Yes, they are.'

THIRTEEN

Bharat clenched his fist around his reins angrily as he took in the scene ahead. So this was the drama that was being played out.

He saw two women and two boys and the sacred stallion. The boys were beside the stallion, which seemed to desire their company. The horse displayed no signs of restlessness or nervousness that it would have, had the boys captivated it against its will. Bharat distinctly saw the horse nudge one of the boys in the shoulder, demanding his attention, a gesture Bharat himself knew well from his own lifelong experience with horses. There was no capture here, nor any challenge that he could see. Not by the Ashwamedha's interpretation of the terms. It was obvious that the gang of horseriders had deliberately coerced the horse to ride in this direction, somehow knowing that these forest dwellers would come across it sooner or later, with the express intention of blaming them.

Then he saw who the boys and the women were and his mouth opened in surprise. It helped that one of the women, the one clad in the red-ochre garb of a sadhini, looked up at him as he approached, and her face flickered with the unmistakable glimmer of recognition too. The hefty woman looming beside her glared up protectively as well and her face changed as well, showing that she recognised him as well as Lakshman and Shatrughan beside him.

Even after a decade, there was no mistaking his sister-in-law. That was Sita Bhabhi, he was quite certain.

Her old bodyguard he recognised from Nakhudi's unique physical appearance and the fact that she was with Sita Bhabhi. Which meant that the two boys standing by the horse could only be...his nephews! His throat leaped in his throat as he swallowed with difficulty. Yes, it was definitely Sita, there was no mistaking her. And the boys were her sons.

'Surrender or die, jungle vermin,' said the man with the trimmed beard arrogantly. 'Those are the only two choices before you. This is the last chance I offer you before I decide that you are not worth capturing at all.'

One of the boys shook his head and drew an arrow from the quiver over his shoulder with a fluid action that impressed Bharat.

Now there's a boy who knows how to handle a bow, he thought. *Reminds me of a bhraatr who was as efficient with a bow and arrows at less than this boy's age.*

The bearded man swore harshly at the boy.

Bharat recognised him as well. He was the same craven who had stuck Sumantra from behind with a pike. Neither he nor his horsemen paid heed to Bharat, Shatrughan, and Lakshman as they approached on their left flank, but the stilted way he was speaking and acting suggested what Bharat had already suspected, that the man and his companions were only playing elaborate roles in some scripted scenario. Evidently, the scenario involved Sita and her sons as well, which was something Bharat had never expected or dreamed of. He had never even associated his banished sister-in-law and her boys with anything that had occurred until now. But the fact that they were apparently being 'staged' as the alleged challengers of Rama's authority and stealers of the sacred horse suggested that this drama's playscript was far more elaborate than he had expected. It could hardly be a coincidence that of all the people in the world, Rama's sacred sacrificial horse would be allegedly captured by none other than his own two sons! Something here smelled rotten as a musk melon cut open and left out for a week.

Bharat waited to see what the response was to the gang leader's last call.

'What say you, Kush,' said one of the boys, keeping the arrow notched and ready but still pointed at the ground. 'Shall we surrender to the authority of a king who has never done anything for us, not even protect us as is his dharma by law, or shall we let his murdering soldiers kill us just as they slaughtered the innocent rishis and brahmins of Valmiki Ashram, including the brahmacharya acolytes, many of whom were younger than us?' The words were delivered calmly, but with a rich accent of irony.

The other boy feigned a shrug, keeping his bow strung and the arrow notched but pointing downwards. 'I don't know, Luv. It's such a difficult choice to make. Hmmm. What do you recommend?'

'Enough banter,' said the ruffian who had murdered Sumantra, evidently losing patience. 'Step aside and let us reclaim the horse, and we may yet let you live long enough to be taken before Samrat Rama for pronouncement of judgement. This is your final warning!'

The boys exchanged a glance. Bharat sensed something pass between them and recognised it as being similar to the instinctive telepathy that developed between comrades at arms over long periods of time and intense threat. Except that these two boys possessed the ability to communicate without words naturally, they were probably born with it. He glanced sideways at Shatrughan and Lakshman, and sensed that they understood this as well. After all, they were not just identical twin brothers like Sita Bhabhi's sons, they were also blood relatives to those two young boys.

Luv raised his chin to stare insolently back at the horseman. 'If your Emperor Rama wants his horse back, tell him to come get it. As for you, you craven wretch, you must pay for what you did to Valmiki Ashram and the innocents you massacred!'

And without further ado, he raised his bow and released the arrow.

And then all hell broke loose.

* * *

Luv's arrow was dead on target. But his words and actions had forewarned the leader of the king's guard sufficiently. When Luv released, Aarohan raised his sword up quickly, deflecting the arrow. At the same time, he shouted a command to his men to attack. The entire company charged at once.

Kush released his arrow a fraction after Luv did, also aiming at Aarohan. But because they had both aimed at the same spot—the gap between the horserider's chest armourplate and helm which left the man's neck and throat exposed, his arrow was deflected by the same sword action. The charging horses, only a dozen yards from where the boys stood, left them no time for a second shot. In perfect coordination, both brothers leaped on the back of the black stallion and clapped their heels to its flanks.

'Go! Ride!' Maatr shouted at them, seeing the danger.

Nakhudi added her voice to the furore: 'GO!'

The sacred horse needed no further urging. He shot forward like a bolt, whinnying with excitement. The other equines pounding after him excited him greatly, after having been alone for several days. He screamed his excitement as he charged through the forest at a pace few horses could have matched. The king's guard's horses, burdened as they were with over-muscled men each weighing more than Luv and Kush combined, as well as their armour and heavy weapons, and tired from being ridden hard the past few days, couldn't even hope to catch up. Luv and Kush disappeared into the shadows of Southwoods in a moment, the rump of the black horse invisible in the dim gloam of the dense woods. There would be no catching them by speed alone.

But Aarohan wasn't accepting the fact. He shouted to his men to go after the stallion and they rode after it, following in his wake.

They did not go far.

Bejoo and his PFs rose and stepped out from their hiding places, aiming bows, and throwing blades at the oncoming king's guards.

Sita and Nakhudi raised their weapons as well.

And from the left flank, Bharat, Shatrughan, and Lakshman rode forward and came around to face Aarohan. Bharat's horse lurched ahead, but Lakshman reached out, took hold of the bit and gave Bharat a firm stare. Bharat looked into his brother's eyes, nodded once, and stopped his horse, allowing Lakshman to go forward to speak face to face with the king's guard captain.

'Captain Aarohan,' Lakshman said. 'That is your name and title, is it not?'

The man glared down at him. The menace in his eyes was venomous. 'Get out of my way. You are obstructing the emperor's personal guard.'

Lakshman looked at him coldly. 'I am the emperor's brother. I am also the Protector of the sacred horse.'

'A fine job you're doing then, letting it be stolen by vagabond children!' The man spat to one side.

'Those boys did not intend to steal the horse. They were provoked by you and your men. I witnessed the incident myself.'

This time Aarohan hawked and spat in Lakshman's direction, aiming the produce of his mouth at the foot of Lakshman's horse. The mare snickered softly, but held her ground, too well-trained to respond to such an obvious taunt. 'It is a well-planned ambush. Look around you. These are traitors, men dismissed from service of Ayodhya, now turned against their own motherland. This whole scheme to steal the horse and shame the Suryavansha throne is a plot against the emperor. If you were a true loyal son of Ayodhya, you would see the truth for yourself!'

'I am one of the heirs to the Suryavansha throne,' Lakshman replied. 'I do not need to be reminded of my loyalty. Nor do I need to be fed the truth by the likes of you, Captain Aarohan. My bhraatrin Bharat and Shatrughan say they witnessed you murdering the former Pradhan Mantri Sumantra a short while ago. How do you respond to that charge?'

The light blue eyes glittered like diamonds in the shadows of his helmet. Aarohan made a sound of arrogance. 'I spit on their claims. They are dishonoured and penalised for transgressions against the throne.

Their loyalty is also questionable. I would not be surprised if they too were part of the plot in which Sumantra was involved.'

Lakshman stared at him in disbelief. This fellow was truly testing his patience now. 'You claim that Sumantra was involved in this? Sumantra!'

Aarohan looked at him pointedly. 'Perhaps you were involved as well, Yuvraj Lakshman. Why else would you be obstructing Samrat Rama Chandra's personal guard from fulfilling our dharma.'

'That's enough of this claptrap!' Bharat said, urging his horse forward. 'I won't stand here and listen to this arrogant ass spout every vile thought that comes into his stinking mouth!'

Lakshman knew how Bharat felt. He looked at Aarohan. The man was clearly in no mood to talk sense. But he also knew how quickly Bharat's anger reached flashpoint and could go out of control. Under these circumstances, it might not be wise to let his brother unleash his temper.

'Just a moment, bhraatr,' he said aside to Bharat. 'I am still trying to clear this up.'

Bharat pursed his lips and kept his silence, but Lakshman could see that it took all of his self-control to do so. He continued to glare at Aarohan who in turn glared back. If not for the number of men as well as the three of them blocking their way, the king's guard would not have stood still a moment longer. As it was, they seemed ready to fight even Lakshman and his brothers if need be. Bharat was astute enough to recognise this and to agree to be patient a while longer.

Lakshman turned his attention to the two women. Again, looking at his sister-in-law's long-familiar face brought back feelings that had lain beneath the surface for too long. But he also knew that to acknowledge her for who she really was might well complicate the situation further. Aarohan would not care that she was his precious emperor's banished wife; if anything, he might consider that a reason to abuse her or attack her instead. Also, the way Nakhudi was glaring at the horsemen and hefting her sword, he could see that a fight was only a single insult distant at this point.

'Sister,' he said, choosing a noncommittal greeting. 'Were those your sons who rode away with the sacred horse?'

Sita's eyes gazed up at him calmly, and he saw that she understood his choosing to err on the side of discretion. 'Yes.'

'And did they lure the horse in this neck of the woods with the intention of capturing it and challenging the emperor?'

Her mouth twitched in something that might have been humour, although it could as easily have been a bitter smile. 'Emperor?'

Aarohan started to say something in his arrogant insulting way, but Lakshman raised a clenched fist in warning, telling him to shut up. The man shut up, though he didn't like it, and Lakshman knew that even his own cache as Rama's brother would only buy him a little more time and patience—very little.

'The horse was sent on an Ashwamedha yajna on behalf of Samrat Rama Chandra's claim as emperor of the Kosala nation and its allies. You know the law. Anyone who stops the horse or seizes it, challenges the authority of the owner and as such—'

'As such, is liable to be put to death on the spot,' Sita said with a trace of bitterness. 'Yes, I am aware of the law. But my sons did not lure, capture, or steal that horse. They have no interest in challenging the authority of your emperor. They were merely trying to get away from that man and his gang of murderers,' she stabbed a finger at Aarohan and the rest of the king's guard behind him, 'who, by the way, were sent by your precious emperor this morning to find and massacre all peaceable people dwelling in these woods, including but not limited to the brahmins, rishis, sadhus, and sadhinis of Valmiki Ashram as well!'

Lakshman stared at her, astonished. 'What? These men?'

Nakhudi stepped forward, pointing with her sword. 'Yes! These men! Either you are blind or you are also a part of this cowardly conspiracy! Don't pretend you were not aware of their mission. They rode through this morning and wiped out an entire village of innocent unarmed people.' She was sobbing angrily, tears spilling freely down her face as she went on, 'even the frail, elderly and the young! They did the same at Guru Valmiki's Ashram. They slew every last brahmacharya, some as young as seven!'

Lakshman turned in his seat to look at Aarohan. The captain of the king's guard was looking in the direction of a tree branch, which he appeared to find exceptionally fascinating.

'Is this true?' Lakshman demanded. 'You and your men did all this? This adharmic slaughter?'

Aarohan turned his cool blue gaze back to Lakshman. 'These women are whores and outlaws. Every Arya knows that the Southwoods are fit only for asuras and outcastes. No decent Arya people reside here. The whole region is aranya, wilderness, and as such comes under no legal jurisdiction.'

Lakshman heard Bharat curse and come up beside him, unable to listen silently any longer. 'Who do you think you are, you arrogant ass? Do you know whom you speak of? What gives you the authority to go where you please and kill who you wish in this fashion? No Arya kshatriya would do such things! Not on the honour of holy gurus or our sacred Vedas!'

Aarohan smiled coldly. 'Whatever I do is under the authority of Samrat Rama Chandra of Ayodhya. I answer to him and him alone. Now, I have had enough of this bantering. While we stand here chit-chatting about outlaws and their pathetic kin, the sacred horse is getting farther away. Stand aside and let me do my job.'

'No,' Lakshman said, reaching a decision. He drew his sword slowly and calmly, with deliberate care. The steel sang out as it scraped the rim of the sheath, the sound ringing out ominously in the sudden stillness of the forest afternoon. He held the sword across the saddle of his horse, not raising it or brandishing it just yet, but keeping it ready to deploy in an instant. 'You have done enough already. I am taking charge here. You are ordered to return to your superior officer and report to him until further notice. I shall go after the horse and retrieve it myself as protecting the stallion is my task. Turn back and leave here, Captain Aarohan. I command you in the name of my brother and by my right as a Suryavanshi Ikshwaku. I command you on pain of death!'

And now he raised the sword and pointed it directly at the king's guard captain. Aarohan didn't flinch or react in any way. He stared directly at Lakshman, his eyeline in perfect level with the length of the sword. Their eyes met over the yard's length of burnished Mithila steel and Lakshman, accustomed to looking his enemies in the eye before a battle, saw that the man held no fear or anxiety at all. Instead, Aarohan lowered his chin, deepening his gaze like a predator marking its prey, and smiled with supreme confidence.

'I shall go for now, Yuvraj Lakshman. But I shall return soon enough. Not just with half a company,' he gestured at the fifty-odd men behind him, 'but with an army. The entire might and power of Ayodhya shall be with me when I come back. And then we shall see who gives the orders here, and who comes first to a painful death.'

And he snapped his horse around and barked a single word to his men. As one, they turned and rode out of the woods, in the direction of the raj-marg. Every single one glared in Lakshman's direction as he turned, and Lakshman realised grimly that the captain of the king's guard was not merely bluffing or speaking idly. He meant every word he said and he had the authority to do exactly as he claimed.

'Devi help us,' Lakshman muttered, then sheathed his sword and turned back to face the others. 'What is going on here?'

A man stepped forward. It was one of the PFs. Lakshman recognised him at once as former Vajra Captain Bejoo, most recently employed as a grama-rakshak.

'I believe I have a fair notion, Yuvraj Lakshman,' Bejoo said without much joy in his tone. 'And if you do not act quickly and contact Maharaja Rama Chandra before Captain Aarohan does, I think this brewing conflict may well turn into a full-blown war. That is the intention of those who have put this devious plan into motion.'

FOURTEEN

L uv and Kush slowed the horse and looked back.
'Nobody's following,' Kush said.

Luv agreed. He couldn't hear or sense any signs of a pursuit.

'Maatr and Nakhudi and the olduns must have stopped them dead in their tracks,' Kush said, with complete confidence. 'Maybe those three strangers helped too. I saw the way they were looking at Maatr. They know her. Maybe they're rishis in disguise, or they took up arms and became kshatriyas.'

Luv turned to look questioningly at his brother.

Kush shrugged. 'Parasurama did it. In the story Gurudev told us.'

'Those are Puranas, Kush. Those things happened eons ago, in the Satya Yuga. This is a modern era, Treta Yuga. Brahmins don't go around riding horses and pretending to be kshatriyas. Besides, those three were royalty of some kind, did you see their insignia?'

Kush frowned. 'The embroidering on their clothes and saddlebags?'

'Yes, and the markings on their armour and their sword sheaths. If they're not princes or kings of someplace important, I'll eat this horse.'

The sacred horse whinnied in protest. Kush patted his neck affectionately. 'Don't worry, big fella. I won't let him eat you. He's just exaggerating as usual.'

'You're the one who's always exaggerating, not me.'

Kush cocked his head. 'You're the one who just said he would eat the horse!'

Luv shrugged. 'Well, I would. If I were wrong. But I'm not wrong. I'm right. Those three strangers were royalty! I bet you this whole forest they were!'

Kush looked around doubtfully. 'Do you own this forest?'

Luv frowned. 'Well, it doesn't belong to anybody. It's just aranya. Uncivilised wilderness.'

Kush grinned. 'Aha. If it doesn't belong to anybody, it can't belong to you. So it's not your forest! So how can you bet it away?'

'Well, I haven't lost it yet, have I? I'm just saying, if I was wrong about those three strangers being royalty, then I would give you this forest. But I'm not wrong, I'm right! So it doesn't matter whether or not I owned the forest in the first place!'

Kush giggled. 'I bet you the moon and the sun!'

'What?'

'I bet you the moon and the sun that those three weren't princes or royalty. They were probably just...house builders!'

Luv gaped at him in astonishment. 'House builders?'

Kush shrugged. 'Or sculptors. Or road-repairmen. Or army cooks. What difference does it make? I'm just saying!'

'And if you're right—though I'm not sure which one you would be right about, since you named half a dozen professions—then you'll give me the moon and the stars?'

Kush wagged a finger. 'No stars. Just the sun and the moon, that's all.'

Luv laughed. 'Okay, so you have yourself a deal.'

He spat on his palm and proffered his hand.

Kush spat on his own palm, then slapped it against his bhraatr's damp palm. 'If they're royalty, you get the sun and the moon. If they're not, I get the forest.'

Luv smiled. 'Done.'

'There's only one problem, Luv.'

'What?'

'How do we know who they really are?'

'Kush, they're going to come after us sooner or later. We'll find out in time.'

'Okay then. What should we do now? Until we find out, I mean?'

Luv looked around thoughtfully. He looked at Kush's rig and touched it. 'Get ready for the murderers. They'll be coming after us sooner or later, probably sooner. We should be ready when they come.'

Kush's eyes brightened. 'A real fight!'

'Yes! A really real fight. We'll need LOTS of arrows. And other stuff. And traps. And hidey holes. And tree machans. And tunnels. And...'

'Yes, yes, I know,' Kush said happily. 'Let's go to work on it. We don't know how much time we might have.'

'Oh I know exactly how much time we have before they come after us.'

'You do? How?'

Luv gestured upwards, at the slivers of sky visible through the dense tree cover. 'It'll be dark soon. They won't risk coming this deep into the woods after dark, especially not after a black horse in the deep woods. All we'd have to do is stand still and they wouldn't find us for days.'

'You mean they wouldn't find us for nights.'

'Yes. That's what I meant. So they'll come in the morning, at sunrise.'

'Long before that,' Luv said scornfully. 'They probably expect to have caught us by sunrise.'

'By dawn then? Even before that?'

'Just before. When it's just light enough to see and yet too dim to be seen easily. They'll probably assemble at the same place around two hours before sunrise, then try to track us...'

'At which time, we'll be ready and will lead them on a wild and wonderful merry chase!' Kush said. 'All right, let's go.'

'Wait, what about Maatr and Nakhudi?'

Kush thought for a moment. 'All right, once we've made our arrangements, we'll go back and check on them.'

Luv twisted around and looked eastwards. The sun was low on the horizon, only an hour from sunset. 'There isn't much time. It may be too late then.'

'So you think we should go back and check on them now?'

'Yes, but we can double back by a wide circuit, leaving confusing tracks at the same time.'

Kush patted the side of the horse and whispered in his ear. He made a horse sound that sounded remarkably like a girl chuckling. He turned of his own accord and began trotting back the way they had come. In moments, he was cantering then galloping as if he had lived in the deep forest all his life and knew his way about as well as a dray horse knew the city streets.

'He's enjoying this, you know, the rapscallion,' Kush said.

Luv patted the rump of the horse affectionately. 'Good for him.'

'So are you,' Kush said. 'I can tell.'

'That's because you are too.'

They galloped through the woods.

* * *

'What? How could this have happened? What were Yuvraj Lakshman and former Pradhan Mantri Sumantra doing at the time?'

Rama's dark skin seemed to grow more bluish in hue when he got angry. Which had been a rare occurrence in the earlier days, but had increased in frequency of late. Right now, for instance, he was displaying the first warning signs of a rising temper.

He rose from the travelling throne on which he had been seated and paced the spacious royal tent that had been set up on the north bank of the Sarayu just beyond Mithila gate to accommodate the royal entourage for the night.

Bringing up the rear of the great procession, they had barely covered two yojanas' distance from the capital. *A whole day, to travel less than eighteen miles from Ayodhya,* Kausalya thought as she watched her son pace the carpeted floor of the tent. *A pleasure trip would have been more useful. Devi knew Rama could have used one rather than this uncalled-for campaign.*

The courier explained to Rama that Sumantra was dead and Lakshman feared missing in the deep Southwoods, last seen in pursuit of the stolen sacrificial horse.

'What other word do you have of the incident?'

The man shook his head to indicate that he had exceeded the extent of his knowledge. Kausalya knew that royal couriers were not wont to hold back messages or information; they usually blurted out everything they knew the instant they were permitted to open their mouth. That was their job, after all. Rama's question was pointless. She was saddened by the news of Sumantra's death. That old sweet man…what a pity!

'At least he died fighting like a kshatriya,' whispered Sumitra softly. Kausalya and she were watching from the far side of the tent, where they had been about to partake of some light refreshment together with Rama. But Rama had barely bitten into an apple when the courier had arrived. And he would not simply let the man deliver his news and depart as was the usual practice with couriers.

He persisted even now: 'Come, come, man. You must know something else of what happened. Who were the parties who stopped the horse and issued the challenge?'

'Unknown, sire.'

'And where exactly did this occur? On the Mithila border?'

'No, sire,' the man replied, glad to have a question he could answer, 'well away from it. In aranya territory, no man's land.'

'I see,' Rama said thoughtfully. He paced another few steps, then swung around again. 'But that does not make sense! Why would anyone capture it in undeveloped territory? If nobody claims that region, then in turn, nobody can challenge the authority of the throne there! It's a completely pointless act of political aggression.'

'Not for some people,' said Pradhan Mantri Jabali as he ducked his head to enter the royal tent. He turned and dipped his head slightly to indicate respect for the royal Maatrs, then turned his attention back to Rama. 'The aranya territories may not belong to any kingdom per se. But precisely for that reason, they provide a lawless haven where unknown numbers of brigands, dacoits, highway robbers, outlaws, outcastes, Magadhans and other such undesirable elements gather and proliferate. As you know, Samrat Rama Chandra, I have repeatedly proposed to you that we clean up those territories once and for all.'

Rama shook his head impatiently. 'There is nothing to clean up. The Southwoods are deep, savage, inhospitable forests. Those few who venture within out of sheer desperation struggle to stay alive, let alone flourish. Those poor dregs of society pose no threat to the Arya world.'

'Ah,' Jabali said, glancing at the repast spread out before the Maatrs and examining it with the air of a man who actively disliked food, his lanky skeletal frame testifying to that fact. 'I forget that you yourself once lived among these very dregs of society, during your years of exile. You must have come to depend on these sordid elements, for reasons of survival. Every Ayodhyan continues to bear a deep regret for the long suffering you endured during those years. But, sire, it does not change the fact that it is in places where such dregs and filth proliferate that the seeds of rebellion are often sown and flourish.'

'Rebellion?' Rama looked doubtfully at the prime minister. 'Nonsense! The aranya folk are too busy surviving each night without bothering their heads with plans of political opposition!'

Jabali wagged a long bony finger in disagreement. 'Nay, sire, do not underestimate them. Even the lichen and moss growing on the backroom wall seems benign for years until the day it suddenly sprouts poisonous mushrooms. Who knows what dark hatreds ferment and fester in those dark woods? Perhaps you do, of course, having lived among them. Tell me, were they all filled with universal love and affection for our Arya ways and our polished, noble society, ruled by the four precepts of Artha, Kama, Dharma, and Karma? Were they not driven by some modicum of resentment and loathing for the society which had cast them out and of which they could never be a part again?'

Rama picked up the apple from which he had taken a single small bite and looked at it. 'I had hoped to be able to rehabilitate those people one day.'

Jabali made a sound of impatience, clicking his tongue. 'Such beings cannot be rehabilitated. They are tainted, beyond the purview of decent, civilised human society.'

'They are humans too. And many were Arya once. Ayodhyan even.' Rama's tone was declarative but tinged with sadness, rather than argumentative. *As if he knows he is rehashing a debate he has already lost a long time ago*, Kausalya thought.

'Once, perhaps. Not anymore. They are no more than insects now. Venomous, barbed insects beneath our consideration.'

Rama protested. 'They are people. Fellow mortals. With families.'

'Criminals. Unforgiven. Exiles.'

At the last word, Rama flinched. It was very slight, not a visible reaction, barely a flicker in his pupils, but for a man so well in control of his senses, that was as much as a grunt of pain from most ordinary men. Kausalya felt her own heart ache with empathy. Exiles. That word had applied to her Rama as well, along with his brother Lakshman and wife Sita, not long ago. Almost a third of his entire life had been spent in exile. The very word must sting like the metal tip of a lash.

He turned and looked at Jabali with the same calm steady expression with which he greeted everything, but Kausalya knew his heart must ache a great deal more than her own. For while she could empathise with his past suffering, he had endured that suffering himself. Nothing could compare. And what he was saying now with his silent reproachful look was that Jabali should know that and be more considerate of how he spoke. But the prime minister appeared to have deliberately turned his face away from Rama for a moment, under the pretext of looking at something or other.

Rama turned to the courier, who was still standing and waiting patiently.

'You may go,' he said.

The courier left with obvious relief. There were courts in which men who accidentally overheard important matters of state or king's secrets were often executed in order to preserve state privacy, such executions performed with an air of sorry-but-you-know-we-have-no-choice but which were nevertheless quite final all the same. That had never happened in Rama's court but that was only because Rama did not approve of what he termed 'excessive danda'. It was a concept and term that Kausalya herself had taught him as a boy, and she was proud to see that he still adhered to the precept. It told her that her Rama still lay within the body of this man, this emperor of dharma who sought to rule the known world. She could still appeal to him then, when the time came. And it was approaching soon, she knew.

She felt Sumitra's hand clasp her own in sisterly commiseration and squeezed back, thanking her sister-queen for her continual support.

Since their husband's demise two-and-a-half decades ago, the First Queen and Third Queen had been inseparable friends, and during the years that Kausalya governed Ayodhya as a Dowager Queen-Mother, Sumitra had been a valuable asset in court as well as in matters that required careful thought and interpretation of law. She had a particular gift for such matters and Kausalya was glad to have her with her now, for law played an integral part of the plan she had come up with to try and turn Rama back from this empirical course he was set upon.

Rama turned to Jabali the instant the courier had left. 'What further word? Have you heard anything? Has Bhadra returned yet? You did say he had gone to find out why the alarms rang out, when you stayed me from going myself.'

Jabali dipped his bird-like chin and nose once, acknowledging that he had indeed done so. 'It would have been pointless for you to inhale the dust of the marg and ride all that way just to learn what we could learn just as well sitting here in the command centre. That is why you have such vast resources deployed. You are an emperor now, Samrat

Rama Chandra, not a chieftain who must ride out and check on every emergency yourself.'

Rama sighed. 'Yes, I understand. Now speak, have you any news from the frontline? The courier could tell me nothing beyond what we had already guessed.'

Nothing? Was that what he called the news of Sumantra's death? The man who had once sat him upon his knee as a very young boy and answered his every question about kings and courts with infinite patience. Kausalya shook her head, sighing softly despite herself. Rama glanced briefly in her direction, but did not say anything further.

Jabali placed his palms together and rubbed them briskly in that manner that Kausalya had always found pretentious. A skeleton rubbing two tinders together to kindle his own funeral pyre, was how her late dear Dasaratha had described it, with his customary wit. She remembered that now and stifled a laugh. It would not do to actually belittle the man in his presence; ridiculous as he was, he was nonetheless a powerful political figure and she could not afford to antagonise him in any way whatsoever.

'It is as we feared. Your brothers have all gone missing. The excuse given is that they were in pursuit of the sacred stallion. But of course, we know better.'

Rama frowned. 'My brothers? You mean Bharat and Shatrughan too?'

'Indeed. Is that not peculiar? That they, all three of them, should go after the horse together and disappear together?'

Rama shook his head slowly. 'Not particularly. They are Suryavanshis. The yajna may be conducted by me, but it is for the future and stability of the Suryavansha throne. They have a great vested interest in preserving the sanctity of the ritual and ensuring its success.'

'Exactly! A vested interest. For if the horse were to be captured and a challenge issued in that aranya territory, by whose authority would it be?'

Rama shrugged. 'Nobody's. Since the Southwoods do not come under any kingdom's jurisdiction.'

'Aha. But what if your brothers had secretly formed an alliance with the aranya folk, the poor misguided mortals you expressed such sympathy for just a while ago, and conspired to capture the horse and challenge your authority?'

Rama looked coldly at Jabali. 'These are grave accusations. Do not make them unless you have strong evidence to back them up.'

'Strong evidence?' The hawkish nose all but sneered at Rama— although that sneer-like expression was one Jabali displayed naturally— and he turned and clapped his hands, issuing a command to someone waiting outside the tent.

At once, several armoured men, dust-covered and bloody from obvious close fighting, entered, pulling a corpse with them which they laid down on the floor. Even Kausalya and Sumitra stood and peered in horror to see whose corpse it was. It was Sumantra, the poor old man's body and face mutilated by multiple wounds and punctures. Sumitra and she both gasped in horror at the sight of the old and long-beloved prime minister.

'Sumantra!' Kausalya said. She could scarcely believe her eyes. Yet there was no doubt it was Sumantra. Beside her, Sumitra clutched her arm hard enough to hurt, unable to even voice her own reaction.

'Is this sufficient to begin with?' Jabali said, pointing a long bony finger at the body of his predecessor. 'The corpse of our beloved ex-prime minister, brutally murdered and stabbed in the back by none other than your own brothers as the first gambit in their bid to unveil this shocking plot and conspiracy against your throne!'

Rama stared down at the body, his own face revealing the intensity of his shock. 'Did anyone witness this?'

Jabali gestured. 'King's Guard Captain Aarohan, sent on a mission under your own seal to roam the frontlines to ensure the security of the yajna stallion.'

A man stepped forward from the group. He was exceptionally tall and well-muscled, even among the other well-built warriors. He wore his beard in a very distinctive style.

He saluted Rama obstreperously. 'Samrat Rama Chandra, sire. I saw with my own eyes Yuvrajas Lakshman, Bharat, and Shatrughan inflict these wounds upon Sumantra.'

Rama stepped forward, eyes blazing with sudden fury. Despite the height difference and the superior build of the taller man, Rama seemed to tower over him by dint of sheer force of personality. 'You saw them? Where were you when it occurred? If you saw them, why did you not seek to stop them?'

The man did not answer instantly. He seemed, Kausalya thought with a twinge of suspicion, to be irritated by Rama's tone and manner. *Even though this is his emperor speaking, he still resents it!* She had also noted the lack of honorific before Sumantra's name, not a common lapse among the scrupulously disciplined Arya kshatriyas. Who were these king's guard anyway? She dimly recalled hearing of them once or twice in some Council session but their precise purpose eluded her. How odd that such a man should be the only one to come forward as a witness to such a significant event. And to blame Rama's own brothers? She could not even entertain the possibility of such an accusation being true. It was instantly obvious that there was something amiss here.

'I was riding towards Sumantra's chariot,' the man said after a pause, 'I saw the murder as I approached. I shouted to them to stop, but they saw me coming and rode away into the woods.' He added after a moment, 'They had accomplices waiting for them ahead, who had captured the sacred horse. Outlaws of the forest.'

Rama stood before the man a moment or three longer, breathing upon him. Though the man was stone still, yet he seemed to be restraining himself, while Rama who was on the very precipice of utter rage, appeared perfectly in control of his faculties. Kausalya realised that she was looking at a man who was the very inverse of Rama. She did not know what that meant, but she did not like it one bit. *That man is dangerous,* she thought. *And he is lying, I'm as sure of it as I am that I am Kausalya.* She felt Sumitra squeeze her hand in as if in silent agreement, and knew that her sister queen-mother also saw exactly what she saw.

Finally Rama turned away, showing his back to the soldier and to Pradhan Mantri Jabali. In that instant, Kausalya saw something pass between Jabali and the man named Aarohan. She did not like that either. But her misgivings were washed away in a flood of emotion when she heard Rama pronounce his next words with the finality and grim commanding tones of a death sentence.

'Hunt them down,' Rama said. 'Hunt them down and bring them before me, dead or alive. Do whatever you have to, use whatever force is necessary. Send the entire army into the Southwoods. But find the murderers of Sumantra and bring back the yajna stallion. Whatever it takes.'

⟨⟨KAAND 3⟩⟩

ONE

In the early hour before dawn, the Southwoods lay as still as a predator in waiting. The inhabitants of its tree-shaded sanctuary were more numerous than the citizens of the most populous Arya city—and the cities of Aryavarta were more densely populated than any place in the mortal realm, including the rough but developing lands far to the west across the great oceans, whose envoys and traders frequently made the long and arduous journey across land to purchase the precious spices, silks and precious objets d'art of the subcontinent and the civilised nations farther to the east.

Yet unlike the bustling metropolises of Ayodhya, Gandahar, Sumer, Akkad, Babylon, Assyria, Cathay, Ayutha, and other great kingdoms that lay scattered like caches of precious jewels upon the Asian seaboard, the denizens of the great ancient forest went about their daily deeds as discreetly as the secret guilds of assassins in the desert kingdoms went about their dark missions. To one another, the bustle and hustle was plain to see: the panther saw the ants, who in turn saw the anteater, who saw the rabbit, who saw the lion, who saw the deer, who heard the cricket, who stopped chirruping when the lizard approached, and so on in an endless circle of infinite inter-dependence.

There was no individual independence in this world. Every living being depended on every other being to sustain its environment and by doing so, its daily sources of nutrition and survival. Like the assassins of the Arab kingdoms, the predators of the deep Southwoods needed the hustle and bustle of everyday forest life in order to go about their own violent missions.

But unlike the great cities of the mortal world, the deep forest had certain codes by which it endured. One of these was the tacitly agreed-upon rule of mutual co-dependence: when an intruder or intruders entered its environs, every denizen was obligated to issue a warning and intimate its fellow animals, avians, and insects of the presence of the outsider. For outsiders always spelled danger; there were no exceptions to this rule. Be it ever so miniscule a threat as the careless ass that stepped on an ant's nest and destroyed half a summer's toil, or the overt menace of a pack of wild dogs seeking a fresh kill, any creature that chose to enter the dangerous perpetually twilight world of the dense jungle did so only for one reason: self-preservation. Whether that meant fleeing from outside enemies or seeking prey or food here, the end result was the same: the newcomers would fight, kill, feed or otherwise commit some form of violent aggression in order to survive and sustain themselves. It was the only way they, or any living being, could possibly survive in this ruthless world. The way of the jungle, the poets called it. And so it was: the only way to survive in here was to kill or be killed.

The men who poured in from the raj-marg and entered the Southwoods that hour before dawn intended to kill. They were trained for it, equipped for it, and even bred for it: not merely kshatriyas, they were Ayodhyan kshatriyas, and Ayodhya's war cry spoke their own motto and conviction: Ayodhya Anashya!

Ayodhya, the Unconquerable and Undefeated.

For Ayodhya was the one city in all the known world that had never been besieged, attacked, or invaded—successfully, or otherwise. Because it was impossible to besiege, attack or invade it, no sane force in the world would dare to attempt such a suicidal feat. The only one that had tried, once, had been the asura hordes of Ravana, and they had made it only as far as the outskirts of Mithila, which was a long way from Ayodhya.

That great invading force of supernatural demoniac beings had been thwarted by a brahmastra, a sacred weapon of the devas, unleashed by an Ayodhyan, none other than the same Samrat Rama Chandra whom these kshatriyas served today. That was part of the legend of Rama, the fact that he had halted the only known attempt to attack Ayodhya over twelve yojanas away! It was not even fit to be called an attack, let alone a siege.

And now, with Ravana gone, the asura hordes extinguished from the mortal realm forever, even the severely weakened rakshasa race of the lord of asura's erstwhile capital, Lanka, diminishing in number with each passing year, there were no other forces, mortal, asura or otherwise, who dared or desired to challenge the might of Ayodhya by attacking the greatest Arya city on earth.

But today, the enemy was not coming to invade Ayodhya. Ayodhya was coming to invade the enemy's domain.

And this domain, the fabled and dreaded Southwoods of mythic lore, until only twenty-four years ago the domain of the fearsome yakshi giantess Tataka and her hybrid offspring, was unlike any battleground, field or city these brave soldiers of Ayodhya had ever visited or fought upon.

In its own way, it was as indomitable as Ayodhya herself, even if it did not boast seven great moats filled with ravenous predators, seven tall stone gates manned by awe-inspiring war machines, and all the mechanical and architectural marvels that mortalkind was capable of creating.

The forest was a living breathing force as powerful as the great military might of Ayodhya.

In its own way—and on its own terms—the jungle was a formidable opponent unto itself, not merely a theatre of battle, but part of the enemy's armoury itself. The fact that it did not appear to be an armoury, and could be assumed to be a staging ground or battlefield, was part of its sinister threat.

Ayodhya might well be unconquerable, never-besieged, indomitable. But so was the Southwoods.

* * *

The first regiment of soldiers was not unaccustomed to forests or forest warfare. After all, the world was not so old and jaded as to have completely forgotten the forests from which mortalkind sprang not long ago. Many of these kshatriyas had spent their childhood and youth roving the wild countryside of Kosala, hunting, farming, herding. They were familiar with woods and with forest environments. They moved slowly and carefully, unburdened by the heavy armour that cavalry regiments like the king's guard wore, bearing lighter pikes and swords. There were archers among them too, with fine Gandahari longbows. And they were told to expect an ambush.

But to their surprise, they met with no resistance at all.

They went further and further into the forest, the dim grey of the sky visible above the tall treetops turning slowly whiter as they went, and even a full hour later, when dawn broke across the eastern part of the forest, not an arrow had been loosed or a sword swung in aggression. It was puzzling but not entirely surprising. Their commanding officers assumed the obvious: the challengers had been all bluster and intent, but lacked the guts to follow through. It was easy enough to filch a horse, quite another thing to face an entire army, leave alone an Ayodhyan army. They had probably retreated or were in hiding, quivering with their blankets pulled over their sweating faces. There were some sardonic grins and shaking of heads as the forward regiment went a mile then two miles then three without meeting any resistance.

As dawn turned to daybreak and the first golden rays of sunlight twinkled through the trees, the men began to relax their guard, feeling that this would be an easy assignment after all. The only reason they went on at all was because the horse still had to be retrieved and the culprits put to death, their bodies brought back nailed to wooden posts to caution future challengers.

Soon, the mood lightened and the men began to chat softly among themselves, even joke and relax their guard. Due to the nature of the forest, they were spread out considerably, and their commanding officers could not see or hear every single one at all times, so it was easy for them to simply squat against a tree trunk and smoke a beedi or chew some betelnut and chat softly about the pointlessness of this mission.

The first inkling that they had of danger was when a peculiar sound came to their ears. It was a sound that was vaguely familiar yet not easily recognisable. At first, many assumed it was only insects or perhaps even the wind. But as it grew louder and closer, they became aware that it was neither of these things.

The sound was a constant hissing. A susurration similar to the sound of the wind shirring in trees in autumn or the ocean surf rising to the shore and falling back. Yet it was neither of these.

A man smoking a beedi was the first to grow certain he knew the source of the sound. He sat bolt upright against the trunk of the tree where he had been resting, dropping his beedi. It fell onto a damp patch of earth and was luckily extinguished at once. He reached out and snatched hold of his spear which he had left standing upright against the tree trunk.

'Snakes!' he said aloud. Then even louder, so his comrades could hear as well: 'SNAKES! It's snakes, coming towards us!'

The word was repeated and passed along the frontlines, moving with surprising speed. The commanding officers heard it too and frowned. Snakes? What did the man mean? Had he seen a snake or perhaps even a nest of snakes near his position? What did that have to do with the rest of the army?

They shrugged and ignored it.

But as the sound grew larger, closer, and omnipresent, seeming to come from every direction at once and all around them, they grew uneasy. Men stopped chatting or lounging about and took up their weapons. Eyes scanned left and right, seeking out something, anything that would provide a more believable explanation for the sound.

Slowly, as the hissing grew so loud and close that each man realised it could be nothing but snakes, they began to panic. Men retreated slowly, stepping backwards, seeking to get away from the wall of approaching sound. The HISSSSSS pervaded the entire forest now, it seemed.

'Hold your positions!' ordered their officers.

'Stay your ground, you lazy ruffians,' growled sergeants gruffly, passing on the officer's orders.

But many of the officers were sweating nervously as well. Some were old enough to have heard stories at their father's and grandfather's knees of the dreaded Nagas and Urugas in the last Asura War. Snakes were not the most popular forest creature and every year on an allotted day, oblations and offerings were given to the snake deities to appease them and persuade them not to unleash their venom on mortals. Of course, everyone knew that the last of the asuras had been exterminated when Rama had unleashed the brahmastra at Mithila twenty-four years ago. But these were the Southwoods, dreaded site of so many fearsome fables and cautionary tales from ancient itihasa, and who knew what beings might still reside in this dense jungle?

Suddenly, one of the archers cried out. They were the ones with the sharpest eyesight and he had seen something in the alternately shadowy and sunlit forest.

He reacted by doing something no kshatriya was ever supposed to do: he threw down his bow and rig and turned around. He ran past his fellows, ignoring even his commanding officers who were too surprised to order him to stop. His face betrayed his terror at whatever he had seen.

'Flee!' he yelled. 'Flee for your lives!'

The others stared after him, then at each other. The officers shouted sporadically to hold the line and hold their positions and the usual claptrap that officers were expected to shout, but none of the men was listening. They were all thinking about how the archer, one of the finest Ayodhyan bowmen, which made him one of the finest in the world, apart from the Assyrian horse bowmen and chariot archers, whom, it was said, were the best in the world, had thrown aside his bow and rig as if it was so much useless baggage rather than the beautifully shaped polished and resin-waxed Mithila bow, a treasure to any kshatriya of the archer varna. It was a bow worth giving up one's life for, and if the archer had thrown it aside, it could be for only one reason: the bow, fine as it was, would be utterly useless against the HISSSing thing that was approaching them, and while running away, would be an impediment especially when making way through the close-growing trees and shrubbery. And if a bow and arrows, which could be used to kill or wound any enemy from afar, was useless, then what good were a sword, pike or axe which required close quarters to be effective?

The officers had realised this as well. And sweating with anxiety though they were, they were still commanding officers entrusted with a mission. It was their dharma to fulfil that mission or die trying. Under Samrat Rama Chandra's 'Ram Rajya', failing to do one's dharma was itself punishable by death. So they roared instructions that nobody was to abandon their weapon, and every soldier must hold the line and engage the enemy. Failure to comply would result in the severest danda: on-site execution.

That worked. Terrible though the HISSSing sound was and the thought of what it might be caused by, the fear of facing the wrath of danda was greater. Face the unseen menace and they might yet live. Run from it as the archer had done, and they would certainly be put to death.

So they stayed, reluctantly but bravely. And raised their weapons when their officers told them to, and prepared to fight.

A moment later, the source of the HISSSing was revealed. And it was every bit as terrifying as they had feared.

The forest floor was writhing with a carpet of snakes. All racing along at considerable speed, winding their sinuous way across the ground, slithering over and under each other, intertwining, hissing at each other or at everything in general, some pausing to strike at one another, fangs lashing out angrily, milky white drops of venom flicking off their gaping pink maws. For as far as the eye could see, the ground was writhing with the creatures. They were all coming as fast as they could, towards the frontlines of Ayodhya's finest.

Too late the officers gaped in disbelief and thought that perhaps they had given the wrong orders. Perhaps it was acceptable to retreat. After all, how could they fight such an enemy? And why fight it at all? The snakes of the Southwoods were not responsible for the abduction of the sacred horse! But their own orders, received from the chief of the king's guard, Captain Aarohan himself, had been crystal clear: no surrender, no retreat...on pain of death.

So they stood their ground. A few soldiers were unable to stand and watch the writhing monstrosity slither towards them, like some enormous beast spread out across acres of forest ground, and they turned and ran. They were caught and despatched a mile or two back, by men of the king's guard, deployed to ensure the obedience of the army. A few others attempted to climb trees, forgetting that many breeds of snakes live in trees. But the majority of the frontliners stayed where they were, weapons in hand and ready to use. And watched as a terrible slithering death approached them yard by twining yard.

The line of snakes and the line of soldiers came closer together, until finally, they met, converged, and overlapped.

TWO

Luv and Kush smiled grimly at each other as the sound of soldiers screaming reached them on the forest wind. Their first tactic had worked better than expected. They had known of the existence of the snake nest ever since they were very young: it was a legend in these parts of the forest. A great nest, larger than any ever known had always existed here near a grotto that led to a network of underground caverns. The nest itself only housed the few thousand snakes that still chose to remain in the open rocky basin at the mouth of the grotto. It was said there were tens of thousands, perhaps even hundreds of thousands inside the deep cavern. They constantly slithered up and down through the tunnels, presumably in search of food and water and sunlight, which as cold-blooded creatures, they required in order to stay alive. From the sounds of it, they had succeeded in disturbing a good number into leaving their subterranean home and travelling in search of safer climes. If those migrating serpents happened to come across several hundred armed soldiers and consider them an obstruction to their seeking of safety, well, too bad for the soldiers.

It had been the work of moments to light a fire and throw the blazing debris down the other end of the great hole that joined up with the one at the back of that same grotto. They had not known how many snakes might be disturbed by the smoke and fire into climbing up and emerging into the open but any number would be sufficient to cause trouble in the enemy ranks. But even as they glanced down at the grotto from the top of the overhang—the only place safe enough to view the nest—they had been astonished at the sheer masses of writhing snakes that were emerging from the cave mouth. Thick sinuous green-black ropes of intertwined snakes fell in a constant stream, like a waterfall of serpents, to land on the leaf-strewn ground below, then work their way out of the nest and into the forest, snaking away at the heightened speed that their species resorted to only when faced by natural disaster or fire. They knew better than to follow the fleeing snakes to view what happened when they encountered the incoming soldiers: once let loose in the open jungle, panicked out of their minds, those snakes were an army unto themselves.

As the screams of the soldiers continued, they climbed back down into the canyon through another route which avoided any caves or open holes which might be filled with more escaping snakes. Reaching the ground several moments later, they were greeted with sighs of relief by their Maatr and Nakhudi.

'That was the most dangerous thing possible,' Maatr admonished. 'What if those snakes had turned on you?'

Kush grinned. 'We would have ordered them not to harm us by the authority of Emperor Rama Chandra of Ayodhya!'

'Yes!' Luv agreed. Both brothers laughed.

Nakhudi glanced at Sita's face when the boys mentioned Rama Chandra. 'You boys shouldn't speak so insolently of the king.'

'Emperor!' Luv corrected. 'Why not? He's nothing but a kshatriya corrupted by his lust for power.'

Nakhudi started to reply but Sita raised her hand. 'Enough talk. That ploy with the snakes, clever though it was, won't keep them back for long. This time they'll come in force and when they do, it will take more than tactics to stop them.'

'It's all right, Maatr,' Kush said. 'We have a plan.'

Sita looked at each of them in turn, her face filled with some undefinable sadness. 'I'm sure you do, my sons. But you will need all the help you can get. Just the two of you alone, brave soldiers though you are, can't keep back the entire Ayodhyan army.'

'Actually, Maatr,' Luv said, 'in the right circumstances, it's easier for a very small force to elude a very large army. In this part of the jungle, with this defensible position, knowing the terrain as we do, having made arrangements for such a contingency, we stand a better chance of survival than a regiment or an akshohini of defenders.'

'Yes, Maatr,' Kush added, deadly serious now. 'You know this to be true. And so do you, Nakhudi.'

Nakhudi nodded slowly. 'Aye, true it is. But I did not intend for you two to make this stand alone.'

Kush shrugged. 'Nobody knows this terrain as well as we do. We have the advantage of being difficult to spot and quick to move. They will be expecting a much larger force, not just two defenders.' He spread his hands. 'What do I have to say to convince you?'

'I'm convinced,' Sita said, struggling to rise to her feet. 'Except that there will be more than just two of us defending.' She got to her feet and stood, swaying a moment, then her eyes rolled up in her head and she collapsed soundlessly.

Nakhudi caught her without any effort and lowered her gently to the ground. After placing her comfortably on the ground, she rose and looked at the boys.

'She will be all right, but she has lost a great deal of blood. She needs rest and treatment.'

The twins nodded, staring solemnly at her. 'You must stay and care for her, Nakhudi. You do see the wisdom in that, don't you? You must stay and protect all the survivors of the attack on the ashram.' Luv gestured at the band of wounded and exhausted brahmins and brahmacharyas clustered at the back of the box canyon. Rishi Dumma had taken charge of tending to the wounded and his bulky form was visible moving from pallet to pallet, doing the best he could to ease pain and suffering.

Nakhudi sighed but nodded. 'Yes, in the event that the Ayodhyan forces do track us down, I could hold them off at the mouth of the canyon. I will stay,' she finished shortly, not happy about it but not arguing either.

'You will be safe here,' Kush added. 'The only way the enemy can get in here is if they get past us. And they won't.'

Nakhudi nodded slowly, passing a hand across her face which looked more weary than they had ever seen her before. 'If they get past you, even her wounds won't keep your mother down,' she said. She meant that if the enemy could enter the canyon it would mean Luv and Kush were dead and if that happened, Sita wouldn't care to live another minute. 'Nor I.'

They looked at her steadily. 'We will return. Once the enemy leaves. Or surrenders.'

Nakhudi's hand flew to her mouth involuntarily. 'Surrenders!' she said. The word brought a smile to her face. The very idea!

They neither laughed nor smiled. They had meant what they said. 'Surrender is always an option for them,' they said. 'Just not for us.'

That much was true. While she doubted that two young boys could bring the mighty Kosala empire to its knees in surrender, there was absolutely no doubt that the enemy would never rest now until they were all dead. It made her wonder if she was doing the right thing by letting the boys go out to fight this battle on their own. Every instinct screamed to her to order them to stay and go herself. But she knew that they were right for once. Somehow, this was their fight and they had every right to wage this war. Whatever the consequence. Even Guru Valmiki had given his assent earlier.

'There comes a day in every child's life when he or she must become a man or woman. For a kshatriya child, that is the day you become a kshatriya. Today is your day, boys. Go and do what you must.'

They bowed to Nakhudi, took her blessing. Then left at a run. She watched their lithe bodies go, wondering if she would ever see them alive again—or they her.

* * *

Bejoo cringed at the sounds of the Ayodhyan soldiers screaming. The forest rang with their misery and fear. He and his men had been in mortal fear that the fleeing snakes might pass their way but mercifully there was water between his position and the Ayodhyans' and the wave of serpents had passed them by with several hundred yards to spare. Even so, each time an Ayodhyan came stumbling to the water, lips blackened and eyes staring wildly, he cringed, praying to Shaneshwara that such a death never befall him. These were the stragglers who had been fortunate enough, if you could call them fortunate, to be bitten by snakes with slower-acting venom. Already consumed with fever and madness, they sought out water desperately. But no amount of water could save them. They would die slower and less painfully than their less fortunate comrades, but die they would, whether it took minutes more or hours. He estimated that several hundred must have been bitten by the fleeing wave of snakes. The distant spiral of smoke had told him how the boys had caused the snakes to flee this way, but he could not imagine venturing even close to a nest large enough to house so many deadly reptiles. No doubt about it—the sons of the Lady Vedavati were truly extraordinary in every way.

Now, he waited in the woods across the stream as the sound of hooves announced the arrival of new troops. Metal glittered and flashed through the trees, catching the morning sunlight and from the looks and sound of it, he estimated that this was the main body of the king's guard he had seen earlier. A familiar lean face came into view, riding a huge stallion, and Bejoo immediately recognised the villain who led this newly conscripted legion. Captain Aarohan. He had heard tales about the man that he had not paid much heed to at the time. As a simple grama-rakshak, the politics of the army and city no longer concerned him overmuch. But now that he was involved again, the very sight of the man made his stomach churn. He knew now that the tales he had heard were probably true. The devastation at Valmiki Ashram confirmed it. What manner of monster would attack and slaughter innocent unarmed brahmacharyas, boys and women included, without provocation or cause? Had he been thirty years younger—fifteen even—and still in charge of his Vajra, he would have gladly led a lightning attack against that monster. The man deserved to have all the snakes in the Southwoods set upon him and left to die.

He watched as Aarohan questioned the groaning and half-poisoned remnants of the first wave with growing impatience turning to outright anger. He heard the sound of the man's raised voice and saw his whip curl out and lash men mercilessly as he vented his anger at the unexpected thwarting of the advance. Bejoo's lips curled back grimly, not relishing the sight of army men being abused thus, but taking pleasure in Aarohan's frustration. He was too far away to hear much of what was said but the overall gist was quite obvious.

* * *

'What do you mean, retreat?' Aarohan snarled. He lashed out with his horse-whip again, leaving a welt rising on the cheek and neck of a sergeant in charge of one of the forward platoons. The man took the beating with stubborn resignation, either accustomed to such abuse under the new empirical army or simply too terrified to care. 'Our orders are to flush out and destroy the rebels, whatever the cost!'

The sergeant spoke without looking up at the mounted officer. He knew better than to match gazes with the notorious new captain, allegedly the right-hand man of Pradhan Mantri Jabali himself and already notorious by his nickname, Spike Hand Aarohan, owing to an incident in which the captain had used a spiked handguard to beat a man until the very flesh was ripped off his face, rendering him unrecognisable even to his own family. 'They have Nagas fighting for them. And who knows what other breed of asuras. They are demons in human guise. We cannot fight such creatures.'

Aarohan stared at the man for a moment as if unable to absorb his words. Then he lashed out with greater ferocity than before, whipping the man mercilessly as he lost his temper. 'FOOL! They were only snakes. They must have flushed them out of some pit. No doubt they bred the wretched reptiles for food. There are no asuras or Nagas left on earth, don't you know that? This is the Treta Yuga, not the ancient world!'

The sergeant collapsed wordlessly under the beating. He had been bitten by mainly only non-venomous snakes, but he had attempted to suck out the poison from the wounds of several of his men and in the process some venom had entered his bloodstream as well. Now, under the barrage from Aarohan, he suffered a fatal collapse and sprawled on the ground, body quivering, legs lurching, foam oozing from his open mouth.

Several of the men under the sergeant's command ran up to help him. 'BACK!' shouted Aarohan, using his whip to warn them. He saw a spear clutched in one man's hand and said, 'Hand me that!' The man handed him the spear, looking dazed.

Aarohan turned his horse around, rode the few yards back to where the sergeant lay in the throes of the venom-induced attack, and drove the spear down through the man's throat. The sergeant died, gurgling and gasping. His men reared back in horror.

Aarohan wrenched the spear out of the man's throat and turned to point the bloody end at them. 'The punishment for retreat is death! The penalty for failing in your mission is death! The danda for disobeying or questioning my orders is death! Do you understand?'

They stared at him dumbly. Then belatedly shouted a ragged response: 'Aye!' There was only fear and no respect in their tone, but their response was clear.

'Now, continue in your mission! Track down and find the rebels and kill them all. Spread the word down the lines. Search and kill all rebels! No retreat, no surrender.'

Then, to underline his point, he flung the spear at the crowd of dazed soldiers. It struck a foot-soldier in the belly, driving him back into the crowd. He collapsed, dying. His comrades started to bend to give him aid, then remembered that Aarohan was watching and straightened up again. They stared at him, then turned and began shuffling away, snatching up their weapons. Even the wounded and those who had injured themselves getting away from the snakes, but had not been actually bitten, scrambled to their feet and ran after their comrades. In moments, the clearing by the stream was empty except for the dead sergeant and other men who had collapsed from the slower-acting venom and were eking out their last moments.

'Kill them all,' Aarohan ordered his men. 'I don't care if they will die anyway. Kill them all to drive home the point. The danda for desertion is death.'

As his men went about the grisly task of cutting the throats of the dying and fatally poisoned men lying by the stream, Aarohan summoned his closest and most trusted cronies to him. They came, their sly faces grinning in anticipation. 'Now, listen carefully, this is the day for which we've been waiting. We roll our bone dice right and we will all live out our lives as rich lords of Ayodhya, doing as we please to the end of our days.'

'We'll do what has to be done,' said one of his aides confidently. 'That band of ragtag outlaws and children won't survive long.'

'Even so,' Aarohan said, 'they know this forest well and may have more tricks at hand like the ploy with the snakes. We'll use the main army to beat down the woods. Let them do the dog work and die like dogs if need be. Meanwhile, I want us to split up into two groups and ride around. We have to find the woman named Vedavati, the one who survived the fight at the ashram.'

One of his men spat bitterly on the ground. 'That one? She was lucky to have escaped us there. She killed half a dozen good men. One of them was my brother. I want a chance at her.' He patted his thigh. 'When I finish with her, she'll be begging for the edge of my blade.'

Aarohan nodded. 'You do that. You do to her whatever that pleases you. But I want her and her companion, the other bigger-built woman, dead before the sun sets today. Do you understand? I will give a hundred gold coins to any man who fetches me the head of the woman named Vedavati.'

'What about her brats, the twins with the bows.'

Aarohan turned his head to seek out the man who had spoken. 'A hundred gold coins for each of their heads then. And fifty for the woman companion, the big one.'

The men looked at each other with pleased grins plastered on their faces. 'Easy money, boys.'

'Maybe not so easy,' muttered one of the men. 'I saw those boys use their bows. They ain't no brahmacharya novices.'

'Get the mother, you get the boys,' said Aarohan harshly. He looked directly at the man who had complained. 'Use her as a hostage, or as you please if that works. The boys will do anything to save her. Anything.'

The men nodded, liking the sound of this now. 'That's three hundred gold coins for the mother and sons then,' said another man. 'Right, Captain?'

Aarohan nodded. 'And fifty for the woman companion.'

His aide grinned slyly. 'Sounds like you don't want them saying the wrong things to the right people.'

Aarohan nodded. 'I don't want them saying anything ever again. See to it,' he barked.

'Yes, sir, yes Captain!' replied his men smartly.

They split into two groups and rode in separate directions.

Across the stream, Bejoo watched them go, then turned and melted back into the forest.

THREE

Lakshman emerged from the royal pavilion, face tight with anger. Bharat and Shatrughan watched as he strode to and fro several times, trying to work off his fury, then went over to a horse trough that had just been filled with fresh water for the emperor's own horse and emptied a pailful of water over his own head. He shook his face free of the excess water, spitting out a mouthful angrily. His brothers waited for him to cool down sufficiently to speak.

'He will not listen to reason,' he told them. 'He says he has heard the testimony of the witnesses and seen the evidence and has delivered his judgement.'

Bharat and Shatrughan exchanged a glance. 'But we were there! We can bear witness to what happened. What about our testimony?'

Lakshman dipped another pail and drank deeply from it. Nearby, the tethered horse whinnied in protest. 'He will not hear or see anyone else. He is in consultation with the War Council.' Lakshman clenched his fist around the handle of the pail. 'Jabali is by his side, filling his ear with venom. I heard them talking of war with Videha when I entered.'

Shatrughan sat on the edge of the trough, not caring that the water was sloshing over the edge. 'This is bad, bhraatr. We have to do something. We must stop this madness.'

Lakshman took a deep breath and exhaled slowly. 'I can do nothing further.'

Bharat took hold of Lakshman's arm. 'You can't just walk away! That was Sita Bhabhi and her sons we saw. Our nephews. Did you tell Rama that much at least?'

Lakshman took hold of Bharat's forearm and dislodged his brother's hand from his biceps. 'I tried everything. But he is on a road without any chance of slowing or turning back. There is only one way to go from here—forward.'

'And forward means war with our own allies? This is madness,' Shatrughan said.

'This is Rama, emperor of Kosala,' Lakshman said bitterly. 'And these are the limits to my influence over him. If I try to circumvent his authority, I will be in defiance of the throne as you two are.'

'There must be something we can do to stop this. I know that lout Aarohan and his thugs are up to something.'

'If they are, then it is with the full knowledge and oversight of Pradhan Mantri Jabali himself,' Lakshman said morosely. 'He personally vouched for the king's guard. They function under his command, did you know that? Even the king himself does not have command of his own guard!'

'Let me speak to Kausalya-maa,' Bharat said. 'She talked some sense into Rama's head earlier. Maybe he will listen to her again.' He started to leave.

Lakshman caught his brother's arm, stopping him. 'There is no use. He will see no one now that the War Council is in session. Besides, to back down now would be to lose face before Jabali and the War Council. It would be a tactical error to call on his mother each time he needs correction.'

'Then what do you propose we do?' Shatrughan asked. 'Stand by and watch this juggernaut,' he gestured towards the enormous army camp sprawled along the banks of the Sarayu for yojanas downriver, 'roll on and crush our own relatives and friends across the land? Plunge the entire civilised world into the madness of a war without reason, without purpose?'

Lakshman stood up. 'There may be a way to get Rama to listen. Someone he cannot dismiss as easily as his brothers or his mother.'

'Who?' Bharat asked curiously.

Lakshman looked at each of them in turn. 'His sons.'

They were silent for a moment. Then Bharat and Shatrughan both smiled. Shatrughan slapped Lakshman's shoulder. 'Now this is the Lakshman I grew up with,' he said, grinning widely.

Lakshman shrugged. 'It took me a while, but I finally realised I can't just go on this way. Things are going out of hand in Ayodhya. This madness has to stop.'

'Very well, then, bhraatr, we are with you. What shall we do?'

Lakshman gestured to where their horses stood waiting and ready. 'You two ride back into the forest and try to find the sons of Sita before Aarohan and his men do. If our suspicions are right, that villain will be trying his best to track them and kill them. Make sure you keep them alive. Officially though, you will both be on a personal mission on my direct orders, your goal being to find the Ashwamedha stallion.'

Bharat nodded. 'We understand. What will you do in the meanwhile?'

Lakshman turned and glared in the direction of the royal pavilion. 'I'll wait here for an opportunity to get Rama alone without Jabali or the other ear-poisoners. When you find the twins, bring Sita Bhabhi and them here.'

'And then what happens?' Shatrughan asked, mounting his horse. Bharat did the same beside him.

'Then we shall have a family reunion,' Lakshman said.

He slapped the rumps of their horses, sending them lurching forward and on their way.

* * *

Captain Aarohan studied the valley one last time before turning to his aides. 'This time we have them. This valley is a death trap. There are only two ways out. North, back to the raj-marg, the Sarayu River and then Mithila. The Imperial Army is already on that route. All we have to do is move one akshohini ahead of the main procession and position it so that anyone exiting the forest on that road is instantly captured.'

'But the army is supposed to follow the trail of the Ashwamedha stallion, not range ahead at will,' said one of his aides.

Aarohan made a sound of impatience. 'Yes. And once the stallion is captured, the army does what it must to recapture it.'

'Ah. Of course.'

Aarohan shook his head despairingly. 'Leave the military strategy to me. Just follow orders. Now, as I was saying, there are only two ways out of this valley. The other way is east by south-east. If they go that way, we have them. In fact, it would be best if we force them in that direction.'

His aide frowned, but hesitated before asking the question.

Aarohan cursed. 'Because it leads to a series of ravines and gullies and finally ends in a box canyon.' He looked around to make sure they all understood. 'A dead end. Once we chase them in there, they will be like rats in a trap. We have only to poke them through the bars until they are dead.'

The aides nodded.

'I am so happy we are all in agreement,' Aarohan said sarcastically. 'Make sure the akshohini on the raj-marg covering that patch of forest is prominently visible. The outlaws will most likely attempt to exit using the old grama-train route that snakes through the jungle and rejoins the raj-marg at the Ahilya Bai junction, some miles outside of Mithila.'

The aides exchanged a glance. One spoke cautiously: 'That will put the army on Mithila land. Well into Videha territory.'

Aarohan nodded. 'That's the idea. We operate on the premise that the old minister Sumantra was murdered by Samrat Rama's own brothers along with the Mithilan brigands, who then stole the sacred stallion and absconded with him into the jungle. We have every right under Arya law to rove wherever necessary to recover the stallion.'

'And every acre of land we cover while doing so becomes annexed to Kosala?' said another aide, tentatively adding a questioning note to the statement. 'So we incidentally expand Ayodhya's dominion in the course of this outlaw hunt! That's sharp.'

'Not as sharp as the point of my blade if we fail at this mission,' said Aarohan shortly. He half-drew his sword, keeping his hand on the hilt to let them know he was done chatting and that this was serious business now. 'We all know the upside of success on this job. The downside is not something that bears thinking about, so I suggest you don't dwell on it. Do as I order. Get these outlaws. And we all go home rich and set for life.'

They all nodded tersely, none of them grinning or saying an unnecessary word.

Aarohan looked at each one of them in turn to make sure his message had struck home. When he was satisfied he had made his point as effectively as possible, he slid the sword back into the hilt and leaned forward on his saddle. He pointed down into the valley, jabbing his finger as he pointed and instructed: 'This is how we round them up and herd them,' he said, 'just like running cattle except that this time we don't have to worry about being chased by the cattle owners.' He grinned brightly, light eyes twinkling in his fair face. 'We'll be doing all the chasing.'

* * *

Bejoo started as a lithe figure leaped down from the tree branch to land beside him. 'Boy,' he said softly, 'you gave me a start.' He glanced up at the tree. 'I checked that tree just before I stopped here.' He didn't add 'in case there might be snakes hanging from the branches'. The fact was he could still hear the screams of those bitten soldiers and see their bloodless faces as they gasped and choked out their last breaths by the stream. He thought he would see them in his nightmares forever—or at least as long as he lived.

Luv grinned up at him, squatting. 'I wasn't there when you stopped here. I waited till you settled before coming over. I used the vanar highway.'

Bejoo frowned. 'The vanar highway...' An image flashed in his mind, of Hanuman loping through the trees along the Sarayu near Ayodhya, a sight that had never failed to draw excited cries and pointed fingers, particularly among the children of the city back in the months following Rama's return. Another age, another Ayodhya. The vanar could race along the treeline faster than the fastest horse in the kingdom. Bejoo doubted if these boys could travel as fast through the trees, lacking Hanuman's particular bodily appendages, but he guessed they must be fast enough to have dropped in on him so suddenly. He had only stopped here a moment ago. 'I understand,' he said, smiling. 'You are resourceful little fellows, younguns. I knew you were someone special the minute I laid eyes on you on that grama marg the other day.'

Luv shrugged with some embarrassment. 'Sorry we held you up that day. You did get back the wagon with all its contents, didn't you?'

'Oh yes, Nakhudi returned it safe and sound, thank you very much.' Bejoo reflected briefly that had they not stolen the wagon and Nakhudi not returned it, he would never have got involved in this in the first place. 'Actually, I'm very happy you robbed our grama-train that day.'

Luv crinkled his nose. It was somewhat snubbed, resembling his mother's slightly snubbed nose. 'You are?' He looked puzzled.

Bejoo patted him on the back affectionately, careful not to touch the oversized rig bristling with arrows. 'It was the best thing that happened to me in the last ten years.'

Luv shrugged, making a face that suggested he would never understand the ways and minds of grown-ups. 'We know they're coming. We're ready for them.'

Bejoo stared at him. 'Ready? My boy, from what I saw, you and your brother are very good with your bows, but these are armed, armoured, mounted, and trained mercenaries. More of them than even I have seen together in my life. There are over a hundred mounted men in the king's guard, with another full company of about one thousand on foot. And they know what they're doing from the looks of it. Don't under-estimate that Captain Aarohan. He's a brute, but he's an experienced brute. When he comes at you with over one thousand armed killers, he means business. And that's not counting the Imperial Army at his back for whatever support he needs. You cannot fight these men with just your bows, lad!'

Luv looked undisturbed by Bejoo's speech. 'Why not? It's been done before. There's the famous battle of Janasthana where a band of outlaws stood against a horde of thousands of rakshasas. Berserkers too! And still they won.'

Bejoo realised the boy was referring to the battle led by Rama himself, against the last survivors of the clan of rakshasas that had come to avenge the humiliation of their sister-rakshasa Surpanakha, twenty-three years ago. He wondered if Luv and his brother knew that the leader of that 'band of outlaws' had been none other than their own father. He wasn't going to be the one to tell them. Especially not here and now! The boy had a grandiose enough opinion of his and his brother's abilities as it was.

'Forget tales and legends,' he said gently, 'this is real. These men are worse than rakshasas. They have the power and might of the kingdom backing them. They will not stop until they get what they want.'

Luv nodded. 'We have the royal stallion. We kept it safe. We think they mean to kill it and blame it on us.'

Bejoo spread his hands. 'Yes! That is exactly what they mean to, I have no doubt at all. You see? That's why I must take the stallion back to Ayodhya myself. I have the ear of Pradhan Mantri Jabali. He will listen to me. I will take the horse to him and attempt to sort out this entire situation. It's the only way.'

Luv looked at him with a strangely intense expression that belied his years. 'And what of the ashram slaughter? The extermination of the outlaw camps? The killing of Nakhudi's friends? We thought the bearkillers were monsters, but these men are the real demons. They are asuras in human guise. We cannot let them walk away unpunished.'

Bejoo sighed. 'What do you want me to say, youngun? They are authorised by Jabali himself under Rama's authority. If I try to accuse them, I would be clapped in chains before I could finish explaining. They are too powerful to bring to book right away. But at some point in time, once this is all over, we can try our best to see that justice is done—where are you going?'

Luv had risen to his feet and turned away. He stopped and looked back at Bejoo darkly. 'There is no other point in time. This is the time. This is the place. This is the day they come to justice.' He raised his bow. 'And this is the instrument of their danda.'

Bejoo rose to a half-crouch, his ageing knees and joints protesting. 'Boy, listen to me.'

Luv's face was caught by a beam of sunlight shining through the dense dappled tree cover as he looked back. Bejoo was struck by how much the boy resembled his father at that moment, in that angle and light. Despite his boyish voice, his tone was as stern and forbidding as Rama himself: 'Bejoo-chacha, thank you for everything you have done for us. Leave the rest to Kush and me now.'

And before Bejoo could say another word, he was gone, vanished like a deer into the dark woods.

FOUR

The men of the Captain's Guard were confident of themselves. They were a ragtag band of ruffians who had lent their swords out for hire in half a dozen different kingdoms across the civilised world. Most of them were Mlecchas, barbarians from foreign lands beyond the great Kush mountain ranges or across the great oceans that bounded the sub-continent. Their mixture of skin colour and appearance betrayed their worldly mix as did their accents and languages, and customs. They were a motley bunch with only three things in common—they knew how to kill, they enjoyed doing it, and they had no compunctions about who was at the receiving end of their blows or thrusts. Brahmins or merchants, kings or serving girls, soldiers or other sell-swords, they had killed all kinds. Often enough to know that all living creatures died much the same way and were as easy or hard to kill. They had turned execution into an art, assassination into a craft, murder into a thriving trade and now, as their youth soured into mature manhood, they sought to secure their futures, build a nest for themselves where they could indulge their varied vices and live out the rest of their lives in opulence and luxury. They had seen their numbers ebb and flow any number of times in the past decade itself, for the mortality rate in their business was the highest imaginable and it was time now to settle down and reap the fruits of their adventuring.

As the ancient jest went—what happens to criminals when they retire? They become politicians. Politics would do very nicely, thank you. And the totalitarian regime that dominated Kosala now made Ayodhya the ideal place for such men to settle and make their homes. After all, the courts of kingdoms across the world were filled with over-dressed overweight nobles and aristocrats who had risen through much the same means: by doing whatever they had to in order to get there. To them, the end always justified the means and today, their end was to kill the woman named Vedavati and her twin sons Luv and Kush... by any means necessary. It was a mission simpler, by far, than most they had undertaken until now. Even the handful who had been with the band since the beginning—Aarohan and his aides—could not recall an assignment that had seemed less daunting and which promised greater rewards. The mood was good, morale high, and an air of certain victory reigned among the company as it poured into the valley.

They moved through the valley in a familiar pattern they had executed several times before, laying out a grid on which men moved in trios, each one positioned diagonally to the other two at all times, thereby enabling them to watch one another's flanks and rear. The valley was perhaps a mile from the highest point of the eastern hill to the peak of the western hill bounding it, most of that distance at ground level. It was a little more than a mile long, the two hills converging in a series of wadis and gullies that wound and crisscrossed until they led to the box canyon surrounded by sheer crumbling rock faces. It was impossible to climb over those rock faces and there was no way to ride or walk or climb around them. Once a person entered the wadis and gullies from any point, they would either end up going in circles until they came back into the valley, or enter the box canyon and be boxed in.

Aarohan had deployed the full thousand men at his command into the valley at once, determined to flush out and finish off the prey within the day rather than prolong this hunt. He and his hundred horse-mounted cavalry stayed on the hill-rise overlooking the valley, watching from above. It was difficult to see much with the dense tree cover, but unlike the jungle outside the valley, there were gaps in the trees here and even a few small clearings, and he could glimpse the reflection of noon sunlight on weapons and armour and buckles and helmets as his warriors moved in threes. He smiled as he watched the frontline cross the halfway point. There was less than half a mile between them and the box canyon now. Already the prey was trapped. It was only a matter of time now.

* * *

Bejoo waited until the last possible moment before ordering his men into action. He knew from experience that a larger company attacking a smaller target would be more cautious and wary when they first entered the new environment. The further they went into hostile territory without encountering any resistance, the more complacent and less alert they grew. In this case, he could hear the occasional gruff laughter of Aarohan's men and see the flash of their teeth as they jested and laughed their way up the valley. It was evident that they did not think much of the target they intended to acquire and were already assuming that the target was probably skulking quietly, sweating it out and hoping not to be found. It was a common mistake made when fighting outlaws and refugees. It was true that these were people who had run away or chose to stay away from civilised society. But that did not mean they were all cowards or that they could not fight. Push them too hard, invade their territories, *slaughter their loved ones and friends*...and they would fight back more fiercely than trained soldiers. He knew that these arrogant mercenaries were in for a surprise once they finally came face to face with their quarry. But he also knew that once that happened, the fight would be over very quickly. Short and fierce. Because there were thousands of these brutes. And only a handful of defenders. And of those defenders, very few could actually fight. Which was why most of the bearkillers and Nakhudi herself were in the box canyon, protecting the survivors of the ashram massacre. And the sacred horse.

So Bejoo had positioned his small band of grama-rakshaks with their backs to the canyon, at the end of the valley. In order to get to the defenders, Aarohan's men would have to get past them. And that would only happen when Bejoo and every last one of his men were down.

He had spoken briefly to his men before they deployed into the valley. His scouts told him that Aarohan's company would be here in moments, so they did not have much time. They were barely a few hundred yards ahead of the enemy. Still, he needed to say what he had to say—and to give them a chance to respond, should they choose to do so.

'You are all olduns like myself,' he said gruffly. 'So I won't unload the usual wagonload of uks offal on your heads the way they do with younguns. If nothing else, we've all earned the right to hear things said plainly and directly.'

There was a chuckle or two at his colourful reference, but for the most part the band of grizzled, white-bearded, white-haired and bald-headed veterans gazed back with apparent indifference at him. These were men who had seen too much to get excited over anything anymore. The fact that they were here was enough.

'What we are about to do is foolish and heroic. We are likely to die doing it. And even if some of us survive, we will either be killed on the spot or be executed later. Not to put too fine a point on it, we are going up against suicidal odds and our action will probably be termed treasonous.'

He looked around to see if there was any reaction to those words. One oldun hawked and spat a mouthful of supari juice; another with his hair tied behind his head with a cloth band scratched his backside, but mostly everyone just looked old and disinterested. Only the newest man in the group, that big-built fellow who had joined them only a few days earlier, seemed to display a modicum of reaction. The man had been a gatewatch sentry all his life, Bejoo recalled, a familiar face at the First Gate for as long as Bejoo could remember. He had been retired involuntarily, he had said, yet another modern development brought in by the new regime. In Bejoo's time the only way a soldier 'retired' was when he died in battle. There was no other form of retirement. *So long as I can raise my sword...* went the old kshatriya tavern song, with a second

line that descended into ribaldry...*And so long as I can raise my sword...*
The gatewatch retiree was the only one whose face showed some
semblance of emotion and that emotion was a familiar one. *He wants
to fight the bastards who retired him, the new order that seeks to change the old ways
and bring in a 'better' Ayodhya for all. He wants to show those young idiots backed
by venal old war-mongers that real soldiers don't retire and don't go out looking for
trouble: they just do their job quietly and when trouble comes, they don't back down.
What was the man's name again? Somasra. That was it. Old gatewatch Somasra.*

'I am going to fight for these people because I believe they are being
unjustly hunted down and slaughtered without cause or provocation.
That goes against everything I know about kshatriya dharma. It is an
affront to Ayodhya that these so-called king's guard wear our national
colours and claim to be acting in our national interest. They represent
everything that is wrong with our kingdom and has been growing steadily
wronger over the past decade. With all due respect to Samrat Rama
Chandra, I think he does not know the half of what some of his people are
up to and if he did he would not condone their actions or endorse them.
But since they act in his name, and since there is no time to seek out the
Samrat or his advisors and beg for this action to be halted, the only way
is to stand and face them down.'

He looked around, indicating their numbers. 'Or at least hold them
off as long as possible. Now, I do this out of my own choice. You don't
have to. Those who wish to turn back can do so now, before the King's
Guard arrive. Slip out through the forest and go farther north or south
or wherever you please. Those who wish to stay and die with me today...
well, all I can say about those who do stay...' he shrugged, then raised
his voice to heckle them furiously: '...*is that you're a bunch of farting old fools
with more pride in dharma than love of life.*'

At this, they perked up a little, some snorting, others rubbing
moustaches and slapping arms and thighs. Old Somasra showed his
teeth: they were quite yellow and the front two were missing. *Sign of a
man who stuck his face where it doesn't belong—or where it does,* Bejoo's wife used

to say when she saw a kshatriya like that. Then she would look at him as if to say silently: *Like yourself.*

'Are we going to fight now,' said the old gatewatch Somasra, 'or are we going to stand around here all day talking and polishing each other's swords?'

This brought a few guffaws. Bejoo grinned. At least he had got through to them, with Somasra's help. 'Very well. We take a defensive position at the end of the valley and only show ourselves at the last moment, when they are almost upon us.'

'And then we kill them with our bad breath,' said another oldun with only one arm and one eye. He had lost the limb in the last Asura War and the eye in a childhood fight, and while he had once been able to wield a sword with his good arm better than most men with two good arms, he now had to use a lighter shortsword because it was all he could manage to lift. The man would probably not survive his first clash with the enemy, yet here he was, tossing off a quip as if he were teaching new recruits on the training field.

'You do that, Yuddhajit,' said one of the others, stuffing a fresh plug of tobacco in his mouth. 'You're armed for it!'

Guffaws all around. Then they disbanded and descended into the valley. Barely had they entered the treeline when Bejoo made out the distant thunder of approaching hooves. Soon after, he had turned back and peered cautiously through a gap and saw the familiar half-shaved, half-bearded face of the captain of the king's guard. *See you at the end of my sword,* he thought, then continued working his way through the undergrowth with greater stealth. The element of surprise—if even that—was about all they had on their side.

That, and two young boys with big bows and even bigger hearts.

But he had fought and lived long enough to know that even the biggest of hearts couldn't overcome odds like these.

It's just not possible, he thought morosely. *Once they knock us down, there'll be nothing to stop them barging into that canyon and finishing the slaughter they began yesterday.*

All the more reason why his olduns and he had to do whatever damage they could. Perhaps if they caused enough casualties, Aarohan would withdraw and leave the regular army to flush out the rebels. If they did that, then at least there might be a chance, however slender, that the commanding officer would honour kshatriya dharma and not cut down brahmins, women, and children out of hand.

It wasn't much but it was all that he could think of and hope for. And die for.

Time now, he thought, as he glimpsed and heard the frontline of Aarohan's guard approach his position. He glanced to right and left. Somewhere over there in the shade of those trees was the old gatewatch Somasra. Yes, there he was, a hulking shadow no less a tree trunk in his own right. The man must have been formidable in his youth. Bejoo nodded at the shadow, not sure if Somasra saw him.

Then he raised his sword and launched himself at the nearest trio of the approaching King's Guard.

FIVE

'Jai Shree Shaneshwara!' Bejoo cried as he launched himself at the closest trio of the King's Guard.

Somasra had seen the grama-rakshak's sign and was prepared. Even as Bejoo leaped out, shouting loud enough to send cockatoos screeching in panic from the trees overhead, Somasra stepped from his hiding place and began slashing with his double-sided sword at the next trio.

They were momentarily distracted by Bejoo's cry—which was the reason why the grama-rakshak had shouted a battle cry in the first place. It served to inform his own men that the attack had begun, and to distract the approaching enemy frontline for that brief instant. Somasra took full advantage of the distraction.

He leaped into the centre of the triangle formed by the three king's guards, slashing sideways at the first. He caught the man completely unawares and had the satisfaction of striking aside the man's drawn sword and feeling his own blade bite deeply. The man collapsed, gouting blood.

But that was all the advantage Somasra got. The other two immediately moved to take up positions on either side of Somasra, forcing him to fight on two fronts at once. That was a deadly game. It had been a long time since he had seen active combat. Most of his decades on gatewatch had been spent breaking up brawls, dealing with angry traders, and offensive foreigners who thought it their birthright to enter any city they pleased and act as they desired. But there had been a fair share of good fights as well, mostly with armed and dangerous men, some drunk, others just mean enough to take satisfaction from gutting a guard or two, even though they knew they would be caught at once and thrown into the dungeons. Casualties among gatewatch guards weren't high, but they did occur and Somasra had seen a fair number of fellow gatewatch guards cut down on the job. Enough to make him stay relatively well enough in shape and practise every chance he got.

Now, he had to work for his life. The two king's guards were shrewd and young and experienced enough to have taken down men like him before. They made him dance, toying with him, one coming in and pretending to get past his guard, forcing him to turn and swing to defend himself, the other doing the same on the other side, until all he was doing was swinging this way and that like a dancer at a king's court. He would soon tire like this and sooner or later, one of them would get a point in and then the other would finish the job. Already he felt his old lower back injury protest as he swung from the hip, trying to keep both in sight at once and failing because they were smart enough to know just how far apart to stand.

There was only one way to end this dance and he resorted to it. When one of them feinted, grinning with the knowledge that he was a foot closer than the last attempt, Somasra lunged at the man. They were prepared for this move—it was the cue for the other fellow to step in fast from behind and run his sword through Somasra's kidney—but what they weren't prepared for was what he did next. He grabbed the first man's sword hand, then the man's neck and shoulder, turned and swung the man towards his oncoming comrade. The other man, rushing in to aim at Somasra's kidney from behind, realised what was about to happen and tried to turn away but was too late. His thrusting blade punched into his own fellow's belly, running the man through. The first man collapsed on the ground, heaving in his death throes. The second fellow's sword, trapped in the man's stomach, required a moment to be pulled free. That moment gave Somasra's ageing muscles and feet enough time to cover the few yards of ground and hack at the man's exposed neck with the power of his bunched arms. He nearly took the man's head off.

Leaning on his bloody sword, gasping for breath, he heard the cries and shouts of outraged men from all across the valley. It seemed the element of surprise had worked for them after all. Those to him sounded like the king's guards dying—the olduns would just grunt and die, they wouldn't waste their fading breath trying to shout. Some of them probably couldn't shout, their throats hoarsened by overuse and chewing too much supari. They were old enough to know when a man died he died alone even if he was on a battlefield surrounded by a dozen akshohinis of his own. Only the young mercenary fools would shout to warn each other and call for help. Somasra grinned at the screams that rang through the noonday stillness. Maybe old gold was as tough as young steel after all.

He heard a sound behind him and turned to see two men in King's Guard uniforms approaching. They had blood on their anga-vastras and swords, and since there were only two of them, he could only presume they had met one of his comrades and come off victors. They approached him cautiously but confidently, secure in their youth and knowledge of superior numbers. He sighed. Now he would be obliged to kill these two in order to avenge his fallen fellow as well as defend his own life. Oh well. If he hadn't wanted to dance he wouldn't have come to the wedding feast.

'Come on, littleuns,' Somasra said, forcing his tired shoulder and back muscles to heave and raise the lowered sword. 'Time for your bloodbath. Don't forget to wash behind the ears.'

* * *

Bejoo finished cutting down his second trio of enemy and took a brief moment to catch his breath. He leaned against a tree trunk spattered with the gore from a slashed throat. He looked back and found himself unable to believe that those six corpses were his work. Six young men of the King's Guard? Really? Either these mercenaries were out of practice or they had grown too accustomed to easy pickings. Although, he admitted ruefully as he worked a broken tooth loose from a socket and examined it, they hadn't seemed out of practice when he was surrounded by them, three at a time and fighting for his life. In fact, come to think of it, they had been quite good. Perhaps he simply had more experience and knowledge of swordcraft? Or perhaps—and this was more likely— he had more reason to fight than they.

The cries and shouts from across the valley had ceased. Only the cries of the birds remained in the still afternoon air, calling out in plaintive tones as they circled the valley, wanting to return to their roosts if the wretched humans below had finished killing each other. *Not yet, winged brothers, but soon it will all be over. Very soon.* He was old and experienced enough to know that killing those six men had taken everything he had. Now, he would be lucky if he was able to keep the next trio at bay for more than a few minutes before succumbing.

A sudden silence fell upon the valley. He frowned. That was odd. Then he tilted his head and listened. The faint sounds of clashing weaponry had ceased as well. That could only mean one thing: the enemy had retreated. And he knew that his old veterans, however bravely they might have conducted themselves in the first clash, were not enough cause for a force of a thousand king's guards to retreat. No. They were simply regrouping and changing tactics. They would attack again soon and this time, they would cut through Bejoo and his dirty dozens in a matter of minutes.

He wiped his face clean and held his sword ready, taking up a position which afforded him cover on at least one side. It meant he would be boxed in if they came at him in numbers but this was likely to be his last stand anyway. He would rather be taken from the front than from behind.

A sound came to his ears.

He frowned but it was gone as quickly as it had come.

He waited and listened.

There it was again.

And again.

And yet again.

Then it continued almost non-stop, a rhythmic repetition. The same, or similar sounds, repeated over and over again, like some distant drummer's beat. For an instant, he wondered if it was a drummer's beat. But that was no drumbeat. It was…something else. Something he had heard infinite times before and knew intimately well. He clenched his free hand, frustrated at not being able to identify the sound.

Then a man's sound came on the still afternoon air. A choking wet cry, as a man might make if struck in the throat with a blade. A quick explosion of air before the blood rushed up and spurted out the hole.

A few minutes later, there was another man's sound, this one a distinctive death rattle in a dying man's throat. As if he had been cut down but the message that he was dead had yet to reach his flailing limbs. It ended with another repetition of that sound. The first sound.

After a few more moments, Bejoo understood that men were dying across the valley. Not his men, not the dirty dozens. The sounds of dying men were coming from several yards further out, from the enemy frontlines. So the men who were dying were king's guards. No mystery to that. The question was: who was killing them and how?

He didn't think his olduns would have gone after the retreating frontline. They wouldn't have had the energy for one thing. And they might be suicidal, but they were not stupid: at best, they had dealt with four score or five score of the enemy. There was still the better part of a thousand more out there, across the valley. To hold them off was madness enough: to try to push them back was ludicrous. No. Bejoo was dead certain that all his men were to his left and right, spread out in a long ragged line across this end of the valley. The sounds and death rattles were coming from farther down. It had to be King's Guard men dying.

Then it came to him.

The sound.

It was the sound of a weapon being deployed. One so familiar he berated himself for not recognising it at once.

'Arrows!'

That was the sound of an arrow whickering through the air across a long distance. It should have been almost silent except to the bowman himself, but the sound was amplified by the bowl-shape of the valley, which was why he heard it at all. And those death rattles were the ones that hadn't killed their targets instantly. Which meant all the others had struck home dead to rights. This was the sound of arrows being shot from somewhere behind him and at the King's Guard soldiers spread out across the valley. Being shot with deadly accuracy and lightning speed.

He began to count the rhythm of the loosing and was astonished to find himself unable to keep up. How fast were they shooting? How was it possible to shoot that fast and with such accuracy? Then he understood: *there are two of them. They shoot alternately, so at any given instant, there's always an arrow in the air. That way, they cover each other during the moment between shots.*

He marvelled at the skill and training that had gone into perfecting such a system.

Then, after he had mulled over that for a moment, he wondered how many enemy soldiers they were actually hitting.

SIX

L uv and Kush were a single being and that being's entire existence was dedicated to a single task: destruction. They had found a position on the top of the rock face above the box canyon, overlooking the valley, yet still high enough to cover most of the low-lying basin. It had taken them time to climb up here, carrying their heavy burden for they were carrying their entire store of arrows. Ever since they had learned to loose and Maatr had taught them the importance of replacing what they used, they had taken to crafting at least a certain number of arrows each day. They used many during their practice play each day, developing their own methods for various angles of attack, for shooting from low positions upwards and from high to low, through leaves and foliage, across water, into water, against the wind, downwind…every imaginable situation in which it was possible to fire arrows, they experimented with, mastered, and then perfected. Whenever possible, they reused their arrows. But many were damaged in use, or not retrievable. That was when they thought of the possibility of someday requiring a store of arrows for defending the ashram. They would require perfectly made and stored arrows, not reused ones chipped or bent or damaged in any way. And when that day came, it would be too late to start making and storing.

So they had taken to making a certain number every day for their practice…and setting a fixed number aside. They made the best arrows they were capable of making, honing the fletching and shaft and head after much experimentation and use in various situations. Finally, they had begun saving their store carefully in bales of straw to avoid warping from moisture and then stored the bales themselves in the box canyon. They had retrieved the bundles earlier and then carried them up here to this position which had been chosen months earlier, in case of just such a contingency. At the time they had never seriously thought that they would literally be fending off an army. But just in case, they thought it wouldn't hurt to be prepared. Besides, arrows could be sold at the city markets or to the occasional grama-train—the ones they didn't waylay—for a small profit. If nothing else, they had intended to sell their store and buy Maatr something from the market or a trader. A new veena perhaps to replace the old moulding one she played on. Luckily for them, Maatr's naming day was a good few months away and their store was intact.

Now, they depleted that store at a prodigious rate. They were loosing faster than they had ever loosed before, and for longer, and across greater distances and with unerring accuracy. For one thing, they had never actually aimed to kill before. They loved the creatures of the forest and could never dream of killing them for sport—or for food, which was, in a sense, worse. They had always practised on inanimate objects, resorting to clever tricks to increase the challenge when practising. One of them would spin a stone in the air, for instance, and the other aimed at it. Or a piece of driftwood rushing down white waters served as a moving target. Or objects hung from trees a hundred yards distant. Over time, the stones flung in the air had become smaller, the driftwood reduced to a mere chip, the objects hung from trees merely dots and painted leaves. The use of natural challenges had only sharpened their skills.

But killing actual living beings was a different experience. They had not anticipated the shock they felt when their first arrows punched into the throats of the first two men. This had happened immediately after the clash with Bejoo's men, when the King's Guard frontline had retreated to regroup and prepare for their next attack. Luv and Kush had seen their opportunity and fired their first two shots, aiming at two men standing in a clearing with drawn, bloody swords, hacking at a badly wounded, but still alive veteran. The veteran wasn't making any sound or crying for mercy and that was probably what irked the two guardsmen. So they had taken to chopping and poking at the fallen man in a bid to evoke some response. Luv had pointed out the men using the terse short form they had developed over the years when practising together.

'South-south-west, one and one,' he said, naming the direction in which the targets lay when viewed from their position and the individual targets themselves.

'I see them,' Kush replied, his bow already turned and aimed, string taut and ready to fire. 'You first?'

'Loose,' Luv said and released his arrow. As he bent his hand back to pluck another arrow from the rig over his shoulder, Kush released his arrow as well. By the time Luv's second arrow was notched and strung and ready to loose, Kush's hand was reaching for his second arrow.

That first time, they had paused and looked at the results of their shots.

Both the guardsmen clutched their throats, blood spurting brazenly between their fingers, and collapsed on the ground, the first dying instantly, the second shuddering once, then laying still.

The wounded veteran sat up slowly, staring at the corpses with arrows standing from their ravaged throats and looked around in grim amazement. He seemed almost disappointed to be alive as he staggered to his feet and hobbled towards Luv and Kush's side of the valley. The twins lowered their bows and followed him until they saw three or four of his comrades emerge from their hiding places to assist him. Then, moving as one, they raised their bows again to seek new targets.

Both of them paused yet again, lowered their bows completely, letting the drawstrings go limp, and looked at each other.

Both of them had tears in their eyes.

'I killed a man,' each of them said at exactly the same time.

'But I had to,' each one added.

They cried for a moment, the tears running freely down their faces. Their throats hitched once, then they wiped their faces clear with the length of cloth they kept to keep their hands clean and sweat-free during their practice sessions. They knew now that this was no more a practice session. This was the real thing. It was war. They thought for a moment silently, their faces hardening, the tears replaced by a new emotion.

'They attacked the ashram and slaughtered everyone in sight,' Kush said.

'They would have killed every last person if we didn't arrive with the bearkillers to stop them,' Luv said.

'They were even going to kill the cows and calves.'

'They killed Sarama and most of her pack.'

'They wounded Maatr badly, almost killed her.'

'They mean to kill us all now. And nobody else is going to save us or stop them.'

'There are thousands of them.'

'Hundreds of thousands.'

'Crores and arbo even.'

'There are hardly any of us.'

'We have the right to defend our home, our loved ones, and ourselves by any means necessary.'

'It is the law of survival,' Luv said.

'It is the duty of a kshatriya to take arms when needed,' Kush said.

'It is our dharma,' they said together.

Then they raised their bows as one.

Tracked and found targets. This was easy because the valley was crawling with hundreds of easy-to-spot targets. While the soldiers might be partially covered by the trees and foliage when seen at ground level, from this vantage point they were as easily visible as carved bone shapes on a chaupat dice board.

At first they called out targets to one another:

'North by north-east.'

'Due west.'

'West by south-west.'

'South by south-east.'

After a while, they stopped calling out targets. It seemed pointless. By then, they were in the grip of battle fever. Their hands, their shoulders, their back muscles, their eyes, their necks, all moved in concert as a unified whole. Like a single organism dedicated to only one function, they aimed and loosed, aimed and loosed, aimed and loosed, over and over again.

They kept count silently, only because they had been taught that as well by Maatr as well as by Nakhudi. It was part of the lesson on war which began: *Know Thy Enemy*. Knowing the enemy included knowing his strength in numbers and by extension, how many of that number your forces had succeeded in killing.

* * *

Aarohan stared down at the valley, speechless with rage. The runner who had just come up the hill to bring him word stood several yards away, out of sword reach. The man was familiar with Aarohan's temper.

'How many did you say?' he asked again.

The man glanced around nervously, then said, 'Over four score dead or dying in the first clash. And now, another three score downed by arrows.' The man paused, then cleared his throat. 'And as Sergeant Manasvir said to tell you, the arrows are taking lives at the rate of one every few seconds.'

'Yes, I heard you the first time,' Aarohan said, then seethed silently for a moment. He saw a flurry of movement in a cluster of trees then had an unmistakable glimpse of a man collapsing. The man's limbs fluttered then ceased movement. That was deadly accurate shooting. Whoever was loosing this barrage of arrows, they had the aim of an eagle-hawk swooping down on prey. Aarohan had once worked for a great lord of the desert who bred eagle-hawks. The desert lord had trained the birds to fly over his city of tents when he camped in an oasis for a few weeks at a time. The birds would fly so high overhead, one had to constantly keep looking up at the sun to spot them, and even then they circumscribed such enormous arcs that one could never locate the camp just by looking up at the birds. But if any stranger made the mistake of coming too close to the desert lord's camp, and if the stranger and his entourage met certain requirements—such as a large number of men bearing metal weapons—the birds would swoop down on them and attack. The clincher was in how they attacked: the birds were trained to swoop down and pluck out only the left eye of each man then fly back to their master and present him with the ripped-out eyeballs. Aarohan had witnessed the birds attacking a caravan in which he was travelling once and it had seemed as if a gust of wind blew out of a clear sky, tore out a man's eye and carried it away. The bird itself was barely a blur of feathers and talons and beak.

Now, for the first time since that day he saw another creature at work with the same deadly efficiency. An archer who possessed the ultimate level of perfection: the ability to spot a target, judge distance, bow-pull, pressure, wind, and then loose a killing shot…all within the space of half a heartbeat. It was impossible. No archer he had ever heard of possessed such speed and accuracy. It must be a platoon of archers. A company of archers, perhaps even a whole regiment, taking turns to loose, while spotters called out targets to them. But he knew that too was impossible: No group of archers could be loosing with such perfect repetition, over and over again. No, this must be a small band of truly gifted bowmen. A handful even. Perhaps even…

'Two young boys!' he said, and his mouth stayed open with awe and amazement. He felt a rush of excitement such as he had not felt in years. The sons of Sita! For who else could they be? The rumors he had heard whispered were true then. These were the heirs of Rama born in exile. And apparently they were heirs of his gift as a yoddha as well. They had to be the archers responsible for this killing wave. He had seen them briefly in action and they had certainly been quick enough. He had not thought them capable of such a concerted attack—nor of taking so many lives with such impunity. But apparently they were and could. Yes. It had to be them.

'Backtrack,' he told one of his aides curtly. The man nodded and rode off downhill to do as he bade.

'Pull back and use tree cover. Lay low until I give further orders,' he barked to another aide. This man too rode downhill at once. His aides were the men who had stayed the longest with him in service. And nobody stayed in service with him for long if they were prone to arguing or debating his orders.

Aarohan leaned over the rock on which he had been standing, peering down at the far end of the valley. It was too far to see clearly, but he thought he could faintly glimpse the thin lines of the arrows as they streaked down towards their targets. He could certainly see patches of foliage where the arrows cut through leaves and twigs to reach their mark. He estimated the shooting range to be at least four hundred yards, perhaps even five hundred.

For arrows to cover that distance and still punch through armour and bone...no, he corrected himself...*not armour and bone, merely flesh and cartilage. That's why they're aiming only at throats. So long as it arrives with enough force to punch through the larynx and sever the main blood vessels, it would be fatal everytime.* He admired the strategy and the execution both. *They must be firing from a high position, someplace from where they can see the whole valley and glimpse my men moving through the forest. And they must be standing and aiming downwards, with heavier-weight arrowheads, to give their arrows sufficient momentum and accuracy to cover such a long distance.*

But no amount of calculation and positioning was worth a pie if the archer's hand and eye were not perfect enough. To shoot ten or twenty times in a row with such accuracy was impressive. To do so three score times and more was unheard of. And that had been the tally several moments ago when the runner was despatched up here to bring word. In this much time, their tally must be twice as much!

Even if they missed occasionally, which was inevitable, it still meant that they were reaping a terrible toll. The olduns had put up stiffer resistance than he would have expected—not that he had been expecting them at all. Their very presence in this fray was a surprise.

But the fact that they could hold their own against his thousand was even more surprising. Still, more than half of them had been killed or severely wounded in that first clash. The second wave of attack would have finished them off. They would have been rolled up and packed away without further ado and his men could have taken the canyon thereafter.

But this was a new twist on the game. The sons of Sita, tallying deaths by the score, without taking a single casualty for their side. He would not have believed it possible had he not travelled widely enough and seen all the various ways in which men could kill and wage war against one another. Yes, two exceptionally good archers perfectly attuned to one another could keep up a killing barrage such as this for a length of time. But sooner or later, arms would tire, bows would lose their pulling strength, and arrows would be depleted. All he had to do was reduce their accuracy while continuing to force them to keep loosing. Hence the two orders he had issued: *pull back and use tree cover.* Which would starve the boys of targets, forcing them to shoot at movements behind trees, missing more and more often, wasting precious arrows and energy. Backtrack. Which would send his best scouts scouring around their flanks to find their exact position and mark it. Archers were well and good so long as they were shooting from a distance. The moment the fight came to them, up close and personal, they lost their advantage. And in a close fight, two striplings were no match for his elite hundred. All he had to do was slip in through their deadly circle of fire and attack man to man. The whole thing would be over in moments.

He grinned. At last he had an adversary worthy of his talents.

He waited for the next runner to bring word as he watched the hail of arrows continue.

SEVEN

When they were each past a hundred-count in enemy fatalities, something changed in the theatre of war.

They found it increasingly more difficult to acquire targets. At first they assumed that the invading forces were retreating. But that would mean moving backwards. Instead, they had simply gone to ground. They glimpsed flickers of movement behind tree trunks or through gaps in the foliage, but the men were apparently smart enough not to reveal themselves. The two hundred or so corpses with arrows sticking out of their throats probably acted as good motivation. As the seconds turned to minutes and then became a half-hour of the afternoon sun's westward progress, they realised that this was a stratagem by the enemy.

Suddenly, a man burst from cover and sprinted to the shelter of another tree. He was visible only partially for perhaps two heartbeats.

He fell, sprawling, with an arrow through his neck before he could reach halfway to his destination.

After several moments, another man in another part of the valley moved his position, showing his back and part of his head to them as he leaned against the trunk of the tree he was squatting behind. He was dead before his body hit the ground.

This continued for another half hour or so, the occasional target showing partially here and there. They took every shot they could get and their aim was true seven times out of ten. The three times they missed were only because the arrows struck armour or sword hilts and that too only because they were risking shots based on guesswork rather than clear acquisition.

After that, the soldiers seemed to grow more disciplined and even these occasional lapses ceased.

Finally, as a whole hour passed without their acquiring a single target or loosing a solitary arrow, they sighed together as one.

'We will have to change our position,' Luv said. 'It's the only way.'

Kush nodded. The predator could not simply wait for the prey to come to him: he had to go where the prey went. That was the basis of hunting.

Still, he was reluctant to leave their carefully chosen perch. Once they climbed down from here they would lose this panoramic view of the valley and be at the same level as the enemy. Which meant that the enemy would be able to see them too. Outnumbered as they were, once the enemy marked their position and attacked en masse, they could not possibly repel them for long. No. Up here, they were unapproachable except up the same crumbling rock face they had climbed to get here. The soldiers burdened with their armour and weapons would have a hard, slow struggle coming up and would make easy targets. Only so many could climb at a time after all. There was no other access by horse or on foot either. They were kings of this hill. Once they climbed down, they would lose their greatest advantage.

'No,' Kush said at last after weighing all options. 'They will still have to come forward and get past us as well as the old veterans in order to get to the canyon. If we wait them out, they will have no other option but to charge. We should remain here.'

Luv nodded. He too had reached the same conclusion. 'You speak truly, bhraatr. They are only testing our patience in the hope that we will show ourselves. So long as we wait them out, they will be forced to come to us eventually.'

'Then we are agreed. We stay here and wait.'

And so they waited. They decided to take turns watching the valley, one resting or refreshing himself while the other watched.

Another hour passed. The sun dipped lower in the western sky. Early afternoon moved slowly towards late afternoon.

Still, no soldiers advanced. The valley was as still as a graveyard.

* * *

Bejoo cursed. Somasra and the others looked up at him. They had spent the afternoon resting in the shade of the thicket near the rock face as a handful of their number took turns standing watch. It had been a dull afternoon after the action of that morning. More than half their number had died in that first clash itself and many who survived were nicked or wounded more severely. Only about a score remained fit enough to fight and perhaps half that number could lift their swords a time or two in defence. Considering the number of enemy amassed in the valley, it was a pitiful band. But the surviving fighting fit in the canyon were even fewer and once the enemy charged in full force, they would sweep all aside in a single attack.

The only reason they had survived the day at all was because of the sons of Sita. They had all marvelled at the skill with which the boys downed the enemy. Although they could not clearly tell how many casualties had been taken, they were in a position to see the arrows passing overhead and from their profusion alone they could estimate that a lot of the enemy were falling. The very fact that the advance had halted was itself proof of the efficacy of the archers. Bejoo had grinned each time he heard a muffled cry or throaty gargle across the valley, signalling the death of another of Aarohan's prized king's guard. How appropriate that the King's Guard should be cut down by the king's own sons! He grinned at the irony of the situation and enjoyed the brief respite.

Now, he saw something that made him curse and rise to his feet.

Somasra and the others reacted as well, rising and taking up their swords at once. Old they might be. Wounded and tired too. But they were neither careless nor foolish. Each man was willing to face death itself today, but only after he had exacted a great price from the enemy for his life. They had taken their respite but known that no battle could remain suspended for long, not when one side boasted such vastly superior numbers. It was only a matter of time before fighting resumed.

And now that time had come.

Bejoo cursed again and peered through the trees. The high afternoon sun threw the trees into deep shadow, making it difficult to penetrate the gloom of the thick undergrowth.

Somasra looked at him laconically. 'You want to tell us what you're cursing at, or is it a private matter you wish to keep to yourself?'

Bejoo gestured with a jerk of his head at the rock face behind. 'They've tracked them back, the bastards. They must have achieved a fix on their position by using their men as bait to draw their fire. Now they're moving in for the kill.'

Somasra peered through the shadows of the thicket. His old eyes glimpsed a flicker of movement that could have been a ladybug leaping onto a leaf, but his warrior's instincts told him that it was no ladybug that caused that leaf to stir. 'You're right, Vajra Captain. They are moving forward again but stealthily, seeking to circle around the surround the rock face.'

Bejoo shook his head. 'Even so, what good will it do them? The boys will only cut them down as they come, unless…'

Somasra waited for him to go on. When Bejoo stopped and looked up and then back again, thinking intently, Somasra finished for him: '…unless this advance is only meant to be a distraction. The real attack on the boys will come from another position. Is that what you meant to say, Vajra Captain?'

'Yes, yes,' Bejoo said impatiently, 'and stop calling me Vajra Captain. I haven't led a Vajra for decades.'

Somasra grinned, revealing teeth flecked with fragments of the betelnut he chewed incessantly. 'This is a Vajra you lead right now, in a manner of speaking,' he said.

Bejoo looked around at the old tired men leaning against tree trunks and on the hilts of their own swords, white-bearded faces and balding heads gleaming with perspiration, and he grinned back at Somasra. 'I suppose it is, in a manner of speaking.'

Somasra laughed softly and clapped Bejoo's shoulder. 'You're a good man, Vajra Captain Bejoo. Would have liked to have fought with you in a real battle back in the day.'

Bejoo smiled, acknowledging the compliment. 'What do you call this?'

Somasra looked at the valley scornfully. 'This? I call this wiping our backsides with poison leaves, that's all! Not a real battle, oh no, sir!'

Bejoo shook his head, laughing softly. 'Well. If they're advancing again, we won't be wiping ourselves for long. Get ready, men. If they're doing what I think they're doing, they'll be rushing us again and this time, they won't stop or slow down. This is likely to be our last stand.'

The men got to their feet wearily, faces suggesting they would rather be in a tavern swigging large containers of soma or any cheaper alcoholic fluid they could afford to buy in great quantities. 'At my age,' said one ancient fellow who looked as if he had already died twenty years earlier, 'every time I stand is the last stand. It shall be a relief to finally lie down at last!'

They stood together and shuffled forward, swords at the ready, prepared to die fighting.

* * *

Luv and Kush watched with guarded expressions as the enemy advanced man by man, tree by tree, gauging the pattern. So attuned were they to each other's minds they did not even need to glance at one another to share a thought.

'Ready,' one said.

'Ready,' replied the other.

They began loosing. This time the rhythm was completely different from before. No longer was it a non-stop barrage. They could only shoot when they visually acquired a target and so they were limited by the appearance of targets. In only a few moments and about two dozen arrows loosed, it became evident to both of them that this itself was being carefully controlled and monitored by someone. No. Not by someone. By the enemy. The manner in which the enemy soldiers appeared and ran from tree to tree, advancing down the valley in twos and threes rather than all at once, the pattern in which they ran forward, not two or three in the same place but at different spots across the valley, made it very clear that the enemy was trying to keep them shooting in all directions at once.

'They are testing us,' one of the boys said.

'Yes,' replied his brother tersely, loosing an arrow. He saw a tiny spurt of crimson against the dark green backdrop of the dark afternoon shadows and was already turning in search of the next target.

But after another half dozen arrows, a suspicion began to form in their minds.

And slowly, it grew until it became a realisation.

Then that realisation coalesced into conviction.

'They know our position,' said Kush, turning to his brother for the first time in over an hour.

Luv lowered his chin, brooding briefly. His dark eyes flashed. 'Yes,' he said.

'They are keeping us busy without actually launching a full-scale attack,' Kush said.

Luv loosed another arrow, saw another man fall. 'Yes,' he replied without looking up this time. 'They are trying something…this forward movement is just a diversion.'

Kush agreed but could not think of the next logical conclusion: *What were they trying? If this was the diversion, what was the main action?*

The answer came a moment later in the form of an arrow whickering sharply past Kush's left ear. He blinked, missing his first shot of the day so far—the ones that had struck hilts and armour didn't count as misses—and his arrow went a whole foot wide of the mark. The soldier who had run from tree to tree glanced back at the arrow embedded in the ground with an expression of disbelief then fell to his knees, clasping both palms together in supplication.

The arrow that had narrowly missed Kush struck solid rock a few yards further, then clattered to the hard stony ground. Both brothers stared at it for a moment.

Then they turned as one, tracing back the arrow to its origin.

The hillside nearest to the rock face was less than a hundred yards away due to the narrowing of the valley at this end. Arrayed along that hilltop was an entire company of archers, bows drawn and arrows notched. It was an astonishing sight to see that many where there had been not a single man only moments earlier. They knew because they had been checking, expecting something like this sooner or later. The enemy had been smart enough to wait until the last possible moment, then move the entire company of archers forward the last few yards up the slope until they were visible from the rock face, and immediately give the order to string and pull. Now, the leader of the enemy appeared in view, atop his horse, light-skinned face grinning widely as he raised his sword, preparing to give the final signal to the archers.

'Maatr…' Luv and Kush both said as one, not even aware they were saying the words. '…Save us.'

Then the enemy captain slashed his sword forward at Luv and Kush and the first wave of arrows flew at them through the air, perfectly aimed at their unprotected and wholly exposed position atop the rock face.

EIGHT

Bharat and Shatrughan had tracked Aarohan's company to the hills overlooking the valley, avoiding direct contact until they were able to discern what was happening. They had passed the dead victims of the snake exodus and blanched at the sight of the venom-blackened corpses, then cursed as they saw the survivors with their throats cut, understanding the situation as perfectly as if they had been there and seen and heard everything that transpired. They came up the slope to the top of the rise just before the King's Guard archers unleashed their first volley. Veterans in warcraft, both brothers took in the scene in a flash: the archers ready to loose, the two boys on the rock overlooking the valley, the corpses strewn across the valley basin…and Aarohan with his sword held raised, ready to give the signal to loose. They reined in their lathered horses, staring intently across the valley.

'Sita's sons!' Shatrughan said. 'They are completely exposed on that rock.'

Bharat saw. But there was nothing he or Shatrughan could do. They were on the far side of the valley. To reach Aarohan they would have to ride around the valley and that would take time. The rock on which the boys stood was detached and reachable only by climbing directly up the rock face, as the boys themselves must have done. It was a brilliantly selected vantage point for archers to position themselves and accounted for some of the corpses that lay in the valley, but he knew bowcraft well enough to also know that only the most exceptional archers could have leveraged that advantage to rack up such a high body count. It was no wonder that Aarohan was furious with them, furious enough to launch this counter-attack. But the reaction was more devastating than the action that had provoked it. That first volley itself would rain down on the boys like hail on an exposed snail. There was nowhere they could hide and nothing they could do to protect themselves. The instant that first volley was unleashed at them, they would be dead.

At that instant, Aarohan's sword slashed forward, giving the signal to loose.

'No!' Bharat cried, his words lost in the wind that whipped around the hillside on which they stood.

The distance from the far hillside to the rock was not much more than a hundred yards. Close enough that the longbow archers of the King's Guard did not even need to raise their bows. They aimed directly at the two targets on the rock, and their volley of arrows shot forward unerringly, all bunched close enough together that from this slightly angled viewpoint they resembled a single dark missile with a hundred individual barbs, racing to deliver death to the two sons of Sita.

The time needed for the volley to cover the distance to the boys was barely a heartbeat.

But before that heartbeat could elapse, something extraordinary happened.

* * *

From where he stood, Bejoo could glimpse the line of archers on the hilltop, silhouetted against the late afternoon sun with their bows raised, arrowheads pointed directly above him. He could not actually see the top of the rock face behind his position, but he knew that was their target. His heart was in his mouth too as he assessed the situation and came to the same obvious conclusion: the boys would not survive the first volley. More frustrating to him as a kshatriya was the fact that they had no way to defend themselves. That was a terrible way to die, far worse than being bitten by a dozen venomous snakes.

But before the first volley could be loosed, the sounds of men advancing through the valley came to him and he swung around, bringing his attention back to his immediate surroundings.

'They're advancing, all right,' Somasra said a few yards to his right. The surviving veterans of Bejoo's group had formed a single ragged line across this side of the valley, forming a one-man wall of resistance. It was unlikely to impede the progress of the enemy by more than a few moments but as soldiers it was their duty to stick to their mission to the end. *Not just our duty,* he reminded himself, *our dharma.* For they were not merely fighting a desperate suicidal action to save a few brahmins and sadhinis. They were fighting to uphold the values for which Ayodhya had once stood and which men like Pradhan Mantri Jabali and King's Guard Captain Aarohan were trampling over like they did not matter anymore. This action itself was proof that those values mattered. To pit a whole company of archers against two boys, no matter how brilliant they might be at bowcraft...was it really necessary? He could not recall hearing Captain Aarohan calling out a demand for surrender. Clearly, the man intended to inflict his own summary judgement on the two striplings for having cost him so dearly. Never mind the fact that the boys had only been defending their loved ones and unarmed friends and doing what they had to in order to survive. Never mind the fact that kshatriya code required the captain to at least ask them to lay down arms before taking action against them. Never mind anything anymore: this was the new way and the new age of Ayodhya. Either you are with us or against us. No middle path. No compromise. No mercy.

And no dharma.

Then, the captain's sword caught the sunlight as it slashed forward and Bejoo glimpsed the volley of arrows, thick as an elephant with a hundred barbed points, flying through the air to deliver the captain's verdict of summary execution.

At the same instant, the soldiers waiting in the valley launched their attack with an explosion of noise and furore. It was obvious that the two actions were coordinated to be unleashed with the same signal: the release of the volley and the advance of the army.

They will cut down the sons of Sita up there as they ram through us down here, Bejoo thought grimly as he raised his sword to meet the rushing line of invaders. They seemed to come at him as thickly as the volley of arrows, holding nothing back this time. This would not be a fight anymore, it would be a juggernaut rolling over a minor obstacle. His mind flashed back to a moment similar to this one in so many ways: the siege of Mithila, when he had led a ragged but proud force of defenders against the overwhelming ocean of onrushing asura hordes despatched by Ravana, Lord of Lanka. He still recalled that day with crystal clarity. The asura wave had come at him like a gigantic tsunami wave. He had remembered thinking at that instant that he would not last a moment, that this stand was pointless, that they may as well have stayed in the city and awaited the invaders there. But he knew then as he knew now that, of course, it mattered, it mattered not whether they won or lost, but simply that they stood, proud men and warriors, shoulder to shoulder, facing certain death with raised chins and clear unblinking gazes, swords ready to inflict whatever damage possible, no matter how miniscule, upon that overwhelming enemy horde.

Just as it mattered now.

Even though they were rebels fighting against the very colours they had once defended with their lives, they were still fighting for the same cause. That cause was dharma, which Ayodhya had once stood for. And in their hearts, would always stand for. If anything, it was they who represented Ayodhya here, not that shiny-tunic band of ruffians with no more sense of dharma than the snakes that had thinned their ranks. The real Ayodhya was a place of the heart and mind and soul, not merely a city or kingdom-state. The real Ayodhya was the capital of the kingdom of dharma and it was that Ayodhya they had fought for all their lives, and for which they would die now.

He raised his sword and cried with all the force he could muster from his age-hoarsened throat: '**AYODHYA ANASHYA!**'

* * *

Luv and Kush saw the captain of the King's Guard slash his sword forward, giving the signal to release. And the first volley of arrows was loosed. Never before in their short lives had either boy seen such a sight. They had been in a fair number of scrapes, exchanged arrows with hostile archers on more than one occasion. But that had been forest fighting with uneven, but still manageable, odds. This was different. There were at least a hundred archers loosing at them at the same time, and they were only two, and there was no place to hide, nothing to shelter behind or under. There was nothing to do but watch as the barrage sped towards them, the very air seeming to grow still and the hail of death seeming to take eons rather than the single heartbeat required to cover the mere hundred yards to where they stood, waiting.

| *arvaci subhaghe bhava site vandamahe tva* |
| ⌊*yatha nah subhaghasasi yatha nah suphalasasi* | |

The shloka spun in Kush's mind unbidden. It rose from his lips like hot breath exhaled. It filled the air around himself and his brother like a cloud of expanding smoke.

| *arvaci subhaghe bhava site vandamahe tva* |
| ⌊*yatha nah subhaghasasi yatha nah suphalasasi* | |

The arrows still continued to advance towards them. But surely far more than a heartbeat had passed since their loosing? Surely they ought to have reached their targets by now, and Kush and he ought to be riddled with arrows, bleeding from dozens of fatal wounds, slender young bodies pierced beyond repair or rejuvenation? *Surely we ought to be dead,* Luv thought, mildly astonished.

| *arvaci subhaghe bhava site vandamahe tva* |
| ⌊*yatha nah subhaghasasi yatha nah suphalasasi* | |

Now Luv saw and heard the same shloka issuing from his brother's lips and mind, taking the shape of midnight blue smoke as it spewed forth. The dark smoke expanded outwards like a great cloud, covering the whole of the top of the rock now, then this end of the valley, then the entire valley…still continuing to spread. With each repetition, it grew farther until he knew that the whole world, not merely the mortal realm but all Creation itself was consumed by the cloud of brahman, for that was what it was, pure brahman shakti, the stuff of which all matter was made, as it had been in the Beginning when the Great Egg burst to release the cosmic brahman energy that made the universe. And despite the smoke, Kush could see clearly, could view Luv standing beside him as clear as daylight, even though the sun was lost in a miasma of blue brahman energy, could see the archers across the gap, bow-strings still rippling from the force of the loosing, see the arrows in mid-air, travelling as sluggishly as snails across a glacier see every mote of light, every blade of grass, every insect, animal, hair and hide, being and unbeing that existed, had ever existed and would ever exist for all eternity.

| arvaci subhaghe bhava site vandamahe tva |
| ⌊yatha nah subhaghasasi yatha nah suphalasasi | |

And Luv could feel every emotion ever felt by every sentient creature, know everything that had ever been known, hear every sound, see every colour…it was magnificent, it was beyond description, it was the heart of all existence itself. What else is God then but a collective of us all, living and unliving, being and unbeing, together in love and harmony forever? And that which you feel I feel, and your pain is mine and mine is yours and all we do affects us all, for God is love and we are love embodied and to hurt myself is to hurt you as well for there is no place where I end and you do not begin.

| arvaci subhaghe bhava site vandamahe tva |
| ⌊yatha nah subhaghasasi yatha nah suphalasasi | |

And Kush saw his father upon a great throne made of sunwood, the back of the seat shaped to resemble an effulgent sun spreading carved rays outward in every direction, and his father's face was as foreboding as the sun itself at noonday, merciless and relentless in its heat of tapas, dark as the night yet lustrous as the moon, and in that face was a terrible fury, a rage as devastating as the anger that ended the cosmos at the end of each day of Brahma, as unendurable as the rage of the Three-Eyed One himself. And in that terrible rage, Luv's father said a single word more unbearable than speeches, more heart-rending than volumes. The word was: '*Exile*.' And it reverberated through the length of time like the beat of a dhol drum in a dark empty chamber. And Kush felt the word pierce his heart like a hundred arrows at once, like a hundred thousand arrows, like a hundred thousand times a hundred thousand arrows. And Luv felt a tear leave his right eye as Kush felt a tear leave his left eye and both tears combined to form a single tear large enough to drown all Creation, and the sins of all beings past, present and future were washed clean by the innocence of that single tear.

| arvaci subhaghe bhava site vandamahe tva |
| ⌊yatha nah subhaghasasi yatha nah suphalasasi | |

And the being that was Luv-Kush felt a stirring in his heart and an answer to that single word spoken by his father, that word that had reduced his mother from a princess to a vagabond, from a devoted and loyal wife to a widow-in-all-but-name, from a proud and magnificent Queen Mother to a penniless sadhini in a remote forest ashram. And that answer was not rage, not fury, not frustration or a desire to respond to harm with more harm, but simply…denial. A refusal of anger, more terrible than anger itself. A denial of rage, more powerful than rage. A deflection of violence, against which there can be no defence and which renders violence itself meaningless. For what good is a blow if it never strikes its intended victim? Or an arrow that never reaches its target?

And then suspended time flicked back into existence and the world resumed its journey on the path to ultimate destruction.

NINE

Aarohan's face lost its grin as he watched the impossible happen. The first volley of arrows was loosed at his signal. He slashed the sword forward, bringing it down on the heads of the boys a hundred yards away, wishing he was close enough to smash open their skulls with the same blow, and watched the volley fly to its targets.

And then the volley slowed in mid-air.

And time stood still.

And a strange darkness descended on the world.

And the heartbeat of an instant which it should have taken the volley to reach and kill the boys stretched out into an eon.

He did not know how long time stood still—for how can you measure the passage of time when time itself is absent?—but all at once, it resumed.

The only sign that it had happened at all was a crack in the substance of reality, in the fabric of memory, a gap in consciousness, like a day one knows one lived through but can summon up no memory of at all.

And then the volley changed course.

Almost at its target, it passed over the rock face, missing the two boys by a yard, then turned sharp right and descended into the valley, retaining the same velocity and intensity of momentum.

Aarohan lost his grin as he gaped.

The volley of arrows flew down like a flock of birds descending with ominous intent, like a murder of crows hellbent on violence—and parted into a hundred individual arrows, each seeking a different target.

The arrows flew at the advancing King's Guard forces charging down the valley at the ragged line of veterans.

He saw and heard the impossible sounds of the arrows finding their mark, each striking a target with a mortal wound, each punching into breastplate and through bone and sinew and muscle and flesh and blood with as much impact as if it had just been shot straight from ten yards away, not travelled two hundred yards diverting this way and that like a sinuous snake.

They may have travelled like arrows from a mythic tale, but they struck home like normal everyday arrows, each taking a life with brutal efficiency.

A hundred of his own men died in the valley, downed by his own arrows.

Upon the rock face, the two boys stood, bows in hand, untouched, unharmed, uninjured.

Aarohan turned to look at his aides, sitting forward on their own horses, faces drained of blood, gaping and staring with faces as shocked as his own felt. He looked the other way, at the long line of archers, standing and pointing down at the valley, trying to make sense of what had just happened—and *how* it had happened.

He was filled with a sudden rage.

'Archers!' he cried out. 'Ready again!'

He looked left to make sure they had heard his command.

They had. But they were confused and shaken. Most did not even raise their bows, let alone take arrows in hand.

'ARCHERS!' he roared, pointing his sword at them threateningly. 'OBEY OR DIE!'

That got their attention. They knew that Aarohan did not threaten punishment idly. If he threatened death, he would, in fact, kill those who did not obey at once. The threat of death was enough to overcome their bewilderment.

A hundred bows were raised again, arrows ready to loose.

'AIM!' he shouted.

They took aim. This time those who had taken the shot for granted earlier took greater care to make sure their missiles were perfectly targeted, in the event, however unlikely, that the cause had been merely a strong gust of wind or…or something inexplicable.

'LOOSE!' Aarohan yelled, dropping his sword forward.

Again the volley flew out across the gap between this hilltop and the rock on which the boys stood. This time there was no break in time and consciousness. Nothing discernible happened.

But again, the arrows turned as one—and swooped down into the valley.

Again they parted ways to seek out their own individual targets. And struck home with unerring efficiency.

Again, a hundred of Aarohan's company died with blasted throats and ruptured hearts and lungs and spleens, thrashing and bleeding on the jungle floor.

Aarohan could not accept it. This was not possible. There was some mischief afoot. He would not condone such treachery—not from mere mindless wooden arrows!

Again he gave the command to aim and loose. Again, another volley was released. Again the arrows diverted. Again, a hundred men died.

And yet again.

And yet again.

And yet again.

* * *

Bharat and Shatrughan watched in smiling disbelief as the impossible happened again and yet again. After the first few times, they shook their heads in commiseration for the men in the valley below. 'Those poor fools,' Shatrughan said. 'They are dying because of the arrogance of that idiot Aarohan.'

Bharat turned the head of his horse. 'I think it's time to teach that idiot a lesson.'

Shatrughan grinned. Both brothers rode away, taking the route that would lead them around to where the captain of the King's Guard stood, slashing his sword forward and yelling 'LOOSE!' over and over again.

* * *

In the royal camp, Rama emerged from his tent, a strange expression on his face. He looked like a man who had woken from a long deep sleep and strange dreams.

Strange dreams indeed.

Lakshman was waiting for him outside. He saw that Rama's eyes glowed with deep blue illumination from within, the way they had once glowed in the darkness of Bhayanak-van.

Rama looked at him and saw a fainter illumination of the same ilk in Lakshman's eyes as well.

'Bhraatr,' Rama said, holding out his hand to his brother. 'Ride with me.'

Lakshman took his brother's hand without hesitation.

They strode towards Rama's chariot together.

* * *

Bejoo whooped and cheered as the corpses piled up. Beside him to either side, the ragged line of veterans cheered as well as another volley of arrows swung by overhead, zinging through the trees, even zipping *around* tree trunks and *over* obstacles to reach their intended targets.

One shot by Bejoo's right arm, pursuing a soldier of the King's Guard who ran screaming for mercy. The arrow caught up with him and punched through his armour's backplate with enough force to send the man flying several yards to crash into a tree.

Bejoo laughed, unable to believe that he had survived yet another stand where merely walking away had seemed impossible. The arrows had not touched him or his men—it was almost as if they knew which men to avoid and which to strike.

The valley was littered with corpses now. He had estimated that each volley consisted of around one hundred arrows. Thanks to Aarohan's arrogant insistence on loosing volley after volley, he guessed that almost a thousand men must have died by now. The entire King's Guard was wiped out, all except the archers on the hilltop and the elite One Hundred that sat on their horses beside their captain, staring down in disbelief at the mayhem caused by their own company's arrows.

Somasra was chuckling beside him too, sitting on a tree trunk and swigging from a leather skin. From the odour that wafted to Bejoo, it was definitely not water though the old gatewatch guard was drinking as if it was. Bejoo held out a hand. 'A taste for a comrade?' he asked.

Somasra grinned and handed the skin to Bejoo. 'Go ahead. Finish it.' He pulled out another small skinbag from somewhere in his garment. 'I have another. It's Chandra Pujari's best.'

Bejoo paused in the act of raising the skin to his lips and laughed. Somasra watched him, his own grin widening. 'Ah,' he said. 'A fellow worshipper at Chandra Pujari's temple?'

'Ever since I was weaned off mother's milk,' Bejoo said, then drank long and deep from the bag. Soma had never tasted this good in his entire life.

* * *

Luv and Kush watched as the captain of the King's Guard lowered his sword at last. Even from a hundred yards away, it was evident that the man was burning with frustration and anger. He pointed his gloved hand at the rock and issued a string of curses and threats.

'Methinks the good captain is a little upset,' Luv said.

'Methinks you may be right,' Kush replied.

'Let us give him something to really be upset about, shall we?' Luv said, raising his bow.

Kush was already raising his own bow. 'Yes, bhraatr, let's.' They loosed together.

Both arrows rose up into the sky, then converged, joining together into a single arrow. The single arrow curved downwards then raced ahead with renewed speed, flashing like lightning towards the archers on the hilltop. The archers saw the arrow and some started to turn away to run. They had barely turned when the arrow struck. The arrow turned at the last instant, punching into the chest of the man to the far right. It passed through his breast on the right, entering just beneath his armpit, and emerged from the other side, out his other armpit. It passed through bone and flesh and muscle as if passing through air. It emerged from the breast of the first archer—then struck the second. It emerged from his breast too, moving with as great force as before, and struck the third. It continued down the line, taking the lives of every last archer in that row. Finally, barely a moment after it had been loosed, it emerged from the armpit of the hundredth archer, the man nearest to where Captain Aarohan sat astride his horse.

The horse reared and neighed in fright, sensing a supernatural force at work.

The arrow hovered in mid-air, rose and floated before Captain Aarohan. His aides reacted more violently than he did, turning their horses and riding away. The captain himself sat frozen, staring at the arrow hovering in mid-air before him. He clutched his sword tightly, his knuckles turning white as he gripped it harder, but he made no move to raise it or strike out. He tilted his head an inch to the left and the arrow adjusted its angle just enough to account for the tilt. He tilted it the other way, experimentally, and the arrow turned that way an inch as well. Realisation grew upon him that no matter what he did or where he moved, the arrow would follow. Slowly, as the moments stretched out, his rage melted into fear and then into stark terror as he stared at the blind unseeing pointed tip of the arrow.

Suddenly, the arrow darted at him directly. He cried out and slashed out in panic with the sword. He missed the arrow—and the arrow missed him too. It nicked his ear, drawing blood in a small splatter on his left shoulder, then zipped on past him. It took him a moment to realise that he was not mortally struck. When he did, he turned to follow its course and saw that it was chasing after his aides who were riding away furiously. The arrow punched into the back of the nearest one and emerged from the man's chest. The man fell off his horse, spewing gore. The arrow continued onwards, reaping another bloody harvest. By the time it was done, every last man under Captain Aarohan's command lay sprawled dead on the hilltop. Their horses milled about in confusion, then began to ride away, glad to be free at last of their ill-tempered masters. Several corpses stuck in the stirrups were dragged along for miles, their heads bouncing along merrily.

Captain Aarohan saw his chance when the arrow was killing his men and turned to ride away. He broke into a gallop with expert ease, racing alongside the hilltop with the desperation of a man pursued by demons.

He glanced back from time to time to see if the arrow was following. He saw it finish off the last of his elite One Hundred and turn around, seeking him out. He rode faster, yelping like a dog in pain, as the arrow spun after him, making a buzzing sound like a bee at work on a honeycomb.

He had not gone far before two riders appeared before him, riding as hard towards him as he was riding in their direction. 'Help me!' he cried. 'Mercy!'

Bharat and Shatrughan stared as they approached the captain of the King's Guard riding desperately towards them. They saw the sprawled corpses of his archers and men lying on the hillside behind him. Then they saw the arrow chasing the man.

Captain Aarohan saw their faces, recognising them from a distance.

He stopped crying for help.

He looked back and saw the arrow come flying at him like a flying demon from the lowest level of Naraka.

Crying out in pitiful terror, he turned the head of his horse...

And rode off the hilltop, straight into thin air.

Moments later, his neighing horse and he crashed to the floor of the valley, landing in the rocky wadis behind the rock on which Luv and Kush still stood, watching.

Bharat and Shatrughan slowed and looked down at the dead horse and man below. Captain Aarohan had landed with his horse on top of him. His body was broken in a hundred places. He lay sprawled like a drunk, eyes staring sightlessly up at the sky.

Bharat shook his head. 'It seems he has learned his lesson after all.'

'And a bitter one it was,' Shatrughan said.

They turned their horses and rode back the way they had come.

* * *

Luv and Kush ran to their mother, embracing her fiercely. Sita gasped, her wounds still fresh, but smiled through her pain as she embraced her sons, tears spilling from her dark-underscored eyes.

'My sons,' she said. 'What have you done?'

They looked up at her. 'What we had to, Maatr. They left us no choice.'

Behind them, Bejoo and Somasra both nodded, supporting the boys. Nakhudi and the other survivors of the ashram massacre as well as the bearkillers who had been protecting them, heard details of the battle from various members of Bejoo's group and marvelled.

Maharishi Valmiki rose to his feet wearily, leaning on his staff. The great guru had aged another decade that day itself. 'Time to return home,' he said.

TEN

The thunder of hooves and chariot wheels overcame the crackling of the chandan wood as the cremation pyres consumed the dead. The royal chariot was preceded by PFs in their familiar purple and black uniforms, the original and true King's Guard. The ashramites who were clustered around the cremation pyres with Maharishi Valmiki at their head looked up with hostility as Rama and Lakshman dismounted.

Sita was standing with her sons before her. At the sound of the approaching hooves, they had immediately wanted to take up their bows, but she had stopped them, indicating the pyres. It would be disrespectful to leave the ritual half-done. They subsided but still kept their eyes on the pathway down which the intruders arrived. The instant they saw the soldiers with spears and swords, their backs tightened and it was only their mother's hands, firmly squeezing each boy's shoulder, that kept them from racing for their bows and rigs.

Rama's eyes met Sita's as he approached. He was raising his palms in a gesture of supplication at that instant and it appeared as if he were greeting her first and foremost, the pain in his eyes speaking volumes. Sita tried to glare daggers at him but for some reason, the very sight of him melted her heart. *How tired he looks, how much he has aged, he looks ten years older than his age, why has he become so thin, so drawn...does he not get enough sleep?* Instead of anger and hostility, these were the thoughts that came to her mind in that crucial moment. The heart's capacity to love always exceeds its capacity to hate. Anger fades in time, genuine affection stays bright forever.

He held her gaze a moment, then moved on to Maharishi Valmiki. He bowed to the Maharishi, offering the appropriate greetings and gestures.

'Forgive my intrusion, Mahadev,' he said. 'I do not mean to disturb you at your time of grief but my business here is urgent.'

Maharishi Valmiki finished the last part of the cremation ritual without comment. When all was done and the pyres had almost completely consumed the bodies, he turned his tired face to Rama. There was no space left for anger or recrimination in his heart. When he spoke, it was with sadness and regret, not out of a desire to apportion blame. 'You know that this was the work of men deputed by you, under your own authority?'

Rama bowed his head in shame. 'I regret that these lives were lost. I am told the men responsible have been killed as they deserve to have been killed.' His eyes searched for and found the two boys standing before Sita like proud cubs defending their mother lioness. 'I have heard the entire tale of the battle of the arrows and seen the results with my own eyes.' He turned and indicated Bharat and Shatrughan who stepped forward to greet the Maharishi as well. Valmiki acknowledged them all.

'And now what business brings you here?' asked the guru. 'How have your feet found the way to my ashram after these many years?'

Rama looked at the face of his old friend and fellow exile, the man he had once known as Ratnakaran and whom he had once fought against when he was known as bearkiller. Valmiki's mangled face, ruined by the claws of a bear in youth, was mostly covered by his flowing white beard now, and the intense hatred in his eyes had been replaced by an enduring sadness and deep philosophical acceptance of the way of the world, but beneath all that great store of learning and acquired wisdom, there was still the core of the man whom Rama had once stood shoulder to shoulder with in a jungle called Janasthana, battling against impossible foes and unbeatable odds—and winning.

'I feel as if I have been asleep these many years and have only awoken today. As if the cobwebs of a decade have been washed away and my eyesight cleared suddenly.'

Valmiki considered this a moment. 'And how did this sudden change come about?'

'A great resonance sounded in the world this day, shaking me out of my slumber,' Rama said. 'It was someone using dev-astras in the service of dharma.' He turned and looked directly at Luv and Kush. 'The shakti of brahman cascading through creation cleansed my soul of all confusion and doubt. I was as a man refreshed by a cold wave that falls upon him unexpectedly. I remembered things I had not even thought about for years. I saw the mistakes I had made and desired to correct them. I saw the error of my ways and sought to redress those errors. But most of all, I saw the unjustness I had meted out to a loved one and knew I must act quickly and do what was right.'

'And what exactly does doing right mean?' Valmiki asked.

Rama's eyes found Sita, standing proud yet tragic in the stillness of the evening. In the trees above, birds cried out and called as the day approached an end.

'I intend to beg my wife's forgiveness and take her and our sons home, if she will agree to come,' he said.

Sita's knees buckled. Both her sons looked up in alarm as they felt her weight shift, and they caught her arms tightly, holding her up. She regained control of herself and nodded to them. Still, they remained alert in case she should lurch again.

Maharishi Valmiki looked at Sita. 'What say you, Lady Vedavati? Do you think Lord Rama Chandra deserves forgiveness?'

She looked at the guru, avoiding Rama's gaze for the moment. 'I cannot say if he does or does not deserve it. I will not judge him. I *cannot* judge him. I can only speak for myself.'

'Then will you or will you not forgive him?' the Maharishi asked gently.

Sita was silent a long moment. Everyone gathered around waited as well. Luv and Kush looked up at her face, holding her hands tightly.

'I will,' she said at last.

A great cheering rose from the ranks of the Ayodhyan army. Word had spread through the army of all that had transpired that day and everyone knew that Rama had found his long-exiled wife and sons. To the masses, it meant that Ayodhya had found her queen. After the threat of war hanging over their heads and the likelihood of war against their neighbouring kingdom of Videha no less, it was a treat to see their liege's martial obsession diverted into a more gentle preoccupation. Kings who loved were easier to love than kings who warred.

The expression on Rama's face as well as Sita's showed nothing but love.

A white-cloaked figure strode forward with a stern face. Pradhan Mantri Jabali gestured at his king. 'Samrat Rama Chandra, you cannot simply take her back.'

Rama shot Jabali a cursory glance. 'I can do as I please. She is still my wife.'

'She is an exile. And she was exiled for good reason. Her secret kinship to Ravana, Lord of Lanka, and the fact that it was kept hidden from us for so long, endangering not just our kingdom but all mortalkind, is partly the reason. But there is also the matter of her purity.'

'Purity?' spat Nakhudi, stepping forward angrily. 'You speak of purity? How pure are you? How pure is any man? Why do men only speak of purity when it comes to their women!'

Jabali gestured dismissively at Nakhudi, ignoring her outburst. 'As a husband, you may do as you please. But as King of Ayodhya, you must also uphold dharma. And dharma demands that any woman you choose to instate as Queen of Kosala should prove herself worthy of that position and respect. You cannot expect your people to respect you, if they do not respect your wife.'

'Why should they not respect her?' Rama asked, forehead creased, but his tone not angry, not yet.

'For the same reason that any husband hesitates to respect his wife if she stays for even one night under another man's roof.' Jabali pointed accusingly at Sita. Luv and Kush glared angrily back at him. 'Your wife was abducted by Ravana and stayed for months under his control.'

'Yes,' Rama admitted, 'but we learned later that he was her father by birth.'

'That is irrelevant to the question of purity. Who knew what transpired with her during the time she was incarcerated in Lanka? A den of demons, lair of rakshasas and all manner of vile asuras.'

Rama's face hardened. 'She underwent the agni-pariksha as was required by our customs. She passed the test of fire successfully.'

Jabali shook his head. 'The error you made, if I may call it that, was in holding the agni-pariksha without any witnesses present.'

'There were witnesses by the millions,' Lakshman countered, stepping forward. He gestured at Hanuman, standing to one side quietly, watching the debate with his arms folded over his greying chest. 'Our friend Hanuman was there. As were the entire vanar nations and rksaa nations.'

Jabali's face twitched in a half-smile. 'I meant civilised witnesses. Aryas. The noble folk. Not monkeys and bears!'

Hanuman bristled at the tone of derision but made no comment or move. After a decade spent with mortals, he had probably become inured to their racist epithets although it was evident that he did not appreciate them.

'Then take my word for it,' Rama said. 'And my brother's. We were there. We witnessed her succeed in the agni-pariksha.'

'And what of the past ten years?' Jabali asked slyly. 'Once again she has been away from your house, who knows where or with whom?'

Rama had no answer to that. Even Lakshman was silent. Bharat and Shatrughan looked on angrily but said nothing because they could not offer anything worthwhile in such a matter. It was Maharishi Valmiki who spoke up then.

'I will vouch personally for the reputation of Lady Vedavati whom you know as Queen Sita,' Valmiki said. 'Her honour is spotless.'

Jabali laughed harshly. 'We cannot take your word for it, Maharishi. The people must be appeased. And the people are not easily appeased. They have been betrayed too often. The conniving late Queen Kaikeyi, the scheming asura-worshipping Daimaa Manthara, the intrusions into Ayodhya, the near-invasion by Ravana's son Atikiya.' Jabali spread his arms, affecting a guileless expression. 'It is not I who questions the authenticity, Samrat Rama. It is the people. They would need to see it with their own eyes in order to be certain.'

'See it?' Lakshman asked angrily. 'Do you mean we should hold another agni-pariksha just to appease the people's doubts?'

Jabali shrugged. 'If she is truly innocent of wrongdoing, and pure as you claim, there is nothing to fear. Besides, it is not I who demands this test, it is dharma.'

'Dharma!' shouted Nakhudi. 'You change your interpretation of dharma to suit your own interests!'

Jabali wagged a finger of warning at the oversized woman warrior. 'Mind your tongue, woman. Otherwise you may well be compelled to undergo an agni-pariksha as well.'

'Enough!' Rama said angrily. 'If this is the only way, then it must be done.'

He looked at Sita. 'I know you are spotless and beyond reproach but what Pradhan Mantri Jabali says is true, a king serves his people and the people will talk. We set very high standards of morality in Ayodhya and in order to enforce those standards I must prove that my family and I abide by them as well. Nobody must have the right to raise a finger and say a single word about you or anyone else in our house once you return home. Therefore, I ask you to do this, not for my sake or even for your own sake, but for the sake of the people we serve. For the sake of dharma. Do this one last thing and we shall be together again, forever.'

Sita looked at him sadly. 'I thought you might have changed after all. I thought you genuinely meant it when you begged my forgiveness, that you sincerely wished to undo your mistakes and do the right thing at last. I kept my love preserved like an acorn in a bushel for ten long years, in the hope that someday perhaps we might be reunited, that someday you would see the light of reason. But today I realise that it is not possible. You never truly desired forgiveness. You were never sincere in your proffer. You did not ask with genuine intention. All you desired was a queen, not a wife. A figurehead to place on the throne beside you, like the stone statue of me your army carries before it. A pure, perfect idol of a woman. Not a woman herself.'

'Sitey,' Rama said, 'you misunderstand me entirely. I came here to ask you to come back. But I live in the service of my station. A king serves the people. Yatha raja tatha praja.'

'"As does the king, so do the people,"' Sita translated. 'So do it. Show the people that you believe in my fealty. That you do not need a fire sacrifice to prove my...*purity*! Do this and prove to them that to doubt an honest woman is itself a stain on her reputation. To point a finger is itself a sullying of honour. To gossip and speak about someone without their being found guilty of any wrongdoing is itself a crime. Deny this unfair demand and prove to your people that dharma comes from conviction, not compromise. Dharma breaks but does not bend. Dharma is the same for men as well as women. Do this and show the praja that you are truly a raja of dharma. Not merely a servant, but a king of dharma. Do this, Rama. Do this for the sake of all mortalkind for you are as close to a god as it is possible for a man to be. Do this one thing and you shall be pure yourself, unsullied, and undoubted by history for all time to come. The eyes of countless generations watch you now. You are the one being judged, not I. Do this and prove to all humanity forever that Rama, King of Dharma, can pass this final agni-pariksha. The test of trust. Prove that you believe without question in my so-called *purity* and need no superstitious ritual to confirm it for the naysayers and doubters of the world.'

Rama was silent for a long moment. Even the birds in the forest seemed to have fallen silent as if listening and waiting now for Rama's response. The entire army, arrayed out for yojanas behind Rama's royal chariot, waited silently as well, word of mouth having passed on the urgency and import of what was being discussed here. The world itself waited.

Finally, with head bowed, Rama sobbed a single sob and said two simple words, 'I cannot.'

Sita was silent for a long moment, even longer than the time Rama had taken to respond. Finally, she raised her head, lifting her hands from the shoulders of her two sons who looked anxiously up at her. And she said in a voice that cracked like thunder: *'Then be a broken god forever!'*

ELEVEN

The earth heaved and cracked beneath Sita's feet. Luv and Kush cried out and stumbled, reaching out for their mother, not asking for her help, but in order to help *her*. To their surprise, Maatr pushed them away with a firm, but not unkind gesture. They staggered back even as the entire section of ground on which Sita stood broke free of the surrounding earth and rose up high into the earth, as if shoved by an invisible fist from below. Everybody around her fell back, staggering and stumbling away from the rising fist of ground. Debris and stones fell, and packed dirt crumbled and spilled over as the ground split. Everybody moved back, away from the heaving earth. A great gaping hole opened in the ground, cracking in a rough circle over three yards wide that forced everybody to move back. Then the cremation pyres heaved and lurched, and fell into the gaping hole! At once, fire leaped up, huge gouts of flame blazing up, as if the smouldering pyres had ignited some underground fuel. The fire roared over a dozen yards high, rising steadily.

Luv and Kush went berserk with panic. 'Maatr!' they cried out together, scrambling to their feet. They ran forward, halting at the crumbling edge of the rough circle that had appeared and which separated them from the fist of risen earth upon which Sita still stood. Flames roared upward from the circular gash in the earth and dirt, and pebbles crumbled and fell away from beneath their scrambling feet.

Nakhudi saw the danger and leaped forward, grasping hold of them with each meaty arm. She held them tight, pulling them back. Great archers they were and gifted with the power of brahman, but when it came to simple muscular strength, they were no match for Nakhudi's wrestler bulk.

Still, they struggled mightily. 'MAATR!' they cried, young boyish voices almost girlish in their panic.

Sita turned and raised a hand, palm outwards, to comfort them. 'Do not fear for me, my sons,' she said affectionately, 'I am safe in my mother's arms.'

As the other ashramites moved back out of the way, guided by Dumma and the other rishis, Rama and his brothers came forward to try to help. Bejoo and Somasra came forward as well. But the distance was too far to leap, the flames too ferocious and each time anyone came close to the edge, the flames seemed to leap higher, almost as if forbidding anyone from trying to save Sita.

'Stay back, my friends,' she said, her voice clearly audible to all in the ashram clearing. Word of what was transpiring was constantly being passed on from soldier to soldier through the long lines of Ayodhya's army. Those who were within viewing were gawking with amazement, unable to comprehend what was happening. 'Prithvi-maa, the earth herself is my birth mother. It was she who was seeded by Ravana resulting in my birth. That is why Maharaja Janak of Mithila found me while ploughing his field. I was literally born of the earth in a furrow. And now, to that same earth I shall return.'

'MAATR!' cried her sons. Nakhudi's powerful arms strained to hold them back as they fought and kicked and struggled to break free. Had she let go, there was no doubt they would have tried to leap across the cleft to rescue their Maatr—and would surely have died trying.

'Sitey,' said Rama from beside them. 'Sitey, forgive me! I know I have transgressed against you. I came here today to try to make amends.'

'And you failed, Rama,' she said sorrowfully. 'You failed utterly. That is why you will always be a broken god. Revered and worshipped, honoured and admired, but also doubted and despised. Each time someone speaks of your great works and exploits, another will remind them of your banishment of your wife and ask what god would do such a thing, and question your divinity. Today you had a chance to answer them once and for all, to silence those doubters, and you failed yet again. Now, for as long as your memory shall live, you shall be adored as a deva yet doubted as a man.'

'I *am* a man,' he said, dropping to his knees before the fiery pit. 'Just a man. Know me as a man. Understand me as a man. Not as a god.'

She shook her head sadly. 'That is the eternal dilemma of heroes and those who worship them. How can greatness have flaws? How can perfection contain a blemish? How can a deva do wrong? And eternally, in answer to those questions, people shall answer a single name: *Rama*. They shall offer you prayers, yes. But they shall do so knowing that they are prayers offered to a broken god.'

'Come to me, Janaki,' he said, tears rolling from his eyes. 'Join with me again. Make me whole.'

'Don't you want your agni-pariksha?' she asked bitterly. And the flames roared up, engulfing her.

'Maatr,' her sons cried.

'Cry not for me, my sons,' her voice said from within the flames. 'These fires shall not burn me, nor the earth suffocate. The heat of the sun will not blacken my skin, nor the cold of winter freeze my blood. My bones will not turn to dust with the passing of time nor will my hair shrivel and come undone. I shall return to the earth and shall be eternally present in her every aspect. Think of me every time you see a flower bloom, a tree offers you shade, or the ground provides you with sustenance. I go home to my mother's bosom. For that is our sanskriti. When a woman is not accepted at her husband's home, she must go back to her mother's house. And this is home to me. From whence I came, thither I return. Before I go, witness my agni-pariksha, tell all in Ayodhya of me, for even in parting, I remain Rama's wife, and lest a single finger be raised in accusation or a single gossiping tongue speak with doubt, let all see and bear testimony that the sacred agni did not singe a hair on my head or harm me. Pure, did you say, Pradhan Mantri Jabali? Is this pure enough for you? Or do you need to ladle ghee upon my body to satisfy yourself further? Perhaps what men like you truly

desire is to cremate women alive rather than accept that they are flesh
and blood and human as you are. If Rama is a broken god, it is because
of this one flaw: he could not accept his own wife without questioning
her purity!'

And the flames shot up impossibly high, reaching for the sky, until
the pillar of flame was visible all across the land, across the length and
breadth of the kingdom, and every man, woman and children paused
and stared skywards, and saw upon the top of the pillar of flame, the
figure of their long-banished but beloved Queen Sita Janaki of Mithila,
standing on that searing flame, yet untouched and unharmed. And every
heart went out to her and every voice spoke in veneration. 'Devi-Maa,'
they said, the highest exaltation possible. Mother Goddess. And if she had
not been until then, she became in that moment, Mother Goddess Sita.
Then and now and forever.

The pillar fell. It descended as suddenly as it had risen, and plunged
deep into the earth. As Sita returned to ground level, the pillar paused, as
if her mother Earth permitted her daughter one final goodbye. And she
reached out to her weeping sons and blessed them. 'Ayushmaanbhava,
sons, rule as one, live as one, and follow this one law at all times: one
dharma for all.'

And then she descended into the earth and was swallowed whole.
The flames were sucked in and vanished. The cracked earth heaved
again and moved together, with a grinding sound that resembled a great
stone sil-butta being churned. The broken pieces fit together as perfectly
as a china pot fitted back together. And a moment later, the ground
was as it had been before, without a single crack or wisp of flame or
trace of anything that had happened.

Only the absence of the cremation pyres served as reminder that
indeed, Sita had been here only moments earlier. And was gone now.

samaptam

The doe leaped out of Rama's arms. He had enfolded her in a gentle embrace, careful not to grip her too hard, and when he sensed her muscles tensing for the leap, he made no attempt to stop her. She jumped upwards and away, bounding across the grassy knoll in the direction of the river. Reaching the rim of the knoll, she paused and turned her head. Her ears flicked as she looked back with wide alarmed eyes. He smiled and rose to his feet, speaking softly, his voice barely audible below the sound of the river.

'Did I scare you? That was not my intention, little beauty. I was only eager to be your friend. Will you not come back and speak to me again?'

The doe watched him from the edge of the precipice, her body still turned towards the path that led down to the river, only her head twisted back towards him. She made no move to return, yet she did not flee immediately.

Rama took a step towards her, then another. She did not run. He took several steps more, but when he was within twenty paces or so, her flank rippled and her ears flickered at a faster rate.

So he stopped again. He called to her. She stayed where she was, watching him. For a long moment, they stayed that way, the man and the doe, watching each other, the river rushing along, the sun breasting the top of the northern hills to shine down in its full glory. In the distance, the city caught the light of the new day and sent back a thousand glittering reflections. Towers and spires, windows and arches, domes and columns, glass and brass, silver and gold, copper and bronze, crystal and shell, bead and stone, all were illuminated at once, and Ayodhya blazed like a beacon of gold fire, filling the valley with a luminous glow. In the light of this glorious new day, it was easy to dismiss the nightmare as just that, a bad dream. And yet...he could still hear the sound of Sita's voice, hear her last words, see her engulfed by the pillar of fire as it descended into the embrace of the earth—

He stopped and sighed.

He straightened and stared at the city. His beloved Ayodhya resplendent in the sunlight of a new day, a new season, a new harvest year. He walked forward, eyes fixed on the blazing city. Before they had grown old enough to be sent to gurukul, he and his brothers had spent any number of days here in the shade of this mango grove. Playing, fighting, racing, all the things that young boys and young princes alike were wont to do. He had come here today hoping these nostalgically familiar environs would cleanse his mind of the nightmare that life itself seemed to have become. So far he hadn't been entirely successful. He hadn't expected to be.

His feet found the edge of the knoll and he stopped, poised ten yards or more above the raging river. It was the point where the Sarayu roared around a bend in the valley, tumbling over rocks and boulders with the haste and energy of a river still in the first stage of its lengthy course. The sound was thunder sustained. He spread his arms, raised his face to the warm golden sunlight, and laughed. Droplets of spray drifted up slowly, catching his hair and simple white dhoti, like diamonds glittering in the sunlight.

'Bhai.'

He turned to see Lakshman standing behind him. Clad in a white anga-vastra as was Rama.

'It is time.'

They walked down together to the riverbank. There were great numbers of people lined along the bank on either side. The lines stretched back to the raj-marg and all along its length back to the city itself. Tens of thousands upon thousands…lakhs…millions, in fact. The entire population of the city. He looked at the city one last time, intending to fix it in his memory. But from this angle, the overhang of the bank on the far side obstructed the view. The deep red light of the setting sun in the west obscured what little was visible. Perhaps it was better that way. To have seen those familiar towers and arches, the palace, the walls, the Seer's Eye…perhaps they were better remembered in his mind's eye as they were. As all things were. In memory, evergreen. Perfect. Immutable.

Maharishi Valmiki had agreed to preside over the ritual. The other purohits of the city were present as well. At his nod, all the brahmins began chanting the ritual Sanskrit shlokas together, their voices rising to rival the roar of the river. Yet as Rama walked towards the edge of the bank, the Sarayu's song was louder by far. She was calling to him. *Come to me, my son. Come and sleep awhile. A season of rest.*

Perhaps Sita would be waiting for him there, beyond the river's end, beyond sleep.

He entered the river. The water was icy cold, but that was good. The shock awakened his senses, made him aware of every sensation. The wind on his fevered scalp. The fading sunlight on his cheek and ear. The smell of jasmine blossoms on the evening air. The sound of parrots or monkeys, or both squabbling in the trees.

The brahmin's chanting reached a crescendo. Everybody had joined their palms together and was chanting along. Rama saw Hanuman looking at him, hands joined together in supplication. The vanar's eyes were shedding tears freely. Rama smiled sadly at him. Hanuman did not smile back: vanars could not smile. Yet they could cry. Strange, wasn't it?

Rama stepped further into the river. So this was samadhi. The ritual immersion into flowing water as a voluntary end to one's life.

A literal crossing over to another state of being. What had his karma in this and previous lifetimes earned him thus far? The right to be reborn as another mortal or some other species? The right to moksha, that final liberation from the cycle of birth and rebirth? He saw Luv and Kush, faces drawn and severe, standing with Nakhudi and Bejoo, who was now elevated to Minister of Peace, a new post he, Rama, had instated before stepping down from the throne. Nakhudi was personal bodyguard to the twins, captain of the new King's Guardians. With the help of Saprem Senapati Shirisha Kumar, great-grandson of Senapati Dheeraj Kumar and grandson of Senapati Drishti Kumar, perhaps they might usher in a new era for Kosala and Ayodhya. An age of peace. He hoped the twins would learn more from their newly discovered adoptive grandfather Janak of Mithila than from himself. Ram Rajya was a great period in the city-kingdom's history, but its time was past. Perhaps there had never been a time for it at all.

He took another step and the water embraced him like a cold lover. She swirled around him, dancing and rushing and washing over him with icy tendrils. He felt his extremities grow colder, his heartbeat slow, his pulse slow, his brow feel more feverish, almost burning hot.

The decision to take samadhi had been his own. His brothers had insisted on following in his steps. None of them wished to rule in his stead. And the entire populace had chosen to follow as well. He had considered issuing some kind of a writ or diktat, forbidding everyone from doing as he did, but it would be pointless once he was gone. Besides, *yatha raja tatha praja*. They had lived by that law and now they were willing to die by it.

Except that this was not death. Not exactly. It was transmogrification. They believed that by following their god-like emperor into the afterlife they would be achieving transmogrification of their mortal souls into eternal states of being. Who was he to disprove their belief? The truth was even he did not know what lay beyond. All he knew was that there was nothing left in this world for him to live for. He had come to his senses in the nick of time, but had Sita and her sons not intervened and Jabali and his evil cronies Aarohan and his men not tried to hasten things by force and manipulation, he might have authorised a war against Videha. And after Videha, perhaps even the other Arya nations. And after that, what? Then what would be the difference between Rama and Ravana except a few syllables?

Samadhi ensured that he sought a higher plane of existence. It was an honourable way to pass on. He could not have endured the idea of Vanaprasth Ashram, forest retirement, as was the custom among kings of his line. For he had already spent the better part of his life in forest retirement—*forced* retirement, that too, without so much as a pension. Nor did he wish to remain in Ayodhya and watch his sons rule—every moment with them would lead to questions of whether to do things Rama's way or their way. Now, nobody could raise that question. There would be only their way, and that was the way it ought to be. He would have liked to watch them grow to manhood but each day with them would have been a day without Sita. And in their eyes he could still see the flames of Sita's final agni-pariksha reflected, burning deep in their hearts, just as his own youthful anger at his mother's treatment had burned in his eyes when he had looked at his father Dasaratha in days gone by. Because he had been a son himself, he knew what they felt. Because he had seen his mother suffer his father's mistakes, he knew how they felt about him, their father. And he could not live with that knowledge nor could he make things right with them. That moment had passed. That opportunity was lost forever.

The only way ahead for him was to seek other worlds, other lives. Samadhi.

He took another step and the water closed completely over his head, submerging him. He heard a collective gasp from the assembled crowd and the word was passed on that Rama had gone under the river. He heard no more except the gurgling of the water and the buffeting of the tide which felt oddly like a powerful wind. The water was crystal clear and he could still see the evening sky. Birds flew overhead, silhouetted against the evening redness. He saw faces and bodies moving, heard the murmur of voices—or perhaps they were only the voices of the river speaking to him.

His feet found the bottom of the river. He was yards underwater now. The sky was no longer visible, the rushing water overhead obscuring all vision. He heard and felt a splash beside him and saw another man's form sink slowly to land on the bottom of the river beside him. It was Lakshman, his eyes open as well, still holding his breath. He gestured at Rama. Rama nodded and gestured, indicating that they should move forward.

Then a strange thing happened.

A great blue light blazed up from the depths of the river, like a standing rectangle of deep midnight-blue illumination glowing brightly. Like a doorway without any substance, just inky blue light spilling through. From where? How?

He did not know. The inky blue light shaped like a doorway stood ahead on the floor of the river. Behind it was pitch darkness as if the river itself ended there, although he knew that was impossible.

Vortal. That is a Vortal. The name came to him unbidden. He had no idea what it meant.

I have been expecting you, Ayodhya-naresh. Come towards the Vortal.

He did not look around to see who had spoken. The voice was in his mind. He glanced at Lakshman and saw from his brother's face that he had heard the voice too. It had spoken in Lakshman's mind as well.

Two more splashes behind them: Bharat and Shatrughan. They came up beside Lakshman and Rama saw that they were looking at the Vortal too. They had heard the voice as well.

Yes, this is the way. You are to go through the Vortal now. One by one. Come.

They looked at one another.

Do not fear. This is inevitable. It was ordained for you from eons before your birth on this realm.

Rama nodded to his brothers then walked towards the Vortal. If this was what he was meant to do, then he may as well do it. In any case, he had come here seeking something. He had not known what. It seemed he had found it.

At the place where the blue light met the Sarayu's water, the effect was most peculiar. As if the water and light met...and merged. There was a point where he could see that the molecules were neither entirely water nor entirely light. They were...something else.

Brahman. Pure brahman.

Yes, Vaikuntha-naresh. The Vortal is composed of pure brahman. It is a portal between possible worlds. Go on through. It is the reason why you chose this way to end your mortal existence in this plane.

Rama stood before the Vortal. He felt Lakshman come up behind him, waiting.

Rama stepped through. It felt like stepping through water into...

Light. Bright infinite light. Light of no colour. Perfect. Extending in every direction. Originating from nowhere.

He felt a strange sensation within himself, then a repetition of the sensation, then another. It happened thrice in all.

When he looked back, his brothers were gone. As was the Vortal. As was the river itself.

The entire mortal world had vanished.

And so had his brothers.

Because here we are all one being...I.

His voice sounded strange in his own mind.

He heard a fluttering from above and looked up to see a great magnificent being descending. He knew instinctively that this was Garuda, his friend and carrier.

Garuda bowed down before him.

Rama climbed aboard.

Garuda flapped his wings and rose up into the air, into the infinite light without beginning or end, origin or limit.

Take me home, Garuda, Vishnu heard himself say. **My heart longs to see my Devi Lakshmi again. I have been too long away from her, playing this game of gods and demons. My work there on earth is done for now. Take me home.**

His voice no longer sounded strange to himself. It sounded natural as it had always sounded.

The bird-carrier rose up into the infinite light, carrying the being named Vishnu who had once been Rama.

In a flash of an eye-wink, they were lost to human sight and mind, passing beyond the extent of mortal understanding or knowledge.

Jai Shri Vishnu.
Jai Shri Lakshmi.
Jai Shri Hindmata.

āti-samāptam

He emerged from the water into the effulgent white light, naked and blind as the day he was first born. Stumbling, he climbed onto land, bare feet scrabbling for purchase. He slipped and allowed himself to sprawl on the soft cool sand, its gritty texture feeling like nothing he had felt before. Yet he remembered this shore, this sand, this place.

Not from his life as Rama, but from long before that.

He lay, recovering upon the glittering white sands of a great shore, the susurrating sound of a mighty ocean tempting him to sleep a while— or an eon or three.

'Welcome back, Vaikuntha-naresh!' said a voice.

He had no desire to look up but forced himself to do so. The voice was familiar, the face doubly so—quadruply so, in fact. The being that stood before him on the white sand shore was clad in a white anga-vastra and dhoti, his head framed by four identical faces on four sides, each with an identical beard. An elaborately shaped gold crown encrusted with precious gems and magical objects gleamed and caught the translucent white light reflecting off the great ocean.

'Brahma-dev,' he said, almost to himself, as if remembering the being's name. In a sense, he *was* remembering, for his identity as Rama, Lakshman, Bharat and Shatrughan—the four-fold division of Self—

had not entirely faded. From past experience, he knew, it would never fade entirely. He still carried vestiges of memories, fragments of half-remembered sensations and experiences from past avatars and amsas— Matsya, Viraha, Vaman...Rama and his brothers was his seventh mortal form.

'It is good to have you back again,' said his old friend and elder god. 'Your mission was a great success. It is our great fortune that you have returned to us.'

He rose to his elbows, then with an effort, to a sitting position. He turned and looked out, beyond the four-faced figure standing before him. The white sand shore sloped down sharply to the ocean from which he had emerged moments earlier, the ocean into which he had passed when he had entered the Sarayu River and travelled through the Vortal that had been waiting to receive him. The great ocean of milk that filled the view as far as his eyes could see.

Brahma glanced back, not needing to turn and look over his shoulder as most beings did: he simply used his other faces to look. While they looked that way, the face facing Vishnu continued to watch him carefully. There was something in Brahma's eyes that Vishnu had seen before: a certain watchful look and guarded expression. 'Do you seek something...or someone?'

'The people who chose to take samadhi with me...' he corrected himself, 'with Rama and his brothers...they must be provided for as well, we cannot let them simply die and resume the endless cycle of rebirth. They have proved themselves worthy beyond the shadow of doubt. They gave up their lives for my...our...sake.'

Brahma was silent a brief moment, just a fraction of an instant more than was needed to respond. In that instant, Vishnu knew that the balance had changed somehow. During the time he had been gone, something had altered irreversibly. He also knew that it would be deadly dangerous to simply ask what it was: the games of gods were not to be trifled with. Worlds were created and destroyed when gods argued; entire cosmos demolished when they fought; all of Creation threatened when they went to war. He needed to learn what had happened before he said or did anything compromising; he needed to learn these things from someone he trusted indubitably.

'Of course,' Brahma said with apparent cheeriness. 'They have sacrificed everything for Rama Chandra of Ayodhya. All creatures that give up their lives for Rama while thinking of you deserve to live forever in peace. They shall go to the realm known as Santanika. It is a great loka, second only to my own Brahma-loka.'

Vishnu nodded, looking down at the sand. A strong breeze from the vast ocean was blowing landwards, riffling sand, piling it in gentle drifts against the parts of his feet and body that were touching the beach. His ankles were fast being covered by the drifting sands. He thought briefly of what it would be like to simply lie here and rest a season, permitting the sands to blow across and cover him entirely, burying him deep within a great dune. And someday, centuries hence, or millennia even, when he was rested and recovered and all the memories and wounds of his time as Rama and his brothers were healed, or at least scabbed over with scar tissue, then he would emerge, exploding from the mountainous dune, shake himself free of sand, and start walking homewards.

But he had things to do, places to go, and people to see. Something had happened in his absence. Something that mattered. He had to know what it was, and quickly. The future could depend on it.

'The vanars and the rksaas too,' he said softly, simply stating, not demanding.

Brahma chuckled. 'Of course. The vanars and bears too. I created them myself, you know! Some of my best work. I'm very fond of those furry friends. They shall go back to their original forms as nagas and yaksas, for those are the beings I transformed into the furry warriors.' He tilted his heads a fraction. 'I have left a few of their ilk on the mortal realm, but those are deprived of the power of speech or the superior intellect of the vanars and rksaas, they shall be mere brute beasts, acting as reminders of the age of Rama Chandra of Ayodhya. The Age of—'

Vishnu interrupted him, rising to his feet. 'I must go home. It has been a long absence.'

Brahma smiled. Or at least the face looking directly at Vishnu smiled. The other three faces had slightly varying expressions which he could not see precisely at this angle: it didn't matter. 'Of course. How foolish of me, to stand here bantering thusly while you are obviously in need of succour and revitalisation.' He made a gesture and a sound. 'Your faithful mount has been waiting for your return, watching this extraction point, for God knows how long.' Brahma chuckled. 'Well, *this* god doesn't know precisely how long but you follow my meaning.'

A great beating of wings and a shadow fell across them both as a cloud fell from the sky, resolving into a flurry of leathery feathers, razor claws and a beak as deadly as a hundred swords.

'Garuda!' Vishnu said with genuine delight.

The bird-god made a great avian sound of pleasure. There was anguish in the sound as well, and a look in those eyes and the angle at which he tilted his head and made the sound told Vishnu more than a speaking being might have communicated with a long verbose explanation. Vishnu's heart grew cold and his eyes burned. So his first instinct had been right: something *had* happened in his absence.

'Yes, my beautiful friend,' he said, stroking the downy proud breast of the being that served as his companion, mount and aide-in-arms, all in one. 'I am back now and we shall do what needs to be done.'

'Vishnu,' said Brahma from behind him.

Vishnu glanced back wordlessly. He did not wish to speak further with his fellow deva; he wished to gain more information before he said or did anything else.

Brahma's facing face was sharp and intense, with a slight smile playing on that bearded mouth. 'There is another mission, a very urgent and vital one. We must speak of it.'

Vishnu's jaw hardened. He controlled the impulse to hurl questions like arrows. Instead he said quietly: 'First I go home. I shall send for you, Lord Brahma. We shall discuss it at that time.'

Brahma smiled coldly. 'Make it soon. There are war games afoot and enemies amassing. You know that your Rama-avatar was only the seventh phase of the Great Game. There are three more to go, the most important ones yet. Every century we delay between avatars, our enemies grow in strength and stealth and number.'

Vishnu nodded. 'I am aware of these things. I shall send for you, Great One. We shall proceed as soon as possible.'

Brahma nodded. 'Of course. I do not need to remind great Vishnu, the Preserver, whose sole purpose in Creation is to protect and serve of his dharma. After all, you are the Sword of Dharma incarnate. Without you, Chaos would reign supreme.'

Vishnu mounted Garuda, the action feeling so pleasurable, like coming home. 'Well met, Lord Brahma-dev. Until we meet again soon.'

'Soon,' Brahma echoed. Then added: 'Give my love and respect to the Lady Sri.'

Vishnu urged Garuda with a gentle touch and with a mighty heave of his great wings, the bird-companion rose up into the air like an arrow shot from a longbow. The sound of their passage produced a great boom that echoed across the lokas and caused the entire surface of the ocean of milk to ripple with waves of power.

Brahma deva remained standing alone on the shorefront of white sand. His faces looked thoughtful and inwardly directed.

'Soon,' Brahma said. 'For the Great Game of Gods will not wait... not even for the Sword of Dharma.'

AFTERWORD
Death is just the Beginning...

Valmiki Ramayana ends here, with Vishnu back in Vaikuntha, the people who served him on earth during his Rama-avatar ascended to the realm known as Santanika, the vanars and rksaas restored to their original forms as nagas and yaksas.

But as Vishnu Purana and other great mythological texts tell us, that was not the end at all. For Rama was only Vishnu's seventh avatar. His next and, some would say, greatest avatar, Krishna, was yet to come, to be followed by two more avatars before the End of Days, the last phase of the Day of Brahma, and the end of Creation. Thereafter, the entire cosmos would be demolished and rebuilt from scratch as it was in the Beginning.

That story continues in the forthcoming series, *Sword of Dharma*.

RIDER OF GARUDA: *Sword of Dharma Book 1* picks up literally where *Sons of Sita* ends, with Vishnu riding home on Garuda to Vaikuntha-loka where Sri awaits him. But unlike *Sons of Sita* and the Ramayana Series as a whole, the *Sword of Dharma* series takes place not upon the mortal realm, but in the realm of devas and asuras, or as some would say, gods and demons. *Sword of Dharma* is a war epic: a blood-spattered rousing battle adventure story that ranges across worlds and ages, following the heroic exploits of Lord Vishnu himself. Think of it as Rama unleashed. All the power, all the glory that any being could ever dream of possessing...and all the enemies your worst nighmares could summon.

CONSORT OF SRI: *Sword of Dharma Book 2* continues the non-stop action and war-torn adventure.

COILS OF ANANTA: *Sword of Dharma Book 3* takes the epic to a new high.

LORD OF VAIKUNTHA: *Sword of Dharma Book 4* provides an unforgettable climax to a thrill-a-page saga, while also acting as a fitting conclusion to the preceding Ramayana Series, to which the *Sword of Dharma* is inextricably connected, taking us 'behind the curtain', so to speak, and letting us revisit key scenes and moments from the eight-book Ramayana Series which left us with more questions than answers at that time. Just as ordinary mortals cannot hope to understand the ways of gods and demons, so also when we enter the world of gods and demons we leave behind those mortal restrictions. All those questions are answered here, and more shocks and surprise revelations made as well, in the unmissable four-book companion series to the Ramayana... SWORD OF DHARMA.

The real battle has just begun.

Ashok K. Banker
Andheri West, Mumbai
July 2011